He was alone on Mars.

But that was OK, because it meant no one was trying to kill him except the planet itself. XO couldn't reach him. Brack was dead. The habs were intact. And Franklin Kittridge was still alive. He could work something out.

Praise for

ONE WAY

"A provocative premise, with an interesting main character....
Morden brings it together nicely in the last pages, setting up the
premise for an exciting sequel." —*Los Angeles Times*

"Sharp thriller in a crisply imagined near future....Morden
makes the science accessible as he steadily ratchets up the tension and paranoia, fully utilizing the starkly beautiful but utterly
deadly setting." —*Publishers Weekly*

"A claustrophobic, high-tension, survival-against-the-odds
thriller." —*Guardian*

"An intense, gripping sci-fi thriller."
—Adrian Tchaikovsky, Arthur C. Clarke Award–winning
author of *Children of Time*

"A rip-roaring thriller of a book that hits the ground running
and doesn't stop until the final chapter."
—John Marrs, author of *The One*

"Deeply immersive, chilling and atmospheric. An utterly fabu-
lous book!" —Emma Kavanagh, author of *Falling* and *Hidden*

"It's a thrilling tale that grabs you and whips along to the very
last breathless page." —Adam Hamdy, author of *Pendulum*

"A stunning novel that mixes science, fiction and mystery into
an exciting tale." —*RT Book Reviews*

"Morden expertly melds the genres of science fiction and mystery in this whodunit set on Mars." —*Booklist*

NO WAY

By S. J. Morden

One Way
No Way

NO WAY

S.J. MORDEN

www.orbitbooks.net

Copyright © 2019 by S. J. Morden
Excerpt from *Rosewater* copyright © 2016 by Tade Thompson
Excerpt from *Equations of Life* copyright © 2011 by Simon Morden

Cover design by Lisa Marie Pompilio
Cover images by Shutterstock
Cover copyright © 2019 by Hachette Book Group, Inc.

Orbit
Hachette Book Group
1290 Avenue of the Americas
New York, NY 10104
orbitbooks.net

Simultaneously published in 2019 by Orbit in the U.S. and Gollancz in Great Britain.
First U.S. Edition: February 2019

Orbit is an imprint of Hachette Book Group.
The Orbit name and logo are trademarks of Little, Brown Book Group Limited.

The publisher is not responsible for websites (or their content) that are not owned by the publisher.

The Hachette Speakers Bureau provides a wide range of authors for speaking events. To find out more, go to www.hachettespeakersbureau.com or call (866) 376-6591.

Library of Congress Control Number: 2018966636

ISBNs: 978-0-316-52221-2 (trade paperback), 978-0-316-52219-9 (ebook)

Printed in the United States of America

LSC-C

10 9 8 7 6 5 4 3 2 1

In grateful memory of Professor Colin Pillinger
(1943–2014)

1

[Internal memo: Mars Base One Mission Control to Bruno Tiller 11/10/2048 (transcribed from paper-only copy)]

We have been unable to contact MBO for twenty-four [24] hours. MBO appears undamaged. The hi-gain antenna appears undamaged, but the carrier signal is absent. The DV [Descent Vehicle] is also undamaged, and does emit a carrier wave. We have attempted to contact MBO routing through the DV, but the link is non-responsive. There is one [1] body, in an EVA suit, visible nine [9] feet west of one of the surface transports. There is no sign of additional activity visible to our orbital cameras.

At this stage, we can neither confirm nor deny whether the XO asset within MBO is still active.

[transcript ends]

It was mid-morning. The early frost had burned off, and the sky was its usual shade of hazy pink. Frank was outside, dragging a body through the red dust. He'd wrapped Zero in a square of parachute canopy, and was using the crudely knotted end—because knots were really difficult to tie in spacesuit gauntlets—to pull him over to where Declan was, by the buggy. Declan was also dead, shot by Brack through his spacesuit's faceplate. Frank was pretty certain that Declan had died when the bullet had gone through his eye, rather than afterwards when his air had escaped, or after that when his bodily fluids had boiled out.

But Brack was dead too. Frank had stabbed him with a scalpel. He'd stabbed Zero as well, with a short gardening knife from the greenhouse.

Frank struggled with remembering the chain of events, but the details? Those were burned into him. It had taken him two days to recall what he'd done with his spacesuit, and the base wasn't that big. Two days in which he'd wandered the corridors naked, scrubbed his skin raw under the shower, and slept only to wake up more exhausted than he had been before.

Two days to come to terms with the realization that he was the only man left on Mars.

Marcy had been the first to go, when her suit's scrubber had failed and Frank hadn't been able to get her back to the ship in time. That had hurt, and it still hurt when he thought about it. Then Alice, from an overdose of opioid that she had access to because she was their doctor. Zeus had died when Frank had accidentally opened the airlock door on him—something that shouldn't have been possible—and Dee had been killed when the fire suppressor system flooded the Comms room with CO_2.

Then Declan, then Zero.

Declan lay on the cold ground, spreadeagled among the fist-sized red rocks, lying on his back, arms out wide. Behind the broken faceplate, the blood had dried, as had the skin and his one good eye. A wizened face, marred by a stretched-out entry wound on the shattered right cheek, stared out into the dull Martian day.

There was a glint of mirrored light on the ground close by. Frank dropped his handful of parachute, and he knelt down—his semi-rigid spacesuit didn't really allow for bending at the waist—and picked it up. It was a scalpel, the one he'd lost out in the night after he'd cut away the excess cloth from the hole in his own suit, better to apply a sticky patch to seal it. Brack had shot him too, but Frank had survived.

He held the scalpel carefully, remembering not to try to blow the dust off it, or worse, wipe it with his gloved fingers. It was still going to be extraordinarily sharp, and he needed to find a safe place for it. He inspected the blade, holding it up to his faceplate, and noticed the white pitting on the metal surface: there was something in the soil that had corroded the stainless steel.

He carried it into the workshop's airlock. He was standing exactly where Zeus had died. Frank had thought he'd been responsible for that. Frank had been allowed to think that, in the same way he'd been allowed to think that Marcy's suit had failed, Alice had committed suicide, that Dee had been gassed by a malfunction.

The inside of the hab was pumped up with pressurized Mars air, so that it was somewhere that sparks could be made without risking instant immolation. People could work in there, with just scuba gear, and use their ungloved hands. The benches were still littered with parts for the putative steam turbine Zeus had been constructing, and further down, pieces of black glass where Declan had tried to fix the broken solar panels.

For a moment, he saw the other two men crouched over their work, then realized he was never going to see them alive again.

"Sorry," he said. "We didn't…do very well, did we? I mean, we did OK. We did OK, but we didn't look after each other like we should have. We should have worked out what Brack was doing sooner, and stopped him. Would have been easier with more of us, too. Then I wouldn't be stuck here, on my own, wondering what the hell I'm supposed to do next."

Brack had killed everyone. He would have killed Frank too, but Frank had found that he had something worth living for, worth fighting for. Even worth faking his own death for, so he could strike Brack when he least expected. Worth killing for.

Frank had a son, Mike, back on Earth. Frank hadn't seen his boy for what, ten years now? For eight of those ten years he'd been in San Quentin, serving a cool one-twenty for second-degree murder. The last two had been spent training and traveling and building.

Jacqui, his mother, had taken him away after the trial, moved to the east coast, and vanished along with him: Frank had killed a cop's son, and the blowback had been hard. The only contact he'd had with them since were divorce papers. He'd been content with the exchange, until XO had come calling. He'd been sent to Mars by a corporation that just happened to own both a prison and an aerospace outfit, in the company of a bunch of cons—murderers and narcos and perverts—and an overseer. Frank had believed he'd been promised a lift home if he toed the line, built Mars Base One, and looked after it. He'd kept his end of the bargain. There was a fully functioning set of pressurized habs, with a greenhouse, med bay, crew quarters, kitchen, stores, power, light, water, air…what there wasn't any more was a team of caretakers. Or that ticket home.

He cycled the workshop airlock, feeling his suit stretch around him as the CO_2 was pumped back inside.

He opened the door, and there was Mars. The first time he'd seen it, he'd been speechless. Now, it was just where he worked. He climbed down the steps and pulled Zero in line with Declan, and then went back for Brack.

Brack had worked his way through the cons. Carefully at first, always making it look like there was another explanation. Which had been easy enough, because they weren't the most stable of people, and Mars punished inattention with almost instant death. But Brack had tripped up with Zeus. He could only have been murdered. Sure, Brack had convinced Frank that it had been one of the others, and Frank had been only too ready to take that on trust, what with his trip home dependent on Brack's good report.

Frank took hold of Brack's parachute-shroud and bounced him down the cross-hab steps. All the malevolence and malice in that wiry body had gone. It was just an empty husk now: whatever had made Brack kill and kill again had flowed out with the blood on the base's floor and the fluids evaporated away in Mars's thin air.

He pulled him all the way to the other two, and tucked the ends of the shroud in around Brack's body. Mars had weather. The parachutes might catch the feeble wind. He collected a third piece of parachute and fitted Declan into it. The spread arms were a challenge. Frank may have broken them or dislocated them pushing them down to the sides again, but sound didn't really travel, and he was able to pretend otherwise.

When he'd done, he straightened up. He took in the crater wall to the south, the notch through which the river from the top of the volcano had flowed, the looming bulk of the volcano itself, all fifteen thousand feet of it. He used to drive up that river—Dee had named it the Santa Clara—and take in the view, before heading back down again to the base. Because it was the only place he could go back to. He'd swapped one prison for another. That had been the deal he'd made with XO. Die on Earth or live on Mars.

XO hadn't played fair, of course. There'd been the small matter of being sent to solitary confinement for the rest of his sentence if he'd failed for any reason to complete his astronaut training. The Hole sent men mad, and it had been a hell of an incentive not to crap out. XO's Supermaxes were probably stuffed with those who'd failed, now howling at four blank walls and dreaming of ever more elaborate ways to stay sane.

Frank couldn't help them then or now. He didn't even know if he could help himself. It would only take one thing to go wrong, with his health, his suit, or the base, and that would be it. He hadn't done any of his maintenance tasks since that long, bloody night, and neither had anyone else because they were all dead. As it was, he was carrying a bullet wound in his arm, and a cut on his chest where he'd extracted his XO-implanted medical monitor.

And yes, he'd pulled the bullet out with a pair of sterile forceps, and used a sterile scalpel to slice himself open, but he hadn't

5

cleaned it up properly nor taken antibiotics. Or painkillers—those that were left after Brack had chowed his way through the supply.

Perhaps he should do that, now he'd got the dead guys out of the base.

When XO had trained him, they'd provided only a rudimentary first-aid course. In fact, much of his training had been a gloss. He knew what he needed to know—in his case, how to site the base and bolt it together—and precious little else. He'd had a second, Declan, and he'd shadowed Marcy for transportation, but he knew almost nothing about the power or the plumbing or the comms. Especially not the hydroponics: Zero had guarded his greenhouse jealously.

He re-entered the base through the cross-hab airlock. There was blood on the floor. A lot of blood. Dried lakes of it, with drag-lines leading through to the yard, the main rec area, where Frank had dragged a semi-conscious Brack to the place where he'd died, his legs cut to ribbons, his suit smashed to an unremovable shell around him.

The med bay was the other way. There was no less blood there.

Frank racked his suit, next to Zero's, and plugged his life support into the regenerator. He was naked. His one set of overalls were stiff and black with dried blood, and despite the sub-zero temperatures outside, it was warm enough inside.

The med bay looked like a slaughterhouse, with spatters up the curved walls, across the metal staging and the hanging fabric dividers. Furniture was overturned, knocked aside, and the floor? Zero had died there. Bled out. And it showed. Zero had attacked Frank, thinking not unreasonably that the man convicted of murder was the murderer. Frank had survived. Zero had not. He stood for a moment in the doorway, finally taking in the scene and seeing it for what it was. He clicked his tongue behind his teeth and grimaced. The place was a mess, and he'd always prided himself on keeping a clean working environment. All the same, he was going to have to leave it for now.

Frank looked through the boxes for dressings, and antiseptic cream. He didn't know if infection was going to be a problem: Mars was sterile, but the base wasn't. He guessed that they'd brought their own germs with them, but didn't know enough to say whether they were dangerous bugs or not.

The water they used was sterile too—Zeus had told him as much—so he stood over the sink and carefully washed the wound on his chest. It wasn't big, just a cut through the surface layers of skin and maybe half an inch long, big enough to squeeze the monitor out through. He'd had to cut along the original scar, though, and that might cause problems.

A dribble of pink water trickled down his belly and groin to drip onto the floor. Not that it mattered. A little more would make no difference at all.

He used one steristrip to close the cut, and wondered about putting a fabric pad over the top. It didn't look that bad, and he left it.

The hole in his arm was more of a problem. It was sore. Of course it was—he'd dragged a bullet out of it—but he thought it should be hurting more than it was, even though he'd never been shot before. It also seemed to be healing well enough. Every time he knocked it or even flexed his muscle, he was reminded that it was there, but it hadn't affected his ability to sleep. Far from it.

He cleaned up the edges of the wound, and used a big press-on patch to cover it. He still didn't take any painkillers, partly because he didn't trust them, and partly so that he could tell how much trouble he was in. There was no one else to look out for him, and he found himself extraordinarily ignorant about how to keep himself alive.

He disposed of the wrappings, and tidied away the unused items. There was no one else to do it.

He looked at the med bay again, properly looked at it. He didn't even know if he *could* clean it up. He'd need actual cleaning tools to do that: detergents, bleach, a mop, a bucket, scrubbing brushes. Did they have that? He hadn't come across any yet, and he'd helped build the base, and carry the stores from the supply rockets inside.

He picked up one of the examination tables that had been knocked over when Zero had crashed against it, and set it back on its feet, a simple enough task in the reduced gravity. His arm flexed, and he winced. There was a weakness there that hadn't been present before. Perhaps he should take it easy. Perhaps that was the excuse he was looking for.

Whichever it was, he stopped.

He let his hands fall by his side. Was this it? Was this how it was going to be from now on? He'd killed two more people, for this?

Frank was at war with himself. There were too many things to think about, all at once. He had to strip everything back, deal with the absolutely necessary and immediate, and put everything else to one side, even if delaying it now spelled disaster later.

He'd bandaged his wounds. That was a good start. He could keep them clean, watch for infection, avoid exerting himself until he'd healed. What next?

How long was it since he'd had anything substantial to eat? His confusion could simply be down to low blood sugar. He had food. He had more food than he knew what to do with. He'd probably end up having to throw a lot of it away. So why not go and help himself?

He let himself into the greenhouse and took a tour of the hydroponic trays, taking the time to inspect both the variety and the growth-stage of each. It took a while to get his eye in, but eventually he was able to identify which he could harvest, and which he needed to leave. Some of the crops looked very similar, with only subtle differences, and none of them were labeled: presumably Zero had known what everything was, and how long he'd been growing them for. If he'd kept records, Frank didn't know where to find them.

Unless they were on the computer. Maybe they were. Had Dee said anything about that? He couldn't remember. Declan had chided him for being incurious. He'd probably had a point.

What had he come in here for? Food, that was it. He found a clean container, and picked himself a big bowl of salad: lots of leaves, tomatoes, green onions, and some young green beans. He left that by the airlock door, and took another bowl to the lower level, to where the tilapia tanks were.

Zero had fashioned a net from a piece of parachute fabric. Frank used it to chase the fish through the water and pick out two of the fattest ones. Would he have to cull them? They were going to breed faster than he could eat them, now that there wasn't a full crew roster chowing down on them. Something else he wasn't going to think about for the moment.

Then there was the atmosphere balance in the greenhouse itself. Was that automatic, or did it need him to manually vent the excess oxygen and top up the carbon dioxide? Not going to think about that now either.

He carried both bowls to the kitchen, and stared down at the fish. They stared blankly back. Their gills were still pulsing, and they gave the occasional twitch of their tails. Frank frowned as his stomach shrank at the thought of killing them. This was not the time to get squeamish. The protein wasn't going to come from anywhere else. Beans and nuts and grains, sure. But meat was concentrated calories.

He opened the drawer, took out a knife, and slapped one of the fish down on the counter. He raised the knife, and slowly lowered it until the blade was resting on the join between head and body.

His fingers flexed on the knife handle. He adjusted his grip and started to press down. It was easy, right? He'd done this so often. Cut the head off, slice down the belly, scoop out the guts:

fresh fish. Bony, but he wasn't going to spend time filleting the damn things. Take a deep breath, and push.

The edge sliced clean through, crunching when it met the spine. The sound made Frank gag, and he tried to swallow back on the rising bile, but then his stomach spasmed and he lost all control. He remembered to grab one of the containers from the side as he collapsed to the floor. The tilapia still in it arced away, and he forced his head over the now empty tray and puked pink watery slime until he was weak and gasping.

His throat burned. His eyes streamed. He wiped his mouth with the back of his hand and let the frothy liquid drip into the tray. Then he rolled onto his back and held his aching ribs.

What a mess. What a state to get himself in. He was going to die here, and he'd never get to see his son again.

Declan was standing over him, looking down at him with his one good eye.

"Get the fuck up, Frank. You've got work to do. You got to fix this. You can't let them win."

"Goddammit, Declan, I'm doing my best."

"You're naked and drooling puke. If that's your best, then you may as well toss yourself out the airlock."

Frank wiped his mouth again, and flicked his fingers clear.

"I'll try," he said. "I'll try."

"You'd better. It's down to you."

And he was gone, and Frank was alone again.

2

[Private diary of Bruno Tiller, entry under 11/11/2048, transcribed from paper-only copy]

I don't know what to do. For the first time in my life, I don't know what to do. I thought I'd left this feeling of powerlessness behind for ever. I've dedicated the past decade to becoming the master of not just my destiny, but of others' destinies too. And I was there. I was there. I had the power of life and death over people I hardly knew.

I know that this is not a time to waver. Looking from the outside, no one knows my struggle. I keep up my wall and I keep everyone out. Inside, I'm breaking. If this goes badly, I'm finished. The only choice I'll get to make is who else I take down with me.

[transcript ends]

Frank cleaned up, the best he could. The fish, both dead, went into the waste system, and he levered up the floor tiles one by one and rinsed them off in the sink.

Declan was right. OK, Declan was dead, but that didn't stop him from being right.

He found his overalls where he'd abandoned them, next to the shower stall. They'd dried stiff, and he had to peel the cloth apart. He'd been wearing them inside his spacesuit when he'd got shot, so there was a corresponding ragged-edged hole high up on the sleeve. But he put them in the washing machine and spent half an hour manually cranking the drum around. He had plenty of watts to play with—it was just that the tub was designed for manual use. When the overalls came out, the black patches weren't visibly lighter. They were more pliable, though. The garment would be wearable, even if it would carry its marks for ever.

He draped it over a chair in the kitchen to dry, then picked it up again and followed the blood trail through the yard to the airlock at the far end. It wasn't one they used—the traffic went through the cross-hab connector—but it was there because the base was designed to be modular and extendable.

He dropped his overalls on the airlock floor, closed the door, and pumped the air inside back into the hab. As the pressure dropped, the water boiled out from the cloth. Just like it did with people. He waited for the fog to clear, then bled the air back into the airlock chamber. Once the pressure had equalized, he could retrieve his clothes.

They were cold, cold enough to now attract condensation, but nowhere near as wet as they were before. OK, it was a grievous waste of water, but he was one man living in a base built for eight. He had resources to burn, which was ironic since they'd been short of everything at the beginning. If he needed more water, he was literally sitting on a reservoir of almost limitless supply, and all he needed to do was fire up the water maker and shovel some dirt into it.

Frank slung his overalls back over a chair, then slumped into it himself. He still felt so very tired.

He was, he guessed, around a hundred million miles from Earth. The distance meant nothing, as he'd been asleep the whole journey. He hadn't any feeling of having traveled such a vast distance, just experience of an edit: fall unconscious on Earth, wake up on Mars. But he thought he knew what Earth looked like in the night sky, and if that bright dot was really what he was searching for, then of everyone who had ever lived, he was the most alone human being in the whole of history.

Somewhere between him and Earth was supposed to be a spaceship with some NASA astronauts. He didn't know when they were going to arrive, nor what they expected to find when they did. It was likely they weren't expecting to find a con who'd now killed three people.

What was he going to say to them? How would he know they were here? He might see their fiery entry. He might catch their sonic boom. The astronauts were expecting to be picked up, though if they were too far away, and either he didn't try to, or couldn't, find them, then what would they do? There'd been so many rockets descending recently, it'd been difficult for him to tell who or what was coming down. What they were, he didn't know—Brack had pointed out that XO didn't own Mars. If they'd been supplies meant for MBO, Brack would have collected them at the bottom of the crater, together with the NASA kit.

OK, NASA: if they were all in this together with XO, perhaps getting stranded miles from help or hope would be justice of sorts. But how likely was that collusion? They were the ones who were smart, idealistic explorers. They'd trained for this mission for years—unlike Frank, who'd barely got six months.

Sure, someone had to have signed off on this. Someone high up had to know that Frank and his fellow cons had been sent on a one-way trip as disposable labor. If not the astronauts themselves, then their bosses, or their bosses' bosses, but if it came to a fight, he knew how this would pan out. He'd seen it on the screen often enough, a war between planets, where humans and aliens would duke it out until, inevitably, the good guys would win. He—Frank Kittridge—was the Martians. All of them. And he knew he wasn't one of the good guys.

He started to laugh, because he found the idea funny. He ended up kneeling on the floor, crying, because it was only going to end one way. Eventually, he raised his head, wiped his cheeks with the back of his hand.

What was he going to do?

The only thing he had on his side was time. NASA wouldn't be here for a while, and he might be able to find out when.

A plan. He needed a plan.

From where he was, hunched over, elbows on his knees, staring out at the dried blood smeared along the floor, he couldn't see anything he could do. His situation was hopeless. He was alone. Outside wanted to kill him. Inside was fragile and depended on his continued labor to keep it going. One mistake would be the end of it all. No one was going to save him.

"Goddammit."

He felt shame. He'd been the mark in a con, and he hadn't seen it coming, hadn't seen it at all, until it was too late. The loaded dice had been rolled, and he'd lost everything. He'd killed Brack, but by that point it had been just to save his own skin, just to save face even. It hadn't made anything better. He wasn't going home. He wasn't going to see his son. He was still going to die on Mars, sooner or later.

What the hell: he'd had a choice, and he'd taken the decision to live.

First things first, then. Make sure the base was still running as it ought to be. He could access the information on his tablet, but that was in the cross-hab, clipped onto his suit's utility belt. Comms was just through the end of the yard, and the screens were bigger.

He followed the rust-red trail of blood and sat in the Comms chair. This was Dee's domain, where he'd spent hours just reading the technical documents and looking at the maps. He hadn't liked going outside so much, and he'd gotten comfortable with his role. Right up to the point where Brack had tripped the fire suppressor system and then held the door shut on him so that he'd suffocated.

On the console was Brack's tablet, and Brack's gun. The gun was just a regular automatic, very similar to the one Frank had used to kill his son's dealer, but with the trigger guard removed, so that a fat spacesuit-gauntleted finger could still fire it. He picked it up, carefully. A stray round would probably register on the fire system as a flash-over, and put a hole in the hab skin to boot. The safety was on, but that didn't mean it was safe.

He put it on the other side of the desk, behind the monitor, and propped Brack's tablet against the table legs, on the floor next to his feet.

He clicked the monitor on—they'd all habitually turned any electrical equipment they weren't using off, to save precious watts—and waited for the screen to bloom into life.

OK. Error messages in the base dialogue box. Comms were offline—that was fine, because Frank had tripped the power breakers on the dish himself, to prevent the automatic systems talking with XO, and XO talking with them, with the ship and the circling satellites. But what about this one: Low Memory?

Dee had told him something about only having room for seven days' worth of data, and he had no idea what the kid had done to automate the system. Dee probably hadn't factored in dying, nor for the transmitter to be deliberately taken offline.

Was running out of memory on the computer going to kill him? It could well do if the hab's telltales couldn't report back environmental data to the main computer, and things started shutting down. Could he fix this? Could he fix this without doing more damage?

This wasn't touch-and-swipe stuff. When he'd run his own construction firm, he'd managed his own accounts and hadn't relied on anyone else to make up his books. But this...Dee would have known what to do. Dee wouldn't have got to this point in the first place. His son would have known what to do, too.

With that thought, he dabbed at the alert with his finger. He had to learn how to do this if he was going to stay alive.

He was offered a list of options: automatically free up more memory, manually delete files, cancel the alert.

He picked the first, and held his breath while the screen showed the computer doing things. Then it stopped, and the alert just went away. It had been easy in the end.

He checked through the other functions—air, water, power— and they were all well within the green part of their respective graphs. Power generation was cyclic: the batteries charged up during the day, and there was a base load of three kilowatts from the radioactive generator to keep things ticking over during the night. But because Declan hadn't been wiping the solar panels free of dust, nor turning them every few hours to face the sun, they weren't working as efficiently as they ought. That was a job that needed doing, then.

As did his tours of the base to make sure that none of the bolts were working loose; and maintaining the buggies, and swapping out the air filters when he needed to, and balancing the atmosphere in the greenhouse, and clearing the muck from the recycling plant, and the plants…he had the whole base to run. Breathe. Breathe again.

He was alone on Mars. But that was OK, because it meant no one was trying to kill him except the planet itself. XO couldn't reach him. Brack was dead. The habs were intact. And Franklin Kittridge was still alive. He could work something out.

He still needed a plan.

What did he have? He had Mars Base One. It must have cost billions in development and shipping, let alone the cost of getting people here to set it up. He had XO, and, by extension, NASA and the U.S. government by the balls. They'd inadvertently made a murderer the King of Mars.

So that had to be worth something. If he knew anything about rich people, and he'd worked on building projects for them before, it was that they feared a loss of status over pretty much everything else. So you think you built a Mars base? Five minutes with a knife and Frank could render that brag hollow.

It would, of course, kill him. XO would probably figure that he wouldn't carry out that threat, so he had to give them a credible reason for thinking that trashing the base was an option. What did he want in return?

He wanted to go home. He wanted his freedom. He wanted to be able to hang out with his son again, assuming he could find him. Was that worth a multi-billion dollar hi-tech facility on another planet?

Yes. Sure. Why not?

There was a problem, though. Who the hell was going to give him a ride?

It wasn't like he was going to build a raft and float home. He technically had a rocket ship, but that had been part of the one way deal. It wasn't going anywhere, and he wasn't a pilot. Scratch that idea. He needed two things, and only two things: a berth on a ship capable of getting back to Earth, and someone to fly it there.

Brack had had that. If Brack had succeeded in killing Frank too, then Brack would get a trip home, be paid off, and live happily ever after. Or as happily as a stone-cold murderer could do.

There was a certain irony there, which wasn't lost on him. He considered his own guilt again, and wondered how life might have turned out if he hadn't done what, in hindsight, had been utterly the wrong thing.

So, technically, the two things he needed would be available once NASA arrived, given that Brack wasn't going to be able to take up the space.

Frank dragged his fingers through his hair and scrubbed at his face. This wasn't his forte. He was a man who worked with his hands, not his head. But right now, he couldn't build his way out of his predicament. There had to be a solution here.

How was he going to take Brack's place on that flight home? Presumably the NASA astronauts were expecting Brack to be here when they arrived. That he'd be around while they completed their mission. That they'd take him with them when they were done. That was all arranged.

There wasn't a hope in hell that XO would let him anywhere near that ship as Frank Kittridge, murderer. He knew where all XO's bodies were buried, and the astronaut-scientists? They were going to be asking all kinds of questions that XO weren't going to want answered.

What if…

He sat up with a gasp. The idea was preposterous. Literally insane. He'd never get away with it.

What if he tried to convince everyone that he was Brack?

Had XO any clue as to what was happening in the base right now? He'd turned the dish off. There was no data leaking out. All they could do was look down from above. What would they see? Three bodies, lying out in the dust. One man in an XO suit, cleaning up shop. Maybe the lights going on or off. If they'd been lucky with when the satellites had been overhead, perhaps a frame or two with him in it. They'd have no clue as to his identity: all their suits were superficially identical.

"Frank, don't."

He looked up, and there was Zeus. Smoke streamed from his nose, his eyes, his ears, his skin.

"What else am I going to do? I've got to get off this rock somehow."

"When you start lying to people, you got to remember all those lies. Tell the truth, brother. The truth sets you free." When he spoke, thick ribbons of boiling water spiraled up from his mouth.

"You don't get to tell me what to do."

"It's the only advice I've got." Zeus was huge. His mere presence filled the room. "If you deal with XO, you're dealing with the devil."

"They hold all the cards."

"You got a pretty decent hand yourself, Frank. You just got to play them straight."

Frank swallowed. "I killed you, Zeus. I opened the door on you and I killed you."

He was addressing nothing but the space between the desk and the door. It took him a moment to realize that he'd been talking to a ghost. Again.

So what was he going to do? Could he hold out for however long it was, hope that NASA came, hope that he could convince them to take him with them, hope that XO hadn't already decided to poison the well, knowing there was someone in the base who was deliberately staying out of contact? What did he actually know about the agreement between XO and NASA?

Had, in fact, XO wanted them all dead? What if Brack had lost the plot so spectacularly that he thought he'd been acting under orders, when XO were desperately trying to talk him round? Maybe he'd passed off the earlier deaths to his controllers as accidents in the same way he'd fooled the cons.

XO were never going to implicate themselves. Of course they were going to pile the blame for this on Brack. They were never going to tell him the truth now, just as they'd never told him the truth in the past.

Perhaps it was the shock wearing off, that it had taken him until now to even consider why he'd ever been put in the position of being press-ganged to Mars. He'd asked, at the time of that initial interview in jail, why not just take smart young people, and had been told that smart young people dying would cause a stink.

That was what this was about. The fancy lawyer-type had known it then: dying wasn't optional. The choice they had was who they were going to kill. Frank couldn't think of anyone who was more expendable than a bunch of cons that they already owned. And probably, neither could XO.

Perhaps decisions this big ought to be made while wearing pants, but it wasn't like there was anyone watching.

He leaned over and pulled Brack's tablet up onto his lap. It was the same as his—standard issue—but with a different- colored cover. He turned it on, and expected to see some fancy password-protection screen. Finger, voice-print, iris scan. He was certain he'd seen Brack do something like that every time he'd accessed the device. Now, there was nothing, not even a pattern key or a text-based code. The lack of security made Frank think that there couldn't be anything on there worth looking at, and he was about to fold the cover over and drop it back on the desk when he noticed there were icons present that weren't on his own machine. Things that weren't on the main computer.

Folders. Folders full of files.

A mail function. A goddamn interplanetary mail function.

He stared at the screen again, not even daring to touch it, in case they disappeared when he tried. But there was no reason for them to do that. So in the end he reached down and dabbed his fingertip against the mail icon and watched while it opened up and out.

Messages that went back months. All of Brack's traffic with XO, which had presented itself publicly as an uncrackable code that Dee had said wasn't worth even trying to unscramble. And here it was, rendered into plain text on Brack's machine.

He scrolled through, letting the headers blur as they sped past. So many. A whole history.

Frank shrank the mail app down and put his hand over his heart. It was banging hard against his ribs. This was it. This was the smoking gun. He was going to have to read everything, just to see how bad it all was.

He tapped one of the folders. Behind the icon were files, and one of the files had his name. His rap sheet? And there was Marcy's and Zeus's and Dee's. They were all there. And there was other information, some named with strings of letters and numbers that didn't mean anything to him, but others with titles that hinted at deeper mysteries.

What to look at first? Frank scanned the file names on that part of the system. Those could wait, and probably those. This one, this Project Sparta summary. He'd never heard of Sparta, not in this context, anyway. He knew about the Spartans because of that movie, that they were badass soldiers of ancient times, but it didn't have any real relevance to his situation, did it?

He opened it up. And he read it.

3

[Image analysis MBO Mission Control, dated 11/11/2048]

Differences in the last sol:

1. Body #1 still in situ but covered (?parachute canopy)
2. Object #2 (?body) next to Body #1 (?parachute canopy)
3. Object #3 (?body) next to Object #2 (?parachute canopy)
4. Rover recharge lead plugged into fuel cell of rover
5. Hatch on supply cylinder #6 was closed, now open.

Conclusion: there is definitely someone (Subject #1) still active at MBO, able to execute EVA and carry out tasks. We can see no external damage to communications equipment, which does not discount other failure modes. Re-establishing contact with MBO remains the priority, but we should discuss our contingency plans in the event of a LOC [Loss of Control] scenario.

[message ends]

Some time later, he found himself on the floor, looking up at the underside of the comms console. He wasn't certain how he'd got there. He'd been sitting on the chair, which was now, like him, on its back.

He'd fainted. That was it. He'd read something, stood up too suddenly, and folded like a bad poker hand.

Robots. Fucking robots.

For his entire life, he'd been threatened with losing his job through automation. Everyone had. Manufacturing had been first, then driving. Marcy had been one of the last operators of big rigs. Banking, retail, they'd all fired their workers and hired machines. Construction was one of the few places a man could still work with his hands and command a decent paycheck.

The base they'd built, with their own labor and their own lives, was supposed to have been built by robots.

He was here, on Mars, because the robots didn't work. They broke down. They got sand in their joints. They weren't smart enough. They were too far away. Easier to send cheap, disposable people in place of expensive, fragile robots.

Even then, that wasn't the worst of it. XO still wanted it to look like robots had built the base, with just one human supervisor. Killing the set-up crew was part of the package, so of course they had to be expendable. XO got its money, and a foothold on Mars. NASA—who thankfully didn't appear to know anything about Project Sparta—had a base they could use.

Brack's job in the first phase was to make sure the base got built. In the second, he had to make sure everyone else died. And in the third—

That was where he'd fainted. He slid his hand up and felt the side of his face. The hard plastic floor panel was unforgiving, and he'd cracked his cheek hard as he'd gone down. Just bruising, he told himself. One-third gravity meant he'd not fallen quickly enough to do real damage.

He rolled over, pulling faces as he stretched out his skin, and levered himself up using the edge of the desk. He reset the chair on its feet. He sat down again.

Phase three.

Brack had been given three months to get rid of everything that might give the impression that there'd been anyone else on Mars. Bodies. Equipment. Anything that might look worn or used. Data. NASA were expecting a clean base, built by robots, maintained by one man. XO were going to tidy up and pretend Frank had never been there.

He looked over his shoulder at the trail of blood that passed through the doorway and headed out across the yard.

No wonder Brack had been pissed about the state of the med bay. All that work he was going to have to do, cleaning up what had leaked out of Zero. That was what all the storing of the bodies on the ship was about. That was why their personal effects had never arrived. Why all the scientific equipment and NASA-specific material was still in containers at the bottom of the Heights. Why XO had taken the encryption off Brack's tablet: no cons, no need for secrecy.

Phase three even included plans to scale back the hydroponics and then expand production again in time for the new, legitimate crew. Three months.

Goddammit, how could he have been so stupid, so naive, so trusting?

It was actually worse than he'd thought. They'd been treated like they weren't even human. Cattle. They'd been treated like cattle. Herded, used, then slaughtered. It was probably a good job that Brack was already dead. Frank felt as if he should go and hang the body from one of the struts. Let the overhead satellites make sense of that.

His cheek was sore, and his eye felt puffy. The skin tightened uncomfortably when he blinked. He pressed his hand against it.

XO were going to bury him for sure. This wasn't just one man going off the rails because of the stress and isolation. This was no more Brack's idea than it was his. And it wasn't the work of a few, either. This was a full-blown conspiracy.

All the people he interacted with at Gold Hill. The medics, the technicians, the drivers even. They knew what the plan XO had sold to NASA meant. Robots. One crew member. They all had to be in on it, to some degree or other. Dozens of otherwise normal people, who were just there to do a job, who'd go home to their families and their children, and maybe take the dog for a walk, or watch a game, or help their elderly neighbor with their groceries, knew the fate of the seven poor schmucks they dumped in the freeze chambers long before the occupants ever did.

Surely, there had to be someone within XO who'd been just a little bit uncomfortable about the whole "let's kill seven people" thing? Someone who'd say something to their wife, their husband, their mother or their father, and be encouraged to go to the authorities?

Yet here Frank was, knowing that all those opportunities, all those people who had to have been on the inside, had done absolutely nothing. If they had spoken out, he wouldn't have been there.

All that effort. Just to cover up what had been...he didn't know what to call it. XO had agreed to deliver a Mars base a certain way, and found they couldn't do it. Rather than putting their hands up and saying sorry, they decided that the only solution was to fake it. Sure, they'd have to kill some people in the process, but no one would miss them.

It was monstrous. Like he'd blundered onto the set of a snuff movie and then had to watch as, one by one, his fellow actors got struck down. If he'd been stuck on a studio back-lot in downtown Burbank, he could have walked home. But no: they decided to fake it a hundred million miles away where there was no atmosphere and no human being belonged.

He had no way out of this. He might as well trash the place now and have done with it. It would be a shame that he wasn't going to be around to hear XO's explanation for NASA as to why their lovely base turned into so much scrap metal and flapping plastic, but that would be the price of his revenge. Though he had really wanted to see his boy again.

He got up, slowly this time, and hesitated for just a little too long.

What if the NASA people needed the base to be intact, in order to get home again? Anything he did here would be condemning them before they even got to Mars. He couldn't talk to them, either, and warn them off. They'd come crashing through the atmosphere and land, expecting to be picked up and taken to safety. Could he do that to them? He'd never met any of them, but they didn't deserve to die on Mars any more than he did.

He couldn't talk to them: he could only talk to XO, and they had nothing to say to him that he wanted to hear. He imagined the conversation that would ensue, trading threats and recriminations across a twenty-minute delay. Even then, the temptation to tell them exactly what he thought of them was tempered by the fact that they'd be trying to work out how much of the base they could control remotely and how they could use that to kill him. Every tablet had access to the deep and vital functions that kept the habs viable. Only Brack had had the motivation to use them to kill.

Frank righted the chair again, and slumped into it, crouching forward and staring at the Project Sparta summary. There were links in it, which would open other files. Details. Carefully drawn-up, terrible details.

What the hell was he going to do?

He shrank the file and sat there for a moment, tapping the side of the tablet with his fingernail, thinking about the nuclear option of suiting up, running through the base with a scalpel, overturning the trays of plants and barrels of fish, smashing the satellite dish and the solar panels, then driving the buggy out into the desert and finding a chasm to hurtle into.

If it was the only way to do damage to XO, then that's what he'd do. Suicide, taking a multi-billion-dollar investment with him, and there was absolutely nothing they could do about it. He wondered what they were thinking right now, with days of non-contact, their precious base uncommunicative and for all they knew... What did they know from their orbital cameras? That someone was alive. And that three people were dead.

The last message they'd received from Brack was on—Frank

checked—the ninth. *Phase two complete.* That was it. That was what Brack had sent straight after finding both Frank and Zero in the med bay and thinking them both dead. The dish had been offline since, so XO's reply was somewhere in a queue over his head. Along, presumably, with increasingly urgent queries as to why he wasn't responding.

Yes, he could trash the base. But that wasn't going to get him back to Earth, to freedom, to Mike. And maybe his ex-wife, though depending on whether she'd moved on or not, that might be awkward. No, scratch that: of course she'd moved on. Mike, then. Concentrate on his son. Concentrate on the idea of his son, who, in Frank's imagination, had turned his life around and gone to college and was starting out poor but happy in his chosen career. Frank needed to be alive for that. He needed NASA for that.

Just how long did he think he could survive here?

Indefinitely? Not that long. Something would break down that he couldn't fix. If he got the hydroponics wrong, he could go from feast to famine in a matter of weeks. If he couldn't eat the fish, and couldn't replace the protein, then he was going to get sick.

But he didn't need indefinitely. It said there, in black and white, when NASA were coming: three months. That was all. Three months to hang on. Could he do that?

He went into the greenhouse, cycling the airlock that kept the higher CO_2 inside with the plants, and just stood there on the staging by the door. The bright lights, the constant sound of circulating water, the startling greenness of the plants. It looked…complicated. Zero had managed the whole system, from set-up to harvest. Though if the kid could do it, so could he, he guessed.

Strawberries grew well with hydroponics, as did groundnuts. He collected a bowl of each and took them back through to the kitchen, leaving a pile of broken husks and green stalks on the table.

The act of eating slowed him down. It made him concentrate on what he was doing. He chewed, and looked around him again, but this time he didn't see what he had before. The base was supposed to be his prison: that was what he'd signed up for, somewhere to spend the rest of his Buck Rogers sentence. That had changed with the false promise of a trip home and a pardon after a few years' work. That had changed again into a desperate fight for survival against a regime that had been designed to cull him and his colleagues and get them out of the way before anyone knew they'd even been there.

Where he was, was no longer a prison. The warder was dead, the law too far away to do anything to him.

It was a desert island. Like that old movie about the parcel delivery guy. He had everything he needed to survive. Food, water, shelter, heat—if he was careful and made sure everything worked. If he treated it like that then yes, he was marooned at a distance further away than some rock in the middle of the Pacific, but that didn't change the material facts.

There was a ship coming. He knew that too. A ship that could take him home.

OK, so that was positive. He could look after the base as if it was an island where the sea stretched beyond the far horizon. He could explore, and grow, and mend. That would keep him busy. Better than that, it would keep him engaged. There was hope.

Dee had read all the base's manuals, and the other technical documents that XO had sent. Whether he should have was irrelevant now. He, like everyone else, was dead. Frank would have to play catch-up on that, which meant he'd need to schedule his time carefully.

He'd need to learn the things he needed to survive, quickly. Yes, he needed to be able to grow food as well as Zero had, but he also needed to maintain the water system as well as Zeus had, keep the power flowing into the batteries and out along the cables, like Declan had. He already knew about the physical structure of the base, and how to maintain the buggies. The computer system was going to be a steeper task, but the straight-forward jobs he knew he could do.

And if something went wrong, he'd die.

That was always going to be hanging over his head. Probably best accept it, and move on. Every moment he had now was borrowed. No, not quite that: stolen. He was already a convicted murderer; theft was well within his capacity.

But he was missing something: that he was now in Brack's position. Brack had been expected to survive between the end of Phase two and the arrival of the NASA mission. Brack had probably been given far more training than Frank had, and was also going to rely on the oversight of XO. It showed, however, that it could be done. That it was not just possible, but that it was part of the plan.

Phase three. That was all of Phase three. The clean-up, the removal of evidence. The wait.

It all hinged on NASA. They were the only people who were going to help him, but they were expecting Brack. And if he couldn't convince them that he was Brack, all hell would break loose. Hell, on a base that could be controlled by XO, with comms through XO circuits, wasn't a place he wanted to be. Hell, on a base with no comms at all because he'd sabotaged them to prevent an XO take-over, was still going to be tricky, especially when the NASA guys would make repairing those same circuits an absolute priority.

The idea of them not trying to phone home at some point during their mission was ridiculous. These were people, decent people with families and friends who cared about them, and jobs they needed to do. They weren't going to be held hostage by Frank any more than they were by XO. So unless he was going to permanently wreck the dish before NASA arrived, cutting off for ever all possibility of communicating with Earth, then he needed to come up with something else.

The first thing—literally the first thing—that any visiting

astronaut would see would be the carnage on the cross-hab floor. Then they'd dig further, and everything would unravel: the bodies, the drugs, the gun, the suits, the simple fact he was growing food for more than just himself. He was going to have to work through the entire Phase three plan anyway, just to keep up appearances.

Sure. Why not? That was the easy part. Brack was just a name. NASA were expecting him, or someone like him. Though if they'd already met Brack, then his plan would fall apart at that point.

That was a real problem. He could pretend to be Brack only if they accepted that he was Brack.

There was only one solution. He needed to talk to XO. And given that he had their multi-billion-dollar base by the cojones, and their dirty little secrets, they'd cut a deal with him. They could hardly say no. In fact, they could only say yes. Oh, sure, XO would be looking for ways to double-cross him, but Zeus— the ghost of Zeus—had been wrong. Frank inexplicably held enough cards to be reasonably certain they couldn't kill him off before he made it off-planet.

He'd decided. He was going to be Brack and get his ride home.

4

[Internal memo: Mars Base One Mission Control to Bruno Tiller 11/12/2048 (transcribed from paper-only copy)]

We have been unable to contact MBO now for fifty-six [56] hours. MBO still appears undamaged, as are all other components. No change in the external environment of MBO or the DV has been recorded since 11/11/2048.

The reason for the communications silence, and the identity of Subject #1, remains entirely speculative. We have insufficient data to reach any conclusions. Activity inside MBO is consistent with the continued function of automatic systems, but does not preclude the presence of one or more personnel. Regrettably, the likelihood of LOC is now high. Full LOC contingency measures should be implemented as a matter of urgency.

[transcript ends]

Outside. The faint sun had just crested the eastern wall of the crater, and the solar panels were catching the first weak rays. It was cold—Frank's suit was registering an external temperature of minus ninety, and there was white frost covering the ground. As the feeble sun struck it, it smoked and hung low over the rocks as fog that swirled around his ankles as he made his way over from the cross-hab to the satellite dish.

His footsteps were all but silent. He could feel the crunch of frozen soil beneath his boots, but the sound didn't travel. The only noise was his own breathing, and the faint hum of the circulating fans.

He inspected the satellite dish's trip switches. He'd flipped them all off to stop Brack from communicating with Earth. It was time for him to turn them back on. He lifted the cover and snapped his thumb against them, one at a time, giving a few seconds between each one to make sure a power surge wasn't going to take them all down again.

"Nice and easy," said Declan. He was back in his spacesuit, but his faceplate was still broken, his eye still missing, his cheek still shattered.

"I'm doing it, I'm doing it. It's my turn to worry about the power now."

Not that it was the transmitter itself that ate up the watts, but the dish motors used to align it. Two-fifty each: enough to spike the system and turn random shit off.

He flipped the last switch and watched as the dish jerked into life, slowly and silently, and turned from pointing almost due west to face the sky. He admired his work for a moment, looking up at the almost-black zenith and the peanut-shaped moon caught mid-flight, skipping from horizon to horizon like a thrown stone.

In around ten minutes, XO would realize that they had a connection. It was time Frank needed to prepare himself. He'd decided on his tactics, and he retained the right to hit the off button if it looked like they were going to try and kill him.

He went back in through the main airlock, and stowed his suit. He'd spent the last few days walking around the base naked, but for this, he felt he should get dressed. His own blue overalls were still half black with blood: however many times he'd washed them, he couldn't get the stains out. In the end, he'd decided that it didn't matter. Brack had spares, and though he was not as tall as Frank, Frank was slighter. He'd tried one on for size: the cuffs were short of both his ankles and his wrists, and though it had been roomy for its previous owner, for him it was a little tight between neck and crotch. But the fit wasn't as terrible as he'd anticipated, which was good because he'd find the state of his own clothing difficult to explain to NASA. He'd keep them for best, and wear his old ones for now.

He sat at the kitchen table, a scuba mask and oxygen tank in front of him, along with a surgical glove, weakly inflated and knotted at the wrist. That was his early warning sign of decompression, something that XO couldn't possibly know about, let alone hack. In front of everything was his tablet—Brack's tablet—OK, it was his tablet now. He read the Phase three summary again, trying to get his mind around what the job genuinely involved. It was a lot of work, and that was without the extra cleaning now needed. His own, old tablet would have to get junked, or wiped at the very least. That would be in the small print somewhere, as this was just an overview.

Three months, though, to do everything before NASA were due. Three months was a tight time-scale, but there wasn't anything he could do to change that. They were on their way: they were almost here, even, having left six months before in a big transit ship. A proper spaceship, too, no sleep tanks. Too risky to use on real astronauts: they were only suitable for disposable crew like him.

The base computer synced to the orbiting satellite. Messages pinged up on his screen. He was live.

There was the response to Brack's last message, and then several more: initially at the rate of one every hour or so, dwindling as earlier communications had gone ignored to a routine one every four hours.

He'd prepared his own message, one that XO weren't going to be expecting. He moved it from the drafts column and read it through again. He'd spent half the night fashioning it, writing and deleting, pecking out new combinations of words with two fingers.

"This is Franklin Kittridge. From the start, let's get one thing absolutely straight. I will destroy this base and everything in it if you try anything. Any hostile act, anything that looks like sabotage, against me or the base's systems, and I'll tear this place apart. No clean-up. Nothing. I'll just leave it all for the next people to find, and you can explain everything to them."

That should wake them up.

"I know what you did. I know about the robots. I know about bringing us here in place of them, and I know about killing us all off. If you try and deny any of this, you might just make me mad enough to want to trash the base anyway. So don't. I've got all the Phase 3 docs."

He hadn't read them all yet, but he had read enough of them to form an opinion. That wasn't a lie.

"I'm prepared, despite everything, to cut a deal with you. I have something you want—your multi-billion-dollar base, and your secrets. You have something I want—my freedom and a lift home. I think that's more than fair, since you'll be getting more out of this than I will. If this goes south, a lot of you reading this message will end up on death row. And you know it.

"So this is what I'm willing to do for you. I'm willing to carry out your Phase 3. I'll clean up the base, look after it like you were expecting Brack to, and wait for the NASA people to arrive. When they do, I'll pretend to be Brack, and keep things running smoothly. I'm not looking to rock the boat."

That was the bait. Now to extract his price.

"I don't know what you promised Brack, but I'm guessing it's a suitcase full of dollar bills and a lifetime of silence. I'll take that, and a commutation: time served will do. I'm not looking for parole, or early release on license. I want to be done with it. A clean start. Obviously, I get Brack's place for the flight home. I'll play along with the deception as long as you do. When I get back to Earth, you give me my money and my paperwork, and that's it: that's the only contact I want or need from you. You leave me alone after that."

All that was left was the boilerplate, because he was certain XO wouldn't make it this far without figuring out that he was vulnerable in one particular area.

"One last thing. If you threaten, attempt to threaten, or in any way mention, my family in these negotiations, I will burn this base to the ground, without hesitation or thought about myself. I hope that's really clear, because I'll do it, and I need you to know that. This deal is between you and me and it doesn't involve anyone else."

It was simple—plain, almost—but unambiguous and defiant. It wasn't going to leave them in any doubt about what he wanted and what he'd do if he didn't get it.

"Take your time. I'm not going anywhere in a hurry, no thanks to you. But don't take too long, because I'm not lifting a finger to help you until we come to an agreement we can both stick to."

That was about as good as it was going to get. He took a deep breath, and pressed send.

XO weren't going to get it for ten minutes. Then there'd be the time it took for the operators at the other end of the interplanetary phone line to pass the message up the corporate ladder until it reached someone who could actually make a decision.

Part of him wanted to be a fly on the wall for that. And part of him was glad he wouldn't be there, because if their reaction wasn't one of begging his forgiveness for the terrible things they'd done, he wasn't certain what he'd do.

He'd started the process. He wasn't going to sit around and wait for an answer, because he had chores. He checked the list of things he had to do in the greenhouse: it was long, and it was detailed. He could follow instructions, though, if he could work out what everything was.

After some digging, he'd discovered the main computer had sufficient documentation on the hydroponics: there were even pictures, which were incredibly useful. And it didn't go into the theory, either: he didn't need to know about the whys and wherefores of crop management. All he needed was a comprehensive, if simplistic, set of instructions on how to grow stuff to eat on Mars.

Whoever had put this all together had known their shit, even if they were colluding with murdering bastards.

He took the tablet and gave himself another tour of the greenhouse. With care, he could identify the juvenile plants by the shape of their leaves, rather than relying on the obvious fruit they might yield in maturity. He realized that if all the stuff that Zero had planted kept on growing, he'd literally be drowning in food. There were no pests. No diseases. The nutrients delivered to each plant or type of plant were individually tailored to maximize the harvest.

He could literally throw half the greenhouse out of the airlock, and still have too much.

He read further, and discovered that he needed to reserve seeds off some, for growing on. Other plants would fruit continually, and he had to keep them growing, even if he wasn't going to consume the produce. The cereals: those he could harvest in a conventional manner, resow the seed, and build up stocks of grain—rice and wheat, maize and oats. That'd be especially important for him, since he'd still not been able to kill and eat a fish, though God knows he'd tried.

The paradox was that he was going to have to cull them anyway—the tilapia relied on the nutrient-rich waste water to make what was essentially pond scum, which they then ate. Fewer plants meant less water. He wasn't looking forward to that moment.

But for balance, if he put half the area he was going to cultivate into cereals, and then kept the other half for salads, herbs, pulses, and soft fruit, then he'd probably do OK. It was subverting the Phase three plan slightly, but he ought to be able to make it work. Even if he'd never looked after so much as a pot plant before. Sure, he'd served his time cutting lawns, but that was purely mechanical. After the hard landscaping, he'd left the planting schemes to the professionals.

He examined the rice carefully. Each individual plant was confined to its own hole in the tray, and water seeped underneath, continually washing the roots in a mineral-rich soup. The minerals had all been brought from Earth in highly concentrated forms, in sealed containers baldly labeled A, B and C. Each batch of plants needed different proportions of each of the three mixed into their water hoppers, and servo-controlled syringes pushed out the concentrate according to timers.

Some of the syringes were nearly empty. He'd taken his eye off the ball for too long. It was time to get serious about survival.

He needed to identify what he could turn off now, and what he needed to keep going. The simplest choices first: the cereals stayed, the groundnuts stayed, the soft fruit—freeze-drying, why the hell hadn't he thought of that before?—stayed. Start with the salad stuff: half of that could go now, but he needed to make sure that he caught some in all stages of maturity.

Each tray had a valve that controlled the flow of water into the hopper. He turned those he'd identified off, knowing that it'd be some time before the hoppers emptied. He could correct, for a while, any mistakes he made.

Yes, he'd be sad to see the plants shrivel and die. Zero's hard work, consigned to...he hadn't given much thought to what he was going to do with it. Stick it in the airlock, let the water boil out, and then bag the remains? There might be something in Phase three about that.

His tablet pinged at him. A response at last. But when he opened the app and looked, he was disappointed.

"Can you confirm the status of Lance Brack."

Brack had a first name. Of course he did. Probably a middle name too. But was that all they wanted? He supposed that he hadn't actually said what had happened to the XO man, though surely they must have guessed. Frank sat himself in

37

the greenhouse chair, and considered how candid his response should be. He balanced the tablet on his knees and pecked out:

"He's dead. He shot me, and some time later, I managed to stab him to death with a scalpel. He bled out on the floor of Comms. I wrapped his body in parachute cloth and I put him outside, along with Zero and Declan, next to the base. If you want photographs I can probably do that, but there doesn't seem much point: you should be able to see that anyway. If he'd managed to kill me as he was supposed to, we wouldn't be having this conversation."

He tapped send.

He'd read some of the earlier messages, and one word stood out: chimps. Brack had called him—had called them all—that, while he'd been kicking Zero's body. That was how he referred to them throughout. Chimps. He'd seethed for a while, and then he'd calmed down. He now had a plan. He needed to follow it.

There'd be no response for another half-hour. Chimps. He gritted his teeth and went back to work.

He took out a lot of the salad—there was only so many leaves he could eat, and they weren't particularly high in calories anyway. The herbs he kept some of, knowing that he could dry what died and use them like that. The gourds and squashes, the zucchini and peppers, were prolific fruiters, and they wouldn't keep. He left in a couple of those at each stage and wiped out the rest.

The space he'd make could be used for more energy-dense crops. The potatoes in their barrels of de-chlorated Martian gravel seemed to be doing well. That was one thing at least that movie had got right. He could expand the nuts and the cereals, and divert some of the water resources to them. Nut oil. He might be able to make fries. Then again, any oil hot enough to cook a potato was going to be hot enough to set off the fire alarms.

He'd probably done enough for now. What he really wanted to do was try and freeze-dry a strawberry.

He picked one of the reddest ones, put it in a small tray, and slid it into the airlock at the back of the greenhouse. Obviously, he couldn't be doing this on single fruits often, because he'd run out of electricity to power the air pumps, but this was just an experiment. He looked through the window in the door and started pumping the chamber down.

The berry started to smoke and shrink, and it continued to do so until it was the size of a grape. It sat on the tray, small and red and wrinkled. Frank let the air back in, and retrieved the fruit.

It was like rubber, slightly yielding, like a superball. He licked it, and it tasted of strawberries. He didn't know why he was surprised by that. He gnawed at it, and got intense strawberry flavors. The middle was still soft and undehydrated. Maybe slice it next time, and let the vacuum reach all the parts. But for a first attempt, it wasn't bad, and even though he didn't know how they'd keep inside, he could literally just store them outside in some of the unused cargo drums until he needed them. That might even be better, because it was cold outside, and if he put the drums into the area of shade cast by the curved hab, they wouldn't heat up during the day either.

The tablet pinged again, and he went to see what XO had to say this time.

"Can you confirm your status? Your medical read-out is offline."

Well, they weren't going to win any awards for their bedside manner, that was for certain. They were as bad as Alice had been.

So, how was he doing? His arm, where Brack had shot him, seemed to be healing over well enough. The jelly-like plug had solidified into a dark, knotted mass that caused him discomfort only when he used that muscle. He'd cleaned it that morning, wiping away the crusty ooze that leaked from it, and unscientifically sniffing at it to see if it was infected. But the skin around it, though bruised, seemed not to be inflamed or hot to the touch. His chest, where he'd cut out the medical monitor that had been spying on him since he'd been fitted with it, was a bit more weepy, and the edges of the wound were puckered and replete with beads of ruby-red scabs. But it did appear to be healing up too.

It wouldn't kill him. Not today, at least.

And the howling, existential terror at being all alone on Mars, that manifested itself as a sudden tightness across his ribs, so constricting that he couldn't breathe, seemed to have lessened now he was actually talking to someone, even if that someone had wanted him dead, and probably still did. Strange how things worked out.

The message header told him it was twelfth of November 2048. Three months, give or take a couple of weeks, was between the beginning and end of February. February 2049. They had reckoned on Brack clearing up in that time, and it wasn't as if they had spare astronauts up their sleeve.

"I'm well enough to carry out Phase 3 if that's what you're asking."

He tapped the screen to send the message, and went back to work.

He picked the herb leaves until the plants were nothing but stalks, and arranged them on a single tray in separate, loose piles, according to type. He shoved those through the airlock too, and watched them turn dry and brittle.

It felt good to be doing something. To be planning for the future. To be even thinking that he might have a future. Dried herbs. He sniffed his fingers and caught the complex aromas the bruised leaves gave off.

He flooded the chamber with air again, and examined the contents of the tray. When he held up a basil leaf to the sharp LED lighting that hung low over the plants, he could see the individual veins. He crumbled it between his fingers. It shattered like thin glass and turned into fragments, almost dust. Possibly a bit too small: again, some preparation might have been necessary, chopping the leaves before drying them out. But he could just save the leaves whole, bag them up and use them that way.

Franklin Kittridge, gourmet chef.

It was almost as if he'd forgotten for a moment how much trouble he was in. He allowed himself a tight smile, and went through the racks again, turning the lights off he didn't need, the pumps, the syringe drivers, to give his power budget a boost. He checked his tablet, and saw that he'd saved over a quarter of a kilowatt. That wasn't bad at all.

He went back around and looked at the cereals. He didn't know how to tell whether they were ripe or not, so he hit the books again.

"Grains should be firm, but not brittle." He crouched beside what he'd previously identified as rice. The short stems were heavy with blunt heads, curved over between the yellow-green blade-like leaves. "Eighty to eighty-five per cent of the grains should be yellow-colored." OK, they were pretty much all a light brown. That was promising. He teased one of the grains out and into his hand.

He rubbed it between his palms to dehusk it, and lightly blew away the chaff. It looked like a grain of rice. Again, the surprise was real, and he frowned at his own ignorance. Of course it did. Where the hell did he think rice came from if not from an actual rice plant?

No point in beating himself up about that, or anything else. He had expertise in other areas, and he got his groceries from the store like everyone else. Most people wouldn't know how a cinder block got made, either.

He collected another empty tray, and plucked—there should be some snippers around, but Zero appeared to have hidden those—the seed heads one by one until he'd got them all. There were a lot. Enough to eat. Enough to eat and still have plenty over to replant.

The how-to told him he now had to thresh the rice, to separate all the grains from the husks, and do this as soon after harvest as possible. Threshing. He hoped that he'd have instructions for that too, because peeling each grain individually was going to take a while.

And maybe he should have read that section first, because it turned out he should have picked the rice at the bottom of the stem, not the top. It was a rookie error, not one he was likely to make twice, but now he had nothing to hold on to to beat the seed head against anything. Some sort of sealable container with a lid would probably have to do, shake it until...something happened. It wasn't magic. People had been doing this for thousands of years.

He'd just be the first person doing it on another planet.

Ping.

He'd left the tablet on the chair. He picked it up and saw what they'd written this time.

"Franklin. OK, to be honest, we're a little surprised here, and we'd like some time to work out what to do. We don't have the authority to make these kinds of decisions on our own, so we need to go and talk to some people who can help us on a way forward. It's probably going to take a few hours to get everyone together in the same room, and a few more hours after that to be able to discuss your situation and get back to you.

"Nothing is going to happen, good or bad, in that time. You've probably wondered if we can remotely operate some of the basic systems at the base, on a considerable time lag. We can, but you can always override that locally. In any event, no one will be interfering with the base systems at all, and you have my word on that. Please don't do anything that would jeopardize the integrity of the base, or your personal safety. If anything happens to either, it'll mean that any offer we might be able to make to you based on current circumstances will be null and void, and we'll all have to go back to the drawing board. Hold tight, and expect something in maybe four-five hours time, but definitely by the end of the sol. Luisa, XO MBO Mission Control."

He read it, and read it again. It seemed...refreshingly honest. He had no idea who this Luisa was, whether he'd met her.

Whatever, she was right—there wasn't anything they could do to him at this distance that didn't give him enough time to destroy the base before he succumbed. There was a measure of realism in her comments that indicated that at least someone was taking him seriously. Whether the suits would, was a different matter entirely, but even they had to know he meant business.

Frank felt in his pocket for the tied-off rubber glove. It wasn't inflating, and it was fine. He wondered if he should always have the scuba gear nearby in case they tried something sneaky like alter the gas mix. He needed to remember that the XO people at the other end of his message stream had been surprised he was still alive, and that he should on no account trust them.

He'd get a response by the end of the day. He could only imagine the flurry of activity, the panic and argument that would blow up as his message reverberated up and down the XO command structure.

In the end, they'd deal. They'd try to weasel out later on, but they'd deal for now, and Frank would just have to stay a step ahead.

5

[Private diary of Bruno Tiller, entry under 11/13/2048, transcribed from paper-only copy]

I don't often get emotional, because emotions have no place in business. But I admit today to feeling anger, at being so badly let down. Everything is in the balance. Everything. I'm heading down there now, to personally chair the meeting. There will be no reputational damage to either XO, or myself. None.

Any other outcome is unacceptable.

[transcript ends]

Frank now inhabited the gray area between collaborator and victim. He had his agreement. He'd forced XO's hand, and in turn they'd forced his. He wasn't a lawyer, and he'd refused to sign or assent to any kind of contract—they'd got him once before like that, sitting in an interview room in San Quentin—and he wasn't going to fall for it again. What he had was an understanding, a spit-and-handshake. Old-school trust, even where there was none.

Frank would carry out Phase three. He'd clean up the base. He'd prepare for the NASA mission. He'd answer to the name "Brack". In return, XO would clear the path for him to return home. They'd get his sentence commuted. They'd give him enough money to start afresh. And they'd keep on paying a sum, every year, to tie them to each other in perpetuity.

It wasn't enforceable in any way, except that the penalties for defaulting were unthinkable. It was literally their lives on the line. Frank's for sure. The unwitting NASA astronauts' too. And if any of this got in front of a grand jury, there'd be a whole bunch of XO people ratting each other out for a deal. It was in everybody's best interest to see this to the bitter end.

On Frank's part, he was under no illusion that his troubles would be over when he got back to Earth. A company that could base their entire business model around murder were no better than organized crime, and they could come for him at any point. And even if Frank went to the press, or the Feds, then… it was going to get complicated. He was a convicted murderer with a few new scars and a tin-foil hat story about how he got to Mars. The NASA crew could corroborate some of the details, but nothing of what happened before they arrived on the red planet.

He knew he'd be on the clock. He knew what he wanted to do with that time. Find his boy. Give him a hug. Tell him that he loved him and was proud of him whatever. Apologize to Jacqui for what he'd done. That shit had gone down without her knowledge or her assent. The kid he'd shot's family? Maybe not. He was sorry, but it was unlikely they'd want to hear from him, let alone see him.

After that? Fuck XO. Let them come. He'd be pretty much done by that point. He knew he was never going to make old bones. Oh, he could lead them on a merry dance, and maybe they'd give up first, and leave him alone, or maybe he'd give up and let them find him. That bridge needed to be crossed at some point.

For now, he had a deal. And that deal started with driving three dead bodies over to the ship.

In their black-and-white parachute shrouds, they'd been stiff like boards. Easy, then, especially now they behaved more like luggage than corpses, to lever them upright and push them onto the open latticework of a trailer, then hitch that up to the back of one of the buggies. Each one went lengthways, and he'd fastened them down with ratchet straps from the cargo cylinders.

He unplugged the fuel cell from the base power supply. The cold had made the cable stiff and unyielding, and it wasn't going back into its drum container. He dropped the connector inside under the lid and would finish coiling it up when he'd returned and the air was warmer.

Frank set off deliberately slowly across the river delta Dee had christened the Heights. The buggy's wheel plates would be brittle, and he hadn't worked out a way to replace any of them yet: repairing a wheel, out in the middle of nowhere, on his own, wasn't something he wanted to do. He was going to have to be more cautious from now on. No more joy-rides up the Santa Clara.

The journey was barely two miles, but it still took a quarter of an hour. The morning fog had burned off, leaving the cold, hard ground with long shadows from the rough fist-sized rocks that littered the surface. Each shadow twinkled white, a frost-pocket that would soon evaporate away, but dust was now rising from the turning wheels.

The rising sun illuminated the horizon far more brightly than the sky above; the wind blew the dust up into the air where it caught the light. The zenith was still nearly black. Between, the typical pinkish blue was smudged with ribbons of high cloud that seemed to chase towards the night.

It could be called beautiful and perhaps, in the right company, it might be. Right now, though, he knew how lethal Mars could be, even without someone actively trying to kill him. To him, it was a barren wasteland that was indifferent as to whether he lived or died. One mistake, and it'd all be over.

The ship they'd landed in was a bullet-shaped white cone that sat off the Martian surface using four retractable legs. Its off-white color had slowly stained red, and sand, blown by the ephemeral winds, had mounted up against the dinner-plate-shaped feet, burying them completely. It already looked part of the landscape, and Frank was used to seeing it there, either as a small pearl in the distance, or as a landmark as he drove past.

Only once recently had he had cause to stop and go in. That had...ended badly. He'd found the floor swamped with empty painkiller packets and used food containers. He'd found four dead people in the sleep pods. It had been, ironically, his wake-up call that all was not well with Brack.

He let go of the throttle on the little steering wheel mounted on the controls, and the buggy coasted to a halt opposite the steps to the ship's airlock. He jumped down to the surface. The gravity made it seem like he was flying.

Under the ship was a bare area that had been scoured clean down to the bedrock by the landing rockets. It had only slowly been reclaimed by the dust. Frank pulled the bodies off the trailer one by one, and laid them out beneath the downward-flaring nozzle, then retreated again. He'd put them inside only when it was time for the ship to leave, carrying its cargo of evidence. Because rot and decay, that was still going to happen, right?

He climbed up the steps to the airlock, wondered if it was going to cycle, because it was XO's ship and they could still probably control it remotely. But the lights changed and the door opened automatically. If XO really did control the ship, what could they do to him? Nothing in the twenty or so minutes it took for a signal to reach Earth and a command to come back. He ought to make that a rule, not to spend any longer than that inside the ship. Though XO probably had other things to worry about right now.

He entered the airlock and cycled it through again. The outer door slid shut, and slowly sound returned.

Inside was as he'd left it. Of course it was. There was no one but him who could have moved anything. And he didn't really believe there were the ghosts of his dead crewmates walking around: that was just a coping mechanism, along with the dreams of knives and asphyxia and standing naked to the Martian day, screaming as his life's water boiled out of him. OK, not dreams. Flashbacks. He blinked them away.

The floor was still covered in trash. Brack's sleeping mat was still stretched out on the storey above, and beyond that, on the third level, the sleep pods containing four corpses. There were lockers he probably needed to check, see what supplies were still usable, but not today. He wasn't even sure why he'd come inside. Was it to confirm to himself that he really was alone?

Probably.

Lights burned on the consoles, red, amber and green. Blue lights for power. Some were flashing, but he knew better than to touch them. Flipping switches might well cause him more problems than he already had. Why add to them unnecessarily? The base was sufficient for his immediate needs.

There was still something strange—eerie, even—about this abandoned vessel turned into a morgue. It had brought eight people to Mars. One was left. And he didn't need it any more. It was part of his past, not his future, however that turned out and however long it might be. It was a monument. It might as well be made of granite.

He cycled the airlock and felt his suit grow stiff as the air pumped away. He checked his read-out to make sure he had plenty of air and power. Then he opened the outer door, and there was Mars again. Still cold, still lifeless, still red.

While he was here with the trailer, he might as well collect one of the four cargo containers which had all the NASA equipment inside, that Brack had parked at the bottom of the drop-off. They had to come up sometime, and now was as good a time as any. He could stick them all in the boneyard outside the base and then transfer stuff, a few boxes at a time, each time he went back through the airlock. Otherwise, he'd have a week of nothing but lifting and carrying, and continually running the airlock pumps, which was going to exhaust both him and the base's batteries. He wasn't going to be as diligent as Declan at keeping the panels clean; he had enough power for normal circumstances, but repeatedly cycling the airlock? That would quickly leave him in the dark.

It could even kill him. Better not do that.

He hadn't been down to the crater floor for a while. The last time had been early on in that long night, the one he was trying to forget but couldn't. He drove the slope carefully, the empty trailer bouncing and slewing around behind him as it slipped unweighted on the loose sand. Ideally, he'd have enough cable on the winch drum to park up at the top and just pull the cylinders towards him, but the drop was a lot more than a hundred and fifty feet.

Marcy had taught him how to reverse the trailer into position. She'd been the first to die. Not an accident, but such was the situation at the time, Frank didn't know that it would have mattered if he'd been the one with the "faulty" CO_2 scrubber. The others would have carried on without him, just in the same way that they carried on without Marcy. By her dying, there'd been one less mouth to feed, one pair of lungs fewer to breathe the air.

She'd been culled, and Alice after her, so that the rest of them would live long enough to build the base. Goddammit, that was brutal. And these were the people he'd just made a bargain with.

"The devil," said Zeus. "You did it, Frank. I told you not to."

Zeus was in his suit, but that didn't stop the smoke from boiling out of him, swirling in his faceplate like clouds.

"Not now, Zeus. Really, not now."

Rather than look at him, Frank unhooked Brack's tablet from his waist loop and opened it up to check the manifests of the cylinders. Maybe when he'd done, Zeus would have gone.

The map popped open, and there were the four white crosses down where he expected them. But what the hell was this? The hinterland, the immediate parts of the Tharsis plain from where he'd retrieved the cylinders to build the MBO, were dotted with crosses too.

OK, it was an older version of the map. Brack hadn't refreshed it for months. All those cargo drops Frank and the others had collected were still marked in their original positions.

No, that wasn't right. Those were all there, in the boneyard, a bright crowding of crosses that almost obscured the base itself. He refreshed the map anyway, doing a hard reset. The map cleared, and then the crosses all reappeared, inexorably, one by one.

Where had they come from?

Scratch that. They'd come from Earth. Of course they had.

These were XO deliveries. They showed up on his— Brack's—system, but not on Frank's own. He knew that if he touched the cross, it'd give him an overview of the inventory. He touched the nearest one to him, which lay a few miles south of the far end of Rahe.

Solar farm.

"Goddammit. Look at this." He turned and held the tablet out for Zeus to see, but he'd long since disappeared. Then Frank realized what he'd done, and sheepishly turned back.

Spares. They were his spares, dotted about the plain, even more scattershot than the first set of hab components had been. If the map was accurate, some of those were going to be utterly unreachable by a one-man operation.

How long had they been sitting there on the Martian surface? Frank had no way of knowing, but there'd been plenty of activity in the sky above the base for the last few months. Brack had warned them off "space piracy", but he'd known they were meant for the base all along, and that he'd be going to get them as part of Phase three.

The NASA kit could wait. He was going for a power up. He was tired of having to squeak by. Even though Declan had been a complete pain in the ass about his precious watts, he'd kept them all alive throughout the build and beyond. These new panels had arrived too late for him to enjoy the sudden abundance, but he could refer to them as the Declan Murray Memorial Solar Farm, and see if XO bit.

He opened up the message function on the tablet, and pecked out with his fat finger: "Luisa. You should probably have mentioned the extra supplies earlier. You know that, right? Because that's a shit-load of extra work for me to do. Let me make myself clear: you need to tell me everything I need to know, before I need to know it, because from now on, every time I find something out for myself, I'll think you've been deliberately hiding it from me, and that you don't want me to know about it.

"This is going to work on trust, or not at all. And right now, you've got to understand that you've fucked up. I'm going to collect the panels, and when I've brought them back, I'm going to plug them in and turn all the lights on. The rest of the schedule can wait. Don't do this to me again."

He sent the message and closed the app down, then checked out what else was waiting for him.

He tabbed another of the crosses, and there was food. Just food. A whole container—six big drums—full of dehydrated food from Earth. As he checked his way through, there was enough lying out there to almost double the size of the base. Hab sections. Wheels for the buggy. Spare fuel cells. Something— what was an In-situ Resource Management Device? It sounded fancy, and it was now his.

He checked his air, and he checked his batteries. Both were good enough to get out onto the plain and retrieve the panels. As ever, if something went wrong with either his suit or his buggy, he was going to die out there, quickly or slowly. No one was going to come and rescue him, because there was no one. But if he wanted the treasure, he was going to have to take the risk.

He looked up at the sky and, more accurately, the time on the tablet. He'd be coming back at dusk, but he had lights and it wasn't as if he didn't know where he was heading: Sunset

Boulevard was so well used, it had become a groove. He wondered if it could be seen from space. Yes, why not? Dee had named it, and there was no reason why it shouldn't enter the official records. The first man-made road on Mars.

Frank set off, dust pluming out behind him as he rattled along at a steady twelve. The driven surface was darker than the surrounding landscape, which was covered with an undisturbed salt rime—the same rime that collected on their helmets and pitted the metal wheels of the buggy. Two hours to drive the length of Rahe, up the collapsed part of the crater wall Dee had called Long Beach. Another hour out on the plain to collect the container, then the two hours back.

With the ridge of Beverly Hills to his left, he traversed the crater floor. It was long, it was boring. Boring on Mars had become a thing: although the landscape was alien, it just wasn't interesting. It wasn't Mars's fault, but it was what he'd grown to expect. Red rock, red dust, ocher sky, pale sun. The only living thing on Mars, barring the greenhouse, was inside his suit. Outside of it was so little atmosphere as to be nothing but imperfect vacuum. Mars was dead and cold and airless, and people still wanted to come here to explore and work. Of their own volition, and not press-ganged like Frank.

The drive out of the crater was better. It was certainly more engaging, but only because it was more dangerous. The slope was steep, the surface loose, the hidden shelves of hard, jagged rock a menace. It had to be taken at a decent pace to allow momentum to carry the buggy over the more inconstant portions, but too quick, and the wheels would lose traction. If they did that, and spent any significant time in the air, then the buggy would slew sideways. Rolling it was a real possibility. And even with the roll cage and being strapped in, he was almost certain to wreck the wheels and leave himself stranded, far out of walking range of both the ship, and the base.

Monotony and fear. Those were his two default states and he seemed to be flipping between them with very little warning.

For ten minutes, twenty, it was continuously uphill, with Frank forced back into his seat and looking at nothing but the slope and the sky. The wheels turned and the plates bit, growling and clattering against the crater wall. He could hear it as well as feel it as he battled to keep the buggy facing forward.

Then, as always, the sudden burst of speed and the shallowing out of the gradient, followed by the explosion of so much Mars against his faceplate. The endless miles of nothing. The volcanoes rising directly from the plain ten thousand feet into a sky that was a dome of bluey-brown. An utterly blank landscape that, save for a few limp parachutes, was painted entirely in shades of red.

He stopped on the first patch of level ground, and hopped off to inspect the wheels and the trailer, and to check again his gas and fuel cell levels. It was second nature now, something he did without thinking.

It was late afternoon—just the right time for dust devils to rise up from the plain—and the sun was low over Uranius Mons, casting a huge, diffuse shadow through the dusty air. He opened up the map to check his direction, and saw there was going to be a problem. Neither his own location, nor the cargo, were marked.

Then he realized. His suit transmitter was still off. He'd turned it off that night, and had had no reason to turn it back on again. Away from both the main base and the ship, the map app had no way of talking to the satellites above. Did he dare risk turning his suit comms on? Did he dare not? If he couldn't place himself on the map, he might end up traipsing across half of Mars looking for stuff and then not be able to find his way home.

If he was talking to XO, then he guessed he'd already made that decision. He tapped his way through his suit menu until he got to the right tab. He poked it back on, and a few seconds later the map recentered on his position, right at the top of Long Beach, and his targets bloomed on the landscape.

He set off southwards, skirting the edge of the crater, until the cross he was looking for merged with his own pointer. Then he stopped, stood up on the buggy's frame and steadied himself using the roll cage, scanning the surroundings for any sign of the cylinder or its parachute. The map would only put him in the right area. After that, it was up to him.

And even though it was a plain, almost laser flat, the ground was pocked with craters, large and small, young and sharp-edged, old and barely even hollows. He'd had to retrieve cargo from several, sometimes even running a line over the rim and dragging the damn thing out. For all that they'd traveled a hundred million miles and all but crashed onto another planet, the cylinders really didn't like lateral stress. He'd bent more than a couple that way.

There, half a mile distant, half hidden in a slight depression. This was going to be sweet. He'd be able to literally leave the lights on all night if he wanted: a full farm, another two big batteries, a full fifteen kilowatts of generating capacity. Of all the things to get excited about, he'd never thought that scavenging items from the surface of Mars would ever figure.

He drove over, dismounted and went to inspect the cylinder, lying slightly point-up and looking like a thirty-foot-long white pencil. The last solar farm had hard-landed, and over a third of the panels had broken on impact: it had only been luck that the batteries had survived, because if it had been the other way around, they'd have frozen to death. This one, barring some scorch-marks up the side, was intact, right down to the XO logo painted on the side.

He used the tool to open one of the pair of side hatches, and he had enough experience to know that the door tended to blow out when released. He was ready for it when it popped—not an audible pop, more something that he could feel through his feet. Then he helped swing the door the rest of the way, and he rummaged through the layers of insulation until he could read what was on the side of one of the drums. Panels: solar. 5x1kW. This was what he'd come for.

He pulled the hatch closed and relocked it, then winched the cylinder onto the trailer, just past the point of balance so that the end cleared the ground. Done. The parachute was gone, somewhere. Sometimes they detached properly, and ended up miles away. Other times they were still hanging from their lines, and the Martian wind wasn't strong enough to shift them after they'd touched down.

The parachutes were useful all the same. Frank tended to pick up everything he could, and take it with him. It had cost a lot to get the stuff there. There was no point—unless it was actually dangerous—in leaving it. He'd have to leave this one, though, if he couldn't find it easily.

He stood up on the buggy frame again and looked for the telltale black-and-white against the dun-colored ground, but couldn't immediately see it. He checked his air, and the light, and decided that he could afford to spend ten minutes circling the drop site to find it. After that, he'd have to head home. He set off, more sedately than before because he was towing, and drove another half-mile south, before turning slowly eastwards. Every so often he'd stop and climb up, hanging off the roll cage, but he couldn't spot it.

But he did see something. Tire tracks that he couldn't possibly have made, because he'd never been this way before. He parked up next to them, and climbed down to make certain that these weren't apparitions like his dead crewmates.

Squatting awkwardly in the dust, he peered at first one, then the other, of the parallel lines. They were real: when he ran his hand through the dirt that carried them, he left lines on the ground, and red on his gloves. They weren't fresh tracks: in comparison to the ones he was making, the edges of the plate-marks were blurred, and if he looked up and down the track he could see there were places where they'd been obliterated completely, presumably by the passage of a Martian twister. That would make them a couple of weeks old, but not a couple of months.

All tracks made by his wheels had a direction—the central tread was V-shaped. These had the same pattern. They were, in fact, identical, and could only have been made by an XO buggy, heading north. Brack had been this way before, then, presumably on his way back from collecting the NASA equipment. He stood up and stared into the south, past the sloping flanks of Ceraunius and into the haze. There was nothing there, either.

He checked his air again, and the battery level on the buggy. It was time to abandon the parachute to Mars, and he turned the wheels to head back to Long Beach. Something was tickling his mind, giving him a feeling of unease, but there were so many things he was worried about. It was only when he met his outgoing tracks that the thought crystallized.

There were no other tracks leading south.

He stopped. He stood up. He turned around and looked behind him. There was still nothing. He'd driven maybe five miles after turning right at Long Beach, pretty much due south. He'd never driven south before from that point. He'd gone all points of the compass—north, north-east, north-west and west. That had been where all the supplies had landed, out on the Tharsis plain in a roughly triangular area between the three volcanoes. Some of the drops had been beyond the range of one life-support pack, necessitating a dangerous swap-out halfway.

But none had fallen in the south.

Brack may have been south. May. But he would have had to travel east first, then south, then back following the exact same route. Two sides of a triangle, twice, when a shorter direct distance was available. They could literally go straight on Mars, unless there was an impassable geographical feature they had to detour around. The shortest route was always best.

Was it subterfuge on Brack's part? Tire tracks south might have alerted the crew as to the arrival of fresh deliveries. Then again, none of them had been out as far as Long Beach since they'd picked up the very last of the containers they'd needed for Phase one, which was months ago. And Brack had chosen to stack the NASA equipment at the base of the Heights, which was hardly hidden away. Granted, he hadn't been making good decisions by that point, but after that he'd still managed to kill three men and had nearly done for Frank, too. So he hadn't been completely incapable of action.

It simply didn't make any sense. To go south, anyone would have got to the top of Long Beach—which was itself a lengthy drive—and gone straight to their destination. Unless...

Unless there was something hidden in the distance, out on the plain due east of Rahe, that Brack had called at on his way out, and on his way back. That would make as much sense as anything, but he didn't have the time, nor the range, to go and look for it today.

Soon, then. The tracks were there. All he had to do was follow them out and see where they led.

6

I'm sorry, Frank. This situation is very new to us as well. We're trying to keep things professional here, and anything that affects that—of course that includes your well-being—is our number one concern. We'll have to try a little bit harder to communicate that to you, and I can only apologize if you feel we've let you down so far.

Good luck, Luisa.

[message ends]

Frank had to go through each hab, upper and lower levels, and make a fingertip search for anything that might indicate that the base had been the home for eight people and not one. Disposing of spacesuits, tablets, overalls, worn sleeping mats, part-used toiletries, scratched crockery and cutlery, everything. Special attention had to be paid to finding telltales like personalized graffiti or notes—written on what was anyone's guess, as there was no paper. Bodily remains such as hair and skin needed to be removed and disposed of, including a thorough cleaning of the drains.

Then there was all the blood.

Now that the satellite dish was working again, the computer

would purge itself automatically of data: the seven-day cycle of information would ensure that. The rest was up to him.

He'd found out the ultimate destination of the descent ship that had brought him and the others to Mars. When they'd had problems early on with power generation and the lack of spares, Brack had told them, point-blank and without explanation, that they weren't to cannibalize the ship at all. The reason was because the ship was taking off again.

It didn't have enough fuel to re-enter Earth's orbit, nor could it re-enter the atmosphere. Its rockets weren't enough to slow it down, and its heat shield and parachutes had already been used and discarded.

What it was going to do was two-fold. Firstly, it was going to throw up a smokescreen that would cover the lack of robotic base-building machines, under the pretense of returning them to Earth for commercially sensitive evaluation. Secondly, it was going to be used to launch the remains of seven dead people, and all evidence they'd ever come to Mars, into the heart of the Sun.

Frank had blinked roundly at that. He wasn't a rocket scientist, and didn't know how much fuel that would take, but he presumed whoever had plotted the course knew their math. It might take a year or two to get all the way in, but as far as getting rid of exhibits that might be used in a trial went, dropping them into a star was pretty final.

They'd literally thought of everything. He wondered how much more effort would have been required to refreeze them all and put them back into Earth-orbit, to be collected by a shuttle doing a round trip, up and down again.

Clearly, too much. The whole thing was just...willfully brutal. The lives of seven people didn't figure in someone's spreadsheet, but faking the existence of Mars-graded robots did. Frank, and the rest of them, were just consumables.

Just when he didn't think he had any anger left inside, it came boiling back up to the surface and threatened to overwhelm him. Why shouldn't he just raze the base to the ground and tell them what he'd done?

Because that wasn't going to get him what he wanted. And, dammit, they owed him.

XO's solution to the blood problem was crude: take the affected floor panels outside and rub them down with sand until they came clean. Frank had been hoping he'd be given the instructions on how to brew up a chemical cleaner—the soil contained chlorate, and that sounded a lot like chlorine, and he knew that chlorine was in bleach. Whatever it was, it was corrosive enough to eat away at the metal plates of the tires.

He'd already levered the panels up in Comms, from the place where Brack had bled out, up to the door that had been held shut while Dee had suffocated. About a dozen in all, and when he'd popped them out and carried them to the airlock at the far end of the yard, he'd gone carefully on his hands and knees to see how much of the blood had seeped through the cracks.

Where he'd dragged the body, not at all. Where it had lain for a while, quite a lot. Some had dribbled through into the void between the floor and the ceiling of the lower level, where the pipework and cables ran. That was...unfortunate. He wasn't going to drain and unplumb the whole system, or even parts of it, just to make certain he'd got rid of every last scab. He was going to have to try and get as much of it off as he could—certainly that which was easily visible—by working from both above and below, taking out the ceiling panels too.

Frank wanted to do a good job, because he wasn't going to be able to explain any quantity of spilled blood to a bunch of curious scientists. They'd unravel his excuses in a heartbeat, and then...that was when things would get difficult, for everybody. He wanted to spare himself and the astronauts that, even if it meant letting XO off the hook.

It was a decent day outside—he'd been on Mars long enough to be able to tell good weather from bad. The early morning fog had burned off, and the high ice-clouds chased away westwards.

The dust-load was less than usual, and the view across to Uranius Mons clear enough to discern the truncated top of the volcano.

There'd be dust devils in the afternoon, after the ground had heated up, and it'd get gradually hazier until the sun started to sink again. A purple dusk was in prospect, and a cold night.

He'd laid out the panels near the satellite dish, their hard plastic surfaces shining in the weak sunlight, and had been using a nut runner and parachute cloth as an improvised flap-wheel. It worked inefficiently, but, if he pressed hard enough, sufficiently well for him to persevere. He had electrical power, and he had a planet-load of grit to use as an abrasive.

Slowly but surely, the dirt shifted the blood. He had to stop often to move the soil around, and to check on his progress, but it was a lot quicker than doing it manually.

He cleaned one panel, shook it free of red soil, and started on another.

When he'd done two, he was tired. He drank some water from his suit, and sat back for a few minutes with his back against the dish assembly. The sun had climbed higher, a small yellow disk against a pink-blue halo, darkening to a light brown at the horizon.

His work was carried out in almost perfect silence. Nothing he was doing made enough noise to propagate through Mars's thin air, although he could feel the vibrations through his hands, and imagined the grinding sounds.

Which was why he missed the start of the thunder, and only when it was too loud to ignore did he get to his feet and look up.

Frank scanned the sky, looking for the telltale line of smoke, or the bright dot of a parachute. He couldn't see it to start with. But he was looking too low, expecting it to be directed over the plain like all the others. Only when he leaned back and craned his neck did he see it.

The black streak of burned re-entry shield—technically an entry shield, because it wasn't going anywhere it had been before—was almost zenith-high, angling in over the top of the volcano behind him. He followed its direction, and there were the parachutes along that line, tiny to the naked eye, but in reality vast red-and-white canopies extending far beyond the smudge of metal that pulled them through the thin air.

It fell, and very slowly detail resolved. The object suspended below the parachutes was ship-like: bullet-shaped and bright. It was difficult to tell how large it was, but it was definitely not the pencil-thin arrow of a cargo delivery.

And he realized that it was coming straight for him. It wasn't just close. It was directly above him and it was falling on his head.

If he'd still had his medical monitor, it would have recorded his breathing and heart rate accelerating away. Two immediate, terrible thoughts.

That this was NASA, and he was screwed. The base was still full of evidence. Full of it, and no way to hide it.

And that they were coming in hot. Hard and fast and they were going to hit the base.

He was paralyzed with indecision. Had he left it too late to get to the buggy and drive off, to save himself for however long his air would last? Or was it simply better to let the fireball take him when the ship hit the Heights?

Come on, Frank. Think, goddammit. Think.

It couldn't be NASA. If it was, they'd be early, and they couldn't be early, because that wasn't how space flight worked. Except he didn't know enough about that to be certain. But this sure as hell looked like a descent ship, and it was growing visibly larger by the second.

Moment by moment, it swelled. It was coming down so very fast. And so very close.

Was it going to crash? It wasn't like that hadn't happened before. Cargo plowing into the Martian surface. Leaving a crater. Was the speed of this normal? Had he come in like this?

By now, the parachutes were huge, blotting out the sky, and it was still hurtling downwards. Dangling from the shrouds was a ship. Big enough to be a crew-rated ship. The air trembled. Dust was rising up all around him as if gravity had gone into reverse. If they were here, it was over. Goddammit, he should have got some warning. What was he supposed to do?

He leaned all the way back. The object had sprouted legs, tiny legs that didn't look strong enough to support the body's weight. It was going to be close, so very close.

Then, from his perspective, the oncoming vessel finally started to slide sideways in the sky. From being dead overhead to a few degrees off, then a few more, then clearly it was coming down to the north. It would just miss the base, and his own descent ship, and it wasn't going to crush him.

The parachutes floated free, turning from taut dishes to sky-jellyfish in seconds. Smoke plumed from the base of the falling craft, and bright spears of translucent blue flame stabbed down. The ground shook as the new ship went from freefall to full stop on the Martian surface in bare seconds.

The rockets cut off, and a wave of dust and exhaust roiled across the Heights. With nothing to stop it, the front blew across the base. The brown fog that had formed during the ship's descent was cleared away.

Two miles distant on the Heights, towards the steep drop-off to the crater floor, was a shiny white blunt-headed cone of a structure. He wasn't ready. He wasn't ready at all. There was still blood all over the floors and unburied bodies, and—

Breathe. Hold. Breathe.

If he was Brack, he would know exactly what this was and when to expect it. XO had told him explicitly that NASA were still three months away. They weren't going to shit the bed. Look. Look carefully. His own descent ship was still here, and it was supposed to leave before the astronauts arrived.

OK. OK. It wasn't the astronauts. What the hell was it? What, in the documentation, had he missed? He was determined that there wouldn't be any panicked messages back to Earth, nothing that would show he was incompetent.

He forced himself to walk over to the fully charged-up buggy, and climb up. He didn't want to go and look. He was scared of what he was going to find. But on the other hand, he knew he had to see what it was. He'd felt like this before, but not for a long time. His own father's funeral. Dread. Sick to his stomach. And yet, it was something he had to do, a door he had to pass through.

He drove off across the Heights, heading in the unfamiliar northerly direction, skirting the big, thousand-yard crater that sat slap in the middle of the shelf. As he got closer, the ship slowly resolved in more detail. The legs—sturdy enough for the job, in a third of Earth gravity—just looked spindly, arranged around the circumference of the fatter cone, which sat so low that its base almost touched the ground.

Frank slowed and stopped, looking up at the structure from a respectful distance away. He could see the NASA logo on the side. There was other writing too, too small to make out from where he was. Sooty streaks ran from dark to light from base to tip, partially obscuring some of the letters. He abruptly realized that he was thinking of it as his Mars, and this new ship was trespassing. That was crazy. Mars was plenty big enough.

He climbed down from the buggy and approached. His heart was still yammering in his chest, and he was sticky with sweat. The ship was perfectly still, perfectly silent. For now.

"Hold it together, Frank."

"Marcy?"

The last time he'd seen her, she'd filled up her helmet with vomit. So that's how it was now. She spoke around the splashes on her faceplate.

"Take your time, Frank. Do it better."

"Right. Better. Got it." He nodded, and that seemed to satisfy her, because she wasn't there when he next looked.

He turned his attention to the drop-off: the ground the ship sat on seemed stable enough. The rocket motors had blasted the dust away, leaving the rocks sitting on a bare, craze-cracked pavement. Mud cracks. They looked like mud cracks.

He was close enough to make out the smaller words. "Dog-wood". "MAV".

MAV. The letters rang a very distant bell.

He circumnavigated the ship on foot, leaning back to gaze up at its blank, sloping sides. No windows, no external features at all to speak of. There was, however, a covered box fixed to one of the legs. Frank undid the catch, and found three buttons: two green, with arrows pointing up and down, and one central red one. He glanced around. No one was going to stop him from pressing the buttons, because he was the only one there. He thumbed the down arrow and stepped back.

A hole opened in the side of the ship and a telescopic ladder lowered itself to the ground. At the top of the ladder was a larger door-shaped outline, and a smaller rectangular outline that was probably the door mechanism. He climbed up, hand over hand, and pushed at the spring-loaded cover until it popped open.

Another two green buttons and one red; this time the arrows were pointing into, and out of, boxes. He tapped the in button, and the door pushed out, almost into his face, before sliding aside. Inside was an airlock.

He had another brief moment when he wondered if he should be doing this, and whether or not he ought to be phoning home to find out what the hell this was all about. Then he climbed up and in, and found the controls to close the airlock door behind him.

The main cabin—there was just the one compartment—was mostly empty. Three poles that went from floor to ceiling were the only furniture. There were mostly inert controls and panels around the walls—a few lights were awake, but none of the screens—and that was it. There was no one inside, and remarkably little room, given the size of the ship. His own descent ship was of comparable volume, and it went over three decks. He glanced down at his suit controls, and registered what his body had already told him: the ship was in vacuum.

He climbed out, and down the ladder, and closed everything

65

up behind him. He walked around it again, and had stopped to look out across the drop-off to see where the parachutes had ended up, when something, some slight vibration, made him turn round. Louvered vents had opened up all around the ship's middle, and two sets of solar panels had unfolded like fans from recesses on opposite sides. The panel arrays glittered blackly, before tilting towards the sunlight. Clearly something was happening, but Frank had no idea what.

But there were no astronauts. He was still on his own, for a couple more months. And that, suddenly, was OK, because he wasn't ready. He needed to prepare the base, get everything sorted and squared away, to get used to the idea that he was going to be Lance Brack.

He was going to have to answer to that name. It was going to be hard.

There was nothing more to do here. He needed to go back to the base and find out what a MAV was, and then get on. This arrival had at least driven home that the timetable was outside his control.

Frank drove back to the base, collected the floor panels he'd cleaned off, and stepped into his own airlock.

He racked his life support, dumped the panels back in Comms, and went to reread Phase three.

OK, so there it was, buried in the small print, because it didn't involve people: arrival of MAV, on or around Sol 529. He had to research what MAV was, and found it in another, even more technical document.

Mars Ascent Vehicle. It was his ride home, or at least off Mars. It was designed to suck Martian air in, and turn it into fuel, a process that would take about one hundred and twenty sols. It would take him and the rest of the astronauts back into Mars orbit, to dock with the transit ship which then would spend two hundred days going home. By which time he'd either be dead or safe.

It was happening. He had a deadline. Either he'd finish in time, or he wouldn't.

7

[Message file #98943 12/3/2048 1843 MBO Mission Control to MBO Rahe Crater]

Thanks for giving the MAV a clean bill of health, Frank. It must have been a wonderful sight, watching it come down—it almost makes me wish I was there with you!

You seem to be making really good progress on Phase 3. I know that this is hard for you, and it's not what you would have chosen, but I think we're working well together now. You've been diligent in your work, and creative with your solutions to problems that have presented themselves. It's great to see you take the initiative.

Remember, wherever in the sol you are, I'm just at the other end of this app. I'll answer straight away.

Take care.

Luisa

[message ends]

Frank had increased the power bank by another battery pack, and plugged in another ten kW of collectors. He'd supplemented his larder with an extraordinary array of instant puddings and drinks powders. He now had spare wheels. And extra fuel cells. And hab sections. He had airlocks, and he'd left one, complete with a spare life support and oxygen cylinders, at the top of Long Beach. Just in case he got caught out at some point.

It should have always been like this. At the start, XO had kept them short. He remembered the early days of not enough power, not enough food, not enough EVA time, of having to make decisions among themselves—no help or guidance from Brack—as to what to prioritize and what could wait. It had been deliberate, and it was one of the reasons he hated them. The second round of launches had shown that they could have supplied everything sooner. He still had to work with XO, though, and had to mute his anger.

There was more out there still: he was just about ahead of schedule in the base, and he needed a day off from the close-work and monotony of scraping blood out of the ceiling voids. He looked at the tablet, and decided that he really wanted to see what the In-situ Resource Management Device did. It was on the eastern flank of Ceraunius Tholus, by no means the furthest adrift of the deliveries, but still twenty miles out from Long Beach. That made it a seventy-mile round trip. Doable on one pack, just.

Not to say that Luisa wasn't nervous about his trips out. She cautioned him to be careful, to repeatedly ask himself if his journey was really necessary. If he died out on the plain, then MBO stayed in exactly the same state as he'd left it. Partially bloody, obviously not constructed by robots.

Maybe that was why he was doing it? Subconsciously subverting the deal with XO. Not wanting to entirely obliterate the memories of Alice and Marcy, Zeus and Dee, Declan and Zero. They had been here, and now he was colluding with the same murdering bastards that had tried to add him to that tally.

He kept on seeing them, in and around the base. It wasn't right, but he was lonely. He'd even taken to reading his way back through Brack's increasingly wayward interaction with Mission

Control, becoming more expansive and flowery as his opioid addiction had grown.

He'd never seen himself as a people person. Yet he'd worked pretty much every day of his life alongside others. It was the isolation that was getting to him. Despite having the whole of Mars to explore, it was still his prison, and still his solitary. It would be over soon. Another couple of months to keep it together, and the astronauts would be here. Just as long as he didn't cry when they arrived, he'd be fine. In the meantime, he had Luisa. He couldn't stop telling her stuff he really ought to keep to himself. But he couldn't tell anyone else because they were all dead.

Maybe he was falling apart in the same way Brack had. Maybe this was just a nightmare and he'd wake up to find…what?

That it was all still true.

He suited up, and cycled the airlock. There was no getting away from it, no wishful thinking that'd lessen his situation. He was marooned on Mars. He opened the airlock door, and there it was. The vast barren slope of the volcano, the pink sky, the red soil.

He unplugged the buggy, checked the trailer hitch was still tight, and drove away from the base. The draft in his face was almost convincing as an analog for speed, except it was constant whether he was moving or not.

To his left was the MAV, tracking the sun with its panels, making fuel. To his right, after a couple of miles, was the descent ship, three black-and-white-shrouded bodies tucked underneath. Then down the slope to the crater floor and onto Sunset. Paradoxically, the sun was just rising, straight into his face. Elsewhere, so he understood—on the Moon, in space— astronauts had tinted visors they could pull down to prevent glare. On Mars, the sun was never more than a luminous disk. It was just about bright enough to cast sharp shadow, but that depended on the dust-load in the sky, and, more often than not, shade was a solid mass, carved from air like a dark slab. Dust. It was always about the dust.

The same dust that was spinning from his turning wheels: most of it fell in an arc like thrown sand, even though the grains were much smaller. The finest particles, however, invisible and impossible, were carried away like gauze, and they stuck to whatever they touched. Particularly his spacesuit's faceplate, but pretty much everything and in everything. In the damp atmosphere of the habs, the dust they carried in ended up smeared on the floor, but outside it just clung.

The ghosts on Mars would be made of dust.

By the time he reached Long Beach, the slope was in full sun. He'd done it in the dark before. It was less fun than advertised. The collapsed crater wall that allowed access to the wider plains beyond was difficult terrain and a relentless climb, fifteen hundred feet at a ten per cent gradient. He squeezed the accelerator paddles and felt himself tip back in his seat.

The motors growled, and the stones clattered. It was an endurance test, for both him and the machine.

The buggy crawled over the lip of the crater, and Frank brought it to a halt next to the airlock. He'd piled loose stones against its sides, and finished it off with a cargo strap that went across the top and into the middle of two cairns that kept the anchors in place.

He did his usual checks—everything was nominal—and opened up the map so that he knew exactly which direction he was heading in. South-east, and up on the lower slopes of the volcano: the lower slopes only, and a good job too, since the summit before the yawning flat-bottomed crater at the top maxed out at twenty thousand feet above the level of the plain.

He followed his already-made track, heading south. His track, and no one else's. He never did find what had caused Brack to take such a roundabout route. He'd checked the most recent satellite maps he had, in case he'd missed something, but there was nothing out to the east but more rock and more craters and more dust.

He could imagine getting lost out on the plain: there were

so few landmarks to navigate by, and if the dust blew up, or the tablet was unable to contact, through his suit, the satellites, he'd be in trouble.

He felt a cold sweat break out across the whole of his body, and his breathing quicken. The planet was so huge, and he was the only one on it. Don't panic, don't panic. Breathe. Hold. Breathe.

The moment passed, but he still wondered if he wasn't taking too much of a risk, going so far from home when it wasn't necessary. He almost turned around. Almost. Luisa would have liked that.

But others were coming soon. It would be fine. Everything was fine.

He consulted his map again and angled the nose of the buggy back towards the volcanic slopes. The quality of the ground slowly changed again: fewer craters, and more exposed rock. Rilles and runnels snaking downwards, like smaller versions of the Santa Clara, almost as if a dusty, crater-pocked sea lapped up against a continent, flowing up its rivers and retreating from its promontories.

He had to be getting close, but how to get to where he wanted to be through what was rapidly becoming a labyrinth of channels? He glanced at the map again, and saw that he was losing his signal. Blocked by the intervening higher ground, his suit was struggling to stay connected.

He could retreat. He could also, looking at the last iteration of his map, go higher still. If he drove up and out of the valley he was in, he'd find himself on the clear slopes above. He eased forward, crossing the unfamiliar terrain until his view opened up again, and he was on one of a staircase of rock steps that seemed to climb, irregularly and imperfectly, all the way to the very top.

Frank had his signal again, and the cross that marked his target was centered on his position. Somewhere, within a couple of hundred yards of where he was, was what he was seeking, but damned if he could see it. He parked up and walked up to the next rock step. Though the riser was blunt, he found out just how difficult it would be to climb in his spacesuit. His knees creaked with the effort, and he used his hands as much as his feet.

He pulled himself upright, and stared out across the lower slopes, looking for a splash of color or scorch-marks from the landing rockets. Right down on the plain, momentarily, he saw a figure in a spacesuit, walking out from behind one bluff and into the shadow of another. From the size of them, it could have been Marcy again, or Alice, or Declan. Definitely not Zeus. He raised his hand, but that was stupid, and he dropped it again quickly. They'd gone, anyway, and they were never really there in the first place.

He was still on the clock, and he had to get on with his search, or abandon it. Where could the cargo drop be hiding?

There was a channel nearby, one with steep, almost cliff-like banks. Wary of going too close to the broken edge, but having to peer down inside it all the same, he shuffled up to it and let his eyes adjust to the dark. There. The parachute had wrapped itself around the cylinder, covering it almost completely, which was a new one on him. And when he looked again, the parachute seemed lumpy. It didn't bode well for the state of the cargo inside, but he was going to see for himself whether there was anything he could salvage.

The best way in was to drive down from the top of the channel. The buggy made heavy weather of the steps, just like he had, and he had to dial the plates to their maximum surface area to get enough grip, even at the slowest speed. The trailer grounded, and he had to drag it, vibrating, until the wheels met the rock again and slowly rolled around the step.

He had to do that twice more, scraping the underside of the trailer frame along hard volcanic rock before it cleared. But then he was able to swing round and into the channel. The banks rose around him, but the valley floor was flat enough. It curved left and right, and finally he was able to park up next to the cylinder.

It looked at first sight as if it had landed safely on the top of the bank, and then fallen the fifty feet or so into the ravine. The cargo doors had burst open, and then the parachute had descended on it, covering it up.

Frank pulled at the fabric, heaving great handfuls towards him as if it was a giant sheet. He was right: the doors were both open, and there were obvious dents and dints in the casing, gouges where the metal underneath had been exposed and shone dully silver.

Half the drums inside were missing, and he turned around, expecting to see the debris scattered down the channel. It wasn't there. He went back to the cylinder and peered inside. Definitely, three of the six drums weren't present. The insulation around them had gone. The straps that secured them in place had gone. The drums themselves had gone.

And yet of those that remained, everything was intact. That…made no sense.

He checked the catches on the doors, the ones he usually used the tool that hung on his belt to turn. The doors hadn't burst. They'd been opened. The parachute: the parachute hadn't fallen on the cargo. It had been placed there, deliberately, to keep the dust out.

His feet. The channel bed was bedrock, with a fine covering of weathered sand and wind-blown dust. Bootprints, identical to his, in places where he hadn't walked. And there, twenty feet away, tire tracks that showed that a buggy had come up the valley, and then three-point-turned back down it.

Brack?

It couldn't be Brack. Brack would have had a trailer, like he had a trailer. He'd have winched the whole cylinder on and carried it away.

Was it...him? Was this Frank? Was he suffering some kind of psychosis?

He put his hand on the side of the rocket. It was real. As real as the boots and the buggy.

In a daze, he left everything as it was and climbed back into his buggy's seat. He clicked the harness on, unconsciously testing the clasp had locked by leaning forward because he could never hear it fasten.

He looked at the tracks in the ground ahead of him, and started to drive slowly, following them down the channel. There were two tracks, overlain. One that went towards him, one that went away. There was no mistake here: an XO rover, driven by someone in an XO suit, had been out this way in the last couple of months, and maybe it was Brack, and maybe it was him.

Frank remembered conversations he'd had with Declan, when they thought that someone had been using the buggies on unauthorized jaunts at night. They'd concluded that all those journeys had been to the descent ship and back, not this far out. But Brack had definitely been out on the plain, picking up the NASA equipment. Declan would have spotted the discrepancies in the power levels a mile off, and a fully drained battery wasn't something anyone could hide from him. So Brack must have recharged the fuel cell from the ship before returning it, masking what he was doing from the surviving cons.

It had to be Brack, and yet...the tracks, once out of the channel, turned resolutely and inexorably south-east, skirting the ragged volcanic rock and following the edge of the dust sea. The buggy had come from the south, and it was returning that way.

There was nothing south of him. Nothing but red desert.

Finally, he came to his senses, and stopped. He was past halfway through his air, and nearly seventy miles on the clock. He hadn't hammered it, but he'd either have to drive quicker to get home, or avail himself of the spare life support at the top of Long Beach. That was now thirty miles away as the crow flew, if there'd ever be such a thing on Mars. Add the fifteen-twenty along Sunset and up the Heights...the range of the buggy was somewhere between one fifty and two hundred miles.

He was no longer safe, even by his standard. And he was towing, which despite being empty added an extra strain on the fuel cells.

And still the incontrovertible evidence of his eyes was that the tracks he was following led south. They originated in the south, and were using their outward-bound journey to guide their way back.

Back to where?

Frank looked at his map, zoomed into the highest detail allowed. It didn't show individual tracks, because the resolution at that scale was too low. Disappointingly, it didn't even show Sunset Boulevard, which had to be the best-delineated and most-used road on Mars. He checked for other features it might show. Not the MAV, which was a recent addition and perhaps the satellite photography hadn't caught up with it. But there was the ship, and the MBO was a clear artifact in pale pink and white.

He searched back south, scooting the map up and down, left and right with his fingers. If there was something there, the map didn't show it.

Those tracks, though. He wasn't imagining them. Something—someone—had been at the cylinder. Someone in XO gear. Someone that came from, and disappeared back into, the wasteland that was south of the volcano. It couldn't be Brack. He was certain it wasn't him.

He stood up on his seat and hung off the roll bars, just looking across the plain until he couldn't see any more. He blinked, hard, and held up the map in front of him, trying to match it to the landscape.

Even standing there, breathing, was pushing his luck. His judgment, his sanity, was flawed. He should turn around and never come this far out again. Stick by the base. Wait for the NASA mission. Stay safe. Survive. Go home.

He hung his tablet back on his belt and strapped himself in again.

Just a little further. Follow the tracks. He rounded a headland, and in the next bay, in the distance, he saw what looked like a buggy, parked up at the end of a channel.

He rolled to a stop. A buggy. A buggy just like his. It was the last thing he'd expected to see. Literally, the last thing.

How was this possible?

8

[Internal memo: Mars Base One Mission Control to Bruno Tiller 12/8/2048 (transcribed from paper-only copy)]

We have a problem.

[transcript ends]

He couldn't tell how long he'd sat there, just staring. Only that when he finally shook himself, he'd dropped a couple of points of stored O_2.

It was still there. It hadn't vanished like all his other imaginings. A buggy. Parked? Or abandoned? There was no way of telling if it had been there for two minutes or two weeks. A moving buggy created dust, and the frames, wheels, controls, were always covered in a film of the stuff. Six weeks. Six months. Longer than that?

Frank eased forward a hundred feet or so. There was no sign of anyone. No reason for there to be. Because he was the only person on Mars, right?

He rolled closer. If this had happened a few months ago, Alice would be in his ears, asking him what the hell was wrong with him and threatening to alter his breathing mix to calm him down.

But she wasn't. She was absent. She was dead. Marcy was dead, Zeus and Dee and Declan and Zero were all dead. Brack was dead. He was the last one alive. So what the hell was this buggy doing all the way out here?

He drove up to it, stopped twenty, thirty feet away. He climbed down, and walked slowly and deliberately around it.

It had accumulated dust. It hadn't drifted, though. If the wheels had been in the same position for any time, the dust would have collected against one side or the other. This...had been driven here. Recently.

Frank reached out. He hesitated, then dabbed his fingers on the frame. He felt solid metal, and jerked his hand away as if burned.

This was ridiculous. But he was terrified. This shouldn't be here. He sipped some water to slake his dry mouth, and clambered up the chassis so he could see the seat. The plastic chair bolted to the frame was identical to his own, except this one was cracked and then fixed with a line of sticky hab-repair patches. It was clear of dust. As if swept. And there: someone had put their hand on the read-outs and wiped them clean. He could see the marks made by four gloved fingers.

He lowered himself down again, and checked the ground. There were faint scuff marks leading up the nearest channel.

Someone was looking back at him from a rock step up on the promontory.

They wore an XO suit. Hard body, integral helmet, back bulge of life support and entry hatch. Light-emitting areas front and top. It was difficult to interpret body language. The bulk of the insulation layer hid a lot of tells. But the way Frank felt he was being stared at made it feel like he wasn't exactly expected, either.

It probably only lasted a few seconds, but it felt like forever.

Then they turned and walked out of sight. Were they climbing back down into the channel and coming to meet him? If they were as real as the buggy was real, possibly.

What was he going to do? He had moments to decide. He could simply drive off into the distance. He'd leave tracks for the other person to follow, just as he'd followed theirs. He could...

disable their buggy—he knew how these things worked, and a few solid blows to the instrument panel would strand the driver out on the plain and condemn them to certain death. He could attack the other astronaut and kill them, then take their buggy—he had an empty trailer, after all.

He took another sip of water and stayed rooted to the spot. He still couldn't quite believe what was happening. His hand had fallen automatically to the nut runner on his belt. It was weighted wrong as a cosh, but it was partly metal and he could get a decent swing behind it. He might actually be better off with an actual rock, given he could lift three times the weight he could on Earth. But being greeted by someone with a huge boulder held over his head wasn't going to start friendly relations any time soon.

Geez, Frank. You can't gut a fish and yet you're still thinking about bashing another guy's brains in. You don't have to kill everyone just because you're scared. You don't know who this is. You don't know why they're here. You don't know anything about them. You can just talk to them instead.

Then the time for equivocation was over. The spacesuited figure emerged from the wind of the canyon and walked towards him. Slowly. With their hands obviously empty. They reached up and tapped the side of their helmet, twice. No comms. Frank had been taught the same hand signal.

The face behind the glass became apparent. A man. Beard, long and patchy. Lean like Frank. Leaner even. Gaunt, almost. Eyes recessed but wide and pale. He didn't seem...well? Frank hadn't looked in a mirror for months. There might be more similarities between them than he was allowing for.

This was the first time the other man had the opportunity to see him properly, too. He took his time studying Frank, his gaze skittering between face and suit and buggy and trailer and back. He seemed to be going through the same mental gymnastics as Frank.

Frank could still turn and run: gun his motors and drive away, try and obscure his route home by finding some rock to break up his tracks. He didn't do that, even though he thought about doing it right up until the moment they met, halfway between the bluff and the buggy.

Frank looked at the contents of the man's utility belt, and he had almost no equipment hanging off the carabiners. Not a nut runner, not a tablet, just a cloth pouch that probably held some patches, and some looped cargo straps. There was something off here. He couldn't put his finger on it, but Frank instinctively took a step back.

The man used his index finger to indicate "you-me-touch-helmets". It was Frank's last chance to bolt.

He could also get his strike in first, especially if the man had no comms—but what if it was a trick, to get Frank within blade range? That was prison-him talking, but prison-him had kept him alive this far. Maybe he should listen to that guy a little bit more, and judge him a little less.

OK, let's calm the fuck down. This guy isn't going to try and shank me. He might even be another con from a Panopticon jail. Someone like Frank, shanghaied in another XO game.

To test that hypothesis, Frank held his fist out, a little to one side. The man frowned at it, and then at Frank. Not a con. A dap would have been second nature. Could this man, whatever he was, whoever he was, be actual XO?

XO. On Mars. This could go very, very badly for Frank.

The man held out his hand, for an actual handshake, between equals. Frank stared at it, then took it hesitantly. The man was real. Not a ghost.

What was he going to do? Play it by ear. See what the score was. The guy had no comms. Frank could afford to try and find out what was going on before deciding anything.

As they leaned forward and touched helmets, Frank put his hand on his nut runner and unclipped it, keeping it down and unseen by his side.

"Hey," said the man. "You Brack?"

What was Frank supposed to say here? The other man clearly knew about him, about MBO, about everything, while Frank didn't even know what this man was doing on Mars.

"I'm Brack, yes."

"Sweet. You got everything set up over there? Everything working fine?"

"We're good," said Frank. Then added spontaneously, "All of us."

"All of you?" There was a telling pause. "OK. Lost track of which sol it was. I'm just picking up gear. That's what you're doing, right?"

Of course, Frank's buggy had a trailer. This man's didn't. If he was picking up gear, where was his?

"Stuff didn't land where it was supposed to," said Frank. "Missing a drop for the NASA guys. Said I'd go and check out a possible from the satellite."

That was plausible, right? If the locator beacon was offline, then it was the only way they could do it.

The man seemed to accept that without a problem. "Tell me about it. Strewn around like fucken' confetti."

"Something like that." Was that useful information? Yes. There was another XO mission on Mars, suffering the same problems as his had. Frank suddenly realized what he'd just thought, and he clammed up. Another XO mission. Fuck.

"You got everything in the end, though?" asked the man. "You got everything you needed?"

All that extra cargo: they weren't spares, replacements for missing or destroyed deliveries. They weren't for MBO at all. He'd stolen this other guy's kit. Other guy: it was a whole other crew at a whole other base. Habs. Panels. Wheels and fuel cells. Food. He'd beggared them.

"You OK?"

This questioning, this real-time questioning, was hard. Frank was used to some thinking time, and then a delay between answer and next message.

"Yeah, fine. Fine." Goddammit, XO. They'd known what he was doing. He'd reported back the manifest of each drop as he brought it in. They could have said stop, at any time. They hadn't.

"And you got everything working?"

That was the second time he'd been asked that. "Eventually."

"Greenhouse? Comms?"

Now Frank's whole skin was itching. "Like I said, we're good."

"Sweet," said the other man again.

All the traffic had been entirely one-way so far. The man, this stranger on Frank's Mars, had told him precisely nothing. Except his mere presence, which spoke volumes.

"So, uh, you got comms problems?" Frank asked.

"Us?" The XO man swallowed. He was really gaunt, behind that beard. Hollow-cheeked as well as hollow-eyed. Starving. And Frank had stolen at least some of their food. "Set-up problems. Nothing we can't fix. There's nothing we can't fix."

"Just that I noticed that you're out here, on your own, without a map. That's making a tough job tougher."

"Set-up problems," repeated the man. "Just set-up problems."

Frank knew when he was being stonewalled. This wasn't a set-up problem. This was an existential crisis. If they didn't have any comms, they couldn't talk to XO, and neither could they find their cylinders. If they couldn't find their cylinders, they were relying on dumb luck as to what parts of their base they could put together. If they had that little, then they were all going to die. Sooner or later.

And Frank had food, heat, light, power, air, water, and space. He had everything.

He almost said something: an invitation to come on over, share what he had, pool resources. But these men, this crew, were XO. And XO had deliberately not told him about this other base, all the while knowing about them, and what circumstances they found themselves in. XO had told Frank precisely

82

nothing, because XO were a bunch of lying, murdering, kidnapping bastards who valued human life even lower than he did. Than he had.

And currently Frank was on his own. This man could replace him as Brack, if he let him. Even if he didn't let him. They could just take him out. He couldn't resist them. The only thing protecting him was their comms failure. XO hadn't been able to tell them that he wasn't Brack. If they got their downlink working again, he was toast.

Frank dissembled. "I hope you get it sorted out real soon," he said. "Comms problems are a pain in the ass. But I got to be heading back. Got my airtime to think about."

"You seen any of our kit while you're out?"

"Nothing to the north of here," said Frank. Well, there wasn't any more, because he'd picked it all up already. "I'd concentrate on the south-side. You spotted anything with a NASA flag on it?"

"NASA? No, nothing like that." He could have been lying. Frank certainly was. "So, the MBO: you can get to it from here? That's where you started from, right?"

"I used a staging post, and even then I'm at the limit of my range. Guessing you are too," said Frank. "Where'd you come down?"

"South," said the man. He'd hesitated. Definitely hesitated. "To the south."

"OK. Good luck. Lance, by the way."

"Good to meet you, Lance." The man separated for a moment, not offering his own name, then touched helmets again. "Looks like you been in the wars."

For a moment, Frank didn't know what he meant, but the patched arm of his spacesuit was more visible to someone else than it was to him. It wasn't obviously a bullet hole: his work with the scalpel on his outer covering had seen to that.

He went for broke.

"One of the chimps. Nothing I couldn't handle." He watched

the man's reaction very closely, and his guts tightened as he realized his bald declaration of murder got no more than a nod. "Still, got to go. Airtime, and I've got to radio the NASA guys. They keep me busy, you know?"

Frank's fingers flexed around his nut runner. He could do it. He could sucker-punch the guy and beat him while he was down. No one would intervene. No one would ever know. His fourth murder. Saving his own skin.

"Busy. Sure. I know all about that. Be seeing you." And it sounded more of a threat than anything Frank had ever heard before. The other astronaut pulled away, and gave him a look: they both knew. Their body language betrayed them both.

Frank backed up to his buggy. No way was he turning round and blind-siding himself. At the same time, the other, nameless astronaut stood tense, rocking from side to side on the balls of his feet.

At the last moment, after he'd put some distance between them, Frank reached up and pulled himself up and onto the seat of his buggy. The man watched him. Watching where he was going. Watching him put down a track.

Frank drove in a tight circle and, the best he could, started along the tire marks that had already been pressed into the dust. He tabbed his rear-facing cameras on, and could see the man still standing, still watching, until he disappeared behind the finger of rock that jutted into the sand sea.

9

[Message file #101862 12/8/2048 0845 MBO Rahe Crater to MBO Mission Control]

You were supposed to be honest with me. No more secrets, goddammit. You hid a whole other base on Mars from me. You let me take their shit. You watched me take things that they needed, that you knew they needed, that you knew would kill them if they didn't have. You said nothing. You let me do it.

So what's it going to be? You want this base standing when NASA turn up? Or do you want NASA to know what you did here? Because if I think—hell, if I suspect you're thinking—that you're trying to replace me with one of them, so help me God I'm taking you down with me. I will find a way.

I am ready to call the truce off.

You've got an hour to start talking some sense, because otherwise we are finished. Got that?

[transcript ends]

His journey back was arduous, crossing unfamiliar and difficult terrain, and he had to rely on his map to guide him. But he thought the risk of breaking a wheel was necessary: he'd been able to travel a significant distance over the lower slopes of the volcano, all frozen lava steps and very little dust. What there had been was thin, and seemed often-blown. The tracks he had made would be resurfaced in a few days. Certainly, it seemed windier on the exposed slopes than it did on the plains.

Praying for a storm that would wipe everything was pointless: either it happened or it didn't. In its absence, he had to make plans.

He'd need to remove the airlock at the top of Long Beach, bring it back, along with all the spare air he'd left with it. It could so very easily be used against him.

What else? He needed to know where the other XO mission had come down, and when. He needed to be able to work out for himself whether or not they could reach him. He also needed to know what they were supposed to be doing there.

He guessed they were, yes, south of him. But how far? Did their ranges barely overlap, or was there the possibility of travel between their descent ship and MBO? He needed to get a map out in front of him, when he wasn't being shaken around on the rock-hard lava. He knew his buggies well enough to know what kind of distances they could manage, depending on the terrain, whether he was towing, whether he needed the lights on, and whether he could take it easy—going fast used disproportionately more watts. If he called it two hundred miles, generously, then that would cover a surprising amount of Mars.

Of course, if it was a round trip, then it'd be half that. And even then, the buggies weren't the limiting factor. Unless the infrastructure was in place to swap out the life support, then somewhere between hours eight and nine a spacesuit would run out of oxygen. Even if the buggy was doing its top speed of twenty, and that was only possible on perfectly flat concrete, that brought the range from base down to eighty-ninety miles.

If the second base was beyond that, he might be OK. Possibly. Closer, and the potential for more interaction was significantly higher. Frank didn't want to interact with these newcomers. He wanted nothing at all to do with them. They frightened him.

Perhaps he should have offed the guy while he had the chance. He clenched his jaw and pulled back his cracking lips. Perhaps. He hadn't. He'd let him go. For all sorts of reasons. And some of those reasons were the same as why he'd held the dying Brack's hand, even though it was Frank who'd killed him.

He was running low on air, and watts. That would normally be a cause for huge concern, and he was never comfortable with letting the reserves get as thin as he had. But it was a good sign right now. The narrower the margin, the less likely that the other guy—the other guys, and he really ought to have tried to find out how many of them there were—could reach MBO.

He'd just about squeak it. He'd traveled the southern edge of the crater, up on the volcanic ledges, and he'd reached the Santa Clara. The map didn't give that many clues as to whether he'd find a route down into it, or whether he'd need to leave the buggy where it was, and hoof the couple of miles across the Heights to MBO. The resolution was decent enough, but in close-up the pictures got granular.

In the end, it wasn't anywhere near as difficult as he'd feared. There was some slumping of material—a landslide maybe, a cliff that had fallen inwards onto the Heights—that let him slither down from the volcano and onto the flat plain that now housed MBO, the MAV and his descent ship.

He eked out his watts to get him to the base, and the first thing he did, even though he was at less than ten per cent air and well within the margin of error that meant his pack could give out any minute, was to scan the horizon to see if anything was coming.

No plumes of dust. No moving shapes. It was like it had always been since before he'd arrived. Still. Desolate. Dead.

Then he plugged the buggy back into the battery, and entered the cross-hab airlock.

His hand went to his nut runner again. Could someone have slipped inside while he'd been away? Of course. There was no way of locking the doors completely—though there was a way once he was inside, he realized. But there wasn't any way of protecting the hab structures themselves. They were composed of a flexible plastic skin, held rigid by a metal frame, screwed together by bolts. Anyone who wanted to wreck it, could. It was what he'd threatened XO with, and now it was threatened against him.

Goddammit, what a mess. He'd allowed himself hope, that he could outwit the company and get one over on them. How could he have been so stupid? Trusting XO? That was never going to happen again.

The airlock cycled. He checked the atmosphere before taking his suit off, and made certain he clipped the scuba mask and O_2 tank onto his belt before he did a thorough search of the habs, upper and lower levels. He'd thought he was done with this. Clearly, he was wrong.

As he went, he opened the inner door of every airlock. Such was their design that the outer, Mars-facing door couldn't now be opened automatically, and not manually until the pressure either side had equalized. And that would give Frank more than enough time to get into his suit and figure out what to do.

His last call was to the Comms/Control hab.

The gun was still tucked in behind the monitor. His hand hovered over it, then he carefully picked it up, painfully aware that a gun very similar to this one was the reason he was on Mars in the first place. It still felt unnaturally light. A gun should have heft, a weight to its purpose, and not feel like a plastic toy.

He pulled the magazine free, and, placing the gun on the desk in front of the keyboard, he clicked the rounds out one by one into his hand. Fifteen. He pushed them back in, and put the magazine in his left pocket. The gun went in his right.

Sitting in the chair, scrubbing at his scalp, he felt... he didn't know what he felt. Like this was the last thing he wanted to do, and at the same time, the only thing he could. No, he knew exactly what he felt. He felt vulnerable. He'd been backed into a corner, and his instinct had told him to pick up a gun and get ready to use it.

It was what, four weeks now until NASA arrived? Until then, he was on his own. No, that wasn't right. He wasn't on his own, he'd only thought he was. This was worse. This was far, far worse.

His tablet was still on his spacesuit. Time to call home. Time to demand some answers.

He typed it out. Oh, he was angry. Angry and scared and just about holding it together. Send. He was going to have to wait to see what Luisa and her team at Mission Control were going to say. In the meantime, he had some maps to stare at.

The question—the million-dollar question—was simply this: could they reach him?

He'd been at the absolute limit of his endurance, both in terms of what his spacesuit could manage, and his buggy. The other guy? Well, he didn't look so good, but he still had a working buggy, and therefore had to have a way of charging it up. Maybe from the descent ship, but maybe they'd got lucky and found the RTG for a bit of base load. They sure as hell didn't have the solar panels that were currently plugged in outside MBO. Had they a second set? Maybe XO had suddenly got a lot more generous.

The guy had said south, and at the time he'd been roughly fifty miles south-east of MBO. The open container was a few miles short of that—the cross showed exactly where that had been. Frank was going to guess that the tracks he'd found out on the plain, the ones that seemed to come from, and go to, the south, were also made by the second crew. Call that the very extreme of its range, because he hadn't found any north of that.

So, if he had two points that he thought were as far out as they could reach, could he calculate roughly where they'd started from?

Ninety miles south was smack out in the middle of the plain, at the far end of the huge cracks in the ground the map called the Uranius Fossae. But realistically, they could be anywhere on an arc going south-east to south-west, from the southern slopes of Ceraunius Tholus to out in the middle of nowhere.

If they were to the south or south-west, they could only get to him by over-reaching. It'd have to be a one-way journey, in the hope that they could recharge and swap out at MBO. And if they were at the south-west end, it was almost inconceivable that anyone would dare make the trip. Frank would be safe.

If it was to the south-east, though, on the southern flanks of the volcano…that would put them just within ninety miles of MBO. They'd have to drive up and over fifteen thousand feet of mountain, and Frank didn't know whether that was feasible. He spent a little longer looking at pixels, measuring distances, then pushed the tablet away.

If he was designing a network of colonies on Mars, then isolating them from each other didn't make any sense—separate enough that they were self-sufficient, that they didn't overuse whatever resources were nearby, sure. But close enough that they could be used as staging posts to the next base, if there were problems. Say if something broke down that someone couldn't fix on site, but a guy in the next base could. What was the betting that XO had deliberately put them within range of a there-and-back journey? When he thought about it, it was obvious. They were evil, not stupid.

What he couldn't get out of his mind was how hungry that other astronaut had looked.

How long had they been out there, on the other side of the volcano? Things had been falling from the sky for months, and only gone quiet in the last few weeks. Certainly, they'd been there long enough to have scoped out MBO already. If they already knew where he was, and that he was alone, and that he'd killed Brack and was holding XO to ransom, why hadn't they moved against him already?

The only conclusion was that they hadn't been able.

The man he'd met didn't have comms. He didn't have comms

out on the volcano, and if he wasn't able to pick up the locator beacons for the supply drops, he didn't have comms, period. Frank's own descent ship had come with all those functions, and the second mission had clearly made it to the surface...

But if the ship was broken, and they had no downlink? They had no way of calling home, and no way of home calling them.

That would explain everything.

It also meant that while they knew where he was, in the sense that they might remember where the MBO was supposed to be situated, they had no maps, and only the sun to navigate by. Compasses didn't work on Mars, either.

So if—a huge if—they couldn't talk to XO and XO couldn't talk to them, they were effectively isolated from everything. From Earth, from MBO, from all their supply drops. All they had was what they'd brought with them or could scavenge, and if Frank thought that his own initiation to the Martian surface had been a hardscrabble, then those guys had to be having it so much worse.

In other circumstances, he'd feel sorry for them.

Frank checked the tablet to see if Luisa had responded. If she didn't reply soon, he was probably going to have to decide what to do about that, too. But it chimed as he was holding it.

She simply said: "Frank, please stay calm. I don't understand what you mean by 'another base'. Don't do anything to jeopardize your safety, please. Can you tell me exactly what's happened, so I know what questions to ask?"

Yes, he could. In no uncertain terms.

"I met another astronaut, wearing an XO suit and driving an XO buggy, out on the eastern side of Ceraunius. There is only one way he could have got there, and that's if XO put him there. The hour I gave you for giving me answers is close to up, and I meant what I said." Send.

Just when he'd got to a level of complexity that he could actually cope with, something else came over the horizon—literally in this case—and pissed all over his parade.

Sitting there, at the comms desk, he was warm, clean, well fed. He had water and air, and the prospect of getting home again. Just over the hill was a bunch of people who had very little and would probably kill him. Should he have struck first? Sabotaged the other buggy? No. Maybe. Just as long as they left him alone.

There was no guarantee of that, though, and if Frank was right, then there could never be a guarantee of that.

Had he made a mistake of showing surprise when he saw the other man? Was that the clue that he'd dropped the ball? A Brack who'd known about the second base wouldn't have done such a thing. Maybe he'd messed it up. But he'd been called Brack by the XO man.

If they knew who Brack was, and what his function was, then that might give them cause to hold back.

Amid all his guesswork, he knew one thing for certain: only he had his own interests at heart. Only he was going to keep him safe.

So while XO sorted their shit out, he was going to suit up again, drive out to Long Beach with a trailer and get that airlock. He had enough daylight to manage it, just, and he wasn't going to leave it out there any longer than he had to. He certainly wasn't going to be heading out to the plain any time soon.

He was bunkering down. Four weeks. Four weeks to hold out. He could do that, right?

He clipped the tablet to his suit, took the gun and the bullets out of his pockets and put them separately but together in his pouch bag, loaded up a fresh life support, and clambered in through the back hatch.

His spacesuit looked as tired as he felt. How many miles did these things have to have on the clock before they wore out? He could very well ask the same question of himself. Fifty-two. He was fifty-two years old and he was on Mars.

And his son was on Earth. Focus, Frank. Focus.

He cycled the airlock, and wondered if he was being watched, even now.

The first buggy was still recharging. It'd take hours for the electricity to strip the water in the fuel cell back into its component gases. He had two vehicles, though. Was that one advantage he had over the others? Maybe not. If they had one, they probably had their second one too, even if they didn't have the power to recharge both simultaneously.

He swapped the trailer over, and drove out to the drop-off, pausing to stare into the distance, along the length of Rahe, trying as best he could to see if there was anything moving down there. It always came down to the amount of dust in the air. Currently, visibility was some fifteen or twenty miles, which was good, but still not enough to see detail at the far end of the crater. He could follow the line of Beverly Hills, but they became nothing but shapes carved into the late afternoon, and the crater wall was a hazy, rosy glow, bright and undifferentiated.

Whatever he thought he saw, he still had to get the airlock back. He drove down the drop-off and onto Sunset.

Worst-case scenario: XO had planned another mission, from the start, in case Phase three didn't work out. They were primed to step in and take over if it went wrong, or something happened to Brack.

That didn't make much sense, because the whole thing about replacing robots with cons was because cons were cheaper, more reliable and ultimately disposable. Putting a whole other parallel mission in place was a ridiculously expensive piece of overkill. They'd have better spent the money making sure that the base actually got built.

Best-case scenario? Frank struggled with this. He couldn't think of a good reason for any other XO mission to Mars. Maybe they did it because they could. Maybe it was as badly run and poorly resourced as his own. Maybe it was so far off course that it had landed in the wrong hemisphere, and out of the whole of Mars to aim at, only accidentally landed close by. Maybe it was crewed entirely by decent, competent people who wouldn't dream of harming a hair on his head, and he really ought to go and help them out with food and equipment.

What was he going to do, if Luisa asked him to do that, to be the good neighbor? That man had looked hungry, so very hungry.

Back to the worst case again—she'd tell him to load up with spare food, go over, and he'd never come back because someone there would know what Brack looked like and would know it wasn't him.

OK, so he'd thought of something even worse. What if they had standing orders to kill Brack? That would make perfect, awful sense. Hire a stone-cold killer to see Phase two through and then get rid of him, too. Brack, with his addictions and his psychoses, was going to unravel in the company of real people, and the last thing that XO wanted or needed was a madman running amok in a thin-skinned hab full of expensive and popular astronauts. Much better to replace him with someone who was technically competent and not a murderer.

Brack was going to be the last victim. And Frank was now Brack.

10

[Message file #103025 12/10/2048 2206 MBO Rahe Crater to MBO Mission Control]

Luisa, this is my absolute bottom line. XO can take it or leave it.

I know XO planned this. The cargo drops happened in the same area the crew's ship was supposed to land. XO deliberately put another base right next to MBO. I've got my reasons for thinking that's a bad thing for me.

I don't trust XO when you tell me that M2 has clear instructions to leave MBO alone, and neither do I think they're going to lie down quietly and die. They know I'm here, and they know MBO has everything they need.

You say no one can talk to M2 because of the comms issue. But I'm not going to contact them either. I think XO are lying about pretty much everything, and I'm not going to risk my life and my chance of getting back to Earth over this. They put me here in this position. So they have to wear the consequences. If M2 stay their side of the mountain, then fine. I won't have to say anything to NASA about this "classified mission". I don't actually give a shit about who gets to play on Mars, but if XO want it kept secret as a condition of my return, then OK.

But you have to understand that I've got about as much control over M2 as you do now. If one of the NASA guys spots them because M2 goes off the reservation, then there's nothing I can do about that. It's XO's problem, not mine. If they bust their cover, no one can blame me.

Like I said. Take it or leave it. NASA are here in just over two months.

[message ends]

He still had to move the bodies into the ship. He hadn't before. He'd not done it so that he didn't have to see them every time he took a new batch of stuff over. Though that wasn't actually true: he did see them every time, because their shrouds were clearly visible under the rocket cone at the base of the descent ship, and they didn't fall out of sight until he was at the bottom of the steps leading up to the airlock.

Now he'd run out of excuses. They were literally the last item on his list, and he'd ticked off everything else. No, that wasn't true either, though there was a very good reason for that.

He drove the short distance to the landing spot. It was his eight-month anniversary on Mars—February 6th. Eight months since he'd been woken up by Alice. Eight months since he'd lost both her and Marcy. Then, five months in, Zeus, Dee, Declan, Zero. Finally, Brack.

Almost three months since he thought he was totally alone.

And eight weeks since he'd discovered XO had put another mission on Mars, just over the hill. Strange that it had been at that exact moment that the ghosts of his dead crewmates had stopped appearing to him. No manifestations since. It would probably scare him to death, thinking it was someone from M2, so he'd been saved that at least.

Even so, Frank was ragged. He snatched at sleep and usually missed, and when he did finally catch it, he'd wake up at the slightest sound, real or imagined. It had been bad enough before, with the nightmares and flashbacks. Now it was concretized: the threats he dreamed about were real. The base being invaded. Him being dragged outside. Held down while his suit was opened up. Because they wouldn't want to damage XO property, would they? On Mars, resources counted more than the people did. Certainly more than a bunch of cons did.

The last few sols had simply blurred together. He no longer knew when he was awake. Nervous energy was the only thing carrying him through. At some point he was going to crash, and crash hard. But not today. He couldn't do that today.

He climbed down from the buggy, and looked around, checking that no one had interfered with the ship—a strip of parachute material caught carelessly in the outer airlock door was his telltale. It was still there. There were no unexplained tracks, no bootprints that weren't his. Time and wind had eroded what lay beyond the ship, out towards the drop-off, into broad, dark smudges, like marks of half-scrubbed pencil lines.

Nothing fresh. Nothing to indicate that M2 had been anywhere near him. That was good, and still he worried. Every day. And especially now. He'd done all of the work. MBO was...not spotless, but it was clean. It had a lived-in look. The floor panels were scuffed where he'd scrubbed them, and the sub-floor voids scratched and shiny after chipping the dried blood out from the framework and utilities. The med bay was orderly once more, and the consulting room empty of everything including the USMC cap that Brack had brought along.

It had been the only personal item from Earth that had made it onto the surface of Mars. The cons' effects—including Frank's few books and letters—had vanished. He had no idea where. And the hat had to go, along with all the other junk—tablets, overalls, spacesuits, hair from the drains and skin in the filters—into the heart of the sun.

His instructions were to just pile it all up inside. He didn't have to worry about tying it down or stop it from banging into the instrument panels. Those wouldn't do anything once XO had taken remote command of the vessel.

He was going to put half an hour on a timer. That was as long as he spent at any one time inside the ship. Not quite long enough for the ship to register that he'd activated the airlock, send a message to Earth, and for XO to trap him inside and take him on a one-way trip into space. Of course, they'd already done that once, but being shot into a star would be a qualitatively different trip.

Maybe they wouldn't do that. Maybe they'd stick to their agreement. But he'd be stupid to bet his life on it, any further than he already had to. When he lay down to sleep, it was clutching a semi-inflated rubber glove, with scuba gear and his spacesuit within touching distance.

And the gun by his side.

He'd decided that he was going to keep it. XO would never know, one way or the other. He'd brought the metal case over along with the rest of Brack's effects, dumped it in plain sight of the ship-board cameras, but the gun itself was currently in the same pouch at his waist as his suit patches.

He hadn't thought so far ahead as to what to do with it when the NASA astronauts turned up. Bury it outside, maybe, as keeping it anywhere on the base would mean he'd always be worried it'd be discovered. And trying to explain his possession of a modified automatic pistol would unravel any lie he might come up with.

He looked up at the ship. He wasn't certain how he'd got there. The buggy was behind him. How else?

Come on, Frank. Keep it together. Just a little longer.

He ducked under the hull of the ship and took hold of the first of the shrouds. He pulled it out, watching how the dust that had accumulated in the folds of the cloth dribbled out into the drag lines. Who was he moving? The twisted package was quite slim, no real bulk to it, and nothing to suggest a spacesuit inside. Zero, then.

He laid him out at the bottom of the steps, and went back for Brack, or Declan. Then again for Declan, or Brack. Both were still in their suits, both with shattered faceplates. Brack's life support had ended up broken. Ended up: Frank had driven an oxygen cylinder into it, repeatedly, like a battering ram, until he'd rendered it inoperable. Declan's should be fine. But he really didn't have the heart to unwrap one, then the other when he inevitably unwrapped the wrong one first, and remove the life support pack.

It was going with the ship, and that was that.

He activated the timer on his tablet, and thumbed the airlock open. He bounced Zero up the steps and inside, then cycled them through. When the inner door opened, he was again confronted by the sheer amount of trash that they'd managed to generate. Brack, specifically, had contributed to much of that, as he slowly but surely lost himself in addiction.

He pulled Zero through the debris, and laid him down near the inactive computer console. He wanted to stand and think about what he was doing, about what he had agreed to do. But the clock was ticking. He turned and went back for the next, and then the next.

Seven bodies. Four upstairs in their sleep tanks, but most definitely dead. Three downstairs, wrapped in their black and white shrouds. His crew.

He thought about sleep. He thought about not having to worry about M2. Not having to worry about being suffocated or stabbed. Not having to worry about every little aspect of the base.

He could finally have some time off. A holiday. He used to look forward to vacations, road trips to various far-flung places, piling into the car and marking their progress on the map. When was the last one? Maybe ten years ago? Twelve? Yellowstone? Sure, that was it. Mike had been fourteen, fifteen, sliding from wonder to cynicism, but the geysers had still taken his breath away.

The alarm on his tablet sounded. Time to stop daydreaming and get the hell out. He cycled the airlock through and bundled himself outside, breathing hard. It was a stupid thing to do, to risk getting caught now. He stumbled as far as the buggy, and leaned against one of the huge wheels to steady himself.

Done it. Escaped. The sun was halfway to the horizon, so it wouldn't be long now. Everything was finished, and he supposed if XO was going to make its move, it'd be now, when he'd done all the hard work and they could just replace him. Today, tonight, and in the morning. Then the next descent ship would come down, and bring relief.

He was so very tired.

But he drove to the drop-off that overlooked Sunset Boulevard and stared out across the crater. Rahe was as empty and still as ever, a huge, deep oval basin with ramparts of broken rock and a central spine of ragged hills. Later craters pocked the floor like afterthoughts.

No telltale dust clouds coming towards him across the shadowed floor of Rahe. No advancing buggies with astronauts hanging off the sides. He supposed that if they were going to try and get to him, and they were somewhere on the south side of Ceraunius, they'd probably try to come over the top. He'd thought of setting up some kind of early warning, but he had no technical expertise to help him. He wondered about all the things he might do, involving automatic cameras, or vibration sensors, or physical tripwires, and he didn't know where to even start.

It was just another day when he seemed to have got away with it. Relying on XO's word was…wearing. Since that moment on the flanks of the volcano, he'd not seen anything of M2. He wondered why. Perhaps they lacked the capacity to get to him after all, with broken buggies or the inability to recharge them. Perhaps they'd already succumbed to hunger, to thirst, to asphyxiation, and their base, what they had of it, what Frank hadn't taken, was derelict. A tomb.

Perhaps it was just that they didn't know where he was. Or

that they did, and they were biding their time, eking out their resources until the hard work was done.

He drove slowly back to the base via the MAV.

The MAV still seemed to be doing its thing. Extracting carbon dioxide, splitting it up, and sequestering the products in separate tanks. It was largely still: every so often the panels turned a few degrees to better face the weak sun, and he knew that at sunrise and sunset the vents would close and the panels rotate all the way back to their starting positions, ready to pick up the first light of dawn.

The NASA astronauts were already up there, above him. Packing and preparing to fall the last few miles from the transit ship down to Mars. Putting one machine to sleep, and waking up another. Those last few miles that had been described as seven minutes of terror on one of the training videos he'd seen, back on Earth and a lifetime ago.

What if they died on the way? After all that time—awake, for all of it—and all that distance, only to burn up in the atmosphere and then plow into the frozen red ground fast enough to leave nothing but a carbon-black smear. There was nothing Frank could do about that. If they fell too fast or too far away, he wouldn't be able to help them, only be a witness to what was happening. And then radio home.

The only preparation that was now useful would be to make sure he charged up the buggies and synced his tablet, and be ready. He knew what was required of him. Be Brack.

He craned his head back, and looked towards the zenith. They weren't going to die. He wasn't going to die either. They were going to live, and take him home with them, and he wouldn't have to be scared all the time any more. It was going to be OK. They would call him Lance Brack, and he'd have to wear the cloak of a different murderer for a while—but that was OK too, because Franklin Kittridge knew what that felt like, knew what the weight was around his shoulders, knew how to straighten up his back under the load.

One more sleep. One more attempt at sleep. There were drugs he could use, and never had before. He'd managed to hold back until now: partly through fear—both of what it might do to him, and what could happen while he was under—and partly through an iron rod of stubbornness that ran through him.

He was better than that. Everyone was better than that, he thought. No one needed that shit to help them cope or do normal stuff like sleep. In his more lucid moments, he acknowledged his approach was killing him, but he wasn't going to give in. Not now.

One more night. One more morning.

The closer it got, the more apprehensive he grew. He wasn't in control of this, and could never be: all he had was the illusion of control, pretending to set his own agenda and write his job list as if he was the site foreman. He wasn't the boss. XO were. NASA were. He was just working off their timesheets.

Like now. He drove south across the Heights to the base, looking at the collection of fragile off-white tubes not as something close to a miracle, but as home. He'd made it. He'd built his own houses several times through his life. This was no different, except it was on another planet.

He parked up, facing the descent ship, and checked his air. He had easily a couple of hours left, which was more than enough. He pulled his tablet into his lap—a tablet that had been purged of any incriminating data: no documents, no files, no past messages between here and Earth—opened up the message app, and started typing.

"Phase 3 complete", he wrote. And it almost wasn't a lie. He still had the gun, and it wasn't going anywhere.

He'd said that he'd tell them when he'd done—that illusion-of-control thing again—but they were going to launch anyway, no matter if he'd carried out his oft-repeated threat to string Brack up in a makeshift gibbet on the walls overlooking MBO. It would be up to him to explain that, and he didn't have the emotional energy to even try. He didn't have energy left for much at all.

He sat on the buggy, and waited. All his work was over. Tomorrow would be the start of Phase four, and he was off the clock until then.

Twenty-eight minutes later, his tablet registered an incoming message.

"You've done so very well, Frank. No one else could have coped like you have, done all the work like you have, kept your composure in the way you have. You're the very best of people, and it breaks my heart that we'll never meet. We are go for DV launch. Luisa."

The ship was two miles away across the Heights, a barely thumbnail-sized white cone set against the flaring red of a Martian sunset. The colors were deepening towards black as the sun sank lower, and the shadows cast in the airborne dust growing more solid. There, if anywhere, was the beauty in the bleakness.

He was looking in the direction of the peak of Ceraunius when the ground suddenly shifted under the buggy. His head snapped around, and already a wall of red cloud was rushing towards him. It went through him, and a second, thicker wind was already on its way. But rising above the long-dead world, balanced on a dirty column of churning gray smoke, was the fleck of the ship.

It drove hard and fast, and as the second storm blanketed him, he heard the boom of the rocket's ignition.

The dust cleared. The air crackled with imperfect combustion. A single incandescent flame continued to climb upwards, all detail of what it was propelling lost already. The sound of distant thunder faded, rolling between land and darkening sky.

Of course, if M2 hadn't known exactly where MBO was, the ragged smoking finger that pointed downwards in an arc was going to be a big fucking giveaway. It even caught the dying rays of the sun before it slung itself over the horizon, turning for a moment from soot to bronze.

High winds started to tug at the smoke, pulling it apart, and Frank eventually looked down. Twilight had fallen, before the proper night began. He drove over to the recharging point, and plugged in the buggy for a top-up. He had watts to play with now, and he could leave it charging until the fuel cell registered full.

His last-thing routine was shot, but he still circumnavigated the base, even if he couldn't carry out the gross visual checks, and then he entered the cross-hab airlock, cycling it and exiting with his hand on the gun. He turned left, and right, and could see nothing that had moved, that he hadn't moved himself. It was, since he started leaving all the internal airlock doors open, the only way in and out of the base. Another precautionary habit that he was going to have to unlearn by tomorrow.

He left the door behind him open, too.

But yes, he was alone, for now, for the moment. He put the gun down on top of the life support rack and checked the external pressure. It read a solid five psi, and none of the oxygen alarms were ringing. He was OK to exit his suit, and he thumbed his way through the flip-down menu on his front until he reached the right command.

He crawled backwards out of his suit, hung it up, racked his life support, and unclipped the tablet, wiping the dust from its screen with his forearm. He probably needed to remember to get dressed at some point, too. In Brack's overalls. He'd sent up his own blood-stained set on the ship. Zeus's overalls would have drowned him, and no one else's were remotely large enough.

But he couldn't walk around like some kind of bum. He needed to relearn that, too, as well as regaining the power of speech. Part of the reason why he went around just in his long johns most of the time was so that he could get into his suit quickly. With the arrival of the others, he could get back to some kind of normal. Whatever that was. Normal for Mars.

He deliberately pulled on the overalls. They felt tight around the shoulders, and up against his crotch. Maybe the cloth would loosen up with more wearing.

The gun went into a pocket, and he collected the scuba gear and his tablet.

Now, food. Coffee. Everything was in place. All evidence of anyone else on the base had been erased. Except for the gun, and that too would have to go by the morning. He'd bag it, so that the alkaline soil wouldn't eat it away, and he'd take it outside and bury it. He'd use the cairn that they'd created when they were building the base, moving the loose rocks that might have punctured the sub-floor matting.

It was a pile five, maybe six feet high, and thin in the reduced gravity. He'd do that. Rebuild the cairn over the top. A marker to show he'd finally, finally left all that shit behind. Tomorrow, he'd be safe. Safer. At least there'd be other people to keep watch for him. He'd never really be safe.

And tonight, he'd keep that gun close at hand. Just in case.

11

[Message file #274-1058 2/7/2049 1437 CAPCOM Ares IV Mission Control to Ares IV "Prairie Rose" Mars Orbit]

Hawthorn, all systems nominal. Surface conditions are good, and Mars Base One is down there waiting for you.

You are go for descent. Godspeed.

[transcript ends]

Frank got the call ten minutes before. He suited up, and went outside to watch. Watching was all he could do. Was it all the astronauts could do too? Would they fall and have to trust the automatics, or could they pilot themselves down? Even then, there might be nothing they could do to correct their course: if something went wrong, it would happen so very quickly. Whatever happened, Frank was only ever going to be a witness.

He clipped his tablet to his waist, and checked he had the pouch of suit patches. Then one last look around. What shouldn't be there? The blue surgical glove. That wasn't necessary any more, was it? And he really didn't have a good excuse for it sitting there, perched on top of the life support rack. He picked it up, and pulled at the knot in the wrist, but undoing knots was about as difficult as it was making them while wearing the spacesuit gauntlets.

In the end, he stretched the thumb out hard enough to create a tiny hole, and then dug his fingers in to widen it. He didn't quite know what to do with the broken glove now, so he just pushed it into the pouch at his waist.

The scuba gear could stay where it was. That was explicable. And he was wearing his one-piece, and Brack's overalls were sitting on a hanger, waiting for him to change into. Slippers too. He'd showered this morning. He'd eaten. He felt OK. He felt he'd done enough.

That didn't mean he'd done it all. Was there something he'd left in plain sight, something he'd grown so accustomed to seeing that he didn't really see it any more, but that would immediately attract the attention of a newcomer—who'd pick it up and want to know what it was? And Frank would unravel.

He'd been over this, a dozen, a hundred times. There was nothing. He was anxious, and understandably so. Accept it, move on.

He stepped out of the airlock into the dull light of a Martian morning. Insertion was due shortly after 0800, enough for the shadows to shorten and the frost to boil off. Nothing outside had moved, and even though he touched his bag, he knew that the gun wasn't there any more, and never would be again. From now on, he could rely on safety in numbers.

He could do this and go home, and the nightmares of blood and decompression would quieten and he could live a normal life again.

He had to stop thinking that, too. That was far in the future, and was too much pressure. He'd been on his own too long, and then threatened with the wrong kind of company.

He needed to concentrate on the mundane, on unplugging the buggy from the power supply and coiling up the stiff, serpentine lead into its container, and kicking the wheels, shaking the frame to make sure nothing dropped off. Changing the wheels—that was a job for two, and now that he had spares, sent or stolen, he was eager to swap out the pitted, leaf-like tires for fresh-from-the-factory ones. Sure, he could have jury-rigged a jack, but so much easier with another pair of hands.

The fuel cell lit up the display, reliable as ever, and he buckled himself into the seat to wait. The time on his tablet showed 0803, and one new message. He tabbed the app open, and it was Luisa.

"Welcome to Phase four, Frank. This is your time, now. It really is all up to you. I know how much you want to come home, and honestly, I'm glad it's you and not Brack. You've become much more than a name on the screen these last few months. I hope I have too. Make it happen, Frank. Come home. Luisa. (I'm going to delete this from the server once I know you've seen it, and resend an 'official' message. But this is how I feel L x)"

Luisa was starting to take risks on his behalf, and he didn't know what to think about that. Did he have an ally at XO? And how far might she be prepared to go for him? Could she get messages out, as well as in? That was something to explore, another day. All he knew was that he'd come to rely on her.

Right now, though, he had one very big thing to worry about, and it was going to take his full attention.

0804. Soon. So very soon. He tilted himself back to catch as much of the sky as possible.

There were clouds, high up and thin, like a gathered veil that stretched in folds from east to west, visibly moving as the ephemeral winds chased them away. The far horizons were blocked by Rahe's rampart walls and the bulk of the volcano, but straight up was where they'd come from.

0806. Had they already left the transit ship, fired their rockets and started sliding inexorably towards the ground? They'd had nine months in space just getting here. Had they argued? Had they fought? Were they still a team? He hoped so. His own crew, seven entirely mismatched cons, had got on well enough. They hadn't turned on each other, except at the very end, and even then that was a matter of life and death. His own, mainly. NASA would have picked these people well. They weren't XO. These were the good guys, right?

They were going to take him home with them.

0807. Come on. His gaze flicked to every aberration in his sight, every floater, every roil of cloud. Nothing. Nothing at all. Maybe he should just close his eyes and pray very hard, but he hadn't done that since he was a kid and it didn't seem right to do it now. Selfish. Wanting something, and not prepared to do anything for it in return. And in any event, if there was a God, then Frank had pretty much plowed his own furrow for his entire adult life, not looking for salvation from outside. He hadn't been turned around or come to any great revelation. He was pretty certain this was it. Zeus would have said otherwise, but he wasn't here and his body was on its way to the sun.

0809. Seriously, what were they doing up there? What could be keeping them? Maybe something had gone wrong. Something, a problem with any part of the descent vehicle, would mean they'd have to abort. If they could fix it, they could try again. Otherwise, they were stuck up there and he was stuck down here. With only M2 for company. But he still had the MAV. If they were willing to stick around for a few more months, perhaps he could climb on board and join the transit ship in orbit.

0810. That hadn't occurred to him before. He knew how long the MAV needed to fuel up enough to take them all back up to orbit, but if it was just him? The payload would be one-seventh of what it had been designed for. He might be able to go now. Did it run fully automatic, or did he need a pilot? Would the astronauts having to abort their landing be the best solution for him? Now he was in a quandary. He didn't know what he wanted any more.

0811. Of course, they'd spent all that time in transit awake, and everything was leading up to this moment. They would

109

have checked and double-checked the ship as part of their routine maintenance. Any problems with it would have been discovered, and fixed, months ago. They were in orbit, and they were coming down. Anything else, and he would have been told. Nothing had been left to chance.

0812. So where were they? Seven minutes, from first contact with the Martian atmosphere to touchdown. That was all. He'd waited months for this moment, and now that it had finally arrived, he was like a child desperate for Christmas. He knew he wanted it. He hadn't realized quite how much. His heart was banging in his chest like it wanted out.

0813. There? Was that it? Could he even see it at this distance? What if they'd over- or under-shot? Hundreds, maybe a thousand miles out, and no way of getting to them. He blinked and wished he could scrub at his eyes. No. Nothing. It was just the fans blowing in his face, drying him out.

0814. Wait. There was something. A light. A flickering, faint light like a match falling. Pulsing. Was that good? All the other deliveries did that too, so it wasn't unusual, but he squinted at it, trying to ascertain whether this was a normal descent, or whether parts were burning up and breaking off. The light grew, both in size and in brilliance. Brighter than the sun. Bright enough to hurt. Or was that the tightness in his chest, and his inability to breathe?

0815. Smoke. There was a trail of smoke. Again, normal, but was this sootier? Was it actually on fire? The first rumble of thunder trembled across the amphitheater of the crater, making the sand dance. The smoke thickened, and the glow changed in quality. No longer blazing, but like a charcoal, a red eye.

0816. The parachutes strung out behind, one, two, three long candles. Then, boom. They opened, taking a great gulp of air each, shivering and clawing at Mars's thin air. The ground, the walls, growled and complained, and the cinder of the heat shield fell away, a black disk tumbling and spinning, sliding and twisting away and downwards, heading towards the plain to the west of the volcano.

0817. It was falling so quickly. He remembered what the MAV looked like, coming down. He remembered the momentary fear that it was going to crash into the base, and it hadn't, and everything had been fine, and he still felt sick. The parachutes were huge, great saucers of orange and white. Then, unexpectedly, they detached, deflated and wheeled away. The dark speck suspended underneath dropped like a stone.

0818. And lit up. Spears of bright fire pointed downwards, and suddenly the air was roaring, trembling. A shadow moved across the sky, eclipsing the sun and then out again, falling, falling, slowing, and it was there, a physical thing, white and smooth and efficient, slowing down, down, slipping out of sight over the edge of the Heights, on the way to the crater floor. Dust, smoke, and then silence.

Frank gasped, dragging in so much air, so quickly, the suit struggled to respond. He deliberately placed his hands on his chestplate and timed his breathing. Slowly out. Hold. Slowly back in. Hold. OK, he wasn't going to faint, not this very moment. The fans cleared his faceplate, and he took a drink of water from his sippy tube.

They were here. He was trembling with relief. He'd done it. He'd survived. Despite everything, despite XO, despite Mars. Despite himself.

The dust cloud was slowly collapsing. The grit pattered down, while the finer material kept on going up and thinning as it went. He'd need to sweep the panels clean after one launch and one descent. How prosaic. He waited until he could trust himself to drive, then reached forward to grip the steering controls.

He squeezed the throttle, and the buggy rolled forward. Had he forgotten anything? Surely he had. Perhaps he should take one last look around...

No. He'd already done that. He was good to go. He was Brack

now. He was playing that part. Brack was going to drive over to meet the astronauts, cool as you like, and pick them up and bring them back to the base, and he was going to be fine. They'd be good people, and he could finally sleep.

He headed out to the drop-off, passing the fresh scour mark from his own reascending descent ship, black spokes radiating outwards and fading into smudges. He drove across them, and the tires made two cords through the wheel of soot. At the edge of the drop-off, he stopped, ostensibly to judge his route down, but actually to check that the NASA craft had really, genuinely arrived.

It had. It was there, well past the foot of the delta, almost halfway to the western edge of Beverly Hills, with a long scour mark of its own as it tracked across the crater floor before settling down on four fold-out legs. It looked smaller than his own ship, which made some kind of sense, since this was just to transport the crew from orbit to the ground, not all the way from Earth. A one-shot taxi, nothing more: a squat, blunt bullet.

The real deal was up in orbit: a now-silent, slumbering spire of a ship. He'd get there, one day.

Frank turned the control column and the buggy angled downwards, traversing the slope that would normally lead onto Sunset. This time, though, he was going to take a left, an unfamiliar direction, and it occurred to him just how little exploring he'd done. The relentless focus on building the base, gearing up for self-sufficiency, then survival...

But of course. XO hadn't wanted the pristine landscape scarred by multiple tire tracks. Frank was supposed to be on his own, supervising the phantom robots and definitely not having the time to wander around Mars.

As it was, it looked just how they wanted it. There was so much of the crater, of the Heights, that he'd never seen up close, and yet it had been where he'd lived, worked, and nearly died, for eight months. He'd never even been to the top of the volcano.

That seemed a shame. If he was going to have stories to

tell, he wanted at least some of them to be good. Everything changed from today, though. He'd have the chance to build up some memories he'd want to keep. Starting from now.

The buggy drifted slightly on the bottom of the slope—rocket-blown dust, nothing more—and he corrected for it. It gave him a jolt, but he handled it instinctively, knowing which way to turn to get the grip back. No danger at all of rolling it in front of the astronauts. He was going to stay frosty, just like his old crew used to tell each other.

He was down on the crater floor, rolling across the pavement of loose rock and angled slabs, heading towards the NASA ship. He knew it was NASA, because the letters were visible on the side, even at a mile distant. No XO branding, he noted. No sign of anyone climbing out either. He hoped they were all OK inside. The landing had looked flawless. The ship was intact. They were just waiting for him.

Shouldn't he be hearing something in his headphones by now? Maybe they were on a different frequency to him. Maybe they hadn't switched over yet. That was it.

Seriously, Frank. Stop inventing problems. They're here. They're finally here.

The shape of the descent vehicle resolved across the plain. He skirted a couple of old, eroded craters, and pulled up outside, looking up at the pale, slanting walls and reading the name "Hawthorn" on the outside. The MAV was called Dogwood. Someone in charge liked their plants, apparently.

The MAV had a box tied to one of its legs, that lowered a ladder to the surface. This one did too. Perhaps that was what they were waiting for. No, they could do that for themselves, from the inside.

Did they even know he was outside? Had he actually said anything, the whole time? Had he forgotten how to speak? He'd talked to the other XO astronaut a few weeks ago. He clearly remembered how, but he suddenly felt mute.

He coughed. He drank some water. He cleared his throat.

"Hello? Anyone listening?"

"Good morning, Lance. We were all wondering where you'd got to. This is Pilot Commander Lucy Davison, and the rest of the team are just as eager to meet you as I am. I appreciate that this could be a little overwhelming for you, so we'll do the personal introductions in stages. I'll come down with Jim, and we'll take it from there."

Another human voice. In his ear. In real time. Someone who didn't actively want him dead.

"Sure. OK." Everything that he wanted to say, that he imagined himself saying, even just playing it cool, had gone. Goddammit, even Dee would have been more articulate. He was still strapped into his seat like an idiot. He punched the buckle, got it at the second attempt, and shrugged his way out of the harness.

The ladder was dropping out of the ship, and the rungs clicking into place. The outer door was opening. There was someone standing there, in the airlock. Two people, one standing behind the other.

Frank climbed unsteadily out of his seat, concentrating hard on his hand- and footholds, but almost slipping nevertheless, having to grip tight as he slewed across the lattice frame of the buggy and banging his back against a strut.

Whereas they were climbing down, hand over hand, effortlessly, practiced, efficient.

He lowered himself to the ground, and turned. The first astronaut paused before they took that last step backwards off the end of the ladder.

– Give them this moment. They won't get another like it. They don't need me shooting my mouth off.

"Mom. Dad. This is for you." She placed her foot down firmly, pressing her boot into the red dust of another planet. She held on to the ladder for a little while longer, then put her other foot down and slowly shuffled to her left.

He remembered his first encounter with Martian gravity.

It had screwed with him, coming straight from sleep, with his body remembering only its Earth-weight. He couldn't walk without feeling like he was going to jump into space. And he'd never trained for it either. XO had deemed that, along with a whole stack of other things, unnecessary.

The second astronaut didn't hesitate. He let go and let himself fall, bending his knees for the minimal impact. "Boom," he said. Then he bounced up, throwing his arms to turn himself around as if he were a gymnast or a figure skater—diver, that was it—and on the half-turn, planted down again.

"Jim, cut it out."

"Yes, ma'am." The man extended his arm again, gesturing towards Frank. "Let's go meet our host."

Pilot Commander Lucy Davison—"Davison" on her left breast, U.S. flag underneath—was pocket-sized and compact next to Jim—"Zamudio" on his—who was long-limbed and lupine.

Was Frank expected to salute? Go through some sort of formal ceremony? Hand the base over using a set form of words? He didn't know. He scarcely remembered his own name, let alone the fact that he was supposed to be using someone else's.

The distance between ship and buggy was barely anything, yet time seemed elastic, stretching out so that the closer they got to Frank, the further they had to go.

Then it all snapped back, including everything that Luisa had told him about this part. It was OK. He knew what to do.

The pilot held out her hand, brisk, business-like. "Lance. Thank you for coming to get us, and letting us share your home."

Frank looked down at his own gauntlet, empty and open. He moved it forward, and she grasped it. Not a dap. A firm, positive handshake. She wasn't a con. She'd never known the inside of a jail cell. It felt...wrong.

"Welcome to Mars," he managed. He could already feel the blood draining from his head, and he knew he was going to faint for real this time. His stomach was cold and his face was hot. His vision tunneled until all he could see was the top of her faceplate, through which he could make out the junction of her beanie cap against her forehead. She was frowning.

"Jim," she said. "Catch him."

12

From: Carolina Soledad <cmsoledad@usach.cl>
To: Miguel Averado <maaverado@usach.cl>
Date: Sun, Feb 7 2049 09:03:29 -0300
Subject: Lava tube project

Hello, Professor.

I was making some measurements last night (couldn't sleep—the rain was so loud!) when I came across this. I looked at previous images, and there's definitely a change in albedo from one to the other at the point marked. I was wondering if you'd seen any evidence of active erosion in this area before that might indicate subsurface settling. Because this could easily be a recent partial collapse of the lava tube, and the brightness of the target due to the uneroded rock fall.

Carolina

[images appended HiRISE2 22 11 54 N 97 39 00 W 8/21/2048 and 22 40 05 N 97 41 25 W 12/16/2048, annotated]

He couldn't have been out for more than a few seconds, and once his head was lower than his heart recovery was almost instantaneous. Even so, he came to with four helmets looking down at him, not two.

One of them, a man with the blackest skin he'd ever seen, was kneeling in the dust by his side. He applied gentle pressure to Frank's breastplate and made sure he didn't move.

"Morning, Lance. How're you feeling?"

It took Frank a moment to realize the man was talking to him, that he was Lance Brack now, and not Franklin Kittridge. He could have told them then, he could have blurted it out and let the whole thing unwind from there, but he held his tongue and covered his actual confusion with an easily faked confusion.

"Good. Good. Sorry. I didn't mean to, you know." The last time he'd fainted was when he discovered that his job on Mars was supposed to be done by robots. Before then? Even with all the ridiculous high-impact tests XO had inflicted on him, he'd never passed out. Thrown up, yes, but not passed out.

"You just take your time, Lance. I'm the doctor, by the way. Fanuel. Everyone calls me Fan."

Frank glanced at the man's label: Perea. The flag of…Cuba? That wasn't right. Panama? Blue triangle, white star, three red stripes and two white. Puerto Rico.

"I'm OK. You can let me up."

"I'm here to fuss over you. Maybe later we can meet up in the medical room, and I can check you over. A lot can happen in eight months, and that sleep process they used? Let's just say I'm not a believer."

Frank's body was a map—the very recent scars on his chest and on his arm—that anyone competent could read. And it was pretty obvious that NASA wouldn't have sent someone less than brilliant to Mars.

"I'd have to talk to XO about that first," he said. Something that Luisa had told him to say. "My medical history is commercially sensitive."

"They're never likely to find out, because of patient–doctor confidentiality, but OK. I'm not going to push." Fan took his hand away and slipped it under the back of Frank's helmet. "Let's get you sitting up, and see how that goes. You been eating OK, sleeping? Noticed any changes in your health recently?"

118

"I'd have—"

"To talk to XO first. Sure. I get that. Reach up. Leland, take his left, Jim, the right please."

Frank found his forearms gripped, whether he liked it or not, and was levered into an awkward semi-sitting position, where the lower edge of his hard carapace dug into the tops of his thighs. He blinked, and remembered these were people and they were holding him, touching him: even through layers of cloth, insulation and rubber, it felt strange, alien.

"I'm good," he said. "Let me up."

"You sure?" Fan must have spotted the flash of irritation cross Frank's face, because he moved behind him and told Jim and Leland—Leland Fisher, United States—to lever him upright.

Frank blinked the spots away and let the fans cool his skin. He wasn't going to faint again, and he had no idea why he'd done so in the first place. Sudden relief, probably. He had been stupidly stressed over the last few weeks, and as he stood there, still held by the arms and propped up at the back, he discovered that his anxiety had pretty much gone. Instead of that knot of worry clawing at his guts, he felt calm. Cotton-wool calm.

"I'm fine. You can let go now."

Both the men waited for confirmation from the doctor to do so, then backed off to give Frank some space. He didn't know whether he should be embarrassed. Instead, he was just grateful.

"You OK now, Lance?"

Lance. Got to remember. Lance from now on.

"Thanks. Good. Sure. Didn't mean to do that." Frank's arms hung limply by his side, and he thought he should do something with them. He lifted them up and pointed vaguely at the crater walls. "So, this is Rahe. It's not much to look at, but it is on another planet. I guess you've got plenty of things planned, so if you want to grab your stuff—you've got stuff, right?—I'll take you up to MBO."

Frank counted heads, came to four, and remembered there should be six. The last two astronauts were climbing down the

119

ladder, one waiting for the other before coming across to join them. He could probably take two, maybe three at a time.

"There's no rush, Lance," said Lucy. Pilot Commander Lucy. Was he supposed to just call her Lucy? She didn't seem the type who'd want to be called by her first name. Let alone have it shortened to Luce. Ma'am? He didn't know. Yet attracting people's attention over the headsets without saying their name first was hard, unless they were the only other person around. "Let them have a walk around, stretch their legs. We had an," she paused, "interesting landing."

"What she means is, we almost missed the crater completely, came down hard, and landed on fumes."

Frank tried to identify the speaker, but wasn't familiar enough with their tone and cadence to make a call. Not Fan. Leland or Jim.

"What she means," said Lucy, more pointedly, "is that despite some unusual atmospheric conditions and anomalous telemetry, the pilot was still able to eyeball the target and touch down safely within a couple of hundred yards of the projected landing site. I will be filing a full report in due course."

"Wait," said Frank. "You flew that? And nearly crashed it?"

"No," she said. "The automatics were going to crash it. I took over and manually landed the ship, which I did perfectly. It's why I'm on this mission, Lance."

"I didn't mean—"

"No offense taken. Armstrong landed on the Moon with less reserves than I had, so I don't even get bragging rights. I'd trained for worse scenarios than the one that presented itself, and what we had was fixable. We're down and safe, and I'm going to leave what went wrong to the engineers for now."

There was a brittle edge to her voice, that indicated she'd come within a whisker of coming down hot and had just about managed to hold it together. She was both furious and relieved, and because she was in charge, she wasn't going to show either. He liked her for it.

"I'm . . . glad you made it down."

"We all are," said Leland. "Makes doing our jobs a whole lot easier." He pushed his fist into Frank's upper arm, close to where the bullet wound was, and Frank clenched his teeth against the unexpected twinge. "Lucy has ice-water where the rest of us have blood, and we're all very grateful for that."

Leland looked up and around, taking in the view. The other astronauts were walking about, testing their bodies and suits against the gravity and the terrain. Bursts of chatter flitted in and out of Frank's ears like birds—everything seemed interesting, the rocks, the clouds, the dust in between, the shape of the land, the way the sun shone through the atmosphere and threw halos and bands of light and dark in the sky.

Only the pilot seemed content to just be. She could, of course, be reliving the last few minutes of flight when triumph and disaster were separated only by her skill and her reactions. But her face was impassive behind the layer of optical-grade plastic.

"So, Lance," said Leland, "you got any advice for us new bugs?"

Again, the mental gears had to mesh before getting up to speed. "Don't fuck up?"

Leland laughed. It was an easy, unpracticed sound, that just rolled out of him. "Well, that's a philosophy I can get behind."

"Here, everything's trying to kill you. Everything. And if you fuck up, it will."

"You've done OK, Lance."

Frank had just about survived. But he couldn't say that. He couldn't say anything about it at all. His mistake—his only mistake—was trusting XO. He wasn't going to make that mistake again.

"That's because I didn't fuck up."

"That'll be music to Fan's ears. Safety first, last and always."

"I'm here to serve," said Fan, "all and equally, according to their need. And to remind them, in the words of our friend here, not to fuck up." He reached out and touched Frank's suit, where the bullet had gone through. "So what happened here?"

"I got a swipe with an unfinished ring section." Frank felt he ought to embellish the story. "The robot's sensor must have been on the fritz." He felt he could pretty much blame anything on the robots, since they never existed and certainly weren't around to examine now.

"Must have been an interesting few moments. But you dealt with it?"

Frank dipped into his waist pouch and held up a selection of patches. "You should be carrying these around with you, too. All the time."

"Just in case. We'll see to that. Thanks, Lance."

He was getting the hang of it. Lance. Lance Brack. That was the name he answered to, even if it wasn't painted on his suit.

"OK, people," said Lucy, "gather round. We've got a schedule, and Mission Control will be wondering what we're doing. Introductions first. This is Lance Brack, XO's representative at MBO. When we all get up to MBO, he can show us around and talk us through any changes to the routines and infrastructure we need to get up to speed on. Lance has been here, by himself, for eight straight months, and having all of us descend on him is going to be a difficult adjustment, so let the man be. If you've got questions that aren't a priority, stow them for now. OK, Lance? We'll keep out of your hair for as long as you need."

They were all now standing in a circle. Seven of them. It was almost like old times, back in training. And it was how it should have been, on Mars. All seven of them, standing and looking at the base they'd made, living and working side by side. Not Brack: he was never part of the team. But Frank's colleagues were. Cons. Misfits. The awkward squad. His team.

Goddammit, he wasn't going to cry.

"Fanuel's already introduced himself. Jim is our rock hound. Isla will be doing all the plant experiments. Yun—Feng Yun—is an atmospheric scientist, and hopefully you've got all her kit. Leland is that thing that no one knows they need until they need it, the appropriately titled "human factors", and I guess you know who I am. These people are my responsibility. Anything and everything that happens to them is my business, because when we go home, we're all going home.

"This afternoon will be orientation and safety drills. Tomorrow, and the next few sols, will be dedicated to unpacking our mission-specific equipment and testing. This has been a long road. For some of us, most of us, this is going to be the high point of our careers, of our whole lives. We've dedicated ourselves to get to this exact point, and we'll never have these moments again, so every hour, every minute on Mars needs to count. Tonight, we get to party. Tomorrow, we start work. OK? Let's get to it."

There was a chorus of assent—someone said "so say we all", echoing back to a sci-fi show Frank faintly remembered from the reruns.

"Leland, Isla," said Lucy. "You're first up. Lance, if you could escort them to MBO, then head back for the next batch."

"I've got two buggies. One of them could drive back with me, pick everyone up."

"We can do that. Leland, you good?"

"I'm magnificent. Lance can show me the ropes."

"You need a trailer for hauling stuff? I've got two of those as well."

"We traveled light. Hand-luggage only."

"OK. You'll have to hang on, and I'll take it as slow as I can."

Frank led the two astronauts to the buggy, and already it seemed normal. He didn't know how that could possibly be. There were six—count them, six—extra people here, and it was just normal. Maybe it'd sink in later, when they were all in his base, making noise, filling up the connecting ways, tramping dirt around and generally being there.

And it wasn't just for today. It was for the next year and beyond. He was going to have to make some big adjustments, and Lucy had been wise enough to start by telling her crew to back off when he needed the space. That was how someone earned his respect from the get-go.

Frank climbed up the usual way, reaching for the lowest strut, pushing a foot against the wheel, and half walked, half clambered over the latticework until he could drop into his seat.

"Hop on up," he said, through the chatter. It was noisy, and he couldn't mute it. Or rather, he could, but it wasn't like he was trying to keep secrets, just the peace and quiet. Isla—Weber, American—just pulled herself up, hand over hand, without using her legs.

"Where should we stand?" asked Leland, looking up.

"We—" OK, stop there. There is no "we". There never was. "Wherever you want, but somewhere behind me, hanging on to the roll bars will be fine. Probably easier if you sit down and you can brace against the struts."

Like we all did. Like I did. Except I can't say that because if I've done it, who the hell was driving?

Frank strapped himself in, and looked at the controls. His mind was inexplicably blank for a moment. He blinked and reached forward, and his hands naturally fell into position. That was better. He felt the chassis rock as Leland joined them. He couldn't turn round to check on them, so he said: "Everyone OK? Holding on?"

"We're good. Take us home, Lance."

One of them patted his shoulder—Frank was going to guess Leland again, who seemed quite tactile—and he took that as a sign that he could move off. He drove them in a broad arc away from the Hawthorn, then back along the base of the Heights to the start of Sunset.

He almost said "we" again, and bit down on the word before he could voice it. "I normally come down this way. The slope's stable here, and not so steep. If you're going out onto the eastern plains, then it's the most direct route. Straight along and up Long Beach, where the crater wall's collapsed."

"Long Beach? You from LA?" asked Leland.

Dee was. Dee had died, but his names lived on. "It was a Mission Control thing," said Frank. "The base is up on the Heights, and the road between is Sunset Boulevard. The ridge of hills down the middle of the crater we called Beverly Hills."

The "we" crept out again, but that was OK. He'd already introduced the idea of Mission Control giving him a hand.

"You know those features have official IAU titles?" It was the first time Isla had spoken. To him, certainly. It might have been the first time she'd spoken, period.

"No. No, I didn't." No one had bothered to tell him, or correct him, because he was supposed to be fucking dead, like Dee. And some of that deep reservoir of anger leaked out in his voice, despite himself.

He didn't know how to apologize, or make it better, so he just shut up and concentrated on not turning the buggy over and killing the new people. He pointed the wheels uphill and remembered to soften the front tires more than he normally would to compensate for the extra weight on the back.

"If it starts to roll, just jump clear."

"You won't roll it," said Leland.

"That's kind of the plan. But, you know. Stay frosty."

"Frosty. Got it."

That was what they'd said to each other. Frank and his crew. And now he was trying not to cry again. His emotions were all over the dial, and he just couldn't control them: from despair to rage to grief, and back again. He was a wreck. An actual physical, psychological car crash of a human being, swinging between extremes with no middle ground.

He widened his eyes, let the fans dry him out, and thanked whoever had designed their suits that the faceplate only allowed ten-to-two vision.

The buggy growled and chewed its way up the drop-off, and leveled out on the Heights—or whatever its proper name was—and he dialed the stiffness back into the tires so that they once more skipped over the surface.

"That's your MAV," said Frank, and pointed. "And there's the base."

"I like what you've done with the place," said Leland.

"It's what we've got. Breathable atmosphere, hot water and enough juice to keep the lights on."

"Sounds perfect. Isla's looking forward to seeing the greenhouse."

She was the plant specialist, right? "I'll give you a tour later on. I just follow the instructions, though, I don't pretend to know what I'm doing."

"You've made modifications?"

"I don't know about that. I did what I thought was right." He probably ought to explain more. "I had problems with the fish."

"Problems? The reports said protein output was right in the middle of the expected mean."

Frank took a moment to work out what she meant. "They grew fine. I, I just couldn't eat them. I couldn't kill them to eat them."

"Oh. So…"

"So I grew more grains and nuts and peas and beans, and cut back on the fish production. I ramped it up again for you guys. I think I've timed it right."

"I'll take a look. We've dehydrated meals to fall back on."

"You won't be short."

"I'll still take a look."

"You won't be short," he repeated, again with far too much venom. "I got drums filled with dried grains and nuts and I freeze-dried my own herbs rather than throw them. I did my job. There's plenty."

OK, so he should probably apologize now. So should she. But she didn't know what she'd done wrong, and he didn't know why he was taking offense so hard.

They drove the rest of the mercifully short way in silence, and when they pulled up outside the base, Isla climbed down, thanked Frank formally for the ride, and walked straight towards the cross-hab airlock without asking for directions.

They'd trained for years for this. They knew the layout as well as he did.

"It's hard adjusting, Lance. No one here hasn't got a massive self-belief in their own opinions: they wouldn't have got picked for the mission otherwise. No harm, no foul. Let's go and get the others."

Frank watched Isla's retreating back, and still couldn't bring himself to say even the simplest sorry.

"Sure. Let's do that."

13

Music. Frank hadn't expected music. He—his old crew—hadn't had speakers, and they'd only arrived later, in boxes that he hadn't opened. Yet it was one of the first things that the new crew had done: find them, sync them to the base's computer and start banging out an eclectic mix of songs, old, very old and new.

Some of them were so new that Frank hadn't heard them before. And when he thought of how new they might be, he realized with a start that for him, new meant "since he'd been in prison". Ten years of popular culture, current affairs, scientific advances, and everything else, skipped like a time-traveler.

He hadn't missed it, until confronted by the fact that he had, in fact, missed it.

He couldn't take it. He felt overwhelmed. Everything was

128

crashing in on him, a perfect storm of absence and recollection, remembering what he'd lost and remembering that other people hadn't had the same experience. In prison, the cons ended up adrift in the past, while the present moved on without them. It was partly why there was such a revolving door of recidivism: it wasn't criminality as such, more future shock. The outside world was a foreign country, with strange customs and a different language.

Frank hadn't paid attention to any of that, since he thought he'd be inside until he died. Suddenly confronted with the truth of how the world had turned without him, he ran away.

Though that was a lie. He didn't run. Everyone, and he was stumbling over that word as much as he was "we", seemed to be in the kitchen area, getting one or another briefing of some sort. If he'd been meant to attend any of them, he was certain that Lucy would have told him. So he suited up and went outside. He didn't ask anyone's permission. He didn't tell anyone. He didn't leave a note. He just wanted to pretend he was still on his own in his own, perfect bubble.

Even that was a lie. He just couldn't stop himself piling on the fictions, one on top of another. He wasn't alone. Even though he didn't have his ghosts any more, there were six astronauts inside the habs—his habs—and there was another XO base, full of XO people, on the other side of the volcano.

He could hear violin strings sing even through his helmet and the closed airlock door, though indistinctly. It was only when the air pumped away that it became silent.

He fell back on routine. He did a walkround of the habs, checked that nothing had come loose, made sure the RTG heating system was still intact, and remembered he had to clean the panels after their two dustings. There was plenty to be getting on with, while the crew settled in and got to know their surroundings.

They seemed competent. He was certain they already knew how to do everything that he did—the basic functions of running the base—and that he could reasonably sit on his ass for how-ever long it was, and then just go home with them. He knew he wasn't going to do that, though. He'd find something to do, in time, even if it was just chauffeuring them around and carrying their bags.

And for now, he still had jobs to do.

He untied the large square of parachute canopy that Declan had used to clean the panels, and had habitually looped around the underside of one of the supports. It was past midday, and the flat black circles were angled to the west. Before he'd set up the new array, the job hadn't taken much time. There were over twice the number now, and it was something that had to be scheduled rather than done while passing.

He worked his way methodically along the rows, cleaning the upslope sides, then brushing off the grit onto the ground from the downslope. They had plenty of watts, even with seven on board.

As he wiped, he relaxed into the rhythm of it. It was some-thing he was used to doing, and by the time he'd finished and shaken out the cloth—upwind, as best as he could judge—he felt calmer.

He spun his nut runner through his fingers and checked the torque on several bolts on each ring; he paid special attention to the workshop, because although he knew there was nothing wrong with the build, he still had the abiding memory of Zeus being stuck in the airlock, boiling his life out into the near-vacuum through a crack in the door that Frank himself had created.

He knelt down in the dirt and examined the pipework that led from the hot-water tank to the habs, pipes that ran under-ground through insulated wraps. There was always going to be a possibility of the soil shifting. Permafrost, which was some-thing that Frank had never had to deal with on building sites across California, had a habit of heaving or collapsing. That was what Zeus had said.

Frank missed the man. Stupid, really. Or not. He didn't know. He even missed Declan, who was by far the most abrasive and awkward of those who'd made it as far as Phase two. And he couldn't talk about them to anyone. They were never on Mars. They'd died, somewhere on Earth, their bodies cremated, their death certificates written up and their effects dumped into storage somewhere. Or burned along with their bodies.

He checked the buggies for charge, and inspected the main dish for dust, not that it had ever caused problems before, but it was worth worrying about. At least, it was if he was looking for jobs to do to avoid going back inside.

Eventually, there was nothing for it. He re-entered through the cross-hab, and as the airlock repressurized the unfamiliar sounds—long, slow chords overlaid by rapidly changing patterns of notes—seeped back in. Voices. Clattering of unpacking and moving equipment.

Frank racked his suit and life support, just like he'd done hundreds of times before. He did remember that he needed to get dressed in his overalls. Brack's overalls. They felt tight, tighter than when he'd first tried them on. It was all he had. He could say that XO had sent the wrong size.

The crew had clearly taken Lucy's warning to heart. They were leaving him alone, but their mere presence was still too much. He let himself into the greenhouse and immersed himself in the damp, green fug.

This was better, running his fingers through the seedlings— apparently it helped them grow strong—and on seeing that the corn was putting out silk, snapping off some of the pollinating tassels and dusting each plant in the block, again working methodically so as not to miss any out.

What he did miss was Isla standing just inside, by the airlock door, perfectly still so that his gaze just slid over her because he didn't expect to see anyone there. Then she raised her hand to indicate her presence, and Frank yelped.

He did more than that. He stumbled backwards, banging

awkwardly against the staging, and had to lose the corn-tassels in order to stop himself from falling. That indignity spared, he clutched at the racks of slowly dripping plants while he composed himself.

He'd thought it was a ghost. Or more than that. He'd thought it wasn't.

"I'm sorry," she said. "I didn't mean ... anything."

He'd be bruised, but that was nothing really. What was wrong with him was what was happening inside, not out.

"It's not your fault," he said. "Nothing is your fault. I'm not saying it's mine either, but I got some stuff I need to work through, and it looks like that's going to take some time." He straightened himself up, felt the pull of his too-small overalls, and took in her scraped-back white-blond hair before looking down for the tassels he'd dropped.

He dipped down for them, gathering them up and discarding them in the compost bin. "What can I do for you?" he finally asked.

"I just wanted to have a proper look around," she said, and pointed at the airlock behind her, "but if you want some space I can come back later."

"It's fine. This isn't mine. You come and go as you want."

"We're new here, Lance. We ... we don't want to crowd you."

Frank turned away, turned back. "It's OK. We're all here to do a job, right? I'm not going to get in your way, and this place is big enough that if I need to escape, I can."

"As long as you're sure. I'll stay out of your way."

She maintained a respectful distance as Frank went round checking the reservoirs and the nutrient levels, topping up those which seemed low; but he could quite easily have left them. It struck him just how much make-work he'd invented for himself, and just how much the routine had held him together. Because of the disruption caused by the arrivals, his tablet was full of missed alarms and notifications, and most of those, if not all, weren't urgent at all.

He climbed downstairs to the lower level, checked the water temperature in the tilapia tanks both with his hand—the fish swam up to investigate, butting against his fingers—and on the digital read-out.

"Holidays are over, kids," he said to them. "They're not going to be as good to you as I have."

"Did you say something, Lance?"

He raised his voice. "Just talking to the fish."

"OK. Sorry."

He leaned over the closest tank. "Nothing I can do about it. Whether it's better you live and eat and do whatever it is you do to make little fishes, or just stay as frozen eggs, I don't know." He looked at his broken reflection in the always-turning water. "I just don't know."

They were going to get eaten. He'd ramped up production to allow for that. What he didn't know was whether any of the new crew were vegetarian, or even whether he could eat the fish himself just as long as he didn't have to kill them. He'd give it a go. Maybe. Goddammit, he liked the taste of it, but that sound of the knife going through the bone: even thinking about it made his gag reflex kick in.

He looked at the floor, swallowed hard, and damped his hands in the fish tank to wipe across his forehead. Did that mean he smelled vaguely of fish now? He'd never really had anyone around before. He sniffed at his fingers, and they just smelled of the nutrient-rich water.

He took some readings of the holding tanks, too, that buffered the system and allowed for contraction and expansion in the external pipework. They were well within the tolerances Zeus had built in, and had remained so for the entire time the system had been installed. It was robust to any variation, and had no moving parts to fail. Make-work. That was all.

He climbed back up to the second floor, and she was still there, inspecting the staging where he grew the strawberries. She saw him, or sensed him at least, and spent time examining the plants both above, where the leaves and the fruits were, and below, where the roots hung into the continually seeping nutrient bath.

Her hair extended in a white, woven rope down her back, almost to her waist.

"How were you told to pollinate these?" she asked, fitting the strawberries back into their tray.

"There's a brush." Frank went over to the drawer where the smaller tools were kept. His hand hovered for a moment, then lifted out what looked like a miniature shaving brush. "I wash it after I've used it, because I don't actually know whether it matters if I transfer the pollen from strawberries to peppers to zucchini. Whether I'd end up with some weird half-chili, half-melon, or something like that: I really don't have much idea of what I'm doing, outside of the list of instructions XO gave me. I didn't starve to death, so I guess I got something right."

That was the longest speech he'd made in months, and he felt almost giddy. He'd remembered how to speak, and not bite someone's head off.

"I guess robots aren't good for everything," she said, inadvertently reminding Frank of why he was there. Did she see him wince? "You said you'd stored grain?"

"Sure. Not in here, though. Too damp. I didn't want it sprouting at me."

"Can I take a look?"

"If you want to."

They cycled the greenhouse airlock together. The last time Frank had done that had been when he and Declan were going outside to try and flush Brack out. They'd both got shot shortly afterwards, Declan fatally, straight through the faceplate. Those flashbacks weren't getting any less, were they? The situation he was in was completely different, and he had to clench his fingernails into the palms of his hands to stop himself from clawing his way out of the door.

If Isla was noticing anything wrong, she wasn't mentioning it.

They stepped out into the cross-hab, and Frank immediately climbed down into the area underneath it. It had seemed as good a place as any for food storage, cool and dry and dark, and away from either the medical equipment or the water reclamation system. The containers he was using weren't airtight, but since he'd pretty much made them himself out of cargo-cylinder parts, he was pleased with them.

There was more room down there than there was in the airlock, but her proximity still made him nervous and he moved right to the back to let her examine the drums, which had shiny words scratched into the still-extant paintwork. There hadn't been any paper on the base, and nothing to make labels with.

"Oats, wheat, rye, soy, groundnuts, corn," she said as she traced the letters. Some of them were, to be fair, hard to make out. She picked up a drum, frowned at its unexpected weight, and carefully opened the lid. "Mercy."

"What?"

"There's so much of it."

The containers, more or less regular sizes, were stacked several deep.

"I got…bored. I suppose. Did I tell you I don't eat the fish? So I changed my diet a bit, and yeah. That. We still seem to have plenty of the ABC nutrients, and there's all the organic waste, just sitting there. I haven't touched that yet. If you want to just take over the greenhouse, that's fine. Like I said, I don't really know what I'm doing."

She looked over her shoulder at him, her plait turning with delayed slow-motion.

"You've done pretty well for someone who says that. XO chose you for a reason. We could make bread. Flat bread, at least. For now. I've got some dried yeast, but we have to keep it under wraps until we know it won't damage the base."

"I don't have anything to mill flour with. I could have made something, I guess, but—"

"I'll look into it. See what equipment we have."

135

"You know a lot about milling?"

She shrugged. "I'm a farm girl. An astronaut farm girl. You?"

Frank's own biography—construction worker, murderer, con—didn't quite fit the expected trajectory for getting onto Mars. The bare-bones of Brack's background—Frank had been told to keep it deliberately vague to avoid close questioning—didn't fit Frank.

"Career military," he said.

"Sure. Which branch?"

"That's, that's classified." It was poor, and he knew it. He didn't even have to fake embarrassment. "Sorry. Orders."

"That's fine. I'm not going to pry. Thank you for showing me this: I think you've done something extraordinary here, and I've no wish to push you out of the greenhouse. It's not like I don't have a whole bunch of experiments to run, and only fifteen months in which to run them, on top of making sure people get fed. If you want, you can just carry on doing what you've been doing, as much or as little as you want." She put the lid back on the container, and eased it back on to its shelf. "It means I get more time to do science. I don't want to make work for you, but if you're happy with that, then deal?"

"That sounds fair. As long as we make sure we don't not do something because we think the other guy's doing it. OK. Deal." He held out his hand for a dap. It was instinctive, habitual, and she just stared at it quizzically. He pulled back and headed for the ladder.

There were so many ways he could betray himself, not even with his words, just his actions, just himself. He went to push some buttons, passing some of the others on the way—Leland and Yun—and they all seemed so impossibly perfect. Fit, healthy, engaged, enthusiastic: physically, emotionally and psychologically in balance.

Whereas he, and his crew of cons, were anything but. Disposable chimps who needed only to last as long as the job. Waking up, being sick, hungry, thirsty, argumentative, exploited and abused.

This was how it should have been. It was how it could have been, with a little more care. Goddammit, XO.

He pulled the cubicle curtain closed behind him, and pushed his overalls down to his knees. He rested his elbows on his legs and his face in his hands. Day one of fifteen months. He'd waited so long for this. So long, and now it was here, he didn't know if he wanted it any more.

"Lance?" It was Leland, just outside.

"Just give me five, OK?" Goddamn it. Declan was always— had always been—doing that: ambushing people in the can, and no one had liked it then.

There was silence, then: "It gets better. That's all. It gets better."

Frank heard his footsteps retreat back up the corridor. That was, indeed, all.

Was it? Was it really going to get better? Or was the accumulated weight of everything he'd seen and done and had happen to him going to break him? No: he was, by any measure, pretty much broken as it stood. All it had taken was the presence of people who wanted him for his skills and experience, wanted to be friends with him, who were willing to show him patience and kindness, who didn't want to kill him, to reveal him as a wreck.

These gods, descended from the heavens, were so far above him, and he didn't know what to do.

Not cry. Definitely not cry. Deep breaths. Blink away the tears.

He pushed the buttons, and washed his hands and zipped. He was going to do the only thing he could do. Carry on, and hope, like Leland said, that it would get better.

14

[Message file #139697 2/15/2049 1708 MBO Mission Control to MBO Rahe Crater]

The team here are going through all the NASA comms, checking that they don't suspect you, or the base, and so far, so good! Just remember, you can always choose to hide behind the "commercially sensitive" excuse if you need. The astronauts know the score, and if anyone presses you, you need to take it up with Commander Davison, or tell me, and I will.

I've been told that we've not seen any activity from M2 in the last week. No movement, no tracks. Still no messages. It looks like they didn't make it. So you probably don't need to worry about them any longer. While it's sad, I'm still angry that we both weren't told earlier.

You're doing great, Frank. The pictures and video footage that come from the base with you in it are digitally altered or edited almost in real-time: you don't need to duck out quite so enthusiastically! I get the raw feed, and I enjoy watching what you're getting up to and see how you're doing. It makes me feel connected with you.

Luisa

[transcript ends]

Yun sat next to him as Frank was finishing breakfast, clutching her tablet and looking expectantly at him. Frank took the hint, rested his coffee mug on the table, and without turning to her, said: "Something you want me to do?"

"You know the rules," she said.

"I know your rules."

"Everyone else is busy for the next four sols, but I want to get the weather stations set up as soon as I can. The more data I can collect, the more we'll know."

"Sure," said Frank.

"I need to show they work in the field. They are, partly, my own design."

"Sure. OK. I'm saying yes." He waggled his mug. "Just let me finish this and go and press some buttons. You've cleared this with Lucy?"

"I will."

She slid her tablet across towards him, and Frank pulled it closer. The annotated photograph showed the volcano, Ceraunius Tholus, and markers marching up the line of the Santa Clara, all the way to, and around, the vast crater at the summit.

Right up on the summit. M2 were down on the far side to the south, but the top of the volcano would be very much within their range. Even if they couldn't get that far any more—even if they were all dead by now, and Frank didn't know how to react to that possibility as his emotions were still swinging between rage and fear—then there might be evidence that they had been up there.

Perhaps he should change his mind, and go up on his own to scout it out. But it was too late.

"You think that's too much?"

Frank circled his finger around the crater. "You've done the training. You know how much hard work it is just to be in the suit. We can give it a go, but I'm guessing we'll need to do more than one trip out."

That might give him time to check out the upper slopes on his own.

"Much is expected of me," she said.

"It's expected that you get back in one piece."

She frowned, as if Frank didn't understand. "A lot of money was spent getting me here."

Frank looked around. No one else was within earshot. "We'll do what we can, but we're not pushing it, OK? Mars is waiting to kill you."

She nodded, taking the tablet with her when she left. He watched her go. She had nothing to prove: to him, to her government, to anyone. And yet that, apparently, brought its own pressures.

The rule was—Lucy's rule, NASA's rule—no expeditions without a buddy. The immediate area around the base was fine, but someone still needed to sit in Comms and listen, just in case they needed to answer an alarm. That made perfect sense. Proper safety procedures, observed at all times.

Then there was Frank, who didn't work under that rule. Lucy didn't like it, but she wasn't his boss, and she had no authority over him. He could go outside whenever and wherever he wanted. He didn't even have to tell her, though he did because he didn't want to shit the bed. And he liked her. She was efficient. She got stuff done. She cared very much about the safety of her crew, and by extension Frank, which frustrated them both but they'd probably work it out eventually.

What she did do was trust him enough to double up with her people. That…that didn't sit well with him. He was a fraud, an impostor, and he wasn't telling her things that she really ought to know.

If she did find out, what would she do? Leave him here? It was a certainty. Rather than spend the eight months with a murderer, on a spaceship that wasn't quite big enough for six, she'd maroon him. Hell, it's what he would do. It was the only sensible decision.

So he wasn't going to tell her. Do the job, go home, find Mike. Nothing beyond that. Nothing outside of that. Keep it zipped up, wrapped tight. He finished his coffee, which was more cold than hot, then went to the can.

Yun was already outside, loading up the trailer, by the time he suited up. She was carrying the weather stations—they were more than that, but that was the name she called them—from the supply rocket in the boneyard to the trailer, fifty yards away. They weren't heavy, but they were bulky, and the longer they spent packing for the journey, the less time they could spend setting up the experiments.

So, Frank backed the trailer up to the rocket. He even managed to make it took easy, which wasn't his intention at all: it was just practice. Marcy had been a good teacher.

Frank strapped the load down, gave them all a shake and tightened the ratchets one more click. They were good to go, and with one last check with Lucy in Comms, they were heading for the entrance to the Santa Clara.

There was no sea level to take as zero—Yun called it "datum"—but the numbers meant that Ceraunius was close to thirty thousand feet high. Because they were in spacesuits, the altitude didn't mean anything as such, just wear-and-tear on the batteries. Still, it was the longest journey he'd made since his encounter with the M2 crew member, and he was heading in their direction.

He felt a tightness in his chest. The Santa Clara river bed was sinuous, with broad, sweeping curves and high arching banks that obscured both the way ahead and the view to either side. Every turn that they took, each new vista that opened up, could reveal a figure in a spacesuit, a buggy.

And every time it didn't happen, Frank would feel a surge of relief that would slowly fade as his anxiety built again. He started to realize exactly what keeping secrets for XO meant. It wasn't that he couldn't manage the lying, the misdirection, the pretending to be someone else: it was the sheer physical toll it was going to take on him.

He'd survived worse. He'd just have to grit his teeth and do it.

It helped that Yun liked to talk. That was fine. Frank didn't mind it so much because she seemed to be in the habit of pointing things out to herself, so she could remember them later, rather than expecting a conversation: there appeared to be no requirement that he listen, let alone respond. If she mentioned his name—Brack's name—he knew to tune back in.

She described the river bed's snake-like track up the slope of the volcano, how the sand had collected at the well-defined edges of the valley and especially in the outer bends of its path, and how the material was still traveling downhill under windpower, as evidenced by the tear-drop shapes around the craters that had subsequently been carved into the dry soil.

If she had noticed the earlier tracks he'd made, she didn't say: but time had smudged them, showing that the processes that were giving the sand surface ripples were still ongoing.

They kept on climbing. Frank had one eye on the direction of travel, and the other on the battery stats: they'd use less juice coming down, but he still wasn't going to go under fifty per cent. It was sixty or so miles to the very top, obviously the same going back. Easily doable on paper, but getting them stranded wasn't such a great idea.

"Lance, can you stop?"

He relaxed his grip on the controls, and the buggy coasted to a halt. Yun extricated herself from the latticework behind him and jumped down onto the ground. She reached for the still camera that was attached to her waist—two cameras side by side, with a supporting frame and a dust-free enclosure that made it deliberately two-handed—and advanced towards the valley wall. She had, inexplicably, gone quiet, and she walked like she was stalking prey.

She raised her camera, framed her shot and took several pictures.

"Have you seen this before, Lance?" She pointed at the ground, at the darker patch of soil that seemed to leak out of the top of the sand bank and spread out downhill.

"I guess I must have done. What is it?" Sure, they were there, most times he'd driven up the valley.

"It's a recurring slope linea. Can you get the ranging pole from the trailer?"

Frank clambered down and retrieved the telescopic pole, locking the sections together as he walked to her.

"So what causes it?"

"Water," she said.

"But water boils away." He turned so he could look into her helmet, at her intent, focused expression.

"When the water is super-saturated with salts, it can exist in liquid form at these temperatures and pressures. The evaporation rate will still be high, but it's believed that being entrained in a matrix of small grain-sized particles will permit the water to flow subsurface. This is water, Lance, melting from the ground. At night it should refreeze, and the dark patch disappear, but once temperatures rise again during the day, it'll restart."

She told him to approach the flow from the side, and lay the striped pole down near, but not on, the stain. Frank did as he was asked. The boundary between light and dark wasn't distinct, close up, and neither did it appear to be visibly spreading.

Yun took more photographs, moving slowly around its base in an arc, then marked the place on her tablet with a touch and some quick one-fingered typing. "When you collected material for the water maker, what did you use?"

"We—me and the robots, that is—just shoveled soil from near the base into the machine. I suppose I assumed that it cooked the rock and drove out water. Not that there was actual water just below the surface."

"It's not everywhere on Mars," she said. "But this is one reason why MBO is situated where it is. It's a resource-rich site, one where it doesn't take much energy to liberate volatiles. Mapping the extent of the resources will help determine the viability of future missions."

"Colonization, you mean. Living here permanently."

"Yes. Do you have an opinion on that, Lance?" She picked the ranging pole up herself, and twisted it back down to its transportable size.

"My opinion?" He clicked his tongue. "I don't think it's for me, somehow."

"You miss Earth?"

"Something like that," he said.

"You may change your mind."

"Would you? Seriously? This planet has tried to kill me so often."

"The Chinese government is enthusiastic about the possibilities for Mars colonization and seeks to establish its own permanent presence before the end of the century," she said.

It was as if she was reading a script. And he recognized that, because it was exactly like he sounded when he had to parrot the XO line. So he laughed: an involuntary response which he stopped as soon as he saw her expression.

"I'm not being mean," he said. "But I understand. I really do."

He climbed back up onto the buggy, and Yun resumed both her position behind him, and her commentary. She pointed out that the further up the volcano they drove, the tighter the turns in the valley became, so that they were almost like overlapping, interlinked C-shapes, with sharp, cliff-like projections into the bed of the river, followed by lazy left- or right-hand turns.

Frank had never been up so high, and they had further to go. At the five thousand meter mark—he had to work out what that actually was, sixteen thousand feet or so—they stopped and carried a box of instruments off the trailer and up the side of the valley, the crate slung between them, each holding one of the straps. The material underfoot was loose, and it was steep.

Frank, who was much more used to being outside, plotted the route up to the top of the bank.

They then walked another hundred or so yards away across the stepped volcanic surface, and put the box down. There wasn't anything left for Frank to do now but admire the view while Yun set up. They were on the north-western flank of Ceraunius, and he could just about make out the wildly broken ground that was, what, sixty miles away due west? Uranius was off to his right. The haze level was, he guessed, about average. Certainly not as fuzzy as he'd seen it before, and some days were unexpectedly clear like glass.

There was little chance of spotting actual features near the base of the volcano: he couldn't even see where it joined the sand sea. Such was the size of the broad shoulder of rock he was standing on, most of what he could see was just slope, up to his left and down in every other direction. M2, whatever state it was in, was going to stay hidden for now. Just as long as there weren't any unexplained debris or bodies up on the top, he'd be fine.

Quite how often Yun had practiced setting up the weather station was something he didn't ask, but he could tell by the speed and accuracy of her movements that she'd trained over and over again until she could do it blindfold. The station itself was mounted on a tripod she assured him wouldn't blow over, and the boom held pressure and temperature sensors, as well as a laser to measure the dust-load. Powered by a palm-sized solar panel, a resin-square of electronics collected all the data and beamed it back to MBO via the whippy aerial mounted on top.

She talked to the device through her tablet, turning it on, running the diagnostics and making sure it talked to the main computer. A quarter of an hour, from start to finish. It was a good piece of kit, and she—and probably a whole team of people—had thought hard about how it went together. Of course it was designed well. Even XO had done that.

But there was such a stark contrast between the ideals of the people who'd designed the weather station and the minds of the people who'd stranded him on Mars. It was probably best that he didn't dwell on such things.

Yun replaced the lid on the box, and they carried it back, sliding down the slope along the path made by their earlier bootprints. Yun seemed particularly keen not to walk just anywhere, as if stepping off the newly created path and leaving more marks would somehow spoil the uniqueness of that place. He didn't really see the problem, but he followed her lead anyway.

Equipment stowed and back on the buggy, he checked his air and his fuel, reminded Yun to look at her suit too, and judged the daylight and weather conditions by leaning back and looking up. There was no good reason not to go to the summit.

The closer they got to the top, the more ragged the valley became: sharper turns, steeper sides, and evidence of waterfalls cascading down from tributaries, even islands, left high and isolated mid-stream.

Frank consulted his map and took a right fork to avoid ending up in a lake bed, and instead drove up one of the feeder rivers, which gradually eased them out onto the open slope of the volcano, near the rim of its huge, flat-bottomed crater.

They were now twenty-two thousand feet above datum, not that it felt like that at all. The volcano's shape made seeing anything but the volcano impossible. The only feature was the far wall of the crater that was still another five and a half thousand feet higher than the one they were on. That was as tall as a mountain in its own right.

They stopped to put another weather station up and tie it in with the network, then drove right up to the edge of the crater. Yun called it a caldera, and Frank let the word glide by rather than reveal more of his ignorance.

The crater, caldera, whatever, was ten miles across, pretty much flat at the bottom, and bounded by steep, broken slopes.

From the maps, the descent to the floor looked pretty much impossible, but standing on the edge of it, it seemed it might be doable in places. The gradient was greater on the far, east side, but twenty, thirty per cent where they'd parked up on the rim.

"I'm guessing that Jim will want to come out here sometime," he said.

"I imagine Jim would probably want to live out here," said Yun. She stared out over the bowl of rock, slowly turning from left to right to try and take it all in. "You see that patch of rougher ground in the middle?"

"Sure." It looked like the rolling boil of water in a pan, suddenly frozen.

"That could be the top of the magma chamber. Mineral rich. What minerals, I couldn't say. But quite probably metals. The area needs surveying, and samples taken, assayed."

"I'll be coming back here a lot, then."

"We do have spare hab sections. If we could erect one here, it would mean considerably greater EVA time. It's a shame the robots have already been sent back to Earth for evaluation."

Frank squinted into the distance until he'd properly formed his reply. If M2 was out of the picture, then OK: it'd be safe enough to come up here without worrying about bumping into the neighbors. And technically, it wasn't difficult to put a hab up. The problems came in keeping the atmosphere breathable and the internal temperature stable. Again, if there really wasn't an M2 to worry about any more, there seemed no good reason for him to block this. He'd have to talk to Luisa.

"I know how to put up a hab," he said. "I've been trained to do it, just in case. If all of us are willing to put in the labor, it'll take less than a day. Inflate it with bottled oxygen to five psi and, I guess, wonder what he's going to do for a can. There's heat and power issues, but if he just wanted it as a daytime lifeboat so he can max out his daylight hours, then that'd be easier."

"He could store samples and equipment here too."

"Why not? Someone could drop him, and his buddy, off in the morning, pick them back up last thing, so we always have the two buggies at the bottom of the hill."

"That's an excellent suggestion, Lance. I'll talk to Jim, and he can ask Lucy. We'll need your input, of course."

"I didn't suggest it. Just, you know. It's not a problem. We've got the kit, and there's no point in it sitting around if you can use it."

She looked back out over the crater. "Can we make the summit today?"

Frank flipped down his suit controls. "Lucy didn't want anyone going below forty per cent, right?" His suit read fifty-one per cent.

"What's the lowest you've been down to?"

Fumes, thought Frank. Fumes and nothing more. And Marcy died that day because Brack had needed to sacrifice someone to ease the food crisis. "Less than that."

Then he did something he used to do with the other cons, turning their mics off so that Brack couldn't overhear them. Sure, it hadn't actually worked, because the medical monitors they all had implanted over their sternums contained microphones that could pick up every word resonating through their chests, and broadcast the information over the still-working suit antenna: but these were the good guys, and they weren't doing that.

The NASA suits were of a very similar design to his: the controls certainly were, and he was able to tab through Yun's commands to knock her microphone out too. He touched his helmet against hers.

"Can you still hear me?"

"Yes. Lance, why are we doing this?"

"Because if we're going to talk about breaking the rules, we don't want to be discussing it over an open channel, which might only have us on it, but might just be overheard by everyone."

"Are we talking about breaking the rules?"

"We will be if we go for the top. I'm on fifty, you're on less, and we're going to have to take the long way round to the south: the map tells me we can't go around to the north, there's some big rock ledges in the way. So we've got a sixty-mile round trip, which is probably four hours, and then we've got another thirty-five back down the Santa Clara. Call that an hour and a half. We'll be lucky to be on ten per cent by the time we get back to base."

"Oh."

"Now, Lucy's not my boss. She shouts at me, I can tell her to whistle. But you? You've been here a week and this is your first long trip out. If you want my advice, I'd play nice, and we can go out again tomorrow, or the next day, to plant the summit."

"But won't we have the same distance to travel as we do now?"

"I know a short cut, straight up the north slope. Probably thirty-five miles to the top. We can be there and back in a morning."

From where they stood, the summit was only ten miles away, straight across the yawning crater. But while Frank was pretty certain he could get down there, he didn't fancy his chances getting up the other side. It looked formidable, steeper than Long Beach and almost five times taller.

"You want me to drive you around, we'll do that. We probably won't get much further before Lucy's going to be wondering what the hell we're up to. Or we can head back, which will take us to close to forty per cent, if not past it. It's your call."

"No, you're right. Tomorrow will be soon enough."

"Good choice." Frank showed her how to turn on her mic again, then did it for himself. "Let's get back."

If M2 had got to the top at any point, they'd have come at it from the south. Their tracks would still be there, and Frank wanted to check that out first, and put some of his own down if he had to. By taking Yun the northern route, he'd avoid any unnecessary complications. He had plenty of those for real.

He waited until she was behind his seat again, and he swung

the buggy around in a wide circle. As he faced south, he peered into the distance. Rust-red rock was all he could see, and he was relieved.

The moment went by like a point on the compass, and he was driving back to the entry point to the river bed. This was fine. It could stay like this, and it'd be fine.

15

[Transcript of private phone call between Diego Ferrar (XO Legal, NYC) and Bruno Tiller 2/18/2049 0951MT]

BT: How much does she want?

DF: That's the problem. What she wants, is to know where her daughter has gone.

BT: People disappear all the time, Diego. We don't want her looked for.

DF: This is undoubtedly true. But if you were able to furnish us with evidence, from a PI, or a police report, that your employee had a troubled work or private life, had got involved in drugs, or perhaps was contemplating suicide, we could arrange to pass it on with our sincerest regrets that nothing was known sooner.

BT: Tell me that will work.

DF: Mothers are strange creatures, sir. Very tenacious. I'm sure whatever I receive will be of such compelling quality as to lead her away from our door.

BT: I'll get someone on it.

[transcript ends]

"Spot for me, Lance."

Frank stopped on his way through the yard. Jim—James the geologist—was climbing off the exercise bike and wiping down the seat with a microfiber towel. An actual towel, not a torn-up sheet made from parachute canopy.

The weights, a metal bar with a set of semi-rigid water-filled drums, paired into different sizes, were a part of the NASA-specific gear that hadn't been available to the cons. It meant that Frank, even though he'd assembled all the gym equipment himself, had a strange disregard for everything in the yard. On the one hand, he felt it wasn't for the likes of him, and he wasn't good enough to use it. On the other, it only reminded him of both prison and the physical tests XO had put him through at Gold Hill. He'd never used a gym in the free world. His work had kept him mostly fit.

"I got stuff to do," he said. "A schedule to keep."

Spotting was a social thing as well as a safety thing. Certainly in prison: it was another way of establishing mutual bonds and determining power structures.

"You're always running from one thing to another. It's OK to slack off, kick it into park for five minutes, then pull out into the fast lane again. C'mon. We don't have to talk."

Frank tucked his nut runner into his belt. Maybe this would be OK. "Five minutes then."

Jim selected the weights he wanted. The largest pair were huge. On Earth, the most dedicated muscle-guy would have struggled with more than a couple of reps. On Mars, where they weighed a third less? The numbers were moot. Two forties went on the bar, secured by a couple of twist-lock cuffs.

Frank assumed the position at the head-end of the bench, and Jim laid himself down on the bench. Frank hefted the bar, back straight and knees bent—he knew what he was doing—and placed it on the hanger. It wasn't that heavy. He'd certainly pressed more in his time, in bags of cement, in scaffolding and tools.

But Jim seemed to think it was a big deal. He gripped the bar, his face a model of concentration. When he took the strain, Frank instinctively reached out with his builder's hands.

"You OK with that?"

Jim nodded. "I'm fine."

"Because it seems like a lot."

Jim straightened his arms, holding the bar over his chest. He lowered it, and slowly pushed it back up again.

"It's my regular weight," he said. "Shouldn't be a problem."

He lowered it and raised it again, smoothly. The muscles on his forearms were well defined, almost sharp. There was no fat on the man. He was lean, marionette thin, yet there was clearly strength in his frame. There was nothing about the man's demeanor that resembled Brack, but they both had that same sparse sculpting.

Was that what this was about? Had Jim sensed Frank's wariness around him, and was trying to do something normal, non-threatening with him?

Jim did another rep.

"How're you finding it, Lance?"

"Finding it?"

"Us invading your space."

"It's OK."

"Just OK, or are you being diplomatic?"

"It's OK," repeated Frank. "I thought we weren't talking."

Jim lowered the weight almost to his chest, then pushed it up again, locking his elbows. They trembled slightly. "Eight months is a long time to get used to being on your own. I hope we're not crowding you."

"You've been very respectful."

"But you'd rather we weren't here."

Frank would rather they took him straight home. He was done with Mars. But he couldn't tell anyone why because he had secrets to keep.

So instead he said: "You're why I'm here."

"Do you resent that?"

What was this? Was he trying to get a rise out of him?

"No," said Frank. "It's different. That's all."

153

Jim did another couple of reps, and said, "OK."

Frank took the bar from him and deposited it on the hanger. He felt his own muscles flex, but it wasn't a strain.

"Could you manage that, Lance?"

"Sure."

"But you've got nothing to prove, right?"

"I've got my chores. They keep me moving." Definitely trying to get a rise. "If I need to lift, I'll swap out the buggy wheels."

"Don't you want to see how high you can go? Fan's got a league table. Balanced for power-to-weight ratio."

"You want me to join your league, is that it? You could have just asked me straight."

"Just trying to see how competitive you are, Lance. You not interested in how you measure up against us?"

"I don't do pissing contests," said Frank.

"I didn't mean it like that."

"Neither did I." Frank lifted the bar out of the hanger and lowered it to the floor. "Your group have been together for a year with nothing much to do but play off against each other. Me? I've been frozen, shipped, defrosted and put to work. I guess I was about ready for you, though there was probably more I could have done. I had to concentrate on building the base, keeping it running and, I guess, not dying. Games? League tables? Maybe one day, but right now I don't have time for that."

Jim sat up on the bench and swung his leg over to sit sideways on it. "Well, I poked a hornet's nest there. Most you've said to me since we got here."

It was getting too close to personal, and Frank wasn't going there. "Unless you need me to spot for you again, I got work to do."

"Lance, I didn't mean anything by this. It was just talk, shooting the breeze."

Frank looked at the man, tried to read his expression. "Sure."

"I've offended you. I'm sorry."

"I'm not offended. Just," and Frank shrugged, "confused. I don't understand what it is you want from me."

"I'm just trying to get to know you. I know I'm not Leland, but there's no harm in trying to work out what makes you tick." Jim gave a half-grin. "Unless that's commercially sensitive information."

"Do you find my personal details funny?"

"It's kind of funny," said Jim. "It's kind of frustrating. It's what we're saying to each other when we want to tell them to butt out of our business."

"Do you ever take the hint?"

"I've already apologized, Lance."

"That's OK. Accepted." Should Frank just go now? Was this painful, difficult conversation finally over? He didn't know. Just how far did he need to go to accommodate the NASA crew, given that he wasn't actually Lance Brack?

"As to whether I can take a hint? Not as often as I should. When they picked us as a team, they made sure that we could all work together. And we're all very different people, so that took some juggling of rosters. We've got some brilliant astronauts kicking their heels Earthside because they get pissed too easily."

"You're saying that's me?" Frank suddenly became aware that he had an audience, and that Jim hadn't noticed his commander leaning on the wall at the far end of the yard, down by the cross-hab connector.

"I'm explaining this all wrong," said Jim. "You were selected because you were resilient, because you could cope with being on your own for an extended period, that you didn't need other people. What qualifies you for that part of the mission is exactly why you think I'm a jerk now."

"We all think you're a jerk, Jim." Lucy levered herself upright and wandered casually through the gym equipment. "Leastways, we all do sometimes. Lance doesn't have to take part in any crew activities, he doesn't have to answer any non-mission-related questions, he doesn't even answer to me on non-mission-critical activities. So you poking him like a hornet's nest—I was here for that, yes—is off-limits. I'm just hoping Lance isn't reconsidering his generous offer to teach us how to build a module up on the summit of Ceraunius, which will benefit you most of all, and which I'm just coming to tell him we kindly accept."

"You're right," said Jim. He threw his hands into the air. "I am a jerk. I'm going to make myself scarce, have a shower, and do some planning."

He gathered up his towel, gave the bench seat a perfunctory wipe-down, and headed in the direction of the cans.

Frank watched him go, and shook his head. "That was..."

"Weird?" offered Lucy. "I need to explain. When they were balancing out the crews, human factors decided what we really needed was a social disruptor. Someone who's not just smart in their own field and dedicated to the overall success of the mission—we're all that—but a joker in the pack. The grit in the oyster. Whichever metaphor you want to choose. It means that Jim can be a monumental pain in the ass, but we actually do need him to behave like that to function normally as a community. Yes, he has a point about how someone who's able to work in almost total isolation for eight months is not necessarily going to easily integrate into a team, but we all knew that and wanted you to move at your own pace, what you felt comfortable with. You're a loner. We get that."

Frank had a sudden urge to start screaming the truth to her. To yell at her, "That's not how it was!" He had had a team, and XO had killed them all. So strong was the feeling that he had to close his eyes and swallow hard and breathe slowly.

"You want the extra hab up on the volcano?" he said eventually.

"Yes. Please."

"When do you want it by?"

"How long will it take for you to train us?"

Frank had a bunch of cons doing it competently within a couple of sessions. "How quick are your crew?"

She laughed. Not unkindly, just surprised by the question. "I guess they're OK."

"If you want to schedule a couple of hours tomorrow, I can walk you all through it, see how you are at the end of it. Then we can head up the Santa Clara whenever you like. Three hours to build it, then it needs inflating and fitting out. It doesn't have to be done in a day: once it's up, you can take your time."

"You put in a lot of suit time, Lance."

"It's how things get done."

"So you don't think about how dangerous it is?"

Of course he didn't. If he did, he wouldn't put himself in the position where the only thing between him and certain, almost instant, death was the thickness of a faceplate.

"I've got other things to think about."

She approved of that answer. She was, after all, the pilot that landed the ship when it looked certain it was going to crash.

"I'll schedule two hours of dirtside training from ten hundred tomorrow. If you think we're ready to go after that, then I'll clear a day later in the week. Otherwise, I'll put us in for more training. You're OK with ordering us around?"

"If you do what I tell you, sure."

"We will. You have my guarantee."

Lucy reminded him a little of Alice: competent, direct, emotionless, honest. Just a lot less murdery. He could certainly work with her. He turned to leave, then turned back. Something had been bothering him for a while. He'd caught the tail-ends of conversations and veiled references, but he'd never got the full story. And he'd worried about its implications ever since.

"Can I ask you a question?" he asked.

"Of course."

"Just how close were you all to crashing?"

She hesitated, and that told Frank all he needed to know.

"You're OK. You don't have to answer." The corner of his mouth twisted briefly upwards. "Commercially sensitive, right?"

Lucy pressed her hands together until her joints went white. "You can, technically, control the MAV from Mission Control. It's not like they don't know the position of the Prairie Rose—that's our transit ship—at any given moment, and though it might take a few more orbits for them to coordinate the docking procedure due to the time delay on the telemetry, they're good at what they do. They'd have got you home."

"Even if you'd all died?"

"There's another crew in training, due to launch mid 2049, arrive nine months later. You'd be over two years alone by that point. You'd be practically a Martian by then."

"The King of Mars," he said.

"You've thought about all of this before. Of course you have." She sprung her hands wide. "Not much else to think about but what can go wrong. The facts are, the training kicked in, I did manage to land the ship, we didn't die. Give me one of a hundred different scenarios and I'd still have landed the ship. Because I'd trained for them all. All I've done for five years is train for those seven minutes. They'll let me fly the MAV, but as previously explained, they don't need me to fly the MAV."

"OK."

"This isn't false modesty. There'd be no point in me being here, being on this crew, if I couldn't get the Hawthorn down. And if you ask me when we leave Mars whether or not it was worth hauling my ass across the solar system for those seven minutes, I'm going to point to all the science we've done, and all the discoveries we've made. I've been a pilot since I was fifteen, and I've never been lucky once. All I did was my job."

"So you don't take compliments?"

"That has been noted before." She gave a rueful smile. "What's more important? That I did a good job, or that someone noticed I did a good job?"

"You wouldn't be here if no one had noticed."

158

"Same for you."

It was Frank's turn to semi-grimace. "Our routes here were… different."

"But you're on Mars. The best of the best. And if you don't mind me saying, older than I anticipated. You must have beaten a whole bunch of people younger than you to get here."

That wasn't a lie. The Supermax had to be full of cons who'd flunked out of the program, for one reason or another. And then there were seven bodies on their way to the sun, with only Alice being older than him when she died.

"Something like that."

"You can't talk about XO's selection process, and I'm not going there," she said. "But none of us are here because we're making up the numbers. Including you. Including me. Including even Jim."

"I get it." Compared with his own team of farm horses ready for the glue factory, these guys were all pure-blood thoroughbreds, highly strung and valuable. The difference was stark, and Frank was only just beginning to appreciate what it meant. "Thanks for your time."

"Thank you for yours. You asked, and I wanted to explain. I didn't do anything special, and I don't want anyone to feel grateful."

"You can't stop them, though, can you?"

"No. I suppose I can't." She nodded down at his waistband. "What do you call those?"

Frank, puzzled, looked down at the items on his belt. He finally held up the nut runner. "This?"

"Yes, that. The electric torque wrench," she said, giving it its proper name.

"A nut runner."

"And that's not the only one."

"I got eight."

"Why've you got eight?"

What would be a good answer here? Why indeed, if he was the only person on Mars, would he have eight of anything?

"For times like this," he said, and thinking, damn, that's not bad.

Lucy seemed to accept that. Why shouldn't she? It made perfect sense, and she seemed more embarrassed at not coming to that conclusion herself than she'd ever shown when stating baldly how brilliant a pilot she was.

"Of course. Evening meal at nineteen thirty, if you want to join us and you're always welcome to. Otherwise, ten hundred hours tomorrow."

"I'll be there." But it wasn't like he could be anywhere else.

16

From: Miguel Averado <maaverado@usach.cl>
To: Mark Bernaberg <mbernaberg@lpl.arizona.edu>
Date: Sun, Feb 21 2049 10:15:59 -0300
Subject: HiRISE2

Hola, Mark.

Just the usual request for HiRISE2 images, this time showing 22 39 59 N, 97 41 25 W. If there's any chance of swinging over that area in the next week or so, I'd be very grateful. There seems to be some recent, if not ongoing, geologic activity.

I'll follow this up with a formal submission: it's the weekend but I know you're working! Raw data will be fine.

Mig

Frank kept on working in the greenhouse. He decided that it wasn't so much the plants, the shades of green in all their varieties, or the textures of the leaves that were organic and not synthetic. It was the water: the sound of it, the smell of it, the feel of it in his lungs and against his skin.

The individually dripping trays merged together to make a liquid static, like that of a river, like that of the river he played next to when he was a kid. And when he went downstairs to the lower level, where the tilapia tanks were, there were additional textures to the soundscape: the bubble of oxygenators and the wet slap of a fish breaking the surface of their tank. It was soothing, arrhythmic, natural, in an environment that was entirely artificial and moved to a mechanical beat.

The rest of the base had a slightly astringent tang on the tongue that he'd got so used to that, after the first few days, he no longer registered it except by its absence. The humidity of the greenhouse seemed to neutralize it, and while this didn't make the section more Earth-like, it made it just a little less Mars-like.

Some mornings, after a night when he couldn't sleep, he'd go to the greenhouse. Sometimes Isla would be there too. She'd cordoned off a section of the upper level, enclosed it in plastic, and was deliberately increasing the CO_2 around what looked like young maize plants, to see if they grew faster. Except that wasn't it: she was as interested in them failing as she was seeing them grow tall and strong. She wanted to know what happened— she'd done the exact same experiment on Earth, and was now trying it on Mars. Was the result going to be different? It didn't matter. It was science. Very different from construction, where the end result was all that mattered.

The greenhouse was big enough that the two of them could be there without it feeling cramped. Without, indeed, seeing much of each other. Isla was a shadow behind the double layer of plastic. Frank was checking the nutrient pumps, topping up those that might run out in the next sol with fresh injections of A, B and C.

The airlock popped, and Yun came in, waving her tablet at Frank.

"I need you," she said.

Frank frowned. Yun was direct. Sometimes that could come out as rude, and he'd had to learn that this was her, trying to do her best. The best for her, the best for everyone back home. Wherever she went on the base, wherever she went on Mars, she seemed to behave as if she had a crowd of watchers looking over her shoulder, silently judging her for every moment she wasn't on task.

"Sure." He found a flag, a piece of stiff wire with some parachute material tied to the top, and pushed it into the gap between the tray and the staging, to mark his place. "What's the problem?"

"Station seven has stopped sending data."

"And…"

"I have to go out and either fix it there, or bring it back to the workshop. Today." She held out the tablet showing the positions of the weather stations, but was moving it too jerkily for Frank to be able to tell which was Station seven, or where it was located.

He took it from her, and put it down on the edge of the tray. OK, so seven was on the far side of the caldera, at about the five o'clock position on Ceraunius. Within range, but not convenient. He tried to remember siting that particular instrument, and maybe he could and maybe he couldn't. After a while, without anything notable happening, each stop resembled both the previous and the next.

The summit. That had been different. Top of the world.

"So if I take you, who's staying with Jim?" Jim would have lived up there if he could.

Yun looked momentarily surprised, as if she'd forgotten that other people had tasks scheduled. Then she was forlorn.

"But this needs attention."

"No one's saying it doesn't," said Frank. Outside, the sun had just crested the crater rim, turning the hab a rosy pink. "But we've got time to sort it. Find someone who'll go with Jim."

"No one else is up yet."

"Isla is."

Frank caught a hesitation before Yun's reply. No reason why everyone had to be best buddies. Just that they had to agree to work together, like Frank's crew had. And he could sense, if not see, Isla stiffen behind the cloudy plastic sheeting. Of course she was listening.

"Isla's got her own work," said Yun eventually.

"And Jim has his. Look, let's leave it until after breakfast. Maybe the cold has knocked out the battery, or something. It might come back online when it's warmed up."

Frank left the greenhouse and filled a bowl with his usual grains and fruits, and even as he crunched his way through them, he was aware of a hovering, hopeful presence, sometimes behind him, sometimes off to one side. Fan wandered in, and went straight to make coffee. Then he wandered out again, as was his habit, to read and plan for an hour before opening up the med bay for consultations. While doctor–patient confidentiality didn't extend as far as astronauts on Mars, the veneer of it had.

Fan had also offered his expertise to Frank, but Frank had already been warned off by Luisa: no going to the doctor except in extreme emergencies. His skin was a map, pointing to secrets that XO would rather leave buried.

Then Frank had his answer. Obvious, really: he'd drop Yun and Jim off at the outpost—CU1 as it was officially known—swap out his life support, and drive around the crater on his own to collect the malfunctioning number seven. He could take it back to Yun, who'd make an assessment on the spot, and all without disrupting anyone else's work pattern.

Sure, Lucy still didn't like him taking solo trips. She never asked him herself, but she permitted the others to ask. Certainly, she could forbid them, but she hadn't. It put a little slack into the system, that was all. Frank thought she found it a useful corrective to the otherwise tight operating rules.

Yun had to compromise. But it took her only a couple of seconds to agree, and she left him alone after that.

He had half an hour before leaving, so he went back to the

greenhouse to pick up where he'd left off. He pulled the flag out and worked his way down the rest of the row.

"Lance?"

"Yeah?" He didn't look up from the tray. These bean roots, they were pretty much mature and the nodules on them were starting to restrict the flow of water across them. Maybe he'd got the nutrient mix wrong, because he'd never seen such dense growth before. Raise the plants slightly, and start picking the longest pods, he guessed.

"You don't have to go along with everything."

"I know that." He straightened up. It was Isla. Of course it was. He'd—just for a moment—thought it was Marcy, even though the accent, and the delivery, were all wrong. He showed her the root network and she peered at it, then started pushing the white fibers aside with her fingertips.

She seemed content to let him care for the food crops. Was that trust? It looked a lot like it. He was certain she checked on them when he was elsewhere, so she was going to pick up any problems before they got serious. But she hadn't said anything yet, and it had been two weeks.

Two weeks and he was trusted. He felt such a fraud.

"Of course you do. Just…" She slotted the beans back into the water flow. "If you feel you're being taken advantage of, you need to say."

"I got the talk from Leland," said Frank. "But I'm supposed to help. It's in the job description."

"All the same," she said.

"It's fine. I don't mind."

She looked down at the plants, and brushed her hand across the top of them, first one way, then the other.

"You're not our employee," she said. "You're crew. However you got here."

What the hell was that supposed to mean? His stomach suddenly knotted up, and threatened his breakfast.

"You like to keep busy." But she didn't press the point, and maybe she most likely meant that he'd got to Mars solo and frozen, eight—nearly nine months now—earlier. But he was never going to be crew. He knew too much, and they knew too little.

"I've got to go. Jim and Yun will be waiting." He put the flag back in the trays, in the new position, and eased himself between Isla and the next set of drip trays. The tightness in his gut slowly started to ease, but it must have shown on his face as he emerged into the cross-hab.

"You OK?" asked Jim, already half into his suit.

"Yeah. I'm going to push some buttons before we go." Talking about bladders and bowel movements was nothing out of the ordinary. The brief delay produced a fleeting flash of annoyance from Yun, but she kept a lid on it and carried on stacking spare life supports into the outside airlock.

Frank wrestled with the zips and flaps, and felt the cold plastic on his ass.

No one suspected him. Not Isla, who he spent most time around, not Lucy, and especially not Leland. There was something about the man that made Frank want to just tell him everything, and that was why Frank studiously avoided spending any time alone with him. Even Jim was preferable, because he was already on his guard with the geologist.

The only person he could be candid with was Luisa. And that had its own problems. He was—how far away now? Ninety million miles?—and the person he was most reliant on, his confidante, worked at the heart of the XO operation. They were both vulnerable. Goddammit, he worried about her.

He scrubbed at his face. His better diet had put some elasticity back in his skin, and he no longer had the gray prison pallor common among inmates. He felt old, though. Fifty-three. He'd missed his birthday in the flurry to get Phase three done: XO hadn't made a thing of it, and neither had he. No birthday candles in a pure O_2 atmosphere, either.

She'd remembered, though.

Frank pushed the buttons and zipped up. By the time he got back through to the cross-hab, it was empty, so he suited up and headed outside.

Yun and Jim were already on the buggy: trailer hitched, life support packs strapped down. Frank kicked the wheels and shook the tow bar, but they'd done the job just fine. Jim was in the driving seat, which bugged Frank: that was his seat, even though Jim had done plenty of driving and there was no reason why he shouldn't today.

Frank didn't like being a passenger. It reminded him too much of sitting behind Marcy. It also gave him too much time to think about it. He guessed he'd have to wear it today.

Jim didn't dick around behind the wheel. He was perfectly safe. He didn't treat the Santa Clara as a racetrack, he didn't try to drive along the banked slopes. He didn't try and bust the top speed. Maybe he did with Yun, but with Frank on board, he was on his best behavior.

It was still a grind to get to the outpost. There was nothing they could do to make the route shorter or faster. The views were only ever going to be of worn rock walls and the trickling dust sliding into the river channel in tiny, slow-motion dribbles.

Lucy wanted waymarkers in the channel, showing the direction and distance of both CU1 and MBO. Frank hadn't got around to that yet. He'd cut out the signage from cargo-rocket fuselage, and made a scriber to write on the information, but installation would take longer.

But despite that, Frank knew when he was getting towards the top: he'd passed that way often enough to know the small tells in the landscape, and without turning round to look back down the valley.

With a final spin of the wheels, the buggy clawed its way up out onto the upper slopes of the volcano. Jim drove the remaining fifteen hundred yards to the outpost and parked up outside.

"OK. Let's unload, and Lance can go and poke Station seven."

Yun climbed down and went immediately to the trailer, eager to get Frank on his way.

"Bring it back here," she said. "Don't try to fix it."

"Even if it's obvious the battery's become disconnected, or the solar panels have gotten clogged?"

"Yes. I need to know why those things have happened, and how to stop them happening in the future."

"OK. If that's what you want." Frank stared out across the crater. "You want to check again, see if it's recovered?"

"I'll still need to take a look at it, find out why it failed in the first place."

"Station seven it is, then." He synced his map with Yun's and checked his air. "I'm going to swap out. It's another twenty miles on from here."

Frank picked up a life support from the trailer and climbed the stairs to the airlock. He cycled it while the others were collecting the rest of the equipment, and stepped inside.

He hadn't been into the outpost for a while: after it was built, and he'd shaken it down, he'd not had a need to. His journeys had been to drop off astronauts or cargo, and they'd often done that themselves.

The hab had got kind of messy, and he didn't like that. Lucy wouldn't like that either. It had unpleasant echoes of stepping into the descent ship and finding the detritus that Brack had created as he slowly, inexorably, lost it.

It wasn't his call, but messy meant sloppy. The one thing that needed to be avoided at all costs was a mistake. He had to work with these people, and snitching on them to Lucy wasn't his style, but he was going to have to say something. He went through his telltales to check that the atmosphere was breathable and warm enough, then thumbed his suit open.

As he went through the rigmarole of climbing out, swapping the pack over, and climbing back in again, Yun and Jim came in separately, stacking the life supports by the door, and unsuiting into the cold dry air.

"You got to clean this shit up," said Frank. "Lucy sees this, she'll blow."

"I don't remember it being this bad," said Jim. "But yes. It could stand a tidy-up."

"Just bag it and I'll take it back down the hill. I'll be back in a couple of hours. Three tops." Frank closed his suit, and if either of them replied, he didn't hear what it was.

The suit tightened around him in the airlock, and he stepped back outside, twenty thousand feet up near the top of an extinct volcano on another planet. And it was ordinary. As was the simple fact that almost instant death was just the other side of his faceplate.

He stood there on the steps, looking out at the gentle curve of the land in almost every direction except towards the crater. Nothing but dust, rock and hazy sky.

Once, a long time ago, there had been a flood, cascading down from the mountaintop. How did that even work? Had there been ice up there, or had the water just fountained out of the ground and spilled down the broad flanks of Ceraunius? It had filled Rahe. A lake. The water was still there, underground. He'd washed in it, drank it, used it to grow plants.

He was using air. He should get on.

He climbed back up onto the buggy, checked that the fuel cell was good for both the forty miles to Station seven and back, and the trip down the hill: not that that needed many watts, as in extremis it could coast most of the way.

He aimed the nose of the vehicle south. He hadn't given that direction much thought recently. M2 had receded from his list of concerns as XO had pronounced them dead, or at least incapable of travel. Luisa had said she'd nixed the idea of him going over to check, at least for now. There was no point in unnecessary trips to prove what they already knew.

But when he did think about it, he still felt uncertain about what he did do, and what he could have done. He was the only person in a position to have helped them, and yet he hadn't, because of the risk that they would have just taken his stuff and killed him.

For him, the decision had been one of personal safety. For XO, it had been a lot more complicated than that. They'd been willing to see one base thrive, and one base die, rather than face the possibility of having both go wrong. Add several layers of secrecy, the company's reputation, and a whole sack of cash, and XO's reasoning got real murky, real quick.

Frank had been put in impossible positions so often, he now just stuck to the simple metric that whatever kept him alive and on track to go home was the best. He hated feeling compromised, and yet everything that XO got him to agree to dug him further into that pit.

It sucked to be M2. But he wasn't going to do anything about it.

He passed Station six, perched on the south-west rim of the crater between the ridge to the east and the "bad lands" caused by subsurface collapse. It hadn't been easy navigating the undulating terrain the first time: craters acting as sand-traps and broken ground all around. The second time, he looked for his tracks, but the wind had already eroded them away, and he had to pick a fresh path through the area.

It took valuable time to work his way through, but there was clear ground from then on, just regular, avoidable craters and rugged, sand-free lava. Station seven was another six miles on.

Station seven wasn't there.

Frank studied his map, and he was definitely in the right area. He knew the locators were only accurate to a hundred yards, so that merely gave him an idea of where he should be looking, but there were no obscuring features, no fresh craters, no debris, nothing. When Yun had planted the equipment, it had been a quarter of a mile from the caldera edge: there'd been no landslides or collapses that could have carried it off.

It had just gone.

He instinctively wheeled south. The ground was open, more

or less all the way down to the plain, and then beyond. The dust-load on the rock was light, and moving even as he watched. Any tracks that might have been laid down had gone, along with Station seven.

The wind wasn't strong enough to blow anything over, though, let alone carry it away, and he should be able to see it. He'd seen all the others. If he drove over to Station eight, then he'd spot it long before he got to it. It was the only artificial object in an entirely natural landscape.

Could there be any other explanation for this? Jim dicking around, maybe? But he wouldn't interfere with science, and neither would anyone else. It made no sense.

M2 were supposed to be in the past. History. And with this one discovery, they came roaring back.

Goddammit.

17

[Message file #147146 3/1/2049 0542 MBO Mission Control to MBO Rahe Crater]

I'm so sorry you've had such a scare. We're working on it. There's going to be a natural explanation for this, and we're exploring what that might be with our NASA colleagues. We're still certain that M2 has failed, but in the highly unlikely event that even one person has survived, it's probable that they're only trying to fix their comms with scavenged parts from the weather station. There's no threat to you or the rest of MBO.

The only thing you can do is tell the truth: you don't know what happened. You don't know how it could have happened. Because you don't. We don't either. All of our models show that M2 is either dead or dying. If there is anyone left, they can't survive much longer. I know that sounds terrible, and that your instincts are to try and help them, but you can't. You mustn't. And say nothing about M2. You'd jeopardize everything you and me have worked together for, and you'd risk your trip home.

Just hang on. We'll clear this up, and things will get back to normal soon enough.

Luisa

[transcript ends]

Eventually, in the darkness of his bed cubicle, light off, tablet on, he found it on one of the satellite pictures. There was something that looked like a trench, or a spillway, or an entrance to a mine where the trucks enter along a sloping road that slowly sinks below the ground until it disappears beneath it.

It had to be a natural feature: it was some five miles long and over half a mile wide, and if XO could excavate such a thing, they didn't need NASA, or anyone, let alone him. But there it was, and the trench deepened towards its western end, where it appeared—difficult to tell from a satellite map—to carry on into a tunnel. Certainly the trench didn't seem to end. Above ground, there were hints of a sagging roof, possible partial collapses, but if the entrance was clear, that was a huge space under cover.

There could have been a solar farm, but it was difficult to tell as it was a few brighter pixels, without definition. He definitely couldn't see any habs, and guessed they'd be set up underground, out of reach of the cancer-causing radiation that he worked and slept in every day. But the telltale shadow of the descent ship was right in the trench, a few hundred yards from the suspected cave. The time of day that the photo had been taken lent itself to long, deep shadows, cast from the west.

It was a straight-line distance of seventy-nine miles away. It was suspiciously convenient for M2 to be just within traveling distance, and Frank was the suspicious kind. Despite Luisa's soothing words, he knew Station seven's disappearance was down to XO's other base. He knew it in his bones. They were lying to her, and she was passing that lie right on to him.

Reporting back to Yun that her instrument had just…vanished, while keeping a straight face, had been hard. Thank God for radio and being alone—at least at that moment—on the volcano. He'd had the majority of the conversations he'd needed to have before he'd got back to CU1.

The chat with Lucy had been excruciating: more of an

interrogation as far as he was concerned. She'd conducted a one-on-one with Yun, then with Jim, and Frank last. He didn't want to lie to her. He knew he'd had to, and felt wretched for the rest of the evening.

The next day, they were on lock-down. Not quite lock-down. Experiments still happened, maintenance was still scheduled. But the daily jaunt up to CU1 was on hold while Lucy talked to NASA.

If he could spot a ship, surely someone from NASA could? He'd messaged Luisa, and she'd told him that Mars was huge, and redacting individual frames in the public domain was straightforward. Just a smudge here and there, and all trace of a landing—a doomed landing—would be erased. There was nothing to worry about.

Frank wasn't at all sure. The growing ease he'd felt had evaporated in that moment on the volcano. He found himself wishing that M2 would just die already, and hated himself for doing so. M2 had a face: a gaunt, hungry face with sunken eyes and a wet, fetid smile. He'd had to put up with that in his dreams as well as seeing his former crew, and now it took center-stage. Hungry, so very hungry.

The fear was that Lucy, or anyone, would work it out for themselves. That the only way the weather station could have disappeared was if someone had moved it, and if it wasn't one of the MBO crew, there was only one logical conclusion.

But as the day wore on, Jim started talking about sink holes and lava tubes, sand-traps, ice lenses, and other geological phenomena, and annoying Yun with the idea that she'd made a major discovery at the expense of one of her instruments. NASA proposed installing the planned seismic net early.

Even if they'd got away with it this time, surely this wasn't a sustainable strategy from XO. If—when—M2 failed, there'd still be something for someone to discover, at some point, even if they died and fossilized out on the plain. There were going to be questions. This? This was just firefighting, and the whole building was in danger of burning down.

Eighty miles. Fifty miles from CU1. There was a danger that, within the lifetime of the current mission, someone—Jim, probably—would want to go out that far and look at the cave. Was Frank going to be expected to clean up M2 too? How was he supposed to explain his absence to Lucy?

He wasn't going to be able. He told Luisa his fears, and she provided his only comfort. He couldn't tell anyone else.

He caught up with his maintenance. He went around the greenhouse. He couldn't eat, let alone sleep. He shuddered every time his tablet pinged with an incoming message, and he dreaded anyone speaking to him. The few times that Isla had tried to engage him, he'd barely heard a word she said. She gave up, and he just hung on, waiting for the all-clear from Luisa. That M2 had either finally made contact, or that they were definitely dead.

In the end, in the middle of the night, he wrote a message:

"Luisa. If you're not going to tell them about M2, I'm going to tell them. You want me to keep it secret, but it can't be a secret any more. I don't even get why M2 is supposed to be a secret: what are they even supposed to be doing out there? It's just a matter of time now before NASA find out, and I'm the XO guy here. I can tell them I didn't know about it, that you hadn't told me, but Leland will open me up like a can.

"I'm not going to tell anyone about how MBO got made. But this is different. Lucy and the others have a right to know about M2, and the right to decide what happens next. They're not cons. They're not chimps. You can't treat them like that, and neither can I."

He turned his light off, and tossed and turned on his bed. At some point, the thought that he'd managed to pull it together enough to stand up to XO, that he actually felt good about himself, allowed him to doze for an hour or so.

His tablet pinged, waking him instantly, and in the dark he fumbled for it.

"OK, Frank. This is serious. Your last message has really upset the suits, and I'm just going to copy and paste this. This isn't from me.

"'Tell that murdering son-of-a-bitch we own his ass. That we own every drop of water, every breath of air, every ounce of food on that base and we will shut it down if he so much as clears his throat wrong. The lives of those six astronauts he's got so pally with are his responsibility. If he fucks up now, they're history. Tell him that. Tell him if he doesn't play along, they are all toast. Got that? Good.'"

He was bolt upright. He'd done a deal with these guys. A nice, straightforward deal: Frank didn't shit the bed; they brought him home. What could be simpler? He'd thought he had enough chips on the table to bargain afresh. Turned out he was wrong. When NASA had turned up, XO had got a whole new bunch of hostages. And he hadn't factored that in at all.

"I don't understand why this has got them so spooked. But you've got to listen to them. I don't think they're kidding, Frank. I think they really mean to do this. Don't say anything. Please. At least, not now, not until I find out why this is so important to them. I'd have quit long ago if it wasn't for you. Just let me keep you alive, OK? Luisa."

Goddammit.

What was he going to do?

He padded through the crew quarters and cross-hab, dim with night-time lighting, and cycled through into the greenhouse. This oasis. The lights over some of the trays had dimmed to mimic the day–night cycle on Earth, and others blazed full, but the sound of dripping water was ubiquitous.

To lose this. To lose all of this would be a tragedy. To lose his life, sure. But to see all this wither and die, starved of air and the pumps silenced?

It was ridiculous, but he held on to the thought. XO could

probably kill them in half a dozen different ways: all the automatic systems like the power regulators that kept them alive, plus all the others that could be misused to make the base uninhabitable. But wiping out their ability to grow food was a more certain death than most.

He found a chair and sagged into it, elbows on knees.

When could they bail? Seven people, one MAV. May? June? XO would know that. It was just March now. So maybe they'd kill them quicker. Mess with the atmosphere while they were sleeping so that no one woke up. Or they could pick someone off, just to teach Frank a lesson. Hell, just take him out.

But wait: they could have done that at any time after he'd completed Phase three, after NASA had landed even. A message of regret, a request to bag the body, even a suggestion that what Lance Brack really wanted was to be buried on Mars. There were people to carry on the functions of the base and…XO would still get paid.

Maybe they couldn't get to him. Maybe they couldn't get to him, but could get to the others. Maybe it was just that they could get to the base as a whole, and not any one person.

He scrubbed at his scalp. This was too hard. He couldn't make a decision. He'd felt the same in the small dark hours before he'd picked up a gun, driven over to Mike's dealer's and shot him. Anything to burst that tension. Anything to simplify matters. Anything to make it stop.

"Lance?"

It took him longer than it ought to respond.

"Yes. Yes, that's…" That's me. I'm Lance Brack, ex-military, XO employee. Astronaut. Survivor. Murderer. He glanced around to see Isla by the airlock, hesitating, before coming closer.

"Are you OK?" she asked. She touched him lightly on the shoulder, and he shivered. "Lance? Are you ill?"

"I just couldn't sleep."

"You should get Fan to check you out. It might be the sign of something else."

"I don't need to take up his time," said Frank. The last thing he needed was Fan seeing his scars. Being kind to him. "It'll pass."

"It's been weeks now." She walked around him, stood in front of him, hands on hips.

He craned his neck to look at her. "I'm fine."

"You need to take some time off."

"I need to keep busy."

"Talk to Leland."

"No." He almost shouted that. No way did he want to talk to Leland. But he'd startled her, and none of this was her fault. XO. Bastard XO. "No," he repeated, mildly, evenly, in case she thought he was losing it—who was he trying to kid? She was thinking exactly that, and he wasn't going to blame her one bit.

"I'm worried about you."

He looked up at her again, looked down.

"No one's looking after you. You were on your own for eight months. You were injured and alone and that must have been terrifying."

He could have said something then. He could have told her the truth. He could have told her everything, and let the pieces of his broken life fall where they might.

Frank took a deep breath, and said nothing.

"Lance?"

"It's just the sleep. You go do whatever it is you got up for. I'm going to check on the tilapia." That was good. The fish were on the next level down, away from her. She was still standing in front of him, so he exited the chair to the side.

He headed for the ladder, and started climbing.

"We're going out again tomorrow. We've been cleared for EVA back on Ceraunius."

Halfway down the ladder, he paused. "That's good, right? Shows there's nothing to worry about."

"You said 'everything's trying to kill you'. Almost your first words when we got here. Why should this be any different?"

She moved in front of him again, even though it was just his head and shoulders above the deck. "The ground just opened up and swallowed Station seven. You should buddy up like the rest of us."

She wasn't wrong. Yet it gave him a freedom that he wasn't ready to give up. Or able, now that the XO suits had dropped the hammer on him. He was pretty much their pawn. If they wanted him to go over to M2, he'd have to. If they wanted him to take one for the team? After all that he'd been through, and done, maybe they knew not to push him that far.

It was brinkmanship. He'd lost this round, but there were going to be other battles. He'd take each one as it happened.

"Lance?"

"I got a lot on my mind," he said. He was looking at her knees, her shins, her feet. "You got up for a reason. It wasn't to keep me company."

Even when he reached the lower level, he was aware of her above him, gazing down the hole in the floor at the top of his head. Then he heard her move away, the flexing of the plastic panels and the creak of the metal beams marking her progress.

He stood by the tilapia tanks, listening to them bubbling away, the aerators and the movement of the fish combining to make the surface seethe.

Isla wasn't going to die. No one was going to die. Not on his watch. If that was the prize, then the price was worth paying. There. Done. His controllers would be proud of him.

18

I refuse to be threatened by a laborer. A common laborer. Beforehand, I don't think I even remembered his name—it was just a line on a spreadsheet—but now, I see him. And he needs to know that the most terrible thing on two worlds is to come to my personal attention. I will crush him, and being a hundred million miles away will not save him.

[transcript ends]

Frank had three passengers: Jim, Yun, and Leland. Enough so that no one really talked to him, and he got to drive. The trailer was loaded with seismometers—which Frank did understand, coming from California—and other equipment, which he didn't. He did know that none of it would take kindly to being thrown about, despite having been launched on top of a rocket from Earth, crashed through the atmosphere of Mars, and dropped onto the surface from a height of around thirty feet.

They had, collectively, decided that the disappearance of Station seven was down to natural processes. And that threw Frank, because he was convinced that M2 had stolen it.

But if a bunch of highly trained scientists, backed up by

whoever NASA could corral, thought there was an explanation that didn't involve someone turning the weather station off, and taking it away for parts, then maybe they were right.

In the clear light of day, perhaps he was the one who was wrong, and he'd fucked up. Lack of sleep? Sure. Paranoia? Understandable. PTSD? OK, the list of his neuroses would keep Leland occupied for months.

There was enough doubt in the situation to send a man crazy, and he had little leeway on that score.

What was certain was XO's threat to him, and to the astronauts. That wasn't his imagination. That was real, M2 or no M2.

When they got to the outpost, Frank spent some time outside. He told the others that he wanted to check the hab over, tighten things up, make certain there wasn't any wear. He did that, but he also searched the ground for tracks that he hadn't made, and bootprints where he hadn't stood.

Now that it wasn't just him, it made things more difficult. The usual crew of Jim and Yun walked around the summit quite freely, and sometimes they had a buggy up with them to reach more distant features. The wind tended to erode tracks quickly up on the top, though. Fresh, unexplained marks might tell him that M2 were still active, still looking for things, still probing north.

And maybe they were. Frank couldn't tell. Tire tracks started and finished in the thin dust almost at will. Scuffs that might be made by boots were everywhere, and when he examined them, nowhere.

Natural. M2 could have had nothing to do with Station seven. He might have jeopardized his trip home over nothing. From now on, he was going to have to tell XO—and tell Luisa—nothing. He was going to bottle it up tight, no matter what, no matter how much he'd come to rely on her. His one prop had been deliberately knocked away, and he was going to have to wear that, because doing anything else was going to get her, and the NASA crew, hurt.

He'd hit the bottom, and he still had to function, still had to put on the Lance Brack show for everyone. He readjusted his face, and came back in through the airlock.

"Everything OK?" asked Leland.

Frank reminded himself that this wasn't a trick question. He'd been outside to shake the hab down. That was what Leland was inquiring about, not the state of his mind.

"It's holding up fine. It gets colder up here. More thermal expansion in the day, but the bolts seem to be taking it."

"If it fails, what will it sound like?"

"Sound like?" Frank frowned. "I'm guessing it wouldn't sound like anything, because all the air will be too busy escaping to carry sound."

Leland laughed, and it seemed like such an odd thing to laugh about. "I guess you're right. I meant before that."

"Oh. You might pick up the bolt heads shearing off. But that depends." Frank pushed himself out of his suit into the cold air of the hab. "You've done your drills, right?"

"Down to twenty seconds. Of course, that's practice. They don't test you under conditions where you might die."

Frank covered his annoyance by turning his back and disengaging his life support. XO hadn't treated him half as well. He was disposable. He still was.

Yun and Jim were testing batteries with a meter down on the ground floor, unpacking them and making sure they'd take and store a current before repacking them for the trip out.

Leland's slow Southern voice was gently coaxing. "So where did you work after serving? JPL? Lockheed? Boeing?"

Kittridge Construction. He was figuring Leland had never heard of it. "You know I can't answer that."

"Doesn't that frustrate you? Us kids getting up in your face with our degrees and doctorates and experience, and you not sitting us all down and schooling us on just what you've seen and done?"

"I got my orders, Leland. And that's that. No point in getting antsy about it. And you're not 'kids', either. You got to be, what, thirty-five? Forty?"

"Thirty-seven. That's two years younger than Neil Armstrong when he first walked on the Moon. He pulled off a landing like Lucy's, too. History could have been hella different." Leland hefted his own life support, and put it against the staging on the upper level. "But you've got plenty of years left in you. You'll get back to Earth and you'll pick up where you left off. You got a life, right? Kids, maybe. A career for sure. You're obviously a senior guy, a consultant, a trouble-shooter. You'll make a good living back Earthside, with XO, or any other company."

"What's your point, Leland?" Frank stacked his life support, and grabbed a fresh pack that they'd brought with them.

"This is our pinnacle, the best thing we'll ever do, and we all signed up knowing this could be the end of us, one way or another. We're here because we think it's worth it, despite all the different ways we could die. But you don't seem to have that same enthusiasm, and I guess I'm trying to work out what you think you're getting out of this."

Hell, they'd been ready to just kill him and fire him into the sun. But now, maybe, just maybe, he might get to live and go home. "Talk to me about it when you've been here nine months, Leland."

"That's fair comment. Well, whatever they're paying you, I hope it's enough."

Frank heaved his new life support pack into place and pushed it home. Making XO pay seemed a pipe dream now, compared with what he'd hoped to extract from them. Having said that, the tables might suddenly turn again and put him on top for a change.

"I'm ready."

Yun handed up the battery packs, and Jim followed.

"Leland, tell me you remember how the seismograph fits together."

"I remember just fine."

"Me and Yun will handle the siting on this side of the volcano. If you and Lance can take the buggy over to the south and west. Meet back here in…four hours?"

South. Why did it have to be south? And why did it have to be Leland? Better than Jim, admittedly, but Yun was good company. He got her, understood her drive, and she didn't ask him personal questions or dick around.

"What about what happened to Station seven?" asked Frank. "Shouldn't we be avoiding that area completely?"

"Sure. If you look at the map, the sites are further south and further west. Give where Station seven was a wide berth—five hundred yards for now. I'm still betting on a subsurface collapse, related to the secondary caldera, marked CT-B, at seven o'clock."

Frank had been there, right there, two days ago. There'd been no sign of a new crater, and he knew it, though he hadn't labored the point. He was still betting on M2.

"What if the whole area is lousy with holes?"

"That's kind of what we're trying to find out. This is a one-off. Just bad timing on our part. And you've got a buddy now. Leland will keep you right, won't you, Leland?"

"I do share Lance's concerns. But you're the geologist. You wouldn't ask us to take any risks you wouldn't take yourself." Leland put in his own fresh life support and propped the suit up, prior to climbing in.

"It'll be fine," said Jim. "Once we've bedded in the network, we get to tour the area with a thumper. Next week sometime."

"OK." The others seemed to know what a thumper was. At this point, Frank didn't mind not knowing. "Let's get to it then. Back in four hours. That's," and he looked at the onboard clock. "Ten past three."

"Fifteen ten. Got it."

They left the airlock one at a time, each carrying a quarter of the batteries. Frank and Leland carried theirs to the trailer,

184

and Jim and Yun stacked theirs on the steps. They divided the equipment, and Frank checked his map.

"I'm thinking we drive out to the furthest point, and work our way back. That way we know that if we're going to run into problems, we're doing so on a full tank."

"Copy that," said Leland. "You driving?"

"Gives me something to do," said Frank, already climbing up to the driver's seat.

Once Leland was hanging off the roll cage, Frank set off towards a point about two miles downslope and roughly four o'clock on Ceraunius's clock face. He had to navigate the bad lands again—formed by the same subsidence that was supposed to have claimed Station seven—and push out onto the broad, blank side of the volcano. Nothing but frozen lava and dust, punctuated by the occasional impact crater and sinuous rille. He could see for miles, and yet could see so very little. The landscape curved in every direction, up and down and around. It made it feel as if the horizon was both far away and close up. Of all the places he'd been on Mars, this was the most alien and the most isolated.

He could drop off the radar up there, just like Station seven had.

Frank wanted to concentrate on driving. Leland wanted to talk about his Huckleberry Finn childhood on the banks of the Mississippi, of the floods and the levee breaches that punctuated his family's slow-motion migration until even the most ornery of Southern families had ended up in the north.

Inevitably, after the almost confessional nature of Leland's testimony to a lost and drowned way of life, he asked: "What about you, Lance? What shaped you growing up?"

Frank knew the bare-bones of Brack's biography. Born. Raised. Educated. Employed.

How many theaters of war he'd served in, both in and out of uniform.

Brack was a mercenary. It was most likely why he was on

Mars. His special talents—his apparent lack of compunction when it came to killing people for money—were what led XO to find him and hire him.

And maybe some of that Leland already knew. Maybe he couldn't quite square the paper Brack with the real-life one, and he was trying to work out why there was such a difference. The explanation probably hadn't occurred to him so far, and Frank wasn't going to give him a nudge.

"I don't have to talk about it, Leland. Stuff happened. I grew older. I ended up on Mars. If you want to tell me more about surfing down Main Street, then I'll listen, but I've got nothing I want to say."

"Most people want to talk about themselves, Lance."

"Most people haven't spent the last nine months on Mars."

"I get that. I really do get that. But don't you think it's healthy to open up now and then?"

Frank thought of XO's threat, not just to himself, but to the rest of the crew. "I'm good," he said. "I'm fine the way it is. I'd like to keep it that way."

There was dead air, then: "You know where I am if you need me."

"I know. Don't take offense. I'm like this with everyone."

When they arrived at the furthest point on the map, they dismounted, and worked amiably together, side by side. Frank knew how to handle a rock drill better than Leland, and he took the first shift while Leland got the other parts together. Even though the ground was lava, rather than soft sediment, the first few inches cut up fine. Then it was lean in and try not to over-heat the drill bit. Back on Earth, they'd be sluicing it down with water. Here, that wasn't an option, so he had to stop frequently and let the machine cool down.

Each hole was supposed to be a foot long. Frank reckoned on making eight inches before having to stop. Below the rime of rust, the rock was hard and gray, flecked with white. A plume of pale dust ascended from the site every time he pulled on the

186

trigger. When he stopped, it had all but fallen away. Just a slight haze in the air. Definitely not like on Earth, where the grinders spewing out clouds of dust were a problem for everyone.

Doing it in near-silence, only feeling the rattle of the drill through his hands. Memories came to him of the huge vacuum chamber back at Gold Hill, where Dee had holed his suit, and Alice had sealed it by cutting the boy and using his blood as a patch.

He hadn't thought about that for months. He had to pull the drill aside and wait the feels out.

"Lance?"

"Just cooling the drill. Another inch and we're there."

Frank returned to the hole and got it to the required depth. He had to assume they had a spare bit somewhere, or some kind of sharpener, because the tip was blunting quickly.

When he'd done, Leland dropped in the anchor and pushed it home with the bolt, then threaded it in through the baseplate and started tightening it up with the crank. The anchor gripped on, and soon enough, the plate was hard against the surface of the rock.

From there on, it was simply a matter of screwing the seismometer onto the plate and activating it. It leveled itself and started sending basic telemetry back to the main computer.

"One down, three to go," said Leland.

Frank wiped his faceplate with his hand, helped pack up the tools and load them onto the trailer, then strap them down. They checked together that they hadn't left anything behind but the seismometer, looked at the numbers on their suits, and headed off towards the second point.

They were already edging towards the end of the second hour—drilling the anchor-hole had taken longer than anticipated, and wasn't that always the way? Whether they could finish today depended on whether the rock in the other locations was as solid as it was in the first. Maybe they'd luck out from now on.

"Yun here."

"Copy that," said Leland.

"Jim's got a suit malfunction. Heading back to CU1."

"What's wrong with it?" asked Frank. He was too far away to be any help. Even if he was close by, he still might not be able to help. Like the last time. With Marcy.

"Comms failure," said Yun.

It was just comms. It wasn't life support. It wasn't a rip in the suit. Jim was fine.

"OK. Abort," said Leland. "We'll abort too. Keep a close eye on him."

"Will do."

"We'll be back in around fifty minutes. Over and out."

Frank drove on, and then said: "Just a comms issue." To get it out of his system. To confirm that he'd heard right.

But Leland thought he was saying something different. "It's SOP. Something's wrong with the suit, get in to a pressurized environment. You were taught that, right?"

"I was taught I could use my discretion..."

"This is how we work, Lance. Something's wrong, we get to safety. Then worry about what the problem is."

"I get that."

"This is protocol. We signed up to it."

"Look, I'm heading back. I'm not even arguing with you." He wasn't. He was actually relieved. So what if he didn't get on that well with Jim? That wasn't the point. The point was that they were all going to live, right? "Let's make it in forty-five."

19

From: Miguel Averado <maaverado@usach.cl>
To: Mark Bernaberg <mbernaberg@lpl.arizona.edu>
cc: Carolina Soledad <cmsoledad@usach.cl>
Date: Wed, Mar 3 2049 12:10:41 -0300
Subject: re: HiRISE2

Hola, Mark.

Gracias! I've passed them on to my research student, Carolina.
If you're planning to do another pass of that area soon, she'll be
interested in the updates—I've copied her in so you have her email.

Mig

They parked outside the outpost, and Frank lowered himself to
the ground. He'd driven hard, and his bones ached. He wondered if they were thinning. They probably were. He wondered
how much further they'd go and how debilitating that would
be back on Earth. Exercise. Actual weight-bearing exercise. He
should do some.

Leland went through the airlock first, and then Frank.

He realized that everything wasn't quite right the moment he
stepped inside the hab.

There was Yun, out of her suit. And Leland, opening up
his own. No Jim. Frank almost blurted out something, but he

caught the position of Yun's finger, pressed against her lips. Don't say anything. No comms.

Frank tabbed his suit controls to open, and crawled out backwards.

"Someone mind telling me why we've gone all Secret Squirrel?"

Leland, cold at altitude, in an unheated hab, dressed only in his thin long johns, batted his arms around himself. Then he spotted a spare insulated jacket, and he struggled into it. "Jim's missing."

Frank looked around the hab, at Yun, at the equipment. "What? But you were with him."

Yun's face contorted. "He said he was going to be ten minutes. Something he'd seen. An outcrop. I said I'd finish off the drilling. After half an hour I called him, in a way that wouldn't tell Lucy he'd gone off on his own. I got no answer."

"Did you go and look for him?"

"Of course I went to look for him! I looked for an hour, and he wasn't there. So...I called you."

Leland was silent. His mouth moved, but he couldn't find the words.

"The suit thing," said Frank. "You made that up."

"I kept on looking for him."

"Goddammit, Yun. You're all supposed to be fucking geniuses and you pull shit like this."

She looked down at the ground.

"It's not the first time you guys have done this, is it?" Leland had finally found his voice. "You did it once, and it felt wrong, but no one caught you, so now it's become a habit. Lance, or whoever, disappears down the hill, and you split up. All you have to do is make sure you're both back in time for the pick-up."

Frank started climbing into his suit again. "Stay here. What you tell Lucy and when is up to you. But I'm going back out to find him."

"We should all come," said Yun.

"No. You two stay here. Which way did he go?"

"South from the second point, a kilometer or two. There's a ridge he thought might be a late-stage intrusion."

The second sentence didn't mean anything to him, but the first part? One k was barely any distance at all. "When I find him, I'll call you." When. When. Jim went south, dammit.

He thumbed his suit closed, and he went back to the airlock. It cycled, and he was once again outside on the hard red rock. There was some dust-drift going on. Maybe afternoon heating, maybe a storm brewing, but his distance vision fuzzed slightly, then cleared, as a band of airborne dust blew past. Upwind of the hab, the rock was bare pavement, with a surface like hammered metal, but downwind, there was some settling.

Being very careful not to swear, even under his breath, he climbed into the driver's seat and set off across the plateau.

Every few seconds, he wanted to spot Jim walking back, carrying a big bag of rocks over his shoulder. But he didn't. He reached the seismometer site after a few minutes. Tools were lying where they'd been dropped, and, almost without thinking, he climbed down and burned some air collecting them together and stowing them on the trailer.

He dialed both his suit lights and his buggy lights up, and stood up on top, holding the roll cage, assuming that being lit up like a Christmas tree would attract Jim's attention. If he was out there. Frank couldn't see him, and evidently couldn't be seen either. But he could see Jim's target, even though it was sometimes partly obscured by the haze: a nondescript line of rock rising ragged from the otherwise ubiquitous lava.

Strap in, go and take a look.

The ridge was barely a hundred feet high. He drove along its base. Unless there were overhangs or caves, Jim wasn't there— he could see down the entire length of the outcrop—but he was also looking to see if there was anything to show Jim had been there: freshly broken rock, tools, bags, markers of any kind.

Nothing.

People don't just disappear. Weather stations don't just disappear either.

M2. M2. Please don't let it be M2.

Then, he thought, maybe he'd gone into that river bed, the one that started about nine o'clock and forked part-way down before spilling its contents onto the plain. The sides were steep at the top, and he might be in the radio-shadow the cliff cast.

He was at the head of the channel. It was sinuous and he couldn't see far down it, but there was no evidence of Jim having gone that way. Not that there was any evidence at all. No footprints, no dust to have footprints in. He'd have to drive into the channel to check.

Frank had been gone, what? Fifteen, twenty minutes. No need to worry. He looked at the maps on his tablet, and saw that if he drove around the western end of the ridge, he could get to the top of it. He was pretty much there already. He carried on, then around, then up. He headed back eastwards, until he couldn't go any further. The gaping maw of the caldera blocked his path, and while he might make it down that wall in the buggy, he was pretty certain he wasn't going to make it back up.

And if Jim had fallen in there? How solid was the slope?

He dismounted and got as close as he dared. The edge was pretty well defined, but he decided he wasn't going to take stupid risks. He paid out fifty foot of cable and threaded the hitch through his belt, before clipping it back on itself. He ran the cable through both hands and approached the drop-off.

That...was a long way down. A thousand feet? Something like that, and approaching a one-in-one slope in places. Blocky and stepped, all the way. Reduced gravity or not, he'd break either himself or his suit if he fell. He tightened his grip on the cable and walked forward as much as he dared.

He got himself in a position where he could see all the caldera floor, left and right of where he was dangling. No sign of Jim. The place was empty, from one side to the other. He turned himself around—carefully—and hauled himself back onto level ground.

Frank's question still stood: where was Jim?

He certainly wasn't where he should be. He wasn't at the bluff, and he wasn't on his way back to the outpost. Frank looked in that direction. He couldn't see it from where he was. He was struck again by the immensity of the planet, the inhospitableness of it. That he was just a fly landing on a vast red face, that he didn't belong there, and in a moment he'd be swatted away.

Goddammit, if Jim was hiding from him, engaging in some practical joke, he'd...let Lucy deal with him. He was pretty certain that whatever he could do or say, what she could unleash would strip paint. Dicking around on Mars was going to get someone injured. Or worse. And he needed to get himself, Yun and Leland back to MBO before they ran out of options.

But there could be other, more terrible reasons for Jim's absence than him being a jerk.

Jim wasn't calling for help. Perhaps his radio was malfunctioning after all. Perhaps he was trapped somewhere. Perhaps the ground had indeed swallowed him up.

Frank reeled the cable back onto the spool and drove slowly along the ridge line. He was getting spooked now. At some point—some point soon?—Jim was going to tip over from having more air than not, to having less than he'd need. He and Yun had walked, and that took more air than just driving. Then they'd put in two seismometers. But they'd had fresh tanks. Calculating how long someone might have to live was something he was used to now, but this felt different.

Jim had maybe four or five hours of air left. He had a part-used spare in the outpost that would see him back to base.

Frank steered the buggy down into the west-facing dry river bed. It was much like the Santa Clara, twisting its way down the flanks of Ceraunius in tight C-shaped curves, between steep walls that seemed to bleed brine.

It was dustier there, on the flat floor of the gully. He drove down a way, and got off to stand in front of the buggy, the lights in his face, staring at the ground and seeing only his bootprints. Jim hadn't come this way.

Had the geologist decided on a whim to go somewhere else, having told Yun that he was going to the bluff? Or had Frank somehow missed him on the wide-open landscape? Sure, there were craters, both big and small, but there weren't any significant obstructions on the route between the bluff and the outpost. If there was a problem with his comms, he might have difficulty navigating. But then again, all Frank would do would be to head upslope until he was in sight of the caldera, and then turn left. He could find the outpost that way.

And if Jim was already back with Leland and Yun, he'd be tempted to take a swing at him. Definitely tempted now. He hadn't had a call, though, cryptic or otherwise.

He backed the buggy up to do a three-point turn, and emerged from the valley, hoping that there'd be a speck in the distance, a figure in a spacesuit, trudging in the direction of the outpost.

Goddammit.

"Leland. Yun."

"Leland here."

"I'm calling it. I'll stay out here as long as I can, but you can be the one to phone this in. And use a different channel. I need to concentrate."

There was a long, long pause, enough for Frank to think that his message hadn't got through.

"Do you copy?"

"Copy that. Good luck."

Frank thought back to the number of times he, and any of the others, had been outside, on their own, maybe miles from the base, and they hadn't got themselves lost, or injured, or incapacitated. They'd inadvertently made XO's job that much harder by managing, against the odds, to stay alive. It had taken someone actively trying to kill them to take them down.

If this involved M2, what the hell was he going to do?

The dust was blowing up thicker, and he didn't know whether that was likely to get worse or not. He'd not been out in a proper sandstorm yet—most of them happened a long way to the south, and they only occasionally got the spill-over—but this one looked like it was threatening to come over the equator. But anything that impeded his vision now was serious: even nebulous clouds of dust blowing past might mean he missed the obvious, and an increased wind speed would erase any potential tracks.

Where would a geologist have gone to, if he hadn't gone to where he said he was going? Frank stood up on the buggy and used its height to scan the bare rock for anything that might catch his eye.

The most obvious feature was the scarp slope to the north, that marked the start of the broken ground at the head of the Santa Clara, where it almost seemed that the water flowing down the flanks was looking for the easiest path down before settling on the one. The cliff was tall, maybe five, six hundred feet from top to bottom, and it was catching the afternoon sun and glowing a bright, almost white, pink.

But that was north. Jim had gone south. South towards where M2 was. Had been. Might still be. And Frank had never warned them to avoid that area, because he didn't feel like he could, because of his deal with XO, and just look where that had got him.

He headed south and east again, going over the same ground that he'd already scoured, looking for anything he might have missed. If Jim'd gone far enough, then maybe, just maybe he was out of radio range.

"Jim. Can you hear me? It's Lance. I'm a mile south of the outpost. Flash your suit lights. Over."

He repeated the message, again and again, driving a little way, stopping, standing up.

No tracks. No buggy wheels. No boot marks.

He stopped, eventually, when his own tank was telling him

he had to. He parked up on the top of a ridge, and watched the dust drapes blow by like chiffon curtains.

"Leland? Yun? Do you copy?"

Leland answered. The signal was choppy, and breaking up. "Go ahead."

"I'm coming back in. I'm running out of gas, and I just can't find him."

There was silence. No static, only the occasional chirruping of data, like crickets, or birds.

Then: "We got it. You had to try."

"I had to try."

"Come on in, Lance. We have to go back to MBO. Orders."

"I could spend another ten minutes out here, maybe."

"Lance," said Leland. "I know. But you've got to come in now. We're relying on you to get us down."

If he stopped now, Jim was dead. If he wasn't already dead. But he'd sure as hell be dead by morning, if he couldn't make it back to the outpost by himself. And even then, it'd get damn cold overnight.

And if Frank didn't turn back now, he might well kill himself. And the people he was responsible for.

"Jim, you goddamn fuck-up," he said. "We weren't supposed to lose anyone. We just weren't. If you can hear this, then: I'm sorry. I'm leaving you here. I've run out of time. I can't put their lives in danger to try and save you. I did what I could. I looked everywhere for you. But what I did wasn't enough. Because I didn't find you. Now you get to stay here, while we go back. And there's not a damn thing I can do about that. I hope that, whatever it was you were doing, it was worth it."

He took the steering column and resisted the urge to rip it clean off. He didn't know if this was an accident, stupidity, or deliberate. The uncertainty burned in him, and made him shake in fear, in rage, in helplessness.

Goddammit.

20

[Internal memo: Mars Base One Mission Control to Bruno Tiller 3/4/2049 (transcribed from paper-only copy)]

Sir, we need to talk. Securely. Urgently.

[transcript ends]

The next day, they all went out—the remaining six of them—to look for Jim. Two buggies. Three people apiece, and the highest-resolution satellite maps downloaded onto their tablets. Frank had shown Lucy where he'd searched, and she'd thanked him for his efforts in such clipped tones, she thanked him again straight after, in case he hadn't realized she was actually thanking him.

He knew what it was like to lose someone. He kept wondering if he might have missed something on his search. Maybe the others wondered that too. That if it had been them, they would have found him. It gnawed at him, at his bones, like a feral beast.

Luisa couldn't help. Her hands were as tied as his. She made all the right sounds, for sure. Conciliatory. Concerned. But she was having to follow the party line at this point, insisting that M2 were gone, were history, dead, incapacitated, dying, couldn't possibly have taken Jim. Station seven had fallen into a hole, and maybe Jim had gone the same way. Mars was an unknown, unpredictable place, full of danger. Who knew? They could have

197

been right, but he sure as hell didn't trust XO to tell her anything like the truth.

In Frank's experience, it wasn't Mars that was the problem. It was people—XO people—who were the problem.

He drove. He had Fan and Isla on the back of his buggy. But no one spoke unless they had to. He'd already been up and out earlier, in the freezing dark, checking the vehicles over, making sure they had a full charge despite the amount of crap that had built up on the solar panels: he'd dipped into the reserves to make certain each fuel cell was at capacity, and that was something they were going to have to watch if the dust kept on coming. He hadn't slept. Hadn't eaten either. He was burning out and only sheer willpower was keeping him going.

As they got higher up, the dust became more mobile, fuzzing the view with haze and causing Frank to keep wiping his faceplate. The walls of the Santa Clara valley trickled with grains of sand like gossamer.

Lucy was behind, driving the second buggy. Whatever she felt about Yun and her complicity in Jim's disobedience, she had at least treated them both like adults rather than shoveling the entire blame onto one or the other. If there'd been shouting, Frank hadn't heard it, and the base was small enough. Perhaps ice was worse than fire, but neither was directed at him.

Frank had some of his lights on. The weather had made everything particularly gloomy, and they were up and out barely a quarter of an hour after sunrise. The shadows were deep and almost tangible, but each buggy had only one fuel cell, and running the lights would eat into the range. They'd brought all the spare life support packs with them, fully charged. He already knew his search patterns, and it was going to be a hell of a long day. And it was only going to go short if someone found a body.

There was no pretending this was a search party. It was recovery. Everyone, when they spoke at all, still referred to him in the present tense. They knew, though. They knew. Jim was dead. It was, perversely, only Frank who wondered if he was alive.

He didn't know which he wanted more. He hoped there was a body to be found so he didn't have to go against XO's directives, and he hoped there wasn't, because that might mean Jim had been picked up by M2. For good reasons? To force someone to go over, and offer help? Would XO double-down on their threats to the NASA team? Or threaten his family? He didn't know.

A body would be closure at least. Fan would examine Jim. Someone else—Lucy?—would give the suit a postmortem. They'd conclude that this was death by natural causes, and Frank could sleep again. He hadn't asked what the protocol was for dealing with a dead astronaut. He presumed it didn't involve them being flown into the sun.

He broached the top of the river valley, driving out onto the broad summit, and caught the stuttering light from the risen sun slanting through dust-laden skies: it was like approaching the gates of Hell. Twilight rather than daylight, and they weren't there for any good purpose, either. Frank wondered if traipsing around in weather he'd never seen the like of before was going to represent an unacceptable risk to NASA, considering all they were supposed to be looking for was a corpse.

But Jim had been their friend. They'd trained with him, traveled with him, laughed and argued and, who knew, maybe even slept with him. Of course they wanted to know what had happened to him, and wanted to do this one last thing for him. Frank would have put his responsibility to the living over that to the dead, though Lucy clearly weighed these things differently. She was in charge: not of him, but still definably in charge all the same.

The volcano-top...it was like it was shrouded in fog. Foggish. Pink Mars fog. It came in bands like rain, as if curtains of material were being dragged over the landscape. One moment it was clear enough to see to the next crater, the nearest scarp, and then the next wall of dust advanced. Continuous, discrete, a conveyor belt of occlusions.

What was most unnerving was the sound. Mars was usually silent. All noise was man-made. Except this. It was like the planet was gently breathing on him.

They parked up next to the outpost and, aware that every moment was a moment they weren't looking for Jim, Lucy kept it mercifully short.

"I'm going in to check," she said.

Was he inside? If he was, had he survived the night?

The answer came quickly.

"He's not here. Put the LS packs in the airlock. I'll transfer them, and then we start." Her voice was controlled, the carrier wave less so. "Let's bring him home, OK?"

"So say we all." Leland? It was Leland.

They piled up the spare life supports in the airlock, and Fan squeezed in with them, helping Lucy move them quickly into the hab. Then they were out again, and ready to go.

Lucy had nixed descending into the caldera. No one had done it yet, and she wasn't going to have anyone try. Sure, Jim could have been buried by a rockfall, standing too close to the edge when it collapsed, bringing a ton of debris down on him, but that became just another reason why they weren't going to attempt it. They had climbing rope, and they had the buggies' cables and winches, but Frank had managed to convince her he hadn't seen anything at the bottom.

That left two sectors, one north and east, one south and west, beyond the immediate area that Frank had already searched. Lucy had taken the north, given the south to Fan, and the doctor seemed content to let Frank do the driving. It was going to take them beyond the ridge where Jim had said he was heading, and down towards a big-ass crater marked on their maps as CT-B, where the pitted ground spoke, according to Jim's own reports, of subsurface collapse of empty lava tubes.

It was maybe a place he might go exploring. It was maybe a place where he could have ended up trapped. And Frank, Fan and Isla were going to have to go there and look. The search area was nine miles out from the outpost, roughly six miles across, centered on the second seismometer. About thirty square miles. It was unlikely that Jim would have gone so far, just on a whim, when he could have waited for a buggy and backup to make the trip properly, safely.

That could be said for whatever he had actually done. He'd ignored that. Now he was missing.

Frank drove to the edge of the designated search area, and Isla and Fan both hopped off. They walked out some hundred yards to either side of the buggy, then turned to face the direction of travel.

"We ready?" asked Fan. He came across choppy, lo-fi.

Frank adjusted the lights on the front of the buggy, so that they shone out not just in front but to the left and right, and climbed back into the driver's seat. "Ready."

The buggy rolled forward, as slowly as walking pace, which was hard to achieve, and harder still because Frank had to keep on twisting in his seat to even see his outriders, who were outside his ten o'clock to two o'clock field of vision. They swept to the river channel that ran down the west side of the volcano, moved three hundred yards down the slope, and swept back.

What had seemed like a good idea back at base was now shown for what it was: ludicrously inadequate. And they were still going to do it because there was literally nothing else they could do. They were looking for a body, in a spacesuit, while wearing spacesuits themselves, on a nearly thirty-thousand-foot mountain in the middle of the worst dust-storm for a year. They had no satellite backup and their radios were starting to get flaky because of the static.

They went backwards and forwards for two hours, covering the area between the outpost and the river. Frank swapped over with Isla. She swapped with Fan. When Frank was out on the left, he could see the buggy, but the other walker on the far side was reduced to the glow of their suit lights.

Mostly, he kept his gaze forward. Scanning the ground, not

for footprints any longer, just a pale spacesuit, banked with blown dust.

The air was beginning to resemble a brown soup. Even with full lights, visibility was atrocious. Frank was having to wipe his faceplate every few steps, and the damn stuff was sticking to everything. Then they moved beyond the river, into new territory, now going downhill on the river's far bank.

Something like a flashbulb went off. He stopped and looked around. Then what sounded like atmospheric entry rumbled overhead.

"What the hell was that?"

"Lightning," said Fan.

"You mean, like actual lightning? Storm lightning?"

"It's the dust."

"We're on top of a fucking mountain. We have no cover."

"We have to keep looking. We need to—" Fan's voice broke. "We need to find Jim."

Frank looked across to the buggy. The figure on top was high up, compared to everything else. Only the top of the roll bar was taller than Isla's helmet.

"Isla?"

"We keep looking," she said.

Did she sound scared? Did he? There was plenty to be scared about.

"OK. Let's do it."

They approached the westernmost end of the sweep, then Isla pointed the buggy southwards to block off the end of their search area. The lightning played above them, lighting up the clouds of drifting dust, revealing their many layers and bands for a snapshot second before everything went dark again, and the mountainside grumbled as if clearing its throat.

Everything that was happening outside of Frank's faceplate told him he was out in hurricane-force winds. The air was granular, and moving, thrashing at his suit with a sound that made him think of the very distant whine of jet engines. Yet he felt no motion. No buffeting. Nothing. It was disconcerting, as strange as when he'd got caught up in the twisters out on the plain.

There, right in front of him, was a tire mark, in the dust that had caught in the lee of a small crater. It was eroded away, was disappearing before his eyes even, as the wind tore at it and stripped away the distinctive ridges and troughs made by the treads.

He stared at it. Had he made this? Had Jim? From what was left—a print barely a couple of feet long, only a foot wide—it seemed to have been heading north at the time.

"Lance? Lance, you've stopped."

Had Jim ever used a buggy out this way? Frank wasn't sure that he had, not recently. And he himself hadn't passed this way, even yesterday: that was closer to the main caldera, and not this far downslope.

Was this what he was looking for? Proof that M2 had been up here? Could they have found Jim? Taken him back to M2?

"Lance?"

He suddenly realized that Isla was talking to him.

"I'm OK. I'm OK."

"Have you found something?"

"No," he said. "No. I thought I might have, but it's just… nothing."

He was going to have to go over to M2, wasn't he? He was going to have to check, or he was going to fall apart under the strain. Unless they found something today, he was going to have to take a buggy and drive it all the way over to the other side of Ceraunius and see what state they were in. With XO's permission or not.

The tracks were crumbling, eroding away, even while he stared at them. He deliberately scuffed at them with his boot, and walked on.

Lightning washed above, in flashes and sheets. Intense and bright. Electric.

The buggy was glowing, a flickering blue-green fire clinging to its metal latticework.

203

"Isla?"

"Lance?"

"What the hell is that?"

She rolled to a stop, and killed her lights. It was obvious now. Startlingly obvious.

"OK, I've had enough," she said. "Fan, Jim was our friend. He was special to all of us. But we can't stay out here in this. Come back to the buggy. We'll drive down into the river where there's some shelter."

She started up again, turned the vehicle around, the pale moons of the headlights washing over Frank. He walked steadily towards it, reaching up to its dust-caked frame and pulling himself up. Fan approached from the other side, climbing up and staring straight ahead, not looking at Frank, not engaging with Isla.

She found, more by luck than judgment, the banks of the river, and slowly rolled down the steep sides to the river bed. The air was barely clearer, but they were below the level of the surrounding ground. There was another flashbulb moment, and a few seconds later a stuttering, growling boom.

Frank habitually checked his air. He had just over half a tank left. They had spares in the outpost, but that was no longer the limiting factor.

"Have we any idea how long this is going to go on for?"

He got no response. In fact, he could see Fan's mouth moving, and he was getting nothing. The storm, the high-sided valley, was wiping out his comms completely. But only *his* comms, because Fan was clearly in a conversation with Isla.

Frank tapped Fan on the shoulder, and then, when he had his attention, double-tapped the side of his own helmet: the universal sign for deaf.

Fan frowned and leaned in so Frank could hear the to-and-fro. It looked like NASA comms were more sophisticated than Frank's own.

"—get this far north," Isla was saying. "We don't know enough about Martian weather to predict it. It could go on for days, weeks even. What we do know is that we're at the extreme edge of the storm: if it shifts even slightly southwards, then we'll get clear air, quickly."

"We can wait an hour," said Fan. "Then start again."

"OK," said Frank, "I'm very sorry about your friend, but there's nothing we can do about that right now. What I'm now worried about is us getting killed out here. We're in the middle of a dust-storm. We can't see shit. We're in spacesuits that rely on complicated electrical equipment to keep us alive. One bolt of lightning and any one of us will stop breathing. Now, we've got enough buffer at the outpost to bank what we've got left in our tanks. We get out of this dust. We can get something to eat and drink. We don't run the risk of getting fried by Odin."

"Thor," said Isla. "Thor is the god of thunder."

"Whatever. Fan, you're supposed to be in charge of this outing, and I'm not going to just walk off and leave you, but goddammit this is crazy and you have to see that."

Fan pulled away and leaned back to take in the slot of sky. Another flashbulb moment, illuminating the dry river bed and the sand cascading down over the banks like living water, followed by, a few seconds later and in the darkness, the gut-rumbling of the sky, seemed to galvanize him into action.

He leaned in again, banging his helmet against Frank's, and the sound was mediated by the dust and grit between the two surfaces.

"I'll talk to Lucy. No. I'll tell Lucy, in my position as senior medical officer, that we're suspending operations."

As far as they knew, Jim was gone: they were abandoning their search for him, and they weren't going to find him any time soon. If he was still on the volcano, maybe a satellite could pick up where the body was, but only when the weather had cleared. If so, they could retrieve him. When it was safe to do so.

If. If he was still on the volcano. What if he wasn't? How could Frank possibly explain any of this?

Isla turned the buggy around and tracked back up to the top of the valley, emerging into weather that had, if anything, deteriorated. She turned her own suit lights to maximum, just to be able to see the screen so she could switch the buggy lights back on.

She headed left, and crawled, barely at walking pace, across the exposed shoulder of volcanic rock that was shrugging itself into the path of the storm. The distance to the outpost shouldn't have been great, but it felt interminable. They couldn't see it. They couldn't see anything except that which was right in front of them. There was more than an element of guesswork governing the direction they were heading in.

Frank started to sweat. The top of the volcano was all but flat, and the drop into the caldera sharp and fatal. Upslope and downslope didn't mean much. His tablet was losing its connection more than it was finding it again, much like his suit, even out of the valley. But it was all they had. He opened it up and held it so that dust would blow against its back, not its screen.

Bear left. A hundred yards, was all.

He held it out in front of Isla's faceplate. "We're almost there," he said. Then repeated it because he'd dropped out again.

"Copy that." She turned the controls and slowly, through the shifting brown haze, another set of lights began to resolve.

The lights dimmed, then grew again. They were signaling.

"We see you," said Fan.

The outpost was just a pale ghost, barely visible, and even with the suit lights on, it was difficult to navigate the steps. They cycled the airlock two at a time, trying to save power. Frank stayed outside with Lucy. He caught her staring out into the void, thinking she'd failed, knowing she'd endangered her crew in trying to succeed, realizing that she'd let emotions get in the way of practical decisions.

He nudged her arm and pointed to the airlock, and she

seemed to just look through him for a moment. He'd been there too, and it wasn't a good place to be. Then she recovered, shaking herself like a wet dog would. She swiveled round and walked into the empty airlock. Frank followed her, closed the door, and waited for the pumps to kick in.

21

[Transcript of briefing given by NASA press secretary, Houston TX 3/5/2049 21:00CT]

It is with profound regret that I have to announce that Dr. James "Jim" Zamudio, geologist and crew member of the Ares IV mission to Mars Base One, is missing. The window of time in which Jim could have been found alive has now closed. We mourn with the surviving crew at this most profound and unwelcome loss.

[transcript ends]

Lucy finally gave the order to abandon the outpost just before sunset. The wind, as insubstantial as it was, was throwing material against the taut skin of the hab and making it thrum like a bass. The sound resonated in their guts, to the point where some of the astronauts started complaining of nausea.

Fan examined those affected, but there was nothing he could do to stop the noise. That it was also stupidly hot inside didn't help either. That was very much against Frank's expectations, as he thought they'd be freezing their asses off as nightfall approached. Yun explained that the dust transferred energy in the form of heat when it hit the hab walls: the more dust, the more heat.

Those weren't the only two factors persuading Lucy down. Even though they'd parked the buggies on the sheltered side, they'd still taken the brunt of six hours in a storm. If grit was going to get into the wheel hubs, or the controls, or abrade cables and weaken joints, today was going to be the day.

There was the lack of air, water, sanitation, and food too. The situation was impossible. She hung on for as long as she could, then pulled them out.

The floor of the hab was red with dust from where it had fallen off their suits. They knocked more off climbing back into them: it would all need cleaning out before it could function as a scientific station again.

Lucy instructed them all to swap out their life supports for fresh ones for the descent. Just in case they had to walk some of the way. It was sensible, but it also underlined the state they'd let themselves get into. They shouldn't have been there. If it hadn't been for Jim, they wouldn't have been.

"Lance? You know the way better than the rest of us. Take us back."

Last in, first out. Frank hugged his old life support pack and walked into the airlock. Someone came in behind him, and Frank nudged the cycle button with his elbow. The pump chugged. Slowly. The batteries were low, but everyone behind him knew how to vent the locks manually.

It was like walking out into a . . . back when he was a kid, someone had had an old-style TV, that worked on broadcast, not digital. The cable had come out of the box, and the screen had filled with static, a moving, hissing storm of black and white. That, only in black and red. Just the other side of his faceplate.

He put his pack down before even leaving the confines of the airlock and dialed up his lights to maximum, then edged out onto the platform. He could see the edges of things. They came and went.

"This is bad," he said. "Stay together."

He turned round and pushed his helmet against that of the astronaut behind him. Isla. She looked absolutely fucking terrified. Maybe he did too. He nodded to her and repeated his warning. She nodded back.

He faced front and worked his way down the steps, remembering to turn right at the bottom, and around to the lee side of the hab. Visibility was marginally better: he could actually see the shapes of the front of the buggies. He went around the other side, and stood in the shelter of the wheel.

"I'll climb up. Pass me the packs when I'm there."

He dropped his again and went hand over hand back into the red static. It was evil stuff. He wiped his faceplate, turning his back to the storm, and took the proffered life support packs, ratcheting them down with straps.

A third was handed up, and he was traveling with Fan again. He fixed the last pack in place, and swept the driver's seat as clear as he could of debris before sitting in it.

The control screen was all but invisible. He wiped the dust to one side, and pushed at the on switch.

A heart-stopping moment when nothing happened, then: lights. The old girl really didn't like the weather, and neither did he.

The last pair of suits went by, on their way to the second buggy. He checked the watts left in the fuel cell, ran the calculations in his head, and decided it was going to be enough. Just. But if it was as bad at the bottom of the mountain as it was at the top, then they weren't going to be recharging them any time soon.

The chassis rocked and settled as he gained passengers, and there was a moment when they were all ready, just sitting in the humming, spitting darkness, waiting for someone to say something.

"Lucy?"

"Copy that. Roll out."

Frank turned the front lights to the max, and eased away. The full—it was wrong to call it force—effect of the storm enveloped him. The lights, normally bright enough to turn night into day, seemed to get no further than just in front of him, and precious little reached the ground. Did he know the way to the Santa Clara? Everything familiar had been obliterated. He could get them close. That would have to do.

So: round in front of the hab, turn north-west. Travel for fifteen hundred yards, and hope.

He set the counter, brought up the virtual compass, and crawled forward. The counter ticked over, the numbers becoming indistinct. He dragged his fingers across his faceplate. And again. He ran across the rims of craters he couldn't see and would normally avoid. The suspension in the wheels responded sluggishly, adding vibrations to the slow lurching of the frame.

Fifteen hundred and two. He stopped, staring out into the ever-shifting wall of red. He couldn't focus on it. He couldn't focus through it.

"Hold up," he said. "I need to find the entrance." He unbuckled himself and pulled himself upright. "One of you needs to drive."

Isla spoke. "I'll do it."

Frank climbed down, and, with one hand on the side, walked to the back.

"OK. Release the winch. Run it free."

He pulled on the cable, then fed it behind first the back wheel, then the front wheel, so that it went directly under the buggy, to the front. He looped it around the frame. Then he fixed the heavy hitch to his waist belt and started walking.

One hundred and fifty feet, minus the fifteen for the length of the chassis. He'd gone thirty when he shuffled round, and he could just about see the pale circles of the headlights. He walked on until the cable went taut behind him.

"Isla? Dead slow. Follow the wire."

"Copy that."

The cable went slack, and Frank advanced ahead of it. His suit lights were almost useless. They illuminated the dust, not what was beyond it. He was going by feel. In a spacesuit. What the hell was he doing? It had gone from guesswork to blind chance. The valley was somewhere. And the only way he was going to find it was if he blundered into it.

"Isla? Hold up."

"Roger."

He took up the slack again, then swung right on the end of it. Nothing but the usual variation in the ground. He swung left, and in a couple of steps found himself stumbling and trying to keep his feet. With no horizon, he slipped, and fell on his knees. He must have made a sound, because Isla was immediately in his ears.

"Lance? Report. Lance?"

"I'm OK. Give me a second."

He pushed himself upright. Was this it? It was impossible to tell. It could just be a deeper crater, but there weren't really any near the top of the valley. Unless he was completely off course. He crabbed on the end of the cable. Definitely downhill in that direction.

"Isla? I want you to go forward again, and give it twenty degrees to the left. Go ten yards, then stop."

"Copy."

His waist belt relaxed, and he pulled in the excess wire, looping it over his arm. He walked forward, and the dust-load seemed to lessen. It was more blowing over him, not around him. There was a rise ahead and behind him, but not to his left, and, crucially, not to his right either, and that seemed to be lower. He paid out more cable, and suddenly, yes: there were fading, multiple tire tracks right under his feet. He'd found the Santa Clara. Goddammit, if anything deserved cracking open a cold one, it was this, and the base was dry. He'd have to make do with a cup of lukewarm coffee instead.

"OK. We're good. Forward one twenty, and watch for the lip."

He unclipped the hitch, but kept hold of it in his hands, then retreated to the far side of the valley. It wouldn't be irony to get run over by the buggy, but sheer stupidity—on his part. After what seemed an age, the moons of the buggy lights waxed over the edge of the river bank.

"Isla? Hold it."

She braked abruptly.

"Reel in the winch, and when you've done that, turn your wheels maybe thirty degrees to the right. The drop is right in front of you."

"I can't see you."

"It doesn't matter. Dead slow. Fan, put some weight on the back axle."

There was a pause, and the buggy nudged forward in a series of stutters, until the front wheels started to crumble the brittle edge of the slope.

"Forward. You've hit it straight on. Just let it go."

She did. She took the brakes off and the buggy rolled into the valley bottom. She steered to the right, presumably having spotted Frank's suit lights in the clearer air.

The second buggy appeared, and he guided it down. Lucy was a pilot. She was good at this, better than probably even Frank, and she even had the wisdom to know when she wasn't at the top of her game. Which was more than Marcy had ever done.

They were all there. All six of them, when it should have been seven. He climbed back onto the first buggy, and threaded his legs through the lattice behind the driver's seat, and next to Fan.

"Don't you want to drive?"

Truth be told, that would have been fine. He could have swapped places with Isla, and driven them all home. But walking through that red-black haze had scrambled something inside. He could see it when he closed his eyes as if it had got into his head, moving, always moving. The valley protected them from the worst that was happening bare feet above their heads, so that it was merely as bad as a smoke-choked room, rather than a living, breathing swarm of dust.

She'd be safe. It would give him a moment. A pause. He was

going to rely on her, rather than think there was no one else to do it.

"Lance?"

"If you're up to it, then I'd appreciate the lift home."

"Roger that," she said.

In the clearer air, where the headlights actually had an impact, they could go more quickly. Even as the valley broadened, the walls got higher, and it seemed to make some difference to be heading north, moving out of the storm. By the time they broached the throat of the valley and spilled out onto the Heights, the worst—the very worst—was behind and above them.

It didn't mean that there wasn't a ton of crap falling on the base. The sky-turned satellite dish was an immediate worry, and Yun hurried inside to turn it and face it away from the main direction of the wind. Sand and dust had drifted everywhere, forming ripples and dunes that squeaked underfoot like new snow.

Frank went to inspect the solar panels. Since they'd not been able to detect the sun, they hadn't turned, but at least they weren't horizontal, so hadn't accumulated a vast load. He spent ten minutes pushing the worst of the dust off the black glass surfaces with the square of parachute canopy that was usually kept tied to the frame, but he didn't think they'd be picking up much sun tomorrow. Or maybe even the day after.

"Lance?"

He kept wiping. "Lucy?"

"I'm right behind you."

He stopped and turned.

"Come on in. We're done for the day."

"I've still got a checklist I need to work through."

"Lance. I'm not losing someone else. I want you to come in."

"You didn't lose Jim, and no one blames you for that." And Jim may still be alive. But Frank didn't say that because he didn't know one way or the other. He didn't even know if it was possible.

"All the same, he's gone." The haze, the rain of dust and sand, thickened between them, then faded away again. "I know I can't make you. But I need to know that everyone is safe inside, and that they're not going out again until morning. Sunset was an hour ago, and it's still above freezing out here. We're going to be fine tonight."

"We're going to have to start turning shit off, and sooner rather than later. You know that, right?"

"Yun and Fan have already started. You're not on your own any more, Lance. You can just come on in."

She was right. It had been a hell of a day. He was beat. And the dust. The goddamn dust.

"Sure. Why not? We can check everything in the morning, right?"

"Of course we can."

He tied the parachute nylon back onto the frame and trooped after her, past the familiar shadows of the end of the med lab, and Command/Control, to the cross-hab airlock. They climbed the steps, and suddenly she was hitting him, slapping him all over.

"Hey. Hey! What you doing?"

"Getting the worst of the dust off before we go inside." She looked at him quizzically, at his raised arms and his defensive stance. "Did you think I was—You did. I'm sorry. I'm so sorry."

She put her hands up and backed away from him, as far as she could go on the narrow platform. He looked at his own hands, his gauntlets curled into fists, his shoulder pulling back and getting ready to punch through.

He had no idea of what to do or say. There was nothing that could convince her that she hadn't seen what she so clearly had.

"Just. Just unexpected. You surprised me."

"I'm sorry," she said again. "I ought to have said something first. Asked permission."

He hadn't actually struck her. That was some measure of how tired, how utterly confused he was. At any other time, he would

215

have instinctively pushed her away, hard, and then followed through with whatever came to hand.

"It's. It's OK. Yes. Some warning." He steadied himself. "OK. You can do it now."

She—initially wary—finished beating the dust away from his soft fabric coverings, then presented herself for reciprocal treatment. They'd learned this in training. Standard Operating Procedure. It was normal for them in high-dust situations. No one meant anything by it, it was just a way of extending the life of the suits, and keeping dirt out of the base.

They cycled in the airlock together, and racked their life support along with the others. Frank hung up his suit on the hanger, and picked up his overalls.

Everyone else seemed to have dispersed, doing chores, turning off equipment, checking systems. Some of those things would have been Frank's job. But they were doing it for him. Instead of him. Who was he kidding? They could run the base without him, even with a man down.

"If, if you don't need me for anything, I'm going to grab a shower."

"Lance? I made the wrong call. I didn't follow the book. None of us did. The others should have pulled me up on it. You dug us out of a hole. And I'm grateful."

She stood there, in her one-piece long johns, and she looked broken. He had nothing to offer her.

"That's . . . fine," he said. "I mean, what else am I supposed to do? This is all we've got, right? We've got to look after each other."

She nodded. "You're a good man, Lance Brack."

No. No, really, he wasn't. He wasn't even Lance Brack.

"Sure." He turned on his heel before a confession came to his lips.

He headed through to the crew hab and grabbed his towel, then pulled the folding door shut behind him in the shower. He rested his forehead against the cool of the partition and closed his eyes. Dust. All he could see was dust.

He hit the valves, turning the water on as hot as he dared, and stripped in the tiny cubicle before stepping into the scalding stream. Heat. Light. Water. He'd had his fill of Mars for the moment. Maybe it would be better in the morning. Maybe he was broken too. Maybe they all were.

He'd had worse days than this. After witnessing, and being a party to, all of that death, he'd somehow managed to hold it together, alone, on Mars. He was still here. He had no idea where that strength had come from, but he knew damn straight that he was now running on empty.

Thoughts of going home, seeing his son again. Thoughts of sticking it to XO. Notions of hope, or revenge, of simply getting off this rock. They'd gone. Everything gone.

The folding door to the cubicle flapped open.

"Goddammit. Give me a minute."

It closed again, but he was suddenly aware that there was someone in there, the other side of the curtain. Then in with him, under the water, pressed against him, arms around him, head against his shoulder.

He had no idea what to do. He probably had known once. He'd unlearned it. Like so many things.

She held him tight, and slowly, slowly he allowed himself to put his own arms around her, his fingertips pressing into her wet, so very pale, skin.

How long they stood like that, he didn't know. Just that when Isla had gone again, slipping out behind the curtain as silently as she'd slipped in, he couldn't work out if it had been real, or just a dream.

22

[Message file #149438 3/5/2049 0334 MBO Rahe Crater to MBO Mission Control]

Luisa, you know about Jim going missing. What you don't know is that there were tracks up on the volcano. Tracks made by an XO buggy, that were recent, and not made by me. You keep on telling me that M2 are gone, they're history, but I'm not buying XO's line on it. Not with Station seven, and now Jim. Is there anything, anything at all, you can tell me that they don't want me to know?

Goddammit, Luisa, if there's any chance that Jim's still alive, I need some answers soon.

[transcript ends]

Twelve hours later, Frank was able to get a message out to XO.

The dish had survived. Yun checked it out, and while the shape of it was slightly warped, the digital signal from base to orbit and back was strong enough to cover for that. It could have been worse. The dust-load could have ripped the dish from its mountings, and that would have left them almost voiceless. The DV had a low-gain antenna. It could have been retuned from the transit vehicle to the relay satellite. But it would still have been a problem.

Frank typed his message out, sent it encrypted, and waited for a reply. While he waited, he went outside—even that, cycling the airlock, charging the life support, had to be budgeted for. It was almost like the old days when he didn't have watts to burn.

The power...Declan would have either loved it or hated it. They had just enough to run the greenhouse. If it hadn't been for the hot water coming from the RTG, and the unnatural rise in the temperature outside, they'd have been sleeping in the greenhouse too. Running the scrubbers, powering the computer, keeping the dish pointed in the right direction, wasn't even break even. The battery banks had plenty of charge, but they didn't know how long the storm would sit over them. As long as usage was greater than generation, then they were simply borrowing from tomorrow for what they needed today.

He cleaned the solar panels. He turned them manually to face the east, because the electricity they consumed turning themselves was almost as much as they were generating. It should have been somewhere near fifteen kilowatts. The colored bars on his tablet showed them getting less than one.

Add that to the base load, and that was less than four kilowatts during the day. It wasn't enough. It certainly wasn't enough to recharge one buggy, let alone two, and that meant they were stuck at the bottom of the volcano until the situation changed.

The weather: looking up, all he could see was dust. The blue-pink of the sky had been replaced with a dirty brown shroud, and the sun was dim enough that he could look straight at it and not even have to blink. To the south, over the hidden summit, the sky was darker still, illuminated by lightning and growling like a distant monster.

XO had specifically threatened him and the NASA mission if he revealed anything about M2 at all. And the niggling worry remained that M2 was specifically there to make sure that Brack didn't survive Phase three. Was that him being paranoid? Possibly, but it wasn't as if XO weren't out to get him.

But if Jim had been picked up by M2, what did they want in return? Food? Shelter? OK, he could probably provide that. He could even put up an extra hab, and extend the greenhouse. It wasn't impossible to imagine, if the M2 crew were decent people who'd play ball. Whatever reason XO had had for putting them there in the first place, they'd abandoned them now, and they'd ordered Frank to abandon them too. M2 would be grateful. However many of them were left. More than zero.

Somehow he was going to have to square that circle.

He rested his fists on the side of the solar farm and side-eyed the sun. Any kind of rescue mission he might throw together wasn't going to happen any time soon, was it? Not unless he drained the batteries and left the base short. And he'd probably need two spare life support packs too, one for him, and one for Jim. One for the possibility of Jim.

He didn't need to explain what he was doing. He'd covered enough silences with the "commercially sensitive" excuse that it had become a joke. The base, the buggy, the power in the batteries, were all XO-owned. It might eat into the trust he'd earned, taking a buggy for a full day, not telling anyone where he was going, but Lucy couldn't stop him if she didn't know.

When he got back, he could just put it down to company business, and that was that. Sure, she'd chew him out. She was as much on edge as he was. But as long as he didn't do anything to jeopardize the safety of the NASA personnel, he was in the clear. He'd take her yelling at him and not say a word in complaint if that's what it took to keep them all safe.

He knew where the base was. He didn't know what condition they were in.

If M2 were dead, he didn't have to reveal anything about them.

If they weren't, and didn't have Jim, then…could he just leave them there to rot? Would they be content to stay there and dwindle away and die, knowing there was salvation just over the hill? Would Frank? Would anyone? No, of course not. That was ridiculous.

If they did have Jim? If he could bring him back with him?

Lucy would probably forgive him everything. Even if he brought the M2 survivors too.

Would XO, though? Not on current form.

What he ought to do, what would get him a straighter line back to Earth, was to simply shrug his shoulders and carry on with life at MBO. Jim hadn't followed the rules. He'd gone missing. He was presumed dead. Tough on everyone, but he'd been an idiot and he'd fucked up. Mars had taken him. Move on.

Frank needed to keep his head down, and spend the next thirteen months hoping that M2 didn't turn up again.

Put like that, it wasn't going to work, was it?

Maybe he could go over and take a look, from a distance, try and see what state they were in. If there was no obvious movement, he could get closer, poke around. If they were dead, then that was that. He could leave them with a clear conscience.

Frank frowned at himself. That word. He was going to do this, wasn't he? Of course he was.

He toured the outside of the base, making sure that the outriggers were still firmly attached to the rock, that the balloon-taut coverings weren't degrading, that the bolts that held everything together hadn't sheared or worked loose. It was his job. And still, after the initial bedding-down phase, it was remarkably robust. The structures, once up, were going to last for…what? Years? What was next? How were they going to make this permanent?

And then, joining the dots—M2 was next. And then, maybe M3. Each base building on the experience of the previous one. More rugged. More sustainable.

Was that what this was about? A land grab? On Mars? For Mars?

They had to be kidding, right? There wasn't any way they could get away with that. But then Yun's parroted words came back to him in a rush. If the Chinese government was enthusiastic about the possibilities for Mars colonization, and sought to establish their own permanent presence before the end of the

221

century, why not XO? Perhaps they wanted to get all the best sites first.

And perhaps NASA had inadvertently paid for them to get their plan off the ground with not just one base, but two. Goddammit. No wonder XO wanted M2 kept secret.

There was nothing he could do or say about that, but maybe he could give hints to Luisa that he might have finally worked it out. In the meantime, he had his chores.

He was round by the RTG pit. Sand had piled behind the hot-water tank cover, and he didn't know whether that was a good thing, adding to the insulation, or a bad thing, putting corrosive soil directly into contact with the container. He went around the windward side, and ran his hand over the white-painted cover, which had been fashioned from a supply-rocket casing. The paint came off, dusting his gauntlet like talc, revealing bare metal underneath. He knew enough about shot-blasting to know what he was seeing.

It had been abraded by the dust-storm. Which meant that the most exposed parts of the habs would also have suffered.

He kept on going around, checking. It was the hard surfaces that had suffered most. The thick plastic envelope they relied on for keeping their air in, and Mars out, hardly at all. He should still report it, both to Lucy and to XO.

The satellite dish didn't look quite right any more. There was nothing he could do about that, unless it involved taking a hammer to it. Which he was more than willing to do, if he could be certain he wouldn't be putting in more dents than he was taking out.

He'd circled the base. There wasn't anything more he could do outside, so he re-entered via the cross-hab, first shaking the dust off his feet and batting down the parts of him he could reach. Pink clouds drifted from him, rising up, and falling down, adding to the steady drizzle of material from above. Like snow. Like ash.

Inside, the base was running on night-time lights.

He went to find Lucy, who was sitting in Comms, staring at the one screen she'd turned on, looking at the power levels slowly draining away on one window, the latest weather reports on the other.

"How are we doing?"

She didn't turn around, as if it was her attention that was the only thing stopping them from descending into the freezing dark.

"We might catch a break in the next sol or two." She pulled the satellite picture forward, colored for wind speed. "Yun has been talking to Earth non-stop. We have a forty per cent chance of the storm going back over the equator by zero hours tomorrow, and sixty per cent by the next. But there's also a twenty per cent chance we get this all week, and after that it's just guessing. Not even educated guessing."

"If you're asking me what I'd do..."

"I know what I have to do. I'm putting off doing it because shutting everything down except core services and the greenhouse is going to put us in a positive energy budget. Which is the good news. We won't have to abandon the base." She screwed up her face. "But we can't restart a full scientific schedule. Not that we could. Not that we'd want to at the moment, either."

"I'm sorry," said Frank. For what felt like the hundredth time. It wasn't his fault, yet it still might be, and he wanted to fix it, and yet he couldn't.

Lucy carried on, unaware. "It's a question of how much to keep in the reserves. I'm calculating what we need: an hour a sol of dish time, tablet recharges, lights, heat, replenishment of resources, even recreation. When I've done that, then I'll tell everyone."

He told her about the abrasion. She told him it had done similar things to the suits. The fogging on the faceplates wasn't just dust. The top layer of the clear sandwich would need replacing, for everyone, which was Fan's job.

He hadn't noticed the vision problem. He'd just gotten used

to it, putting it down to the dust he couldn't be bothered to wipe off any longer.

"I'm going to take some sack time," he said. "Base is sound, for now. I'll go out again later and clean the panels, turn them."

"Thanks, Lance." She did look over her shoulder, and smiled. Forlornly.

One man down. Science all but shut down. No vehicles. Confined to base. It wasn't a great start for her.

"It's going to get better," he said.

"Not going to bring Jim back." She faced the screens again. "I'm getting turbulence from Mission Control."

"The fuckers weren't here."

"No. No, they weren't." She leaned on her elbows. "You lost anyone you were responsible for?"

"Yes," said Frank. "Yes I have."

She turned round again, looked him in the eye. "And it's at that point we're our own worst enemies, right?"

"Pretty much."

She pressed her lips together, then said: "Talk to Leland. It's what he's here for."

"I'm not really the talking type." He shrugged. "Much rather do stuff."

"Point taken. Go hit the sack. If anything happens that you need to know about, I'll call you."

She went back to staring at the numbers and the bars, and Frank walked through the yard into the crew quarters. He pulled the curtain of his cubicle closed behind him and saved the base a couple of watts by not hitting the light switch.

He wiped his tablet screen and nudged it back to life, turning the brightness down so that it didn't glare at him.

There was a reply from Luisa. She was always on duty, whatever the cycle of day/night was on Earth, and it was always she who answered him. Should that worry him? He didn't pretend that he had a "Team Frank" in the heart of the XO machine, but did the relationship he'd built up with her count enough for her to slip him information under the radar?

"We were all devastated to learn of the loss of your colleague. I'm sure you feel that as keenly as the other astronauts, and it's only human that you're looking for anything that might mean his death was anyone else's fault but his own. I'm so very sorry about Jim, but you know deep down that it's a tragic accident, the result of not following orders. It can't be anything else, because there was no one else there.

"We're going to do everything we can to help you locate your missing friend through satellite imagery. That's the best we can do, but we can do that better than most. We've a whole team on stand-by, waiting for the storm to clear.

"Jim's gone, Frank. Please don't go making trouble for yourself or the rest of MBO. I don't think I could bear it, especially after this. You need to stay safe, and come home. Luisa."

They were fine words, but he couldn't ignore the tracks he'd seen up on the summit. M2 had been up there, and recently, and if they'd done that, then maybe they knew what had happened to Jim. Every single message Luisa sent him repeated that M2 were no longer a threat, but Frank knew what he'd seen.

And just how good were XO's satellites? Because he didn't think the photos he saw every day on his tablet were sharp enough to pick out a suit. In fact, that was something he could test right now.

He went into the files, and after sorting through a few dozen thumbnails, found a picture of the Heights. He loaded it up and drilled down into it until the image had dissolved into gray, incomprehensible blocks.

That was the utter limit of the resolution. Each block was somewhere around three feet across. He wasn't going to be able to resolve an object twice that size, but he might be able to tell that there was something there, taking up that space and making the ground a different color to its surroundings.

He pulled back out and examined the picture of MBO from orbit.

The habs were obvious—the greenhouse, the crew quarters, the yard, were all sections that were twenty feet wide and sixty feet long. They cast shadows, too: the satellite dish was a black oval cast on the ground.

The buggies? He knew where to look, and yes, he could just about make them out. They weren't solid objects, though. The terrain underneath showed through the latticework of the chassis. It was the wheels that were more obvious, both in themselves and that they blocked out the light. The tracks the tires made were dark bands on the ground, indistinct and intermittent, except where the road was well traveled.

A guy in a suit? No, that was impossible. Either XO was lying about helping to find Jim, or lying about how good their resolution was.

But if that was what Luisa had told him, then he was going to have to behave as if he believed it all, in order to keep them all alive. That M2 were still out of contact. That they were dead. That they hadn't picked Jim up.

Frank was still going to have to respond with something, though. He sure as hell wasn't going to tell them what he was planning on doing. A man was missing. If there was a chance he was still alive in a base whose existence he wasn't allowed to reveal, then it was up to Frank to thread a way through all the truths and lies.

"Guess we'll just have to wait on a break in the storm, and see what you can see. I don't know if Lucy wants to keep looking. She probably will, and that'll mean going south, closer to M2. But if they're gone, I suppose that means we won't have to worry about running into them," was what he eventually typed. He pressed send, and turned off his screen.

Frank sat in the dark.

The chips could fall where they may. The first opportunity he had, he was going over.

23

From: Carolina Soledad <cmsoledad@usach.cl>
To: Miguel Averado <maaverado@usach.cl>
Date: Sun, Mar 7 2049 08:43:41 -0300
Subject: re: Lava tube project

I don't know what to make of this. I've outlined the area in red.
Please could you say what you think you see?

Carolina

[image appended HiRISE2 22 39 02 N 97 45 10 W 2/27/2048, anno-
tated]

The sky had cleared. Yun's forty per cent had lucked out. The
storm had contracted and swung south. On the other side of the
equator, Mars was still blanketed in airborne ocher dust, and it
could still come back. But Frank had been able to plug in the
buggy for a full day, without worrying about leaving the base
short, and thanks to their surfeit of generating capacity, the battery banks were mostly full.

At some point in the night, he'd dozed. But it wasn't proper
sleep. At least he was already awake for his set-off at 0300. He
hadn't said anything to anyone else. Not to Luisa, not to Lucy.

Not to Isla.

He still didn't know what that had meant. If anything. If it
had happened. If he'd hallucinated it. She'd not mentioned it.

Neither had he. It wasn't as if he could forget it, or wanted to forget it, not like some of the other things. Just that…what was he supposed to do?

It was dark when he stepped outside. He'd made absolutely certain that he hadn't woken anybody up. He'd secreted two fully charged, spare life support packs in the med bay airlock, and he went round and collected them, strapping them to the back of the buggy he was taking.

He'd be at the outpost in an hour and a half; there, he'd swap out his life support, and carry straight on over to M2. The route wasn't certain, and he'd be slowed down by the fact that he was working solely on lights.

That would eat into the energy budget, but he'd kill them as soon as the sky got light enough, shortly before dawn. He could be at his destination by, say, 0700. That would give him some poking-around time when he got over there. Unless their buggy was out and in view, M2 were unlikely to see him approach: they were in a cave, in a deep trench. He thought he could scout them out without necessarily revealing he was there. He could decide, based on what he found, what to do afterwards.

Though quite what he could do, he hadn't worked out. He was going to have to wing it, and that didn't sit well with him. The decision to go—dangerous, reckless, possibly pointless— was bad enough. All his old fears about M2 and what they could do to him came back with a vengeance.

It was still dark. Frank looked away to the south, towards the hidden summit of Ceraunius Tholus, towards the outpost, and towards M2. His guts tightened, and for a moment he had to swallow hard and breathe slowly. He had to do this. He was the only one who could.

He climbed up on the buggy, powered it up, and waited until his nose was pointing towards the dark bulk of the mountain before bringing the headlights up slowly. The ground glittered with frost, and it was hard, cracking under the wheel plates as they dug in and gripped.

He headed up the Santa Clara, and when he'd gone through the first curve of the river, flipped the lights to full. That was better. There weren't many obstacles on what was essentially a flat river bed that was now layered with even more dust, but it was the dust itself that made the going heavier than it normally was. He adjusted the responsiveness of the tires accordingly, so that they were broader and less springy.

It reminded him of his trips out away from the pressures of the base when most of the others were still alive. Driving up alone, and just taking in the view from further up: the sky, Rahe crater, the distant bulge of Uranius Tholus. A few minutes of peace, before descending again. The days before he'd known what XO had planned for him.

Eventually, he worked his way out onto the summit plain, and there, despite his expectations, was the outpost, apparently intact and unharmed. Though he knew with his head that the wind couldn't really exert any pressure, his experience of the storm had been overwhelming. If all he'd encountered was a few shreds of plastic clinging to twisted metal, he wouldn't have been surprised—but a quick tour of the outside told him that it was still bolted down, still under pressure, still functioning. The air was clear—not rain-washed, but scoured—and the cold probably helped to settle what was left of the dust that might have otherwise been blowing around. He checked the temperature, and it had dropped over a hundred degrees from yesterday.

The leeward side of the hab was higher than the windward. Dust and sand had dropped there, and now had frozen into place. The other side was blasted clean down to the bedrock. All traces of tracks and footprints had been erased, wherever they'd lain.

The aluminum supports and rings were almost mirror-like where they were exposed to the wind, enough that he could catch his own reflection. Suit lights and blank face. Unrecognizable as himself.

He picked off one of the life supports from the buggy and

carried it into the airlock. The surface of the door was smoother than it had been. Some of the detailing had flattened. The look of the door seal had changed too, from plump and effective to worn and thin. They had some spares. He needed to swap that out before it failed.

But the pressure held as he pumped the airlock up, and because he was alone, he had to climb out of his suit in order to exchange life supports. His old one still had a good six hours in it. He'd probably swap it out again when he passed this way on the return leg; he just wanted the buffer that a fresh one would give him.

Goddammit, it was cold. Cold enough that the sweat on his feet threatened to stick to the floor panels. He should have thought of that. Everything he touched was at below minus one hundred. He was going to get burns. The main base never got that cold. Even when they hadn't had heating. Stupid to get frostbite or hypothermia. Careless. Dangerous.

Quickly, then. Get one of the jackets the crew used and stand on that while pulling the pack from its clips, and plugging the new one in, then scrambling into the insulated spacesuit as fast as he dared. He thumbed the "close" tab on his control panel, and waited for the heated air to start circulating again while he ran on the spot and clapped his hands together, trying to get his circulation going again.

When he and Zeus had hauled an airlock out with them onto the eastern plain beyond Rahe, in order to collect the last of their wayward supplies, it had been difficult to change life supports in such a cramped space, and cold for sure. On the way back now, it would be day, and the outside temperature would have gone up as far as freezing, and that would be OK. Certainly not as bad as he'd just experienced: he'd done himself some damage this time, because he hadn't thought it through.

He curled his toes, clenched his fingers. He could still feel everything, which was good, but he'd scorched his fingertips and the soles of his feet. Yes, he'd learned, and he'd lived. He was damn certain he wouldn't be doing that again without taking extra measures.

Outside, it was only getting colder. And maybe it was the fact that he was higher than Everest that should have given him the clue as to just how cold it was going to get. Cold things were brittle. He'd have to be extra careful, because breaking plates, or worse, bearings, was going to leave him stranded and in trouble. There'd been no real choice in his route, though: going around the base of the mountain would have been a round trip of over two hundred miles, and completely out of range.

Frank climbed up and restarted the buggy, and headed initially towards the caldera, in order to get past the next river valley. He'd then turn south, around the CT-B crater, and follow the direction of the lava flows down to the plain again. There was a good stretch of flat ground before the trench, before more hilly terrain, caused by a huge impact crater off to the south-west.

He rumbled on, feeling the vibration in his hands and his spine, as the frozen ground hammered under the tires. He kept the suspension loose, reasoning that he needed all the grip he could get. After what seemed an interminable stretch across the broad summit, he started feeling the bite of the straps against his chest, holding him in his seat. Downhill.

He'd gone further than he ever had done before, well beyond the area they'd searched during the dust-storm. No tracks, and neither was there an astronaut's body, encircled with blown sand. His lights deepened the shadows and made them solid, but he could pick out the few craters that he needed to avoid and steer around them.

The headlights, and staring at the patch of illuminated ground ahead of him, ruined his night vision, but even so he could see one of the moons of Mars dash overhead in the dark sky, and the first lightening of the sky over to the east—just a hint, a pinking of the black. He could see faint features out on the plain that stretched from the foot of the volcano, as far as the horizon.

The fuel cell was... OK. The drive up was always draining, and even though he could ease off now, he faced the same climb on the way back. Better keep an eye on that. His suit was good, though, and the temperature, now that he was off the very top of the mountain, was no longer quite as low, while still being triple-figures negative. 0500. Dawn in an hour or so.

He drove on, and on. Features in the distance didn't seem to come any closer, even though the ground was speeding past underneath him. But it did grow gradually lighter, and eventually he killed the buggy lights completely. He was so far from home, in a landscape that was completely unfamiliar to him, even by Mars's standards.

Then he was at the bottom. One last bump of the tires as they dropped off the lava shelf and into the sand sea, and he was within twenty miles of his target. An hour there, an hour back to this point. 0540. He'd made good time.

From now on, he'd be making a dust plume behind him, but it was still very early, and it wasn't likely that anyone would be ranging out beyond the immediate vicinity of M2. He checked his air, and his fuel cell levels again. His suit was still fine. His fuel cell? He made some quick calculations. If he could get back to the top, then there'd be no problem. He could coast down to the Heights, even if he had to walk from there. He wasn't in that zone yet, but he'd have to watch it all the same.

The sun broke into the sky. Shadows, which had grown diffuse and gray, sharpened, and the land turned rose-red for a moment. Then the frost started to boil away, and fog blanketed the ground, so thickly that Frank stopped for the time it took for it to mostly disperse again.

When it had, he could see clearly the hilly country around the big impact crater miles off to the south-west. He wasn't going to miss the trench, which was closer and more or less due south. Everything was going well enough.

There was no evidence he'd been seen, yet.

The quality of the vibrations in his hands changed as he left the plain and drove up onto the more chaotic debris. A surface layer of dust hid blocks of rock thrown hard and fast along with the pulverized and melted debris. It was like driving over broken concrete in places, so seeking out the deep tracts of sand was worthwhile.

Then there it was. The ground in front of him seemed to stop. A few yards more, and he could see across to the other side, the steep cliff edges with their bands of exposed rock, black blocky lava and lighter material sandwiched between. He coasted to a halt, and slowly, stiffly, dismounted from the buggy.

As he walked to the edge, he realized he was closer to the cave entrance than he thought. And it was a proper cave—an overhanging shelf of rock on top gave way to an almost sculpted arch underneath. Smooth sides and a gradual curve down to the floor of the trench, where it obviously continued. Not a circular tube, but oval, wider than it was tall, but even with solidified lava filling the lower part of the channel, it was easily a hundred feet high.

There'd been a rockfall in the past. Big chunks of the roof, some as large as an apartment building, lay where they'd fallen in the approaches to the tunnel, but they didn't block the way. He couldn't see the back of the cave. It could run for a short distance. It could run for miles. There was no way of telling from the outside.

But he could see the top of the descent ship, landed squarely in the middle of the trench, a couple of hundred feet away from the entrance, sitting in a field of broken rock and sand. It looked more or less intact. Slightly at an angle, perhaps, but it wasn't on the flattest of terrain.

And over there, in clear ground, was a small solar farm—Frank guessed at maybe three to five kilowatts—dumb panels already pointing at the rising sun, which illuminated the trench east to west with ruddy light. MBO was supposed to have ten in the initial stages, and it now had fifteen.

It had fifteen because XO had allowed him to think M2's panels were spares for MBO. Of course they had, since M2 didn't officially exist.

How did they expect to keep this hidden again? It was literally right there, in plain sight. Certainly, the descent ship was. Maybe he could make out the pale curve of a hab inside the cave, and maybe he was imagining it. The abrasion on his faceplate made fine detail difficult.

The airwaves were dead. He tried every channel, including the common one they'd all shared during set-up. There was no traffic at all. Not even a hiss. No messages and no carrier. Random clicks and pops. Nothing meaningful. No comms, the man had said. No comms. If they'd taken Station seven, then the parts or the expertise hadn't been enough.

It looked dead. Nothing was moving.

There was nothing else for it. He was going to have to drive down and take a closer look.

It was four miles east to the start of the trench, and five miles back west to the cave entrance. He checked his air and fuel again, and yes, he could probably spend an hour picking over the site before he had to leave to get back to the outpost.

The ramp down into the trench was wide and shallow, pocked with craters filled with sand. It gradually narrowed, and the walls rose to form cliffs: rocks that had fallen from them littered the floor, but they didn't seem to have rolled all the way into the middle of the depression. By the time he drew level with the ship, the trench walls were towering over him, and the tunnel mouth was a black pit.

There. He could just make out a single hab, side on. Presumably there'd be other habs stretching back into the cave. If they had them. If they had the means of inflating them and heating them with such a paltry amount of power. He couldn't imagine running a greenhouse on that few watts, and there was no sign yet they'd picked up their RTG.

They had to be dead. Surely, they had to be. He'd wasted his time, put his cover story at risk, and maybe blown it with XO and put the NASA mission in jeopardy. No one could survive with so little kit, and for how long? Almost four months now?

He almost turned back there and then. But he'd come all that way, and he was going to go and check, just to make sure. Put his mind, finally, at rest. And maybe then he could actually get some sleep.

And there. A single figure, slouching their way towards the panels. Frank sat stock still. They didn't appear to have spotted him, or the buggy. They weren't looking for him, and they were intent on something else.

That wasn't an XO-issue spacesuit, like the one Frank wore. Nor was it like the one the M2 crew member wore who he'd previously met. It was—goddammit—a NASA suit. He was close enough to make out the color-splash of the mission patch.

Jim. Jim's suit.

Frank urged the buggy forward, and got within about thirty feet before he finally entered the astronaut's eyeline. They turned towards him, reflecting the morning sun across their faceplate. They stopped. They took a step back.

Shrugging off the harness, Frank jumped from the buggy seat and clambered down, running across the sand and shouting: "Jim! Goddammit, Jim, you lucky, lucky—"

But it wasn't Jim. It was the man from the M2 buggy. Who, naturally, recognized him. But it was definitely Jim's suit. Name tape. Little American flag. Mission patch on the arm. He wasn't mistaken.

"Where's Jim?" Frank said instinctively. But there were no comms. Nothing over the airwaves. He was going to have to communicate in a different way.

The astronaut peered at Frank through a faceplate that was

as scuffed as his own. He looked like...he looked like shit. If he was gaunt before, now he looked old. A wizened old man, who reached up and tapped the side of his helmet with two fingers.

Frank knew what he needed to do, but he hesitated. This was M2, and at first glance, it wasn't a viable base. This guy—these guys?—should be dead by now. If they were here to stake a claim on Mars, then they weren't doing so great—and were hardly the threat he'd built them up in his mind to be.

But this man had Jim's suit. Frank had to know why.

He gestured you-me-talk, and warily shuffled closer. The man wasn't empty-handed. He had a manual wrench. Light-weight, sure, but all the weight was at one end. Frank had a nut runner, and that was it.

They were within arms' reach. Then closer still. The other guy seemed just as nervous as Frank at this encounter. Surely, he knew what he was going to ask?

Their helmets touched. Frank tried to stand where he could see the wrench. "Jim Zamudio. Where is he?"

"He's inside."

Goddammit. He was alive after all.

"You're wearing his suit."

"Said I could borrow it. I had a problem with mine, right?"

"Sure. In there?" Frank pointed to the hab. "How did he even get here?"

"I was up on the volcano. Found him lost. Anyways, he's in the hab. Go on in."

The man broke contact, but Frank purposely resumed it with a click of perspex.

"You were up on the volcano. And you were, what, ten minutes away from safety, yet Jim let you come all the way back here. Nearly three hours away?"

"I don't know what you're saying. Ten minutes?"

"We've got a hab up on the top. It's got air, and a radio. Jim would have been able to guide you back to it."

"Well, he was in a bad way. He wasn't making much sense."

"You said you found him lost. He had plenty of air. As much as I did." This wasn't adding up.

"The suit was faulty, OK? Just get inside and see for yourself. I got to get on here, and you're using up my airtime."

The man broke contact again, more determinedly, and he gestured towards the hab. His lips were moving, but the sound couldn't travel between them.

Frank dragged him back by the arm. "His suit was faulty, and you're wearing it now. I thought it was your suit that wasn't right."

Then his prison senses kicked in. We want to discuss something, just step in here where the guards can't see you and the cameras don't cover. Frank reflexively stepped away, even though previously, yes, it had been him pulling the man closer.

His helmet rang like a gong, and suddenly, he was down. Tripped. Pushed. And the figure leaning over him was holding a wrench over their head, about to bring it down hard on Frank's suit controls.

Frank kicked out, taking out the astronaut's legs, and rolled awkwardly away, scrambling to his feet. The other guy stood up and closed the distance between them, swinging the wrench, but telegraphing each move so that Frank didn't have to do much in the way of dodging, but instead just backed away.

He'd backed away too far. The other man was now between him and the buggy. He threw the wrench at Frank—badly aimed, and it glanced off his carapaced shoulder on the way past—then started to climb up the buggy's chassis on the way to the driver's seat.

What was he doing? Hijacking the buggy? No. Obviously, stopping him from driving away. Frank jumped, grabbed the man's leg, and pulled. The man's other foot came away from the side of the tire he had wedged it against, and he was now hanging by his arms, with Frank hanging from him. He kicked out at Frank, missed because Frank had moved sharply out of the way, and still he hung on. He tried to carry on climbing with just his hands. Despite his weakness, his furious intensity dragged Frank across the sand. He tried to shake Frank off with another kick.

Frank felt the blow against his chest, a solid punch that nevertheless did nothing but leave a boot mark against the white plastic. He took the foot he was holding on to, and he wrenched it around by more than a right angle. He felt something give at the same time as the man in Jim's suit went rigid. He could pull him off the buggy easily now, and Jim's helmet hit the sand hard.

The wrench was too far away to retrieve, so Frank pulled his nut runner from his belt and pinned the man face-down in the dirt. He banged on the other man's helmet with the nut runner once, twice, three times: hard enough to send a message and perhaps disorientate, but not enough to crack the seals.

He had to turn to check he wasn't being bounced from behind. He'd hear nothing. He'd see nothing outside of the narrow window in front of him. But they were still alone. The hab's airlock stayed closed.

He knelt down, bent his head low until their helmets touched. He could hear groaning, but that wasn't his priority right now.

"What have you done with Jim?"

No answer.

Frank took his nut runner and banged on Jim's helmet again.

"What have you done with him?"

"Go to hell!"

OK. Frank adjusted his position slightly so that he could put his weight on the man's ankle.

"One last time," he shouted through the screaming. "Where is Jim Zamudio? Is he alive or dead?"

He lifted his foot to ease the pressure. He could hear the man inside Jim's suit panting.

"He's...he's..."

How difficult would it be to say "alive" if Jim was actually alive? He clawed his fingers around the mission patch on the spacesuit's arm and ripped it free. He tucked the patch into his belt pouch, reholstered his nut runner, then looked again at the cave entrance. Suit lights. One. Another. Goddammit. Coming towards him. Fast.

Frank scrambled up into the buggy seat, and didn't bother to strap himself in before he gripped hard on the accelerator triggers. The wheels spun before the tire plates dug in, and he jerked away, bouncing over the ground, heading past the descent ship, on his way towards the end of the trench. The rattling of the frame grew too much, and he slowed momentarily to buckle up.

He also activated his rear-view cameras. The tiny screen told him what he suspected. Dust plumes. Two of them. Right behind him.

24

From: Mohammed Aziz <m.aziz@jpl.nasa.gov>
To: Jay Fredericks <jgfredericks@berkeley.edu>
Date: Sun, Mar 7 2049 23:26:21 -0700
Subject: re: interference

Jay,

I can assure you that those transmissions were not from MBO, the DV, the MAV or the TV [transit vessel]. They ran full diagnostics, and there's no leakage. Yes, I know what the next question is, and no, I have no idea where it actually came from. I'll get back to you once we've locked that down. We are definitely working on it. I'm sure you realize it's not our top priority at the moment.

Mo

Even though Frank had been sent to prison for murder, not car-jacking, he was still going to give outrunning his pursuers his best shot, because what choice did he have otherwise? Suffer the same fate as Jim? Whatever that was.

He pointed himself in the direction of the summit of Cerau-nius and tightened the suspension. This was going to get dif-ficult. The vibrations in the frame—constant, with frequent big hits as he clattered against a rock—made it all but impossi-ble to see out of the rear-facing cameras. He managed fleeting glimpses of something, but unless he slowed down, he wouldn't know where the M2 buggies were. He couldn't turn around in his seat. He wasn't going to swerve the buggy to give him a view beyond his ten-to-two. He was never going to hear them behind him either.

He'd just have to hang on and hope that it was enough.

His front wheels skimmed a ridge, and he was airborne. Torque control slowed the motors, and when he landed, he landed hard. It took him moments he probably didn't have to get up to speed again, until the next time it happened. And the next. Would he be going faster if he actually slowed down? Less airtime meant more wheels-in-the-dirt time. He didn't know. He couldn't judge. Marcy would know. Marcy would be able to get him out of trouble because she was a pro, and not a rank amateur like he was.

The plain. Better. Deeper dust, fewer rocks.

The nose of the buggy dipped down, chewed up a plume of red soil, and then dug itself out of the hole it had made.

Frank acknowledged that for all his time on Mars, getting into what amounted to a car chase was something that he hadn't prepared for. No streets, no buildings, no other traffic. He was just being driven down.

He looked at the shaky picture from the rear-facing cameras. Nothing. He could see only the distant horizon. Did that mean they'd given up, that he was sweating bullets running from people who weren't chasing him any more? Did he dare swing left, swing right, to check? Not just yet.

He wondered at which point were they going to give up. When Frank reached the volcano? Halfway up? All the way to the top? If it depended on when their fuel cells or their gas reached fifty per cent, that was nothing he could control. They could chase him all the way home, come to that, except they'd be pretty much out of air. They were all hammering their buggies hard, driving in such a way that wasn't efficient use of the stored energy. Their ranges were decreasing faster than the miles they covered.

Crap. He was going to have to do something, wasn't he?

So, laying it out. He was on his way home. The only thing he needed to worry about was whether he had enough watts and tanked air to make it back to MBO. They were on their outward leg, so they needed to keep enough in store to make it back, and the further they went, the more they'd need. Also, Frank only had to stay ahead, while they had to stop him. That meant cutting him off. Boxing him in at least. They didn't have comms, but maybe they could talk to each other like the NASA suits could, when they got close enough. That meant they could coordinate their attack.

Frank had a pretty good idea of what was at stake for him here if he lost this. His hard-won, if limited, freedom. His future trip back to Earth. Possibly his life. And just possibly the lives of all the NASA astronauts. He still didn't know whether to count Jim among the living or the dead.

Just how much skin did his pursuers have in the game? What did they want from him? His suit? His buggy? Him? He didn't know, and he sure as hell wasn't going to make it easy for them.

He caught movement in the corner of his eye. He turned his head, and just saw more of the inside of his helmet. He straightened back up again, and shifted his hips slightly so he could turn his shoulders.

Goddammit. One of them had drawn level with him, fifty feet off his left-hand side. He checked the right, and as far as he could see, there was nothing there. He glanced down at the camera screen.

Right behind. Right. Behind. He swung left, and right, and it was there, just off his rear wheel.

"OK, I have no idea how this works, but screw you anyway."

He flexed his fingers momentarily, letting go of the paddles, and the other buggy zipped by. He clenched them again, and now it was him who was behind.

Dust was streaming off the tires like spray, and he was in it.

He couldn't see. He nudged the wheel over, and then he was in the clear air between the tracks. Their buggies had no lights. No winch. No cameras. To the guy in front, he'd effectively disappeared.

Which meant he was about to turn and try and pick him up again.

Frank eased off again, letting the distance between them increase by ten feet, twenty feet. The buggy to his left was turning in a wide arc, still ahead, but easing rightwards. The one he was tailing would be told where Frank was, but he wouldn't *know*. The driver would have to make that turn soon. Left, or right?

Left. It heeled over, and the buggy threatened to tip. It slowed hard as it tried to make the curve, and the wheels came up, spinning fast and useless on the side facing Frank. Who squeezed hard and thanked his good sense to strap in.

He rammed the buggy, his nose against their rear wheel, his own tires away from the collision point. The plates clattered hard against the lattice framework, and one sheared off, spinning high into the air, sharp and fast. Frank felt the impact, the juddering as the tire ground against the metalwork, could hear the rattle and the whine of the motor.

He dug in, spreading his own plates wide for maximum traction. And shoved. The other buggy tilted and tipped. He was almost under it now, and they were still moving. If he twisted the steering column left, he'd have most of a buggy on top of him. He'd be a sitting target for the second one. So turn it right.

Higher. Higher still. Now. He pulled the column over as far as he dared, and the M2 buggy was on its side, careering across the dust, wheels a blur, and—it must have hit a rock—took off. It sailed up, tumbling, and came down hard before flipping again, rolling like it was in a barrel. It came to a rest upside down, the driver hanging from their harness, arms extended limply towards the ground.

Frank had no time to check for damage. The other buggy was barreling round ahead of him, and heading back in his direction.

He steered around the wreck and wondered how he should handle this. There was one obvious way. If he got it wrong, they might all die out here. If he called it right, then he could still make it home.

Home. Was that what MBO was? No time to unpack that just now. He looked at the dust plume ahead of him as it turned from something he saw side-on to seeing it head-on.

How brave was he? Honestly, he wasn't brave at all. He'd proved that again and again, taking the path of least resistance at each moment until all he was left with was the extremes. He'd only killed Brack because that was the only thing he could do apart from be killed himself. It had been all very matter-of-fact. He could fight for others. But not for himself.

The M2 buggy stopped. So did Frank. There was no one behind, or to the sides. They were alone out there. No one was going to stand as a witness to this, except maybe a satellite and God, and Frank didn't believe in God. He checked his fuel and air. Tight. Even the air. He'd done lots of hard breathing, and he'd used up more than he'd expected. He had enough to get himself to the outpost. He still had one full life support pack strapped to the back of the buggy, but he needed an atmosphere to change it in. Not really something he could do while being chased.

He started forward. Gradually, he built up speed until he hit about fifteen. The other buggy was half a mile away across the plain, standing between him and the volcano's lower slopes. It started moving too, dust rising up behind it, falling down again like water.

Frank wondered if the other driver had worked out which game they were playing yet.

They were closing on each other, both at quite modest speeds. That wasn't the way to do it. This had to be all or nothing. A cataclysmic crash, or one of them bailed. That was it. Of course, they could both steer away at the last second, but there was no guarantee of survival if they still hit each other.

Forty, fifty miles an hour wasn't really that fast. They'd both probably live through the crash. But their transports wouldn't. They'd be left to suffocate together, out of reach of help. That was the kicker.

There were so many different ways to die on Mars.

Closer. Frank could see the driver's pale spacesuit now. The other guy would be able to see his. There was nowhere to hide. Time to go all out. He squeezed down hard, felt his buggy respond, and he dialed back the suspension until it was taut once more. The ground rattled his bones, and the wheels skipped from crest to crest.

The speedo crept up. Twenty. Twenty-one. Twenty-two.

They were getting close. He saw the driver hunched over the controls, faceless, almost immobile, just like he was, crouched, tense. Waiting for the smash.

Then, barely before it had started, it was over.

The other guy blinked first. He wheeled away, sliding sideways through the soft sand to a halt, and Frank was tearing by, heading for the lava flows as they swept down to the plain.

He was drenched with sweat, but he was laughing. Goddammit, he'd gotten away with it. Chicken. In a spacesuit. On Mars.

He eased off as he reached the volcano, and swung round to take in a view of the southern plain before he pointed himself back north for his ascent.

There, in the distance, were the two buggies, one just arriving at the place where the other had come to rest. Frank didn't think he'd killed the guy: the roll cage would have taken the impact, but it would have hurt all the same. Loosened some fillings at least. He might have damaged the buggy more. He didn't know how much rough-housing one would take, but being flipped over and bounced several times wasn't going to do it any favors. There wasn't much to go wrong, but if he'd bent one of the hubs, that might not even be fixable.

They weren't in a position to chase him now. They'd have to go back to M2. What they'd do after that was anyone's guess.

But the question as to whether he could now tell Lucy about them had been settled. He was going to tell her everything. And by everything, he meant everything. He had Jim's mission patch—proof that M2 had been up on the mountain that day. Proof they'd found him. Beyond that, Frank wasn't prepared to say. But Jim could be alive inside the M2 hab. There wasn't any real wriggle room in that. Oh, he could lose the patch, pretend, but…he'd changed. He didn't know if that meant something else was broken, or that something else had been fixed: he just wasn't the same Franklin Kittridge who'd got himself sent to Mars.

He owed Lucy. He owed them all. And Jim was one of them.

XO weren't going to like that. Maybe he could shut the dish off, like he had before when he wanted to stop Brack from phoning home, while he made his confession. Give everyone the chance to work out what to do, what to say.

He wasn't expecting the news of his and XO's deception to be greeted with enthusiasm. Lucy would be well within her rights to cuff him and kick him out of the airlock. He was guessing she wouldn't, because they were all decent people—better than he was, for certain—and maybe they'd realize he was victim in all of this too.

Or maybe that wouldn't matter. Lucy's role was to make sure her team was safe. She'd know, because Frank would tell her, that she had a killer on the base. Loose. Living among them.

Perhaps this wouldn't be so straightforward after all.

But at least he could use his own name again, and not that of the man who tried to kill him. He wouldn't have to pretend any more to be something he wasn't. Not an intrepid resourceful pioneer on the cutting edge of human endeavor, but a convicted murderer, a liar, a survivor.

When he'd handed himself in to the police, he'd known what to expect. Arrest. Questioning. Arraignment. Trial. Sentence. Jail. Divorce. Death. That path had been mapped out for him the moment he'd pulled the trigger and put that bullet in Mike's dealer. Someone who had only a few years on Mike.

Goddammit, Frank. You really fucked up there.

He was going to leave it to Lucy. He was just sitting there, using air. He needed to get back, whatever the outcome. He turned the buggy up the volcano, and headed for the top. The climb ate hard into the fuel cell, even at a reduced speed, and by the time he'd finally reached the summit, he was nursing the watts. He reckoned he had just enough to get down the other side, without having to get off and push. Probably. There was a mode where he could disengage the hub motors and let the wheels run free, specifically designed to make it possible to retrieve a dead buggy with a live one using a tow unit: he could use that to coast downhill. But if he had to get off and walk, he would. The other buggy would be charged up. Recovery would be easy.

He was going to swap out his life support again, though. The one he'd left at the outpost had around six hours left in it; the one he was wearing had less than two.

"Lance. Lance Brack. Come in. Over."

He was in range of the repeater at the outpost. The signal was choppy, squashed to hell and back, but he could just about make out the words. Deep breath then.

"I'm here. Voice isn't great. Over."

"—hell have you been? Over."

"OK. If I'm going to say anything, I'm going to call it 'commercially sensitive' and leave it at that. I've been doing XO business. Over."

"—told us. You should have told—"

"Who is this? Over."

"—cy."

"OK. Lucy. I'm hearing half of what you say. I had XO business." He was conscious that anything he broadcast now would go into the databank and XO could just lift the information right out of it. He was going to tell them in person, or not at all. Certainly not like this. "I'm going to be back at MBO in an hour and a half. I'll see you when I get in."

"—just wander——where you're going. Over."

Frank had had a hard day already, and it was barely past noon. The signal was crappy, because of storm damage to the repeater, or low battery power, or something like that, and he just didn't have the energy to argue about this shit.

"If you don't like the arrangement, you know who to complain to. Over and out."

He considered turning off his suit's transmitter, but the airwaves remained silent. He looked down to his right, and could see into the caldera: almost at the outpost, then.

He followed the edge at a respectful distance, and crossed the open ground before angling north-west towards the lone hab. It looked entirely different again to what it had seemed in the dark, and what it resembled in the middle of a storm. Just a hab, wind-blown, abraded, pinker than usual due to the dust that had filled the microscopic indentations in the plastic covering. The solar panels—just a kilowatt array, aimed upwards—had either been blown or knocked over, and lay face-down in the dirt.

He parked up next to the array, and on dismounting picked it up and shook it clean, setting it back on its legs again. He made sure the cable was still attached, as he did for the telescopic antenna that served the repeater station. He'd have to come up again, give the hab a full check, over-pressure it and make sure nothing was going to give suddenly. That could be as early as tomorrow, if he was ever allowed to leave the base again. He'd have to have that argument too.

Before heading into the airlock—and he was supposing that

it would be a manual vent—he turned round and looked at his buggy. The life support pack strapped behind the driver's seat told him he'd failed. He'd gone out to find Jim, and bring him back to his friends. Even dead.

But he hadn't even managed that. All that way, all that danger, and all he had to show for it was a torn mission patch.

25

From: Mark Bernaberg <mbernaberg@lpl.arizona.edu>
To: Jay Fredericks <jgfredericks@berkeley.edu>
Date: Mon, Mar 8 2049 05:12:15 -0700
Subject: re: interference

Jay,

Maybe I can help you with your rogue transmission? Research student in Chile spotted this, south-eastern edge of Ceraunius Tholus. You know we weren't allowed by XO to cover Rahe during MBO construction due to "issues pertaining to commercial confidentiality", but if you want to compare that picture with the press shots of the DV, then—that's pretty much the cat out of the bag.

That's an XO ship, or I owe you dinner.

Mark

Frank rolled most of the way down the Santa Clara. He had just enough watts to drive the last half-mile across the Heights to MBO, but the fuel cell warning had been on for five minutes by that point. He parked up outside the workshop, and immediately plugged the buggy into the power system.

Then he inspected the damage. The front was scraped and dented where he'd used it as a battering ram. There were bright ridges along the right side where the tire plates had made their mark. His own buggy's plates were more dinged than before. He'd got off remarkably lightly himself, all things considered. A touch of frostbite on his hands and feet. A few more gray hairs.

He entered through the cross-hab, carrying a life support pack in each hand, and as he expected, Lucy was there, waiting for him. She said nothing while he went through the routine of climbing out, racking his equipment, and re-dressing in his too-small overalls.

He tugged on his ship slippers and straightened up in front of her.

"You owe me an explanation," she said. "All of us. Come through to the kitchen."

"I'm guessing 'commercially sensitive' doesn't cut it any longer."

"Not any more, Lance. Come and sit down. We need to talk."

"It doesn't sound any better coming from you than it did from my wife."

She instinctively glanced down at his third finger, left hand. "Wife?"

"Ex-wife. At least let me make myself a coffee."

"Someone will make you coffee, Lance." She took a deep breath. "Just...come."

He snaffled Jim's mission badge from his pouch under cover of unclipping his tablet, and followed her through the connecting corridor. They were all there. Isla and Fan opposite—Lucy took the spare seat between them, leaving him to sit between Yun and Leland. Lucy gave the barest of nods to Leland, who got up to pour hot water on some coffee granules. He put the mug down in front of Frank, and resumed his place.

Frank looked at the tabletop and screwed his face up.

There was a silence after they'd all settled. No one spoke until Lucy leaned across and into his eyeline. "Lance?"

"Lucy."

"We reported your absence to Mission Control. Wasn't much

else we could do. XO sent through a whole slew of records. About your psychotic episodes. Your hallucinations. Your rambling late-night messages to someone called 'Luisa'. How you think you're really someone called Franklin Kittridge? That you're a convicted murderer sent to Mars as a punishment? Is... is that right?"

Frank looked up. Goddammit. He hadn't seen that coming.

That was actually a stroke of fucking genius. No one was going to believe a single word he said from now on. He could be protesting his sanity from now until whenever, and that'd simply be reinforcing XO's story.

He started to laugh.

"What's so funny, Lance?"

Frank calmed himself down and slurped down some of his coffee. It was only lukewarm, but it was still better than he'd got in San Quentin. A long way to go for some decent joe.

"I give up," he said. "I haven't got the energy to fight this any more. You can do what the hell you like with me."

Lucy glanced at Leland. Perhaps that wasn't the reaction either of them was expecting.

Leland shuffled on his seat and said: "You went dirtside with two spare LS units. In the middle of the night. For hours. Where did you go?"

"I went to look for Jim."

Again, from the tremor of disquiet that moved around the table, not the answer they'd thought they'd get.

"Did you find him?"

"No. I was able to get this, though." Frank reached into his pocket and tossed the mission patch into the middle of the table.

Everyone stared at it for the longest while. Then Fan reached forward and dragged it back towards him. He examined it, the loose threads hanging off the embroidered edge, the dust ingrained on the face, the paleness of the backing. He passed it to Lucy.

"Where," she asked, wagging it at Frank, "did you get this?"

"You're not going to believe a word of this, so I'm thinking why should I even bother." Frank watched Lucy grow even more cold, more controlled. "But this is about Jim and where he is, so you're just going to have to shut up and listen until I've finished."

He caught the gaze of everyone around the table, held it until they looked away. Isla... what was that expression even about? He didn't know.

"Deal?"

"Tell us," said Leland. "We won't interrupt."

Frank pinched the bridge of his nose. "So there's another XO base, eighty miles south of here. They call it M2."

"A manned base?"

"Goddammit, Fan."

"Sorry. Go on."

"It's been there maybe three, four months." He stopped. "Look, this is difficult to explain without giving you the whole backstory, but let me just give you the edited highlights. Half the equipment we're using is theirs. They've got a total comms failure, and they can't find their supply drops. But I could, and XO were so determined to keep M2 secret from me that they told me their stuff was a resupply for MBO. I didn't know anything about it until I happened across one of them out on the plain, east side of the volcano, before you arrived even. XO swore me to secrecy. Said you weren't to know. They were prepared to let M2 fail and everyone in it die if it meant keeping it hidden.

"And I had my own reasons for not wanting to go over there, which you're not going to believe because XO have poisoned that well. Let's just jump forward to when Station seven vanished. I'd been told that there was no way M2 could have survived, yet I knew it was them who'd taken it. I wanted to tell you about M2 at that point. XO said that if I did, they'd sabotage MBO and if anyone died, that'd be my fault. So I said nothing."

Lucy gave him the side-eye. Words started to form, then she pressed her lips shut again.

"Then Jim disappeared. Maybe you were right. Maybe this was something to do with caves and ice and stuff like that. Maybe he'd had a suit malfunction. Maybe, hell, I don't know, he just wandered off. It can be like that some days. And when we couldn't find him, I thought maybe I'll go and see M2. See if they really are as dead as XO says. Turns out they're not."

The silence dragged on, and grew more awkward.

Finally Lucy placed the torn mission patch on the table between them. "Are you saying that someone from this other base, this M2, gave you Jim's patch?"

Frank scrubbed at his face. "I wouldn't say 'gave'. There was a guy outside—the same guy who I'd met on the east side—wearing Jim's suit. He told me Jim was inside their hab, wanted me to go in too. I felt something was off, and when he realized I wasn't going to do that, he tried to beat my brains out with a wrench. We...fought."

"In spacesuits?"

"Of course we did it in fucking spacesuits! He tried to take my buggy. I broke his ankle and ripped the patch off his arm and got the hell out. They chased me. There's damage to the buggy." He scratched at his stubble again. "I got away. I came back here. That's pretty much it. Apart from all the other stuff."

"You know, this is..."

"Sure." Frank swilled the remains of his coffee. Properly cold now. He grimaced. "What are you going to do now?"

She shrugged helplessly. "This has to do with the safety of the base and the mission. That is my responsibility. You disappearing off with mission-critical equipment with no explanation is...And the information XO has sent through? That they didn't tell us en route, or after we landed: their excuse was they thought you were getting better, with us arriving. I'm going to leave that to the people back home. Right now, you're my problem. Fan and Leland are going to take you through a thorough medical assessment. Which I'm going to arrange for you to fail."

"I don't think you'd have to get them to lie," said Frank.

Yun, silent until now, said quietly. "Lance, what have you done with Jim?"

"I haven't done anything with Jim. I don't know if he's alive and in M2, or…not. I just saw his suit. If you want answers, you'll have to ask M2. But they don't seem keen on answering that question. I did try."

"When we first lost him, and you went out on your own to look, did you find him out on the volcano? Did you take his patch then? Was he still alive at that point?"

"I didn't find him."

"Is there really an M2? Or is that a—"

"Yun. I can show you on the fucking map. You can see the descent ship."

"If that's so, then—"

"Enough," said Lucy. "This is about Jim. Where did you get this patch from?"

"I told you. I told you. As much as I'd like to be making this shit up, as much as I'd like to have brought Jim back, it didn't happen. I tried to do a good thing, and, well, I guess it didn't work. But before you drag me away, just remember, the threats that XO made to me, and to you, still stand. We're breathing XO's air. Drinking their water. Relying on their computer to run everything. Talking to Earth through an XO dish via an XO satellite. You probably want to watch out for that."

"Fan, Leland. Go and do what you have to. You can take your time."

Leland put his hand on Frank's forearm, and Frank jerked away. "I know the way to the med bay."

As they left, Yun leaned forward and started to whisper furiously at Lucy. Frank couldn't catch what she said, and with both Leland and Fan at his back, he couldn't linger. They followed him through the cross-hab and into the med bay.

"In here?" Frank indicated the examination room. "It has the only lockable door on the entire base."

"Let's just take it easy, Lance," said Leland. "We just want to take a look at you."

"Sure." Frank pushed the door open, and lay down on the bench. "Do what you want. There's nothing you can do to me that is worse than what's already happened, or is going to happen."

He stretched himself out. He felt his joints crack and click. It was done. It was over. He'd tried to play the game, and he'd lost. He'd just not been ruthless enough: he'd put the possibility of Jim's survival over his own. If he'd left it, not said anything, not done anything, then maybe he would have survived. Gone home. Seen Mike again.

He'd blown all that out of the airlock. He'd fucked up. He hadn't thought it through. Jim going missing hadn't been his fault—it had been Jim's fault. And rather than accepting that Jim take responsibility for that, Frank had decided to try and fix it. History was repeating itself. He'd wanted to fix his son's drug habit, and that had ended with Frank in prison for life. This bad decision might end up with him the wrong side of an airlock door without a spacesuit on.

Was he going to fight that? Or was he just too tired? He didn't know.

"Are you OK with me giving you a physical?" Fan asked.

"Am I going to try and bust you up, and break out of here? I built this place. If I wanted out, I know exactly how little force I need to use to get through the door." Frank sat up and swung his legs out over the floor, and started to unzip his overalls. "Knock yourself out."

"That doesn't fit too well, does it? Have you grown some? Or has it shrunk?"

"It's not even mine." Frank eased himself up and pushed the garment down to his ankles, then kicked it off onto the floor. He started on his long johns.

"Not even yours," repeated Leland. "Whose is it then?"

"You know that story I've made up, about me being a prisoner called Franklin Kittridge?" The examination table was cold, and he shivered slightly. "I don't know how to break it to you, but that's pretty much the bones of it."

"So this is all Franklin's stuff."

"No, this is all Brack's. I'm Franklin. Frank." He watched for the reaction. "Don't raise your eyebrows at me like that, Leland."

He was naked, and he saw Fan frown.

"What's that on your chest?"

"That's where I cut out my monitor. Measured heart rate, breathing. Also, it turned out, worked as locator and microphone, so Brack could hear what we were all saying, even when we thought we were private."

"We?" Leland leaned in next to Fan to take a look.

"I was part of a team. Seven convicts. One guard, Brack."

"Eight of you," said Leland. "Seven…convicts?"

"Let's just stick to the physical for now." Fan snapped on a pair of nitrile gloves, the white dust from them hovering in the air. "You cut out this monitor yourself?"

The steristrip had long since come off, but he still had a raw scar over his sternum. Fan used a head torch as extra light, and pushed aside the hair on Frank's chest to examine the wound.

"You've got two scars."

"Where it went in, and where it came out. I was in kind of a hurry for the second one, so I just cut."

"It should really have been stitched."

"I'd have been sewing my own skin closed. I know people have done worse, but I didn't feel up to that. I've got no training, over some really basic first aid."

Fan's frown deepened. He let Leland take a good close look. "First scar is the pale one. It's a couple of years old."

"I wanted to make Brack think I'd died in the knife fight with Zero. So I had to cut it out. And the bullet." These were just names. More embellishments for his delusion.

Fan moved over to Frank's arm. That scar? That scar was

ugly. Puckered at the edges, indented in the middle, still ruby red and angry.

"This was where you got hit by the pylon, right?"

"No, but that's what I had to tell you. Brack shot me."

"Brack shot you. With a..."

"Gun. Automatic. Modified." Goddammit. The gun. It was still under the rocks outside the hab. The one part of Phase three he bucked. Actual physical evidence that he might not be mad after all.

Fan spent a long time probing the scar, pushing at the skin, watching how it moved and changed color. "What did you do with the bullet?"

"Pulled it out with forceps."

"And after that?"

"It went in the descent ship with all the other crap. Brack was supposed to clean up after he'd disposed of all of us."

"If I'm telling Leland not to do that now, I don't want you doing that now either. This is the physical, OK? I do bodies." He grunted, and lifted Frank's arm up and down, backwards and forwards.

"Well, it certainly looks like a bullet wound," he said eventually.

"Seen many?"

"Worked the ER for five years in Miami. Can I take a look at the rest of you while I'm here?"

"You asked nicer than the XO doctors ever did."

Fan got the rest of the tools of his trade and spent a good long while listening to Frank's heart and lungs, and palpating parts of him. Lights in his eyes, down his ears, his throat. When he'd done, he pulled his gloves off and slapped them in the medical waste bin. Leland stood in the corner, arms folded, observing.

"How old are you?" asked Fan.

Frank squinted at the ceiling. "Fifty-three?"

"And your birth date?"

"January twentieth. Ninety-six."

258

"Almost a millennial."

"I guess so."

"I'm going to go out on a limb here, and say this was your first time in space, right?"

Frank frowned. "Well, yes."

"We're all in our thirties. You'd have been what, late forties, when you started your training?"

"I barely got six months of that. I'd just turned fifty-one when some suit came to the Q. Fan, you got to understand: all they needed to know was, one, whether or not I'd survive the sleep tanks, and two, whether I'd live long enough to do the job. Me, and the rest of the crew, we were disposable. You know what they called us?"

"What did they call you?" asked Leland.

"Chimps. That's what they called us. Not to our faces, as that might have given us a clue what was going to happen to us. But behind our backs. Chimps."

"You're angry about that, aren't you?"

"Look. I know I made some pretty shitty life decisions. Shooting some drug-dealer being the worst. Maybe this is some kind of justice for the life I took. But the others? Especially Dee. He was just a kid himself. They didn't deserve this."

Again, just a name. They didn't believe him. Why was he even bothering?

"Maybe you've heard of Alice," he said. "Dr. Alice Shepherd."

Fan pursed his lips. "Name's ringing some kind of bell. Leland?"

"Involuntary euthanasia. Made a splash at the time."

"That's her," said Frank. "She was here, on Mars, with us. She was our doctor."

"She's in jail."

"If you look, so am I. Or I might have recently died."

Fan took a step back. "You're physically fit. Considering your age, you're actually in pretty good shape. It's too late to really do anything about that cut. There's some cream, for that and

259

the…hole in your arm. What's happening up top is a different matter." He hesitated, looked at Leland, and back at Frank. "Lance, what's going on here? There's something that doesn't sit right."

Leland intervened. "Why don't I take over now?"

But Fan hushed him. "I know. I know. I'm not saying anything out of turn. I just, I've got a feeling. It's nothing, right?"

The door opened, and it was Isla.

She saw Frank, naked, sitting on the bench. Frank didn't move, didn't try to cover himself. In prison, he hadn't had any privacy, and it wasn't as if she hadn't seen it all before. She blinked and looked at the floor. "Fan, Lucy wants to talk to you." Then she left, leaving the door open.

"Leland?" he said. "You're up. I'll be right back."

As he left, he narrowed his eyes at Frank, and Frank knew. There was doubt there. Good doubt. He could work with that.

"Why don't you get dressed, Lance?" said Leland. "Then we can make a start."

Frank struggled back into his clothes, and lay on the bench again.

Then he told Leland. He told him everything.

26

[Internal memo: Mars Base One Mission Control to Bruno Tiller 3/8/2049 (transcribed from paper-only copy)]

Full LOC [Loss of control] procedure is now in place. We've told NASA we've lost contact with MBO, and are trying everything to re-establish. We can spoof their FLIGHT for a while, but as time goes on, this will become more difficult. Do we have an exit strategy on this?

[transcript ends]

At some point, Fan came back in. When Frank had finished his confession, the doctor eased Leland out of the way and stood at the head-end of the bench.

"Lance? We looked at your tablet. There's nothing on it."

Frank glanced from ceiling to Fan. "That would follow. They think of everything."

"It's not just that all the personal files have been deleted. Yun tells me that it'd be trivial—trivial for her, at least—to get those back in some form or other. It's the whole thing. Even the operating system. It's been erased. The entire memory's been overwritten. It's just zeros. Whatever was on there has been destroyed. Did you do that?"

"I might be Californian, but I'm not Silicon Valley."

"He says he's a builder," said Leland.

"Did you wipe your tablet?"

"I wouldn't know how."

Fan gripped the edge of the bench. "OK, so how about this: we went looking for this other base. The photos have gone too. Everything in a two-degree block to the south of Ceraunius Tholus. We've asked for them to be reloaded, and we're waiting for them now."

"And when you get them back, they'll be edited. They know. XO know."

"What do they know, Frank? That you've deleted all your data, overwritten it, that you've wiped out the maps that would prove you wrong?" Fan leaned over him. "There's nothing, anywhere, that verifies your version of events. Everything you say has an alternative explanation. Even your scars. But I would be personally very grateful if you could tell me, if you can, where Jim is, because we intend to bring him home, no matter what."

Frank sat up and it brought him face to face with Fan. For the first time, he recognized how big he was. Tall, and broad and strong. Capable.

"I've told you the truth. I've told you everything."

"No question as to whether you, when you went out on your own looking for Jim, that you found him, and you left him there and tore off his mission patch?"

"Fan, no."

"Or that you found him alive? Unconscious? And somehow what you think happened got mixed up with what really happened?"

"No. Never."

"You got Jim's patch from Jim's suit—that's the only certain thing here."

Frank and Fan were inches apart. "All I wanted to do was go home. That was it. That was what I was holding out for. And now I'm never going to do that."

"Why not?"

"Because now you think I killed Jim. What are you and Leland going to do? Keep me sedated for the next year? Then

262

again on the ship home? That's not going to happen. If Lucy doesn't put me out of the airlock, you're all in constant danger. And you're right, but not for the reasons you think: XO will want me out of the way because I've said too much, and they won't care about how many of you they take out in the process."

"You know that believing that someone wants to kill you has a clinical name?"

"I'm not mad." He looked at his lap. "I am going to ask for one thing before you make a final decision. That someone drives over to M2 and takes a look for themselves. OK, two things. The second thing is easier than the first."

"You want us to check for the gun," said Leland.

"It's right there. Under the pile of rock. While you're digging for it, you can ask yourselves why a man alone on Mars would need a gun. And who might have let him bring it." He brought his head back up, and said to Fan: "I know this isn't looking good for me right now, but you know that there's a chance that I'm telling the truth. And not just because that might mean Jim's still alive."

He could feel Fan's breath on his skin.

"Leland thinks you're full of crap."

"That's not my professional opinion," said Leland quickly. "I'm going to take some time over that. Until then, I'm reserving judgment. Everybody is."

"I know you want Jim back. So do I. That's what I was doing." Frank looked down at Fan's balled fists. "You're not going to beat on an old man, are you?"

Leland put his hand on Fan's shoulder, dug his fingers in and pulled Fan back. "That's not helping. We can do better."

"What the hell is going on here?" Fan turned on Leland. "I don't know what to believe any more."

"We're scientists. We're all scientists. We look at the evidence and we look at the theories and we see what the best fit is. That's what we do."

Fan lowered his voice. "What if he's right? What if he's right about this M2 base at least? Shouldn't we be taking a look, seeing if that's where Jim's at?"

"That's Lucy's call. It's a long way. It's not a risk-free journey. And currently we've only got one buggy on full charge. A trip of that distance, she's going to insist on doubling-up on everything."

"He did it!" Fan jerked his finger at Frank. "He went there on his own."

"He says he did. We've no proof of that."

"How can you be so, so reasonable? Jim is...gone."

"Being reasonable is why I'm on the team. Let's go and talk to Lucy." Leland put his arm around Fan. "Lance, you going to stay here?"

"If that's what you want. I'd rather be in the greenhouse. I've still got stuff to do there."

"Pretty certain Lucy won't wear that. The greenhouse is the very definition of mission-critical equipment. You need something to eat? Drink? The can?"

"I'm pretty tired. I can just get my head down for a bit."

"That's fine. I'll come back if anything new comes up."

Frank lay down and closed his eyes. He heard the door shut, and moments later, the lock click. It was OK. He'd done everything he could. He didn't know if it was enough. What he had to do now was wait, and hope.

In all of that, he suddenly found himself falling asleep. He was even consciously surprised at the speed of it: *I'm actually going to sleep.* It had been such a long time coming.

Then he was awake again. The weak light leaking through the hab walls had changed in quality. It was later in the day. Afternoon, sometime. Leland was standing over him.

" 'Sup?"

"There's some things we need to talk about. In the kitchen." His voice was...guarded. Frank wondered why.

"Give me a moment."

"You want lunch?"

"I guess so. Condemned man and all that jazz."

"No one's reached a decision on anything yet." Leland stood by the open door. "When you're ready."

Frank padded through to the kitchen. The crew were all there again, in the same seats. They all had their tablets on in front of them, and the remains of a meal, and mugs and bottles. And in front of Lucy, a couple of plastic bags, still dusty from outside.

"You want to sit down?" said Leland from behind him. "I'll get you something. Coffee?"

"Sure." Frank slid into his seat, and moved it forward. "You found it then."

"We found it." Lucy pulled the bags towards herself, and away from Frank. "We just don't know what it means."

"You told XO about it?"

"No. No, I haven't."

"Can I ask why?"

"You can ask. I probably won't answer."

Frank looked bemused for a moment, then shrugged. "OK."

Yun slid her tablet across. It had a satellite picture on it.

Frank took it from her, and moved his head back slightly so that it came into proper focus. It was Ceraunius Tholus. He'd seen it often enough. Rahe at the top, the plains to the bottom.

"They gave you back the maps then," he said.

"Yes," said Yun. She leaned across and used a finger to recenter the image on the southern slope of the volcano. "Can you show me where you believe this second base is?"

Frank eased the map up slightly, and zoomed in on the trench. "Right there. The ship is at the western end, a couple of hundred feet from the cave."

Yun expanded the map further, and Frank realized that she'd synced everyone else's tablet to hers: they were seeing what she was. "This partially collapsed lava tube here?"

"That's it. The hab is under the overhang. There are panels on the south side of the entrance."

"You can see that there's no sign of anything you described."

265

"They've edited it out. I said they would."

Yun nodded. "So I went looking for artifacts that might show that there'd been some degree of image manipulation. Cloned textures. Blurring. Artificial junctions. Differences in shadows. All within the single frame."

"And did you find any?"

"No." She inclined her head to one side. "However. These images are composites. Built up from strips of images taken when the satellite passes overhead. As you can see here."

She shifted the whole image eastwards, and showed a brighter grayscale stripe of Mars sandwiched between two darker borders.

"You can also see that each strip is lined in the direction of travel of the camera. This is a feature of the motion of the camera relative to the surface. We see it so often, we just accept it."

Then she brought it back to the trench, and Frank could see the lines cross from the plain, clearly over the floor of the trench, and continue again on the other side.

"If I make a layer, and match the direction of the lines by marking them..." Yun used a stylus to highlight the northern and southern ends of the lines. "You can see something very interesting. It's very subtle. But if I fade this layer in and out, look at the underlying lines."

Frank bent his nose closer. He didn't get it. Then he did.

"This line here. It's broken. It doesn't follow all the way across."

"No. Although there is a line. This isn't to say that the original image doesn't contain errors. But it might indicate that someone has very skillfully dropped a segment of another image into this one. There is no other flaw that I can see. This is only one, or perhaps two, pixels out."

"But that's where the ship was."

"Which is interesting in itself, but not conclusive. There is more."

"Are you dragging this out on purpose?" asked Frank.

"I'm not dragging anything out," replied Yun. "I'm explaining what I'm doing."

"Did you find something or not?"

Yun made a face. "No. I found the absence of something." She scrolled north, almost all the way to the summit of the crater. She zoomed in, almost all the way, until the pixels were blocks and the image grainy. "You can just about make out Station two from the shadow the panels cast. I can draw it on a layer, like so."

She outlined the shadow in the shape of the weather station, with its distinctive boom.

"Now, this is where Station eight ought to be."

Yun zoomed out and in again. There was nothing to see but a bare patch of lava.

"This indicates that XO have sent us a series of replacement images which are not contemporaneous with each other. I know there was an image of Station eight. I saw it myself, when I was checking the latitude and longitude. Now, it might be, in the hurry to reload the deleted files, someone made a mistake, and uploaded an older image. I will ask them to try again, using the most recent images."

"Let's not do that for the moment," said Lucy. She sat back in her chair. "The safety and well-being of everyone on the base is my priority. Right now, I don't know how to best achieve that. On one hand, I've been told that Lance is in the middle of a psychotic episode and poses a genuine risk to us all. On the other, Lance has given a testimony that Leland has determined to be both coherent and internally consistent, but which cannot possibly be true, precisely because it's so absurdly monstrous."

"Thanks, Leland," said Frank.

"You're welcome."

"And on the third hand, there are some disturbing inconsistencies cropping up. We have an automatic pistol. The trigger guard has been machined off. Its presence on the planet is inexplicable. I'm aware that early astronauts had survival knives, flares and even handguns in case they came down in hostile territory, and yes, there have been weapons on space stations. But I can't think of any situation where a gun would be of any use on Mars. It sure as hell isn't to scare the bears away. Neither was I made aware that MBO had one. And I should have been. And I don't know why it was buried outside.

"Then there's everything that Yun's just told us. Mistake? Probably. Artifacts? Probably. Anything else would be preposterous. The mere idea that there's another, simultaneous mission on Mars without us knowing about it, is inherently ridiculous. That it's just over the hill from us is . . .

"Lance has requested that no final decision be made on his mental capacity until someone's gone over and eyeballed the trench where M2 is supposed to be. I've thought long and hard about it. There's no reason at all why I should entertain the idea. We're looking at maps which show precisely nothing. But we still have the possibility—not a real possibility—that Jim might be there. Our missing friend. So I'm going to do that tomorrow, to settle it. I'll take Isla with me. Lance, this is your last opportunity to tell me I'm wasting my time."

"You won't be wasting your time. Just be careful."

Lucy blinked at him. "You busted up the buggy."

"They tried to ram me. I rammed them back."

Then she dropped her head. "I've said my piece. This is what we'll do. Everything else is on hold until we get back. OK?"

Frank couldn't help himself. "You going to tell Mission Control where you're going?"

Lucy fixed Frank with a stare. "We got into this situation because we didn't follow the rules. So we follow the rules."

"You're not telling them about the gun, though."

"I haven't decided yet. Don't push it, Lance."

"I'm done." He looked at the plate of greens that Leland had edged onto the table by his elbow. He'd missed it until now, so he nudged back his chair and picked up the plate. And the coffee that was next to it. "You don't need to set a guard or anything. But it's probably in the rules that you have to."

He took himself back to the consulting room, and sat on the bench, listening to the sounds of the base around him. He'd built this thing. There was that much to be proud of, at least.

27

[Internal memo: Mars Base One Mission Control to Bruno Tiller 3/8/2049 (transcribed from paper-only copy)]

If you review the latest transmissions, we have around twelve [12] hours to decide what to do. If we forbid them to travel, they'll ask questions. If we permit them, they'll discover M2. The third option of Not Yet is our best, but it isn't a long-term solution.

Sir, some guidance would be useful at this point?

[transcript ends]

Frank woke up to an almighty crash from outside, like the racking collapsing and spilling its contents on the floor. Disorientated, with no idea how much time had passed, he screwed his eyes up and called out, "Hey, you OK out there?"

When there was no immediate call of "I'm fine", he slipped off the examination table and put his ear to the door.

There was...something.

Then the door bowed. Frank threw himself aside as it came off its hinges, flying into the wall hard enough to dent it. Fan followed it, arms and legs flailing. He hit the broken door, upended the examination table, and slid downwards.

Someone in an XO spacesuit walked in, arm raised, a length of stanchion in their hand, ready to beat down on a prone Fan.

"The fuck you will." Frank pushed himself off the floor and

into the figure, catching them under the shoulder, wrapping his arms around them. They fell together, tangled up, half on Fan's legs.

Frank snatched at the stanchion, got both hands around it and twisted it hard. Wrists weren't meant to rotate that far, and he broke the hold. Now he had a weapon, and goddammit, he was going to use it. He brought it down hard and fast on the helmet, not caring much about damage, but he was going to make it loud in there. He could see through the faceplate. Not the guy from before, and he'd be surprised if that one could walk any time soon. Different man, same desperate, wolf-like features.

The spacesuit tried to get up, rocking side to side on the curve of the life support to get some purchase on the floor. Frank knew that keeping him down was the thing.

Fan managed to pull himself out of the ruck: winded, he was in no position to help, but Frank already knew how to deal with someone in a semi-rigid suit, and that wasn't by going toe-to-toe with them.

With one final swing at the helmet, Frank switched his attention to the control panel, which was right in front of him. He turned the pipe end on and drove it down hard. The man beneath him saw it coming and twisted onto his side, letting the carapace take the blow. Frank helped him over the rest of the way, and now the other guy found himself face-down, getting smacked around the head with the piece of metal pipe he'd brought himself.

Fan sat up, wheezing, and Frank tossed him the stanchion. He needed both hands free for this. He dug his fingers into the back panel on the suit, heaved the cover aside, and hit the manual off switch on the life support. Then he held the man down while he suffocated, slapping uselessly at the plastic tiles on the floor, clawing his fingers, kicking out. It took longer than Frank thought it would.

"You OK, Fan?" he asked, when the struggling had finally stopped.

Fan, clutching his chest, sipping at the air, nodded.

"He won't be alone."

He shoved the body to one side so he could get out the doorway. Leland—he was on the floor, boxes and crates and the things they contained around him, on top of him, and there was a hell of a lot of blood pooling behind his head. Frank couldn't see anyone else, and ducked back into the examination room.

"Leland's down. Do what you do: I'm going to find the others."

Fan held out the stanchion again, and Frank shook his head. If there was a moment of comprehension, it was then. Fan knew. Fan understood.

Frank crept out, peered around the corner to the crosshab, and could see shapes framed in the doorway to the crew section—chairs, people, stuff—in motion, chaotic and noisy. There was no one in between. No one standing guard. How many attackers? He didn't know. Neither did he care. He would take them all on if necessary.

He grabbed an oxygen cylinder as he passed, because he knew that it was heavy and made more of an impact against the suits. Though there was now a gun in play. What had she done with it? There wasn't any time to think about that. He charged.

They were all armed with makeshift weapons. Most usefully, Lucy had managed to get one of the kitchen knives. Isla had a chair, which she was about to throw. The three opposing them all had better. One, a wrench, one, part of a parachute filled with rocks, and one a makeshift spear, plastic tubing cut diagonally at the end to make a point. That could go through the hab wall if it was allowed to.

Lucy and Isla were backed up against the kitchen units, more or less surrounded, but the one with the wrench had slashes across his arm.

"Get out, get out, get out!" Lucy was shouting, when Frank barreled in behind and used his momentum to skittle two of them over.

He jumped up, swung his cylinder to meet the sack of rocks coming down, and reeled back as the spear end jabbed forward. Then it was just a free-for-all. At least he knew who he was supposed to be fighting. Lucy carved the air in front of her, Isla fended off the wrench, and Frank managed to get inside the spear length and bring the blunt end of the carbon-fiber cylinder up into the man's faceplate, with the guy still hanging on to his length of tubing and trying to bring the point to bear on Frank.

It took three good hits to crack the clear plastic, each time stepping forward to keep within range. The fracture went right across, right to left. The suit's occupant stared at it, rather than Frank, who took the opportunity to smack the hell out of the spear and force it from his grasp.

Disarmed, suit integrity compromised, they pushed Frank away, and ran for the airlock. They were about to find out the hard way whether they had a leak or not.

Then it was three against two, and the odds had shifted back. Rather than being on the defensive, Isla jabbed forward, inviting retaliation, until the rock-filled sleeve wrapped itself uselessly around one of the chair legs. Then she let go, and bundled the suit over while they were still trying to get untangled. Frank brought the cylinder down again, hard, like he had before, hitting the helmet, breaking it, sending shards of sharp plastic spinning away.

Lucy's opponent turned and ran, and, not giving up, she gave chase. They beat her to the cross-hab airlock and started to cycle it.

"Lance, suit up," she shouted. "Suit up. Get outside and find Yun."

"Yun's outside?"

She was right. Suit up.

"Tie them up," said Frank to Isla. "Fan's with Leland in the med hab. You OK?"

Isla nodded. Just the once. She was bleeding from several cuts. "Go."

Frank hefted his cylinder again, and headed for his spacesuit.

Lucy was quick. Frank was quicker still, but when he powered his suit up, all he could hear was Yun calling for help, right in his ear. A mixture of English and what he had to assume was Mandarin. She was fighting them. She was fighting them hard.

Frank and Lucy cycled the lock together. They bundled outside, the usual suit checks not so much forgotten as ignored, and ran towards the open space beyond the Comms/Control hab. There was a buggy driving away in the direction of the Santa Clara; there were figures on the back of it, but the dust, the distance, made it impossible to tell what was going on. Was Yun with them? There was another buggy, with at least two—no, it was just two—people on it, circling round in front of the workshop. Someone was unplugging the charger from one of the base's own transports.

The thing about radio was that it didn't matter how close or how far away it was broadcast from. The distance to the receiver's ears was a constant. Yun's howls of rage, her demanding her release, her eventual begging for mercy, he was there. Right there, next to her. He wanted her to keep resisting and he wanted her to stop. But M2 were trying to steal one of their buggies. That, he could do something about.

He picked up a rock and threw it, not particularly aiming to hit the other guy, but to alert him to the fact he'd been spotted. Frank didn't want to fight him so much as he wanted to scare him away from the buggy.

The rock sailed into the tire plates, and bounced against the man's life support. The man stood up, saw Frank crouching over in that Mars-efficient running stance, and dropped the power cable. He dithered. Climb up and try and get the buggy going, or flee? Neither. He was frozen on the spot as Frank dug his boots into the friable Martian soil and ate up the distance between them. Only at the last moment did the other man try and escape.

Frank struck him from behind, and sent him flying, properly

flying, feet off the ground, turning in the air, arms and legs wide. Frank skidded to a halt on his shoulder, and started to pick himself up. The circling M2 buggy came around and drove straight at him.

But slowly enough that he could jump backwards out of the way, sliding along on his life support. The buggy slowed right down for the interloper to climb up, and then it was off again, dust spurting from the wheels, showering Frank in grit before it was out of range, following its companion in the direction of the river valley. Yun was still calling. Still right in his ears.

"Lance. Status?"

Frank lay on his back, and flipped out his suit controls. Green lights all the way down. "Intact. Yun? Yun, we're coming to get you. Just hold on."

"Yun?" said Lucy. "You have my word on this: we will bring you back home. Back here."

"There were too many of them! There are at least six of them here. I tried. I'm sorry. Please hurry. Please."

Frank stood up, staring at the shrinking dust plumes. "Lucy, if we're going, we need to go now."

She ignored him. "Yun. Listen to me. The more you struggle, the more oxygen you'll use. You have to let them take you. We will come for you. We'll secure the base. We'll call home for help. You will be released. We will bring you back."

"They're getting away!" said Frank.

"There's nothing we can do! We are unprepared for this. So woefully unprepared. And that—that is on you, Lance. Franklin. Whatever your name is."

"XO would have worked their way through your entire crew to get to me if I'd told you everything from the start. I told you as soon as I could. And you chose not to believe me." Frank retrieved the gas cylinder from where it lay on the dusty ground. "Goddammit, sorry, Yun."

"Come and get me. Please. Please, I'm frightened."

"We will," said Lucy. "I promise. Soon, Yun. Be strong."

"If they open up her fucking suit it won't matter how strong she is!"

"That is enough. I'll finish up out here. You go inside." Lucy was standing over by the satellite dish. "Go. Before you say anything else you regret. Over an open channel."

"You're not in charge of me."

"Right now, you are either part of my crew, or you're something I have to worry about. You can choose which it's going to be. But you go off on that buggy, you've made your choice, because you are going to put Yun in more danger than she is even right now. Maybe, 'Franklin', we can come to some kind of accommodation here that doesn't involve anyone else dying. What do you think?" She obviously and deliberately started flicking the fuses on the dish to off, working her way down the line. "You want to help Yun? Or do you want to do the other thing?"

Frank could barely see the two buggies climbing the side of the volcano, hidden within the curves of the valley. A faint haze of dust. Nothing else.

"Yun?" he said. "We'll get you out of this. If Jim's there, tell him we're coming for him too." Frank turned his transmitter off. He couldn't bear it a single second more. Whether or not Lucy had anything else to say to him, he didn't care. He plugged the buggy back in and stalked over to the cross-hab.

He racked his suit. He allowed himself a moment where he could just rest his forehead against the cool, humming machinery of the oxygenator, then went to make sure the base was secure.

The M2 guy subdued by him and Isla was hogtied—literally, hogtied, wrists and ankles bound together with cable ties—on the floor of the yard, away from any of the exercise equipment. The guy twisted his head as Frank passed by, and they stared at each other.

The man peered out through his broken faceplate. A fragment

276

of plastic clattered to the deck. Gaunt. Ragged. Yellow-eyed and gray-skinned.

"I'm sorry. I'm sorry."

"Fuck you," said Frank. He took a knife from the kitchen and checked all of the crew quarters, upstairs and down, including the airlock. He peered inside, saw it was clear, and on leaving, left the inner door ajar. Just like he had done when he was alone.

He re-emerged in the yard, did the same to that airlock, then scouted out Comms, and below it, Control. There were flashing lights on some of the telltales. He'd let Lucy deal with those.

Back through the yard.

"Look, I was made to do this."

"Shut the fuck up. Now."

He went through the greenhouse, top and bottom, making absolutely certain there was no one hiding between the racking or behind the tall green plants. He fixed the outside airlock, and even plunged his arm into the tilapia tanks, just to make certain no one was hiding in them.

Fish squirmed against him, but there was nothing more substantial than that.

He checked the below-deck in the cross-hab, then the part he'd been dreading: going back into the med bay.

Fan was leaning, heavy-knuckled, against one of the gurneys. Isla was next to him, arms around him. There was a shape, a body, covered, shrouded by a green medical sheet. Frank looked around for Leland. Where he'd fallen and lain buried under the staging was rearranged but no less chaotic, but Leland had been retrieved, evidenced by bloody marks that once again stained the med hab floor.

"Fuck."

Frank wheeled away in time to catch Lucy coming back in through the airlock. She cracked the seal on her suit, and crawled out of it onto the floor.

"You didn't pull your punches," she said.

"I've got—"

"The one you hit, who ran out through the gym's airlock?"

"That's not import—"

"Faceplate blew out. He's dead."

"Lucy, just..."

"What?"

"Leland. He. Just go through to the med bay. Just go through." He gestured to her abandoned suit. "I'll deal with this."

She halfstumbled, half ran, and while he racked her life support and spacesuit, he could hear her cry of pain and loss echo down the corridor towards him. Then she was back, marching through to the kitchen area, and he stood in her way.

"You're going to let me pass."

"No, no I'm not."

"I want some answers."

"You'll get them. Not this way, though. He'll tell you anything you want to hear. But if you want the truth, you'll have to wait." Frank held his arms wide, and backed up until he blocked the through-passage completely.

"Franklin. That is your name, isn't it? Franklin? Until I can work out exactly what to do with you, and what your status is regarding this mission, I'm simply not going to listen to anything you have to say."

"What are you going to do? Fight me too?"

"If I have to. Whatever it takes to ensure the safety of my crew."

"Like turning the dish off. Blocking XO from the main computer. I watched you do it."

She balled her fists. "Get out of the way."

"No, ma'am."

"You shouldn't even be here!"

Frank blinked away the sudden pain. "Don't you think I know that? I tell myself that every single day. They killed my crew. Now they're killing yours. You, me, we're on the same fucking side. We always were. I tried—goddammit I tried so hard—to protect you from them, but they fucked it up. They fucked it up, and us with it."

He stood aside, indicated she could go through. She did nothing, just stood there, breathing hard.

"Go on. Get what you can. Slap him around. Torture him if you want. All you'll get is a pile of horseshit that means nothing. Seen that all before. When you toss him out the airlock, everything he knows will go with him, and you'll have no clue as to whether he told you the truth or not." Again, he pointed through to the kitchen. "Whatever it takes, right?"

"What else am I supposed to do?"

"I can get him to tell me the truth."

"Will it get me Yun back? Will it get me Jim?"

"I don't know. If I screw this up, you'll still get your chance at him." He wandered over to the greenhouse airlock, and peered through. The sight of the plants calmed him. Made him less terrified. Less angry. "You were a combat pilot."

"The Stans."

"You do the interrogation technique thing?"

"I survived it, if nothing else."

"Did it work on you? Did you tell?"

"Name. Rank. Number," she said.

"So give an old lag some credit for knowing that I can get more out of a stoolie with kindness than you will with threats."

Lucy stepped away from the now-open corridor. "How long were you in jail for?"

"Eight years in. Out of a hundred and twenty, without parole."

"What did you do?"

"He was a nineteen-year-old kid and I shot him at point-blank range." Frank shrugged. "If you've got any sympathy, save it for his parents. I don't want it, I don't need it. I sure as hell don't deserve it. I did a bad thing and I can't put it right. Give me ten, fifteen minutes. I'll sit where I can give you the sign that it's working, where he can't see you. And I'll need Fan to do something, even though he won't want to. But he's the only one who can."

He told her what, and such were the circumstances that she nodded and went to pass on the message.

Frank picked up the kitchen knife from the top of the life support rack and held it loosely as he walked through into the crew hab. He squatted down next to the tied man, and rolled him onto his side. More of his faceplate fell out, and Frank brushed the shards aside.

The man was wide-eyed and ashen. What did he think Frank was going to do to him? What had he been prepared to do to Frank, that he was imagining the same treatment?

"Do you know who I am?"

The man shook his head. More plastic clattered out.

"What's your name?"

"Jerry."

"Is that Jerry with a G or a J?"

"J."

"Jerry. Jeremiah." Frank stood up and found himself a chair. He set it on its feet and sat backwards on it. "I'm Frank, Jerry. And you tried to kill my colleagues."

"We had no choice."

"I'm going to stop you there, Jerry, because that's not true, and I'm only interested in what's true right now. No time for bullshit, no time for games. When you say 'we had no choice' what you really mean is 'we didn't expect you to fight back'. Am I right?"

"You don't understand what it's been like."

"I don't? That sounds like an invitation for me to listen to some more BS. I'm not going to feel sorry for you, whatever you tell me. We're currently missing a geologist, an atmosphere scientist and there's a dead shrink over in the med bay. Pretty much out of fucks to give."

"But you're the XO man, though. Aren't you?"

"Oh, Jerry. Jerry, Jerry, Jerry. The XO man is dead. I killed him. I'm one of the chimps. That's who I am. I'm the disposable crew who didn't lie down and die." Frank watched Jerry—if that was his real name, and Frank didn't hold out much hope—carefully. The flare of recognition, the recoil away, as much as a man bound hands to feet could manage, told him that M2 knew all about Phase three. "If you think I'm an XO man, I'd think again."

"What do you want from me?"

"What do I want? I wanted what I was promised by XO. That you would leave us alone. That I'd get my lift home. That was what I wanted, and now? I don't know what I really want any more. You've taken Jim, you've taken Yun, you've killed Leland. Perhaps I just want you gone."

"How can I change your mind?"

"I don't know if—"

A scream. More of a yell that tailed off into a whimper. Frank acted surprised, but actually it was pretty convincing.

"What was that?" asked Jerry.

"That's the sound of our doctor operating without anesthetic. You weren't the only person we caught."

Jerry gagged. "You can't be serious," he managed eventually.

"I don't think it's a joke. Do you?"

"What's he doing to him?"

"Despite all the shit that's gone down, I'm not going over there to ask." Frank stretched out and put the knife on the table. "Looks like I won't need that."

"What does he want?"

"He wants to know what happened. Why you're here on Mars. Whether or not XO told you that home invasion was OK. What happened to Jim. What's going to happen to Yun. Stuff like that."

Right on cue, another scream. That one sounded a little over-egged to Frank, but Jerry wasn't in a discriminating frame of mind.

"I can tell you. I can tell you now."

"I don't think it's going to make much difference to what he's going to do to you. He's one pissed sawbones right now."

"I will tell you everything."

"I don't want to hear everything. Waste of good O$_2$."

"Then just ask me questions. And quickly."

"Like I said," said Frank. "I don't know if it'll make any difference. I don't carry that much influence around here. Not any more."

"Oh God, you have to try."

And again, this time cut short with a bubbling choke. Better. Definitely better.

Frank affected a bemused look. "I guess, if it doesn't tally with the other guy, then it's not like we've lost any time or anything. OK, I'll try. I don't know how long we've got. Depends on how long it'll take them in there."

"Just ask me something. Anything. Please."

Was that easy, or was that difficult? Did he feel clean, or dirty? Frank was beyond such considerations now.

"Sure. Let's talk about why you're on Mars, and why you're just over the hill from here."

28

[Transcript of Emergency FLIGHT meeting Ares IV Mission
Control JPL Pasadena CA 3/9/2049]

GT: What have we got? CATO [Communication and Tracking
Officer]?

MA: XO are reporting complete failure of the main antenna.
They say that they're trying to reroute, but that both the HG
[High Gain] and LG [Low Gain] are offline. No carrier signal.
Nothing.

GT: OPSPLAN [Operations Planner]?

TY: Both OPSPLAN and EVA [Extravehicular Activity Officer]
registered that the last authorized external activity was on
Sol 622, where five [5] crew and the XO operative took two [2]
rovers to the summit of Ceraunius Tholus to search for James
Zamudio. All personnel and equipment returned to MBO.
Other than that, nothing.

GT: RIO [Remote Interface Officer]?

LS: I've informed the Chinese government of the situation. I'll
inform them again after this meeting. They are, so far, not
lighting a fire under my ass, so I'm grateful for that.

GT: ECLSS [Environmental Control and Life Support System]?

PO: The onboard LSS of MBO is dependent on the maintenance
of the main computer by ODIN [Onboard Data Interfaces and
Networks]. Likewise PHALCON [Power, Heating, Articulation,
Lighting Control Officer] functions. If there's a fault with
the main box, then they can run MBO LSS and PHALCON
functions manually.

GT: ODIN?

WM: I've been through the logs. There's been no hint of any errors or hardware failures in any of them. If anything, the system has overperformed. I can't rule out a catastrophic failure of critical systems, but neither can I rule it in.

GT: So we wait for them to fix it. In the meantime, ladies and gentlemen, the director of HiRISE2 has sent me this, with his compliments.

PO: Is that what I think it is?

GT: Why don't you tell me what you think it is, and we can take the discussion from there.

[transcript ends]

Frank and the rest of the crew sat back down around the kitchen table. Their prisoner had been put, without his suit, in a chair at the far end of the yard, and retied by a frighteningly efficient Isla—something to do with wrangling livestock on her parents' farm.

The bodies, that of Leland and his unnamed assailant, still lay in the med bay. The other man whose faceplate Frank had cracked was left where he'd died, on the steps down from the yard. The living had priority for now.

On the table were some of Frank's freeze-dried berries. He'd shaken some out into bowls and put them within reach. No one had eaten for a while. Not that they were going to feel like eating much when Frank relayed what Jerry had told him.

He leaned over to grab a handful of strawberry slices, and chained them until they were all gone. Then he sat back up and blew out air.

"Can we get Yun back?" asked Lucy.

Frank thought about it, given what he knew. "Maybe. I hope so. If we don't dick around."

Fan reached out for a strawberry, and toyed with it before nibbling off the tiniest corner of it. "What about Jim?"

"Yeah. About that." Frank felt his guts tighten. "That's not going to be happening."

"I came here with five crew members," growled Lucy. She looked down the yard at their prisoner. "I'm down to two. Two."

"What happened to Jim, Franklin?" said Isla.

"You know what? He can tell you himself. I'm fed up of being XO's messenger boy."

"Who is he? What's he even doing here?"

"OK." Frank squeezed his forehead. "OK. So he says his name's Jerry. That may or may not be true, but that's not really important. They landed mid-November, 2048. Three months before you did. They used the same sleep tanks as we did. Landing was fine, all on automatic, put them exactly where they were supposed to be, which is more than happened with us. But when they woke up, they found that their ship wasn't working right. The comms were down. Fried completely. They couldn't get a message in or out. They couldn't talk to XO, and XO couldn't talk to them."

Isla frowned. "But what about their cargo drops?"

"It was the same problem we had, in spades. Some of theirs were on target. But a lot more of them ended up scattered over the southern and eastern plains. They got their RTG early on, which saved their asses, but it just meant they lived long enough to realize just how screwed they were. They've two habs, but not enough power to run them both. No water maker: they had to make a crude one out of parts. No greenhouse. No comms. No batteries. Between me first seeing the guy out on the plain, and now, they managed to find one food drop. I'd already taken one other. I could see the locators, and they couldn't, and XO deliberately hadn't clued me in. So yeah. I took their stuff. And there's other kit that's still lying out there: something that makes bricks out of the soil, and a three-d factory, but that's not the . . . they had food, but no way to grow any more. They've been on starvation rations for the better part of three months. They don't have enough water or air or power."

"And XO?"

"Had no idea what state they were in, above what they could see from space, and what I told them."

Lucy pressed the back of her hand against her lips, head bowed, thinking.

"Why, though? We're here for the science. What are they here for?"

"Colonization. A land grab. Boots on the ground. Call it what you want. Hell, you paid for it."

"We did what?"

"You paid for it. For what NASA spent on MBO, XO were able to put two bases on Mars. That we know about. I don't know all the details."

"Is that why they didn't just come and ask you for help? They knew you were here, yes?"

"Sure they knew. When the one guy met me out on the plain, he even called me Brack. But in one of those weird strokes of luck, their comms outage meant they didn't even know what sol it was. I told them you were already here, and he bought it. He was clearly XO, and I thought they were here to replace me as Brack—that was why I was such a mess when you arrived. I'd slept with a gun for two months, thinking they were going to swarm in and toss me out the airlock."

"But—"

"You were never supposed to know about M2. They couldn't just sail over any more, even if they wanted to. And the MBO crew was now six fit, well-fed astronauts, and me: Brack, the ex-military guy who'd just seen off seven cons because he'd been told to do it. They didn't have the numbers. And they were so short of both air and watts, they needed to prioritize their supply drops. Searching Mars, manually."

"What were XO doing all this time? Didn't they ask you to go over?"

"I told them to go fuck themselves."

"But they didn't insist."

"No."

"But that means XO were willing to see M2 fail," said Lucy, "and everybody there die."

"Look, if you want to know what XO were thinking, then ask them yourself. Turns out my lie was the best thing I could have done in the circumstances."

Fan rumbled: "What do you mean?"

"They've..." Frank pushed the bowl of strawberries away from him. "They've gone rogue. Worse. It's like the ding wing over there."

"Ding wing?"

"Nut house."

"They've got mental issues?"

"Some of them. Their commander for sure. They fight each other to work out who does the jobs and who gets the food. The weakest do all the work and eat last, if at all. They've been like this since they realized they were never going to get a viable base going. They took Station seven, tried to use it to talk to the satellite. Apparently they kind of got halfway, but they just couldn't figure out how to send a message. That was the final straw. The boss guy, Justin, finally worked out that if they, if he, was going to live, they were going to have to take MBO for themselves. And fuck the people who are already here."

"When did we have the solar storm?" said Fan to Lucy.

"November seventh. We spent ten hours in an insulated cage in the middle of the ship," she added for Frank's benefit.

"Enough to interfere with ship systems. Disable their communications. Maybe something happened to their hibernation tanks at the same time." Fan, still holding the dried slice of strawberry, looked at it like he'd never seen it before. He dropped it back in the bowl. "It's very experimental. NASA wouldn't let us travel that way."

"While XO didn't give a shit about how experimental it was with us."

"I wasn't party to that decision," he said, and Frank realized he was aiming his anger at the wrong person.

"OK. So, for them, it was now or never. They've run out of food. Their systems aren't enough to maintain life. They figured I'd spill the beans about them. And we were a man down. I don't know whether Jim talked before—" Frank looked over to where Jerry sat, bound, isolated, alone. "Go talk to him yourself. I'm done here."

Lucy pushed her chair back, and Fan and Isla followed her. They stood in front of Jerry. Lucy, hands on hips, Fan, arms folded, Isla, pressing all of her fingers against her upper lip, not trusting herself to speak.

Frank kicked his own chair aside and stood at the back, where he could see everything that went on.

"Jerry, right?" said Lucy.

"Yes."

"I'm Commander Lucy Davison. I want you to tell me what happened to Jim Zamudio."

"He..." Jerry nodded at Frank, because that was pretty much the only part of him he could move, "said he'd fix things for me."

"Whatever he promised you, he can't deliver. Jim Zamudio."

"Tell her what you told me," said Frank.

Jerry weighed up his options, and realized he had none. "We. We were out on the volcano. We were looking to see if we could grab some more of your equipment. That was all. That was all we were up there for. Nothing else. We'd almost got the comms working. We needed more parts. That's right. More parts."

"And Jim?"

"He was suddenly there. We came around the corner, and there he was, back to us. Head right down over the rock, looking at it close. He didn't see us at all. I wanted to back up, but Jen.

She lost it. She saw him, drove at him. Hit him hard. Crushed him against the cliff. Knocked him down. Knocked him out cold."

"It wasn't you who did that?"

"It wasn't!" Jerry licked his lips, flexed his arms against the ropes. "She wanted to strip his suit, leave him behind, but I stood up for him. We couldn't leave him behind, could we? Could we?"

"You took him back to M2."

"Sure. We took him back to M2. I thought we'd just keep him for a while, then take him back. Swap him for stuff we needed. But Justin…"

"Your commander."

"He's," and Jerry hesitated. Frank eyeballed him, and he continued. "Scary. He's really scary. We do what he says, because otherwise, it's just not worth saying no to him, OK?"

Fan leaned in. "What happened to Jim?"

Jerry didn't answer. Not straight away. "He's gone," he said eventually. "He's dead. He's definitely dead. He's not coming back."

"He was alive when you took him. How did he end up dead?"

"It was Justin. It was Justin's idea. He made us. He made all of us."

"Tell me. Tell me now, or I'm throwing you out of the airlock, Hippocratic oath be damned. What did he make you do?"

"Eat him."

There was absolute silence. Not even a breath as the words sank in.

Then Fan lunged forward, and Frank, who'd been ready, managed to wrestle the doctor away and held him, hugged him, until he instead sagged onto Frank's shoulders, weeping.

It was poor comfort, from a man who'd now killed five men. Frank didn't feel capable of offering Fan any solace at all. Jim was dead, Yun was about to suffer the same fate, they were down to three of the original six crew, and even if they wanted to bail,

289

the MAV wouldn't be ready for months. It would feel like all hope was lost. And maybe it was.

He could see Lucy and Isla over Fan's shoulder. Both of them looked hollowed out. He remembered that look from that one night when he and Declan and Zero had gathered to talk it out.

"I know that this isn't what you expected. You were supposed to come here, do your science, discover all kinds of new shit, work out how to live on Mars, and then go home to tell everyone how to do it. I know what that feels like. I was supposed to come here, build a base for you all, look after it and serve the rest of my sentence knowing that I was finally doing something good with my life, and maybe, just maybe, making my boy proud of his old man again. I knew I was going to die here, and that was OK, because I thought it'd be in ten, fifteen years' time. I didn't know they were planning to off me within six months. You didn't know that they'd put a bunch of bugs on Mars who'd fight you for every scrap you had. None of us got a choice about what we're facing. But we've got to deal with it all the same."

Lucy took Fan from Frank, and guided him gently back to his seat over at the table. She stood behind him, hands on his shoulders, kneading his flesh, while Isla and Frank stood the other side.

"Frank, we've got fucking space cannibals." She grimaced. "Training didn't cover this."

"So let's work out a way to get Yun back and, I don't know what you'd say, neutralize the threat."

"The way you neutralized yours?"

Frank blinked. "Jesus. Lady. What did you expect me to do? Lie down and die? Goddammit, you were a fast jet pilot, right? In the Stans? How many people did you kill then? Did you lose count, or don't you know?"

"That's enough, Frank," said Isla.

"At least I looked my victims in the eye, which is something you can't do from twenty thousand feet."

"That is enough!" Isla came to stand in Frank's eyeline, so that he had to look at her, and not Lucy. "You're right, but you're being a dick about it."

She let that sink in, and then she turned on her heel.

"Lucy. He's right. We have to get Yun. We have to stop them coming back again. Either that, or we sit here and wait for them to take the rest of us. This is not what we wanted. But this is what we have."

After a minute or two, Lucy slumped into Frank's discarded seat and dragged it back to the table. "So what have we got?"

Isla retook her place, and kicked the chair next to her. Frank sat.

"The four of us," said Frank.

Lucy looked bleak.

"Three of those four are supposed to be really smart. Maybe we could use that to our advantage."

She didn't look any less bleak, but she did at least grunt in acknowledgment.

"We've got two buggies. Power to burn. We've got suits, we've got spare life supports to take with us. We know where they are. We know how many of them there are."

"Do we?"

"They had a crew of eight. Two are dead. We've got a prisoner. Five of them left. One of them won't be in a fit state to fight, because I probably broke his ankle while I was over there."

"Franklin."

"He was trying to kill me, and hey: I'm a convicted murderer. What did you expect me to do? Play patty cake?" He waited for any further objections, then continued. "We know the layout of their base. We know they're weak. They blew everything on taking MBO. All their reserves. They've got nothing left. We know they're in one hab, and their descent ship. Yun must be in one or other of them."

"If she's still alive."

"Lucy." Frank's turn.

291

"OK, OK. Fan, can she get back to, whatever we're calling it—"

"M2," said Frank.

"—M2 without running out of air?"

"Yes. It's only four, four and a half hours away. If she manages to regulate her breathing, she can make it. Whether, in the circumstances, that's a good thing—"

"Fanuel. We're trying to get a plan together here." Frank played with his burned fingertips. "Her suit's still working. We can get a fresh life support into it."

"And what if someone else is wearing it?"

"Then we make them take it off." He glanced around the table. "If any of you are squeamish, now would be a good time to say. Because Yun's relying on us to get her out of there, and we need to know we've got each other's backs on this."

"You're asking me to kill people, Franklin," said Fan.

"I stopped you from strangling Jerry."

"Thinking about it is one thing. Doing it is another."

"You were doing it," said Frank.

"I was angry."

"If I'd lost half my crew and I wasn't angry, there'd be something wrong with me."

Isla put her hand on top of Frank's, and he stopped talking and was still.

"You're not angry, though, are you?" she said. "You never get angry. You just decide what needs to be done, and then you do it. And right now, you've decided that M2 has to go. We can't co-exist, and you'd rather you lived than you died."

Frank pulled his hand away. Slowly, so that it was like the tide receding. "Something like that. Sometimes killing is a purely practical decision. Except when it comes to those stupid fish." He looked at his fingers, then shook himself. "Then there's all of you. I kind of like you. You're good people. Even if I don't get back home, you deserve to. But this isn't getting us anywhere.

We've all got to be prepared to do whatever to get Yun back. Doesn't matter why or what we feel afterwards."

"Accepted," said Lucy. "What have they got?"

"Five people, one can't walk. Limited air and power. Enough to mount a two-buggy attack across an eighty-mile gap once, but probably not again in a hurry. No central comms, but suit-to-suit communication like you have, which is limited to what? Thirty yards or so."

"Weapons?"

"No one shot at me, if that's what you're asking." Frank thought about it for a moment. "At least, I don't think anyone was shooting at me. No one hit me. One guy attacked me with a wrench, and two tried to drive into me with buggies."

"And we've got a gun."

"We can make other weapons," said Isla. "We have piping, and compressed gas. A potato cannon is simple enough. Firing rocks, of course, or bolts. Edged weapons using what we have here, and blunt ones from outside. Shields using drum lids. Reach will be important." She realized the stares she was getting. "I had lots of brothers and cousins, and access to the toolshed."

"We can't spend long on this," said Lucy. "We have to go as soon as we can."

"If we leave now, it'll be dark when we get there," said Isla. "Frank left early morning, and was there at dawn. We can do that too."

She was fierce. Now she'd got over the shock, determined. She was ready.

It went quiet around the table. Lucy eventually broke the silence.

"So this is our plan? We tool up, drive over, kill anyone who gets in our way and rescue Yun? This is a disaster that's only going to get worse." She stood up and looked at them all. "OK. If that's as good as it gets, then we do it. But what do we do about XO?"

"We keep the plug pulled," said Frank.

"That isn't viable in the long run," said Lucy.

"There is no long run with XO."

"We've got to wait for the MAV to fuel up. And we need to tell Mission Control what's going on. Let Jim's and Leland's folks know they won't be coming back. And, if we stay—"

"Do you think they'll let you talk to Mission Control? Knowing what you know? Billions of dollars in fraud? Lying about the robots? Sending seven men and women to their deaths?"

"We can't be without an earthlink, Franklin. Frank. Once we've got back with Yun, we, the surviving members of the mission, will decide what we do next." She faced him down. "We've spent years getting here. Not just the eight months' travel, but the whole of our careers, earning enough astronaut points to just be considered. And yes, you're right. None of us are where we wanted to be. This is not a problem I ever thought we'd have to deal with. But there will be an after for us, and I need to prepare for that."

Frank pushed his hands against the tabletop and levered himself upright. "You saw what they did to my tablet, and the maps. They just reached in and wiped them. You let them in again, and they could do anything."

"They're not going to kill us off, Frank."

"They care more about themselves than you. Of course they're going to kill us off."

"I'm still going to have to talk to Mission Control."

"How? You have to go through XO. You need to talk to Earth, directly. Can you do that?"

Lucy looked down at Fan, who said: "Yun should be able to do something. She's the expert. Without her?" He pulled a face. "I can't do it."

"Then we get Yun," said Frank. "We don't talk to XO."

"I'm in charge, Frank." Lucy was adamant. "If we have to talk to XO, then that's what we do. Perhaps we need to let them try and put this mess right."

"Don't let them in. That's all I'm going to say. Don't do it."

"Thank you for your advice."

"Well, shit." Frank looked down the yard, at the solitary figure still tied to the chair. "While you're making plans, you should probably figure out what to do with him, too."

29

[Private diary of Bruno Tiller, entry under 3/9/2049, transcribed from paper-only copy]

Gold Hill has always been special to me, since we first started this project. I commanded it to be built, and it was. I commanded it to be staffed, and it was. I made sure that everyone here was loyal to me. To me, and not XO. So it seems only right that I'm back here now. We still have so much to prepare.

[transcript ends]

It was an hour before dusk. Frank had used a cutting disk to take off the doors of a cargo rocket and had sliced them into sections to make bumpers, sides and rear, for the first buggy, making sure they protruded further out than the wheels did. On the front, which he anticipated being more of a battering ram, he fixed a drum, piercing holes in its base to thread spare hab bolts through and clamp them to the frame with drilled strips of metal.

"Do you want help?"

He turned, nut runner in hand, and saw Isla. He also saw that the satellite dish was swinging over to the east, to pick up a signal.

"Whose bright idea was that?"

"We decided," she said. "We can't do without the uplink. Lucy hasn't told them everything. Just that M2 attacked us."

"Which part of 'M2 has to remain secret at all costs' passed you by?" He leaned into the buggy frame and tightened a bolt. "You've made a massive mistake. All you'll ever get to talk to is a bunch of XO people trying not to end up in the same jail they fished me out of."

"We can't survive here otherwise."

"You're wrong. That's all."

"We decided," she said again.

"OK, I get it."

"We have to get help from somewhere, Frank."

He picked up the drum lid and pushed it into place, then flicked the clasps over to fix it. "Has Lucy actually talked to anyone at NASA yet? Or has it just been XO?"

There was dead air.

"You just can't quite believe that they did what they did to me and my crew, so you're going to give them another chance to work yours over. Don't think that being NASA will save you."

"They won't do that," she said.

Frank rattled the drum and stepped back to admire his handiwork. "I don't have that much faith in the justice system. I've seen too much shit go down to think it's fair, or even working right. But I do know this: if this ever went in front of a jury, everyone from the CEO down would get serious flat time. They do not want that. Prison isn't for guys like them. And they will turn every trick in the book to avoid it. If that means offing you, they'll do that in an eyeblink."

"Frank. It's just—" She stopped long enough for Frank to turn round and check she was OK. "We have to do something. We can't just hide ourselves away for months, not talk to anyone back home."

"You fucked up, Isla. Lucy is fucking up at this exact moment, talking to XO. Even if she doesn't tell them about knowing I'm not Brack, she's telling them she knows about M2. I don't know how XO want this to go down, whether they want M2 to kill us or they want everyone dead. But we still end up dead."

"Well, we'll just have to see, won't we?"

Frank picked up the cutter and headed off for more cargo door. "You want to put a bet on this? A hundred bucks says I'm right." He was out of the loop. He had no idea if a hundred dollars was still a significant amount in the outside world. "Hell, I'll do your laundry for a month."

"And if you're right, I have to do yours?"

"If I'm right, neither of us will care about that. But at least I get to use one of my dying breaths to say I told you so." He spun up the cutting disk and applied it to the curved surface of the cargo door. He could feel the vibration in his hands and through the ground, but the sound was of a softly growling animal.

"I came out here to help you," she said, belatedly.

"Can you make that cannon you talked about?"

"Probably. With the right fixings."

"I'll do this. You do that. I'm not in a talking mood right now."

She stalked away over to the boneyard, and he kept his head down, working. It actually started to feel good, doing something constructive with his hands, even if it was armoring the buggies for a fight. He could switch off, and just build, and when he'd done, he felt OK. Not great, because he still had the idea that he was going to die along with the rest of the crew, but considering that, OK.

Fan and Lucy were still inside. They had two bodies to deal with there. One outside—he should really ask them what they wanted to do about that—and there was Jerry to feed and take to the can. A cannibal.

Oh, sure, Jerry had used the defense of not wanting to, being forced to. Frank was pretty certain how it had gone down, with the leader of the group, this Justin, making certain that everyone, absolutely everyone ate, taking them all over a line there was no coming back across. He'd bound them to him, like a gang initiation. Blood in, blood out.

Frank had almost spaced Jerry himself when he'd been told. And no one would have blamed him for notching up kill number six. He didn't know why he'd stopped Fan, either. Except that he had. He'd told Jerry he'd keep him from going under the knife, and he'd kept his word, even if the knife itself was a lie.

This was what happened when he was good: it got complicated. Very complicated. What was Lucy supposed to do with a prisoner, someone who'd eaten one of her colleagues? Not Frank's decision, not now.

He went over to see how far Isla had got with her project.

Plastic pipework was the best they had. A good straight metal tube would have been better—would certainly take more pressure, be more rigid and would wear less—but they were beggars and they had to scavenge whatever they could.

The longer the pipe, the more accurate it'd be. And the more it'd sag. But there were ways around that.

At the back end, she'd fitted a quarter-turn valve and a cistern as an air reservoir, and added a couple more fixings: a non-return valve and a separate spigot. She'd also had time to make projectiles: Martian rock wound round with parachute canopy.

"Have we any compressed CO_2?"

"If you want to rip the fire-suppression system apart, yes. But nothing portable."

"Using oxygen seems a waste."

"Do you want me to get you a tank of what we actually have, or do you want to stand around wishing for something different?"

"You've had the time to adjust to what's going on. I haven't. So while I can understand why you're getting pissy with me, I'm also telling you that it's not helping. Not one little bit." She didn't look at him. Just unscrewed the compression fitting at the breach-end of the barrel and pushed one of the cloth-wrapped rocks into it.

"I'll get Fan to dump a tank in the airlock," said Frank. He spoke to Comms, got Lucy, and by the time he'd walked to the cross-hab, there was a black cylinder in the already pumped-down chamber. All Frank had to do was pick it up and carry it back to the boneyard.

Isla took it from him, and plugged it into the cistern.

"This may explode," she said, as she opened the regulator.

From being a cube, the container rounded out rapidly, and well past the point where Frank would have shut the gas off, she kept on going.

"About that exploding thing," he said.

"I've done this before," was her response. Then she cranked the regulator. "You need to be ballast. I don't want to risk it breaking."

"I'm holding on to something that could blow up in my face."

"Yes, Frank. That's exactly what you're doing."

She waited until Frank had hunkered down and wrapped his arms around the taut-as-a-drum cistern, then crouched next to him with her hand on the quarter-turn tap. The barrel was propped up on a pile of rocks so that it pointed slightly above the horizontal. "Don't block the return valve. OK: three, two, one."

Isla twisted the tap in one quick movement, and Frank felt the cistern kick against him. Proper recoil. He looked up to see how far the projectile had gone, and his gaze was drawn through the expanding cloud of mist at the end of the barrel to a fluttering tail of black and white far in the distance: it was still in the air.

"Fuck."

Its trajectory slowly bent downwards, and when it eventually hit the ground, it bounced and tumbled along for another thirty, forty feet.

Frank stood up and tried to estimate the total distance. Now the rock had stopped moving, it was impossible to see.

"Quarter of a mile?"

"Better than we managed back home. Reduced gravity and no wind resistance. And that's at least a third, if not a half." She closed the tap and began unscrewing the breach again. "Overclocked?"

"Depends what we're trying to do with it. But I can't see any situation where less bang is better than more."

"If we had a pressure gauge, and a safety valve...Dad always insisted on those." She loaded up another rock and laboriously screwed it all together again. "And a bolt action. Yes, I know we don't have the parts, or the time to manufacture them. And after this, we hopefully will never need to."

"I'm sorry," he said. "I'm sorry you've ended up in the middle of this. I'm sorry that this is the only way out of it. There's nothing I can do that'll make what's happened go away. None of you deserved any of this."

"We need to mount this on a buggy. Strap it down. Maybe a seat for the loader, too." Then she stopped and turned back to Frank. "They ate Jim. Why would they even do that?"

"I don't know." Frank stooped to unfasten the oxygen cylinder. "I've been in prison long enough to know that people don't make good decisions at the best of times. And I've seen what happens when the screws stand back and let the gangs take over, like you've got to join one or other of them just to make it through the day. There's no place for neutrals. So, what Jerry said rings true—the guy in charge does it, it's taboo but he's trash-talking the others, says it makes him strong and powerful. It's then, when it's many against one, that you need to take a stand, but everyone's fucking terrified of taking this monster on. Then someone sees how afraid they all are and thinks, 'I'll have me some of that,' and they eat, and suddenly it's two of them and they've got this little club going. These guys are hungry, they're weak, they're scared already, and now they've got to live with cannibals, work with cannibals, sleep next to cannibals, and it's just easier to join in than it is to fight them. That's how it happens."

"Frank, I understand it. I just don't want to understand it."

"I get that."

"He was my friend."

"I know. And now we've got to try and stop the same thing happening to Yun."

He hefted the cistern and propped the pipe barrel up against his shoulder. He started to carry it towards the buggy he'd already fitted out for battle.

"How can you be so calm about this?"

"Because I'm already broken, Isla. Your reaction is the normal one. That's what regular people feel in a situation like this. What's wrong with me can't be fixed. So I may as well use it to help you." Frank slid the length of the air cannon onto the buggy, and dragged it this way and that until he was happy with its position. "You want to pass me some straps?"

She didn't, so Frank fetched his own and started tying the weapon down to the frame.

"Takes something to kill another human being," he said. "Even soldiers, trained to do it with guns and bayonets, most of them never kill another guy. They don't want to do it. You sure as hell don't. Someone with a spear and a club trying to bring you down in your own home, and still you don't stick them with something sharp. That's the right way to behave. You know it. I know it because I was like you once."

"What are you trying to tell me, Frank?"

"That you want to leave the killing to me. You get Yun, first chance you can, and you hightail it out of there. You stay clean. You leave these XO sons-of-bitches to me." Frank tightened the straps, and judged what he'd need to chock the barrel so that it fired horizontally. A couple of drum lids, maybe, and a bracket to hold it in place.

"There's more of them than there are of you," she said. "Or is that the point? You're going to be the big damn hero so you don't have to worry about coming back?"

That wasn't the point. The actual point was too ridiculous to articulate: that he'd had enough of spending his time with killers and cons, and he wanted to preserve Isla's—and the rest of her team's—innocence. He was going to do the terrible things so they didn't have to. And if he came back from M2, and if he was allowed to get on the MAV and go home to Earth and... even if it was now unlikely he'd get his sack of XO cash, he was going to spend so long in front of a grand jury that he'd probably have finished his sentence by the time they were done.

So he said, "Something like that," and he was content to leave it there, but she wasn't.

"That's not going to happen, Frank. You're one of us now."

"I'm never going to be one of you, Isla. Get real."

"Frank, will you just listen to me for a moment?"

"We got stuff to do, Isla. We got to get Yun back and we've not got the daylight to stand around jawing. Just let me get on. If you want to talk, we can do it another time. It's not like I'm the important one around here."

He was the shield. The meat-shield that was going to get in the way for the others. Getting Yun out, alive, was the priority. He'd take his chances as they came to him, and no, he wasn't going to throw his life away, because the longer he stayed upright, the more likely it was that the rescue mission would be successful.

He turned round and Isla was still there. They stared at each other through the near-vacuum of Mars and the faceplates of their suits. His was fuzzed by abrasion and dust thrown up during his labors. Hers was clear. It had been replaced by Fan, and she'd been using parachute cloth to wipe it clean.

"I'll finish fitting out the cannon," she said. "You do what else you need to do."

He nodded. She could see that, so he assumed that they were done for now. He started back towards the cargo rockets, to hack off another set of doors.

"Don't think this is over, Frank."

He slowed, almost stumbled. Then he straightened himself

up and got to work, cutting and shaping and fixing, long into the twilight, almost to the point where his air was going to run out.

He carried the weapons that he'd made to the airlock, and took the control columns off both the buggies and stacked them in there too, to make them less stealable. He was pretty certain that M2 didn't have enough resources to mount another raid any time soon. But he wasn't going to take that to the bank.

The sun had set. The temperature was falling. He was dog tired.

Just like the old days. He closed the airlock door, and cycled it.

30

[Transcript of hearing Judge Treynor Williams III (2nd District (Denver) CO) 3/10/2049]

TW: And you believe these violations of the Commercial Space Transportation Regulations are both serious and sustained?

FAA Agent #1: Your Honor, we do. We believe there have been multiple violations of four-one-four [414], four-one-seven [417], four-twenty [420] and four-sixty [460]. The signed affidavits present evidence of a clear probable cause.

TW: I've read them. I still can't quite believe they put men on Mars, and no one knew about it.

FAA Agent #2: Uh, sir. We're pretty certain a lot of people did know about it. That's why we're applying for a search warrant.

TW: Hush, young lady. In all my forty-seven [47] years on the bench, I don't think I've had an application quite like this, so allow me a moment to express my genuine surprise. Well. Application granted. And may God have mercy on your souls if you're wrong.

[transcript ends]

"XO want to talk to you," said Lucy.

Frank took his time racking his suit. "You going to give me a clue, or am I going in cold?"

"They know you've told us about Brack."

"I figured they might. Did you tell them, or did they guess?"

"I didn't tell them."

"We were shouting at each other before you turned the dish off." Frank pulled on his overalls and went back to the airlock where he'd stashed everything. "OK. That cat's out of the bag. So what do they want? Did you get to talk to NASA at all, or did they stonewall you?"

"We went up the semantic ladder, starting with me requesting and finishing with me demanding. I didn't get to speak to anyone I wanted to." Lucy shrugged. "I got comforting bullshit. Oh, sure they were sorry we got attacked. Really sorry we have dead team members. Really, very sorry that one of them got eaten." Her mouth turned into a thin line, and Frank waited for her. She shrugged again. "They're saying none of this is their fault. They deny that M2 was paid for by chiseling the MBO contract. They're telling me they lost contact with the mission while it was still in transit, and they've not been able to re-establish it. What M2 have done and what they do now is nothing to do with XO. And they've replaced their whole Mission Control team with new people. Said the old ones were under investigation."

"They've taken Luisa. Shit." Frank pulled a face. "There's nothing I can do about that, is there? She's going to be thrown to the wolves, just like we are."

"Maybe we can do something about that when I finally get hold of NASA."

"Yeah. She knows too much. They all do. Look, did you get anything useful out of them at all?"

"Nothing. I got nothing. They say they'll pass messages on to Jim and Leland's relatives. They'll pass messages on to NASA, 'reach out' to them, bring them 'on board', whatever they mean by that. I just wanted to get some sort of confirmation that NASA knew about our situation, so that they could come down and take over."

"And what made you think XO would ever agree to that?

Did you ask them what M2 were doing here in the first place?" Frank opened the airlock and started to collect the shields and the swords he'd made.

"Jesus, Frank."

"Points are sharp, and so's the curved edge." He handed her one, and she made absolutely certain she didn't get any part of it anywhere near the hab walls. "We're a hundred million miles away from Earth. This is the best chance we've got. M2?"

"Commercially sensitive," she said, and sniffed.

Frank took the sword from her and stacked it with the rest. "Why don't we go and find out what they want?"

"They said they wanted to talk to you alone. That this was commercially sensitive too."

"Goddammit, Lucy, I don't give a shit what XO wants any more, and you shouldn't either. They're your enemy now. They've been mine for a while. You want to be in the room? Hell, you should be in the room. Maybe you'll see for yourself how they operate."

He walked through to Comms and sat himself in the chair. There was a message pad open on the console, and he tapped a few letters on the keyboard to make sure it was active.

"This is Frank. You wanted to say something to me."

He sent it, and got up. Lucy was in the doorway.

"Got to wait half an hour. You want me to fix some dinner?"

"I'm not thinking of food right now."

"You want to faint? Look, I've tried that whole denial thing. It doesn't make anything better. It sure as hell won't bring Yun back."

She stood aside with a sigh. "Knock yourself out. It can't make it any worse."

"You haven't seen my cooking yet."

"Don't make jokes. Please."

He checked they were still alone. "You got to hold all this together. Isla, Fan, Yun, they're relying on you."

"Save me the pop psychology. I know what I've got to do."

"Then damn well do it. You got a gun. You got a fucking cannon outside. XO aren't going to be any help except to themselves—their best outcome is that M2 wipes us out. Second-best is that we take each other down. The only guys rooting for us are us."

"There should be a way of getting Yun back without a fight."

"You want me to go over and ask nicely? Or have I tried that already with Jim, only to discover. They. Fucking. Ate. Him."

"This is a scientific mission."

"This is war."

They were both shouting. The others would have heard them. Frank didn't care. But it wasn't what he wanted to do.

"So while I wait for a reply, I'm going to make a big bowl of greens, soak some grains, get some fresh herbs and a couple of chilies and see how that goes together. Then we're going to sit down and eat together whether we all like it or not. We get an early night, because we're up again at two, checking our equipment and loading it up, and it is *cold* at that time of night. If you've got a better plan, then sure, I want to hear it. Otherwise, get out of the goddamn way."

"I'm not in it." She was still standing to one side of the door.

"It's a metaphor. Or something like that."

"I'll tell you when something comes in. Otherwise, go."

Frank went and washed up, then rattled around the kitchen for some bowls. He got water onto a bunch of wheat and microwaved it up, and while that was settling, went into the greenhouse for the leaves.

He was on his own. While he was passing the airlock, he heard low voices in the med bay, and presumed it was Isla and Fan. He hadn't asked about Jerry. Maybe they'd decided they were going to toss him at the same time they'd decided they were going to talk to XO. Could they keep him on permanently? As a prisoner? Or even a trusty? Did he want to share living space with this guy? And yet, the irony was, XO had told him right at the very start of this, that the base would be a prison facility. Frank himself was prisoner number one. This guy was just the second.

So sure, he'd worked with murderers and thieves and perverts. Why not Jerry?

He carried the veggies back through to the kitchen and got mixing. He could still do with some oil for a dressing, and by that, a press for the groundnuts, which he still hadn't gotten around to making. He threw a cupful of them in whole anyway, and used the starchy liquor from the wheat to carry the finely chopped chili and cilantro across the whole meal.

At some point, he became aware of Lucy sitting at the end of the table, waiting for him.

"How long you been there?"

"Five minutes or so. Watching you work."

"You could have set the table."

"I could have done. But then I'd just be setting it for four, not seven, and that'd remind me how far down we've gone. Yes, you're right. I need to hold it together. But I'm also a human being and those were my friends, and I'm entitled to grieve."

"I'm not busting your balls, Lucy. You handle this however you want. All I'm doing is giving you advice."

"You're pretty persistent about it, Frank."

"I'm just trying not to die here. That's all. Not yet, anyhow."

"They've responded."

Frank shook his hands and rinsed them over the sink, then in the absence of a working towel, wiped them on his overalls.

"So what do they say?"

"Why not come and take a look?"

She led the way back into Comms, and left the seat free for Frank. He settled in it and moved closer so he could see the screen.

He was quiet for a while, just absorbing what was probably going to be the very last contact he was ever going to have with XO. This clearly wasn't from Luisa. The suits had taken full control of the message feed. He kicked back and thought about his response.

"What do you think? A simple 'go fuck yourself', or something more profound?"

"You think that's a good idea? Yes, OK, I admit I was wrong. XO have no intention of cooperating with us, but willfully antagonizing them?"

"You're going to pull the plug on them after I send this, right?"

"I don't see how I've got any choice," said Lucy, "but telling you that 'protecting XO assets on the Martian surface is your chief priority' and then threatening to sue the U.S. government for the cost of what gets damaged is pretty clear. Just so as I know, are you going to," and she chased down the lines of text with her fingertip, " 'prevent third parties from pre-emptively acting against XO-owned and maintained facilities, without prior authorization and agreement, and in direct contravention of the Outer Space Treaty of 1967'?"

"No, you're good."

"Because otherwise I was going to invoke the Rescue Agreement of 1968, which technically only applies to state actors, which NASA is, but in the circumstances, XO are obligated to help us."

"They've no hold over me. Not any more. I can't help my son, whatever happens. But I can help the people in front of me, here on Mars." Frank flexed his fingers and began to peck out his response on the keyboard.

"Tell me about him."

"He was blond when he was born. Didn't expect that at all. Blond curls. Then they all fell out and it came out dark brown and straight, like his mother's. He was a good kid. Athletic. I must have spent hours sitting on the bleachers while he trained. Then it kind of started to slide when he hit senior high. Got in with the wrong crowd. Stopped sports, started parties. You know. I guess we were all young once. The way I dealt with it all, I made as many bad choices as he did, except mine went way over smoking some weed and taking a few pills. What the hell was I thinking? I could have done so many other things. I just got lost in it all. But I never stopped loving him. I never have."

"And he doesn't know you're here?"

"How could he possibly know?"

"XO really did a number on you, didn't they?"

"Yes ma'am, yes they did." He looked again at what he'd written. "How does that sound?"

She leaned over his shoulder and read his words. "'Dear XO, the deal's off. I quit. I'm going to take my chances with the Feds if and when I get back—just like you will. If you hurt Luisa, you'll answer for that too. She was the only one of you bastards who ever showed me any understanding, and is pretty much the only reason I made it this far. Also, go fuck yourselves. Frank.' You really want to burn all your bridges, don't you?"

"We're on our own here. It's us or M2. Everyone else is too far away to do jack. Unless you're telling me you don't need me."

"Not saying that at all. But as commander, I need to be able to explain to my superiors every decision taken on this base that might affect crew safety. This, this is pretty final. You send this and we're cutting all contact."

"It's your call." He waited. He waited for a long time.

"We're not really losing anything, are we? Send it, Frank. Send it, and let's go eat."

Frank clicked the button, and watched while the message worked its way through the system, to the dish and out. "Really need to be turning this shit off now."

"I'll go and pull the plug. No more traffic until we can get our own secure channel."

He left her to it, and went to find Isla and Fanuel.

They were standing a little way away from one of the gurneys, where a black body bag lay, unnervingly full.

"Lucy's calling you into the kitchen," he said.

They had body bags. More than his team ever had. But someone at NASA had thought ahead, had planned for fatalities, and had used some part of the cargo manifest to send body bags to Mars, on the assumption that those bodies would be coming back to Earth again. Everyone on the crew had known that death was a possibility, and had also known that even then, they'd be taken home and not abandoned.

He could feel his face stiffen, and he blinked rapidly. Of all the things to get upset about, someone showing a measure of respect to a corpse that he'd never got in life had to be one of the stupidest. Yet here he was, working his jaw and trying not to cry.

"Go on," he said. "She's waiting for you."

He felt a hand on his back, fleeting, warm. Human contact that wasn't the prelude to an assault. Then he was alone with the dead.

He leaned his knuckles on the gurney, looking down at the heavy-duty zipper that ran the length of the bag, the write-on patch for identifying who was inside—FISHER Leland 3/8/49. Twenty forty-nine. How the hell had it got to twenty forty-nine? There were plugs and valves on the bag. A NASA logo. A medical company logo. The words "Body Back" and a serial number.

"Should have done more, Leland. I should have done more."

What else could he have done, though? Jim would still have disappeared, M2 would still have attacked, and that was pretty much it. The only thing he could have done differently was tell the NASA crew everything from the very start—and it would still have unwound with XO undermining his testimony.

The only way it would have been better would be for M2 to have found all their gear and not to have turned into a bunch of crazies led by a madman. Them on their side of the hill, NASA on the other. That would have worked out. That would have been fine.

Instead, it was a mess. A goddamn mess.

He went back through to the kitchen. They were sitting around the table, bowls in front of them, cutlery laid out, glasses of water poured. Waiting for him.

"OK, you're going to have to give me a minute," said Frank.

Rather than disturb the place settings, he got another bowl out from storage and used the big plastic spoon to scoop some of the salad up. He went for a second helping, shook the bowl, then carried it, and a knife, back to the med bay, past Leland's body bag, and unlocked the examination room. He'd reaffixed the door himself.

Jerry, curled up in the far corner beneath a blanket, didn't move, though he was clearly watching what Frank was doing. He saw the knife, and perhaps he thought this was it.

"Chow time, Jerry."

Jerry blinked, and rolled himself upright, leaning against the partition.

"Let's see your hands."

"What are they going to do with me?"

"At the moment, 'they' are trying to give you dinner. Beyond that, I don't know. It's not up to me."

"They going to send me back?"

"Back to M2? You want that? Because we can take you with us and dump you there, after we've rescued Yun and taken out your buggies so you can never hurt us again. You'll starve to death in the cold and the dark. Quickly, slowly. Maybe you get to do the eating, maybe you get eaten. What do you think, Jerry?"

"I don't want to get sent back."

"So let me see your hands."

Jerry ass-shuffled so his back was to Frank. His wrists were cable-tied together, and Frank sliced through the tie.

"You came here as a prisoner, right?" Jerry rubbed at his wrists. "Maybe that can work out for me. Make myself useful over here."

"You ate their friend."

"I didn't want to. He made me."

"No one cares about your motives. Just about what you did. They're decent people, and they're not as used to the depths of human behavior as I am. Any one of them could decide living with you is just too risky and throw you out the airlock. They might just decide to do that anyway, in the cold light of day. We don't need you."

313

"I can do stuff. Computer stuff. I'm an expert. And electronics and electrics. I can do all of that."

"Jerry, that's what you did. Maybe that defined you before, with all your certificates and your college degrees and whatever. I know something about that. I was a builder. A good one. I ran my own company and I employed people and paid them on time and together we built houses. Then I shot someone, and all I was was a murderer. And all you are is a cannibal. Accept it. It'll make things easier for you." Frank pushed the bowl over to Jerry. "This is what we're eating. You can take it or leave it. You don't get so much as a spork to eat it with, though: I've seen what a man can do with one. You leave this room, I'll toss your ass myself. You and me, we're never going to be best buddies, but for some reason or other, I'm your best hope of making it through the next sol. Don't piss me off by doing anything stupid."

Jerry nodded. "OK. I get it."

"The door stays locked. You've got a bucket. Use it because we're not checking on you for comfort breaks every five minutes. Try and break out, and it'll be the last thing you ever do. Now, I'm going to eat too, and after that you'll probably get tied up again. So make the most of it. There are no guarantees here. If Lucy wants you gone, I can't save you."

Frank closed the door behind him. He clicked the lock, and pushed one of the empty gurneys up against the opening. If Jerry tried to get out, they'd hear him.

Then he went back and took his place at the table. They were watching him carefully.

"I feel sorry for him, for now. That's all." He took the spoon and helped himself to the salad. No one else had, and no one else did, for a while.

Eventually, Isla reached across and dragged the serving dish over towards her. She gave herself a tiny portion, barely anything, but from her expression it was going to be all she could gag down. Lucy reluctantly followed, and when she'd finished, she pushed it at Fan.

Who stared at it for the longest time.

"That's an order," she said, softly.

He didn't have the willpower to defy her. The fight had gone out of him, and he theatrically clattered the spoon on the edge of his bowl to knock the last few grains of boiled wheat off.

Frank looked around the table, and found that everyone else was doing exactly the same. It wasn't just ridiculous, but painfully, obviously so. He picked up his spork, toyed with it for a few seconds, then said: "You know what? Fuck it. If I'm going to die, I'm going down with a full belly. A couple of cold ones would go down nicely, but some damn fool decided this base was dry."

He took a mouthful and chewed and swallowed, and went back for another.

"My parents," said Isla. "They never drank. Very strict. When I used to come home from college, I had to hide my beer out in the barn, and the nearest place to buy it was some fifty miles away. Those summers were long." And she ate. "It's good, Frank," she said.

After that, the floodgates opened. Reminiscences of childhoods in cities and on islands, on prairies and on air force bases. Things they'd done. Scars they'd earned. Loves they'd lost and hearts they'd broken.

One last normal evening, because they didn't know who'd be coming back tomorrow.

31

[Transcript of Officer Denny Kraft Salt Lake City PD and Dispatcher (Jem Macintyre) 3/10/2049]

Dispatcher: They've all gone?
DK: Every single one of them. I mean, I know this place was a
    ghost town before they got here. But everything's just been
    left. Except the people.
Dispatcher: Doors open?
DK: Nah. Everything's locked up. I'm not going to go breaking
    windows without a warrant.
Dispatcher: No sign of our caller?
DK: There's no sign of anyone, Jem. The whole place is
    deserted. Pete's gone around the lot, same as I have, and it's
    like they've just been raptured. You know?
Dispatcher: You want backup?
DK: I don't know. I mean, it's not a crime to just up and leave,
    but this is thousands of people. And we got that call.
Dispatcher: Maybe you and Pete should come back to the station.
DK: We're out here now. We'll go on to the fence. See what we
    can see. Maybe someone there we can ask.
Dispatcher: OK, Denny. You take care now.

[transcript ends]

Loading up in the dead of night, at the coldest moment, when
everything was glittering with ice, was hard. Plastic was brittle,
rubber was like iron, and their suits were stiff.

Frank hitched up a trailer, put drums on it and when they were full—ropes, straps, life supports, oxygen canisters, weapons in one, shields in another, even Leland's suit in case one of theirs, or Yun's, got damaged—they got ratcheted down. Everything they thought they'd need. Plenty of pre-made ammunition for the cannon. Spare parachute cloth. Rubber patches, a full medical kit even though getting into a pressurized environment to use it was going to be problematic at best. But if they didn't take it, they couldn't pop back for it later.

At three on the nose, Lucy, with Isla strapped into a bucket seat from the kitchen behind her, drove off in the direction of the Santa Clara. Frank followed with the trailer, Fan riding behind him. The tire plates growled and crackled against the loose rocks grown heavy with white frost.

They left the base behind, internal lights barely showing through the dense covering of the habs, the dish pointing blindly up into the sky. Overhead, the stars burned through like holes in a curtain.

It took them two hours to get to the outpost, where they discovered that anything that hadn't been nailed down was gone. Panels, stores, electronic equipment that was vital for Yun's work, scrubbers, gas cylinders, either vanished or gutted. There was little reason in taking some of the stuff: perhaps M2 were just punishing them for their abundance.

Frank made the others stay outside while he checked out the interior of the hab. It was still pressurized—a little saggy but otherwise sound—and someone could have been inside. It was freezing, and he walked through the debris of ransacking with the hope that maybe there was someone from M2 there, so that he could get an explanation as to why all this pointless, expensive waste.

It was silent, except for his own footsteps.

"We're good," he said. "Come on in, but don't touch anything with bare hands or feet, or you'll be leaving your skin behind."

They swapped out their life supports, one at a time, and then remounted and drove on, with Frank in front this time. He knew the way.

The occasional voices in his ear started to chop and eventually cut out altogether. The NASA suits were still linked together, as long as they stayed close to each other. The XO suit which Frank wore wasn't. He was out of range of the main antenna back at MBO, and the one they'd set up at the outpost had been stolen.

It was going to make it difficult when they got to M2, and something he should really have thought about first, not that they could have changed it. He might have swapped into Leland's suit, but Leland had been a different size and shape to Frank. He had to drive on in silence.

He led the way down the volcano's hard, ridged slopes. With the lights on, they would be easy to spot—but only if someone was looking. It was very much easier said than done, standing out in the freezing night, acting as a lookout. MBO had been attacked in broad daylight, and Yun hadn't even managed to warn anyone inside before M2 had started coming through the airlocks.

Bouncing the cave base wasn't going to be the difficult part. Dealing with the occupants while not killing Yun, assuming she was still alive, was.

That was the problem with these long drives. Being in his own head, nothing to do but steer and stare out at a landscape that hadn't changed for tens of thousands of years, and wouldn't for another ten thousand. Nothing they did would make any difference, in the long run. Sure, lives saved, lives lost, but there'd be other Martian missions, other Martian bases. When someone came to write a history of Mars, MBO's fight with M2 might make a paragraph or two. They probably wouldn't even mention anyone's name.

When it came down to it, there was so little at stake. A few people, duking it out on the surface of an uninhabitable planet, when there were countless billions at home. It felt meaningful to him, but in a hundred years' time, who was going to care? He managed to keep his wheels pointing south. What was he in this for? Revenge? Hell, yes. Anything that was going to piss XO off was worth doing. And mercy: Yun shouldn't be abandoned, not to this bunch of psychopaths. Even if it was too late, there was always justice. Which, for Frank, felt strange, having spent so long on the other side of it.

The eastern sky started to lighten, and he looked up to see one moon chase towards the sunrise, while the other seemed painted onto the western horizon. The land slowly changed from a blank canvas to one with black pits and gray rock. Then, as the temperature rose, the ice started to burn off.

Had the others never seen this before? Frank had, not just on his previous trip to M2, but on countless early mornings, where he had to hoard the daylight like a miser and spend it thriftily.

Lucy brought her buggy to a stop as the ground steamed and swirled with fog. Twists of smoke spiraled upwards and vanished, and all too soon the spectacle was much diminished, with only sheltered spots sending drifts of white vapor rolling out and up.

It looked like Hell. It could well be.

The first slanting rays of weak sunlight made more substantial shadows from the buggies, and the figures balanced on them, and Lucy set off again, allowing Frank to pull ahead as they descended towards the foot of the volcano.

They reached level ground, and Frank could, in the distance, see the dark scar of the trench. He pointed towards its eastern end and turned his wheel slightly. He was down on watts from where he'd been at this stage previously, due to the increased weight of towing. He might have to abandon the trailer for the trip back, assuming there'd be one—he might even have to abandon the buggy at the outpost. Someone could collect both later.

He kept watch for any movement ahead of him, but could see nothing. Just miles of dust and rock and craters, like most of Mars. Why would anyone want to come here? Sure, scientists, but a land grab? Get in before the competition? Who would want this? Why throw money and people at a place that was dead, dead, dead?

That was XO's plan: it didn't have to make any sense. Maybe he'd ask Lucy about it.

Now they were out on the plain, he could make out tire tracks: his own, and those of the M2 buggies that had chased him. Easy to follow them round to the entrance of the trench, not so easy to make himself drive that route, knowing what he faced at the end of it.

Then they were there, at the start of the five-mile-long trench that sloped gradually downwards and disappeared into the dark vault at the far end. The descent ship was clearly visible as a white thumb pointing skywards, but not the hab hidden in the cave.

Frank rolled to a halt, and Lucy pulled in alongside him. They dismounted and met in the middle, touching helmets.

"You good?" asked Frank.

"As far as the circumstances dictate."

"I'll hand out the weapons, and detach the trailer. Then I'll just follow your lead. Fan has the spare suit, and I'll run as much interference as I can. And don't wait for me: Yun's the priority here."

"You know I'm never going to agree to that."

"Is this where I tell you to go fuck yourself, Lucy? Because I will if I have to."

"Sure you will, Frank. I make the rules now: no one gets left behind."

They separated, and Frank held out his fist. She dapped it, deliberately and self-consciously. There wasn't anything left to say.

He took out the shields he'd made, handed them up to Fan

and Isla, then went back for the swords. It looked ridiculous, but no one had come up with a better idea. And, to be fair, it looked terrifying as well. The shock of facing armed and armored warriors when all that separated you from instant death was a pressure suit might just be enough to force a surrender.

Frank unhitched the trailer, strapped his shield to his left arm and, for the want of anything better to do with it, passed his sword to Fan. He climbed up to the driver's seat and wondered what it was going to be like.

He started forward, and Lucy matched his speed. Isla loaded up the cannon, and fixed the oxygen cylinder to the cistern.

Everything ahead of them was quiet. No spacesuited figures, no one coming out early to clean and turn the solar panels. Maybe, maybe they'd done everyone a favor and turned on each other, and Yun was inside, just waiting to be picked up. Maybe it wouldn't come to a fight after all.

They swept past the descent ship, and started to slow. Sometime soon, surely, they'd have to be spotted. Not yet, though. Not yet.

Frank put the brakes on some hundred yards from the shadowed hab. He sat in his seat, watching the airlock, and still nothing. Then he stood up in his seat and looked back at the ship.

The descent ship he came in had had cameras on the outside.

Goddammit, they were going to have to go in and quickly.

He climbed down, held Fan's sword while he dismounted, and together they jogged up to the hab's airlock.

It had exactly the same design as their own. XO standard hardware. He ran up the steps, and pressed the airlock cycle button.

Red light.

OK, so the airlock had power, but it wasn't cycling. Someone had propped the inner door open. The only way in was to equalize the pressure either side of the outer door, and Frank knew two ways of doing that. One slow and easy to thwart, and one quick, and very, very dirty. And if Yun was in there, out of her suit, most likely fatal.

He butted heads with Fan.

"We're not getting in that way. We have to go through the wall."

"Do they know we're outside?"

"Yes. Get Isla to fire."

Lucy had rolled her buggy so that it was square on, some fifty feet away. She grabbed Leland's suit, and dashed across the open ground, dragging its heels after her. Then she handed it to Fan, who tucked his sword under the metal steps, to keep it from being used against him.

She gave Frank the OK sign. She turned and gave Isla the OK sign.

They all crouched down, and Isla turned on the oxygen.

It felt like he'd been waiting for ever when there was an audible pop, and the thick membrane of the hab puckered inwards. A fist-sized hole appeared about six feet off the ground, and the rubber rippled as the shockwave whipped through it.

Almost immediately, the warm, moist air inside started to geyser out, turning to ice in the frigid near-vacuum outside. Frank drove his sword through the breach and dragged it down. The gust knocked him backwards, but Lucy was already pushing through, braced against the headwind. Frank leaned in behind.

The countdown had started. They didn't have long. Twenty, thirty seconds to find Yun, get her into a suit, pressurize it.

Entering the hab, Frank didn't know what to expect. What he could get out of Jerry was that they'd partially put the second-storey floor in, but there were no internal walls. Stores, such as they were, were downstairs. Sleeping was upstairs. There'd be at least one ladder up, and he could jump and scale eight feet in open space in any event.

It was far more filthy, more chaotic, than he'd anticipated, but the basic structure was right. Lucy had gone left, to the ladder, so he went right, climbing over a loose pile of drums towards the clear area beyond. The air pressure was dropping fast, and he couldn't hear much, nothing beyond the faint sound of Lucy's boots on the rungs. Fan was through too, looking frantically for Yun on the lower deck.

She didn't seem to be there, so Frank left Fan to search, and reached the open portion of the hab.

No sign of Yun.

He spotted movement above him: outlined by the faint light, two figures were struggling to enter their spacesuits. OK, Frank. Remember what you came here to do. Save Yun. These people made their choices, just as you made yours. They get to live with that, same as you do.

Frank bent his legs beneath him, and pushed off with as much force as he could muster. It was Mars, and he soared.

The edge of the floor passed his eyeline, and he planted his feet solidly on the platform, right arm outstretched so he didn't cut himself on his own sword. But the two people—one man, one woman—frantically trying to seal their suits, were simply intent on finding air to breathe, and not interested in him.

Where the hell was Yun? The emergency lighting didn't show her at all.

Lucy emerged at the top of the ladder and instinctively smashed her shield boss into the faceplate of someone who'd already got their suit on. There was someone else at her feet, moving feebly, trying to crawl away—definitely not Yun, but the guy Frank had faced off earlier, the one who'd taken Jim's suit. The two behind him weren't Yun either.

Where was she?

He knew that letting them get into their suits and then having to fight them didn't make any sense. He put his foot against the female astronaut's side and kicked her over the edge, then swung his sword hard at the second. They put their hand up to ward off Frank's blow—instinctive, but very wrong.

The blade wasn't sharp-sharp, but it was moving fast and it

broke the man's hand as it hit the palm of the gauntlet. The scream was silent, and Frank kicked him away, too, sending him spinning down into the drums and the debris below.

He checked quickly on Lucy—her man was down, cowering, covering his head, his back to her, and the crawler, suitless, had stopped moving completely. Below him, the woman had managed to seal herself, and she was making her way towards the rent, and towards Fan.

Frank dropped on her from above, boots hitting her helmet, sending them both falling apart. They were up at the same time, but Frank knew where his enemy was, while she would only be able to see Fan's suit lights as he pushed and pulled the drums aside.

Frank punched out with his shield, right into her life support, and sent her sprawling. Seeing her in that suit, lying there, arms out, legs spread, reminded him too much of Brack and he could feel himself go into that same cold place where killing was necessary and the only thing that would save him and those he cared about.

Then Fan was there, arms around him, holding him back. Their helmets were touching, and he was saying, "It's OK, Frank. It's OK. You can stop now. You can stop," over and over, and after a while, the urge to keep stabbing and hitting faded, and he was able to listen to reason once more.

He took a step back. Yun wasn't here. That meant one of two things.

Frank went to check on the guy whose hand he'd hacked at. It turned out the man hadn't managed to close his suit anyway. His faceplate was thick with frost from his last breath, and smoke was starting to spiral out through the open hatch as his fluids boiled away. He was beyond saving.

By the time Frank turned back round, Lucy had marched her prisoner down to the lower deck at sword point, and forced him to his knees. Fan stood over the woman brought down by Frank, and he stepped away to allow her to be turned over.

Frank found himself looking down at someone who was just a kid. Early twenties. Wide-eyed, unblinking. Breathing hard, fogging the faceplate momentarily before the fans cleared it. Frank looked at her, looking up at him. The absolute terror. The imminence of death.

He knelt down and he pressed his helmet against hers. He could hear her now, her panicked, whistling breath.

"Feng Yun. Tell me where she is."

"In the ship in the ship she's in the ship with Justin don't don't she's alive I swear she's still alive—"

Frank pulled his head away, and leaned into Fan. "She's in the descent ship with the boss. Alive, she says."

"How do we get her out? We can't cut our way through like we did with the hab."

"Should have brought a can opener." Frank looked around, then came back into contact with Fan. "Let's get these jokers outside. We've got to think of a way, and quickly, or we'll be the ones running out of air."

He hauled the kid off the floor and shoved her in the direction of the rent, which now hung loose. He kept one hand on her shoulder as he pushed her through first, keeping close behind her. He needn't have worried, as Isla was already there, sword poised and looking fierce.

Lucy's prisoner was next, then Lucy, and finally Fan, still dragging Leland's empty suit after him.

They tied the two M2 crew members to the steps leading up to the airlock. Frank and the others put their heads together.

"Does he know we're coming for him?" asked Lucy.

"He knows all right," said Frank. He looked back towards the cave. "I've got an idea."

32

[Transcript of private phone call between Paul Leander (CEO XO) and Marjorie Bellingham (PL's Personal Assistant) XO headquarters, Tower of Light, Denver CO 3/10/2049 0822MT

PL: Mags, has there been anything from Bruno?

MB: No, sir. I've talked to his people—actually, his people's people—and they don't know where he is.

PL: Have you tried Gold Hill?

MB: Sir, I've tried everywhere. Mr. Tiller and the entirety of Mr. Tiller's staff have dropped off the map. They're not answering their phones, or their emails, and no one seems to know where they've gone.

PL: I'm not happy, Mags. I'm not happy at all. This business with the Mars base is dragging on. XO stock is down, and the board are asking questions. Bruno should be in front of the cameras, not hiding from them.

MB: I hear you, sir. I will keep trying every avenue.

[transcript ends]

It all needed to go like clockwork, and there were too many ways for things to go wrong for Frank to feel any certainty at all. But it was literally all they had. Justin knew what they were outside for. If he hadn't wanted a confrontation, he could have sent Yun out to them. He'd had plenty of time, but there'd been no move, no attempt at communication. They were going in.

They couldn't force their way into the descent ship's airlock. There was a manual release, but that could be blocked from the inside. Even with the sliding, rather than hinged, door, they'd need to essentially break it.

And then they'd have to do the same thing again with the inner door. And once they were in, the ship would be depressurizing the same way the hab had. Justin would be waiting for them. They'd have to fight their way past him to get to Yun, and get her into a suit, all within thirty seconds. Max.

It was what they'd been going to do if she'd been in the hab—but access to a plastic hab and access to the interior of a metal spaceship were two entirely different scenarios, and now they needed a new plan.

Frank had explained what he had in mind, and, since time was short, the others had agreed all too quickly. Given that these guys were supposed to be the smart ones, and he was just a construction worker from San Francisco, they were all scraping the barrel. No pressure, then.

In the back of the cave, he found the makings of a second hab, the one that Jerry had told him they hadn't had enough energy to make air for, or heat. Everything was there: the rings, the bolts, the cover. And, critically, the airlock.

The four of them dragged that part out and carried it over to the rocket. Isla disconnected the oxygen cylinder from the cannon, and Frank put both that and the spare spacesuit inside the unpressurized compartment. Then they stabilized it, using ratchet straps wrapped around big blocks of fallen masonry from the cave roof.

It all took time. And the external spaceship cameras were watching them.

Fan positioned himself next to the airlock. He knew what to do. Maybe he'd wanted a go at Justin himself, but since he was the doctor and had trained for decompression injuries, this was his job. It was up to the others to extract Yun.

Frank mounted one buggy, and drove it over to the ship,

327

reversing it up to one of the landing legs. He paid out some cable, and Lucy threaded it around the leg, carabiner locking on to the cable itself. He wound in the slack, and she climbed up behind him, tapping him on the shoulder to let him know she was ready.

What were they going to find inside? Who knew? Maybe Yun was in her spacesuit. And this Justin, this mad leader of a failed mission, was naked to the air. That would make everything so much easier. Maybe Yun was already dead. Maybe Justin was too. That would also be easier, as it would mean Frank hadn't had a hand in killing either of them.

But this wasn't about what he'd find easier to live with. This was about getting a certain result and damn the method. A result that in the cold, pale light of the Martian day stood about as much chance as a snowflake in this particular unpressurized hell.

He turned his rear-view cameras on. In the little picture on the console's screen, he could see the edge of the ship, the leg and, in the distance, Isla turning the second buggy around, ready for her run.

Either this would work, or it wouldn't. Lucy had assured him it would...in theory.

In practice, it was a total crap shoot.

He sat, fingers curled around the steering column, and waited for the signal. Maybe something else would come to him, so that he didn't have to do any of this. So that they could come up with another, better scheme.

Lucy put her hand into his eyeline and gave him the OK.

Well, crap. Time was up.

He squeezed the controls and kept one eye on the screen in front of him.

The cable he'd paid out went abruptly taut and his body jerked forward against his harness. The tires scrabbled for purchase through the dust and against the rock, spurting red fog up and out.

"Come on, you bastard." He gave the wheels maximum grip and gunned the engine.

If this were Earth, he'd be able to hear the tensioned cable sing and the spaceship's metal leg groan. All he heard was a deep bass growl as they started to drag the whole ship across the surface of Mars.

That was not what they'd intended at all.

He glared at the screen and hauled the controls around to the left. There was a crater. If the leg wasn't going to give way on its own, he was going to have to let the terrain lend a hand. Of course, moving the ship was pulling it away from the airlock, and away from Isla, but goddammit, they had to get it down somehow.

Lucy banged on his shoulder, and when he didn't respond, hammered on it again.

He let go of the controls, frustrated, and pushed himself back in his seat.

She leaned her helmet against his. "It's not working."

"You don't say. Unhitch the tow. We'll try again."

"Which leg?"

"Unhitch, and I'll drive round."

She climbed down and walk-ran back to the descent ship. There was no element of surprise. Justin could see exactly what they were doing, and there wasn't anything they could do about that. There wasn't much Justin could do about it either, or at least, that's what Frank hoped.

Lucy unclipped the hitch and laid it on the ground. Frank wound it back in and waited for the autostop to shut the cable reel down. Then he turned the buggy around and examined the geometries carefully.

So, not the leg he'd been trying to buckle. The one that was now between him and the airlock. He gestured to Lucy—waving his hands from left to right, as if sweeping the path ahead of him. Then he settled his hands back on the controls and squeezed hard.

The wheels dug in, and he sped across the surface, dust and rock flicking up behind him. Belatedly, Lucy realized what he was about to do. She scrambled out of his way, and Frank slammed the buggy's cargo-drum battering ram into the side of the landing leg.

He hit it hard. The straps bit down against his hard carapace, and the buggy's back-end came up. He'd forgotten to clamp his jaw shut, and now his teeth hurt. And his neck. And his shoulder. When the dust of the collision had settled, he backed up. The leg had bent, but it hadn't buckled. He drove backwards fifty feet, and gave it everything the fuel cell had.

This time, he tensed up. He clenched his jaw. He pushed himself into the back of his seat and prepared for the bang.

It was more brutal than before. He could feel parts inside of him move in ways they were never designed to, and when they stopped, he felt disorientated and sick. He struggled to find the controls, even though they were right in front of him, and had to remind himself how to put the buggy in reverse.

One more time. One more. He'd buckled the whole support, and he needed to hit it again to bring it down.

He pulled back seventy feet. Eighty. Enough? He didn't know anything beyond the fact that this was going to hurt. He took the column, squeezed the triggers and leaned into the direction of travel.

The impact left him hanging limply over the controls, his harness the only thing stopping him falling out of his seat. He shook his head and blinked hard. He'd felt something tear. At first he thought it was just dust on his faceplate, but maybe it was blood in his eye. Isla was standing up, waving at him, pointing above him.

Frank craned his head backwards. Something went click in his neck, but he didn't have time to faint or throw up, because there was a spaceship about to topple over, and it didn't much care where it was going to end up.

Reverse. For the love of God, reverse. For all his bemoaning the lack of cold beer, he was punch-drunk. It took time to find his hands, longer for them to connect with the controls, and he started by trying to go forward again, knocking against the collapsing leg as it twisted into the fold made by repeated blows from the buggy.

That button. That one there. He mashed his palm against it and squeezed the triggers again. He shot backwards in an arc that terminated in a four-wheel drift across the Martian surface. He had no idea what he was doing any more. He sprang his fingers from the controls.

The buggy juddered to a halt, tilting over, and dropping back on its wheels with an emphatic and possibly final bounce. Frank reached up and slapped at his chest, once, twice, three times to release the harness.

The ship was falling, its leg bent beyond use. It tipped, and, in what appeared to be slow-motion, went past the point of no return.

Frank tumbled over the edge of the buggy, hanging on to the frame. He pulled himself upright just as the fuselage hit the ground. It crumpled against rocks and boulders, sending out clouds of dust and waves of sand, all in almost perfect silence. Frank could feel it, though, through the soles of his already unsteady feet. The nose cone dug itself in a yard from where he stood, and he didn't have the wit to flinch.

The nose rose again, towering over him, and he watched it go, open-mouthed.

It settled, rocking backwards and forwards in ever-decreasing cycles, and Lucy, not realizing just how damaged he was, thrust his shield and sword at him. Frank stood there, staring at these items that he knew meant something but couldn't work out precisely what.

He took them anyway, and let himself be dragged to one side.

Behind, Isla turned her buggy in a tight circle, and drove directly at the side of the fallen ship.

It tore through the flimsy metal skin and composite core like it was foil. Gas erupted in a white cloud around the front of the buggy, and when Isla reversed out it revealed a rent, a hole punched into the flank, big enough to climb through and access the inside.

And Frank came back to himself with a sudden realization that the clock had started. Thirty seconds to save Yun.

He fumbled his shield onto his arm and dragged his sword point off the ground. Lucy was ahead of him, and he scrambled to catch up. The edges of the ship's wound were turned inwards. Getting in was just a question of pushing through the gale.

He knew the layout. He remembered it. Sleep tanks at the top. Middle storey with a mesh floor. Bottom layer with storage and controls and the airlock. They were in the middle level, and there was Yun, gasping and gulping as the air streamed out into the insatiable void beyond the circular walls.

He barely had time to register her presence when he saw a spacesuited figure launch itself at him, coming from his right. One of the mesh floor panels came loose and struck him hard on the shoulder, and while the momentum wasn't enough to knock him down, it was enough to momentarily blindside him.

Frank's helmet sounded like a gong. He raised his arms, and the second blow accidentally struck his shield. It hurt, but it still gave him a moment to recover and reorient.

Justin was in a spacesuit like his own, and he was attacking him with a hammer. A geology hammer. Jim's. Justin's face was…not impassive. Determined. Serious. Intent on killing him, and moving on to the next job. He brought the hammer down again, and Frank interposed his shield, and it hurt again, jarring his arm, making his shoulder burn.

Frank couldn't see what was happening behind him. He could only assume that Lucy had grabbed Yun and pushed her through the opening to the willing hands beyond, that Yun hadn't panicked and fought her off, that she hadn't already died from an embolism, or sheer fright.

The hammer kept on rising and falling, smashing into Frank

when he couldn't get his shield in the way, and into his arm when he could, pushing him back and back towards the ceiling of the middle deck until the only way out was to fight or die. Justin seemed oblivious to his hopeless situation, to the reason he was still attacking Frank, to the whole fact that his ship was now lying on the sands of Mars, gutted and open to the outside.

He just wanted to kill Frank.

And maybe that was OK. Frank had done what he'd come here to do. Goddammit, he was tired of all this shit, and maybe signing off was something he could contemplate. He saw his own derangement mirrored in the eyes of another—it was the same look he'd worn in the rear-view mirror moments before he'd got out of his truck, gun in hand.

He slipped to one knee, shield over his head, the blows against it steady and methodical, like a metronome. His left arm was numb. His shoulder on fire. Justin wasn't going to stop. He absolutely wasn't going to stop. Was Frank going to do any thing about that?

He was going to slowly, surely, get battered to the ground and have his faceplate cracked open, and all the air in his lungs and liquid in his body boil out through the wounds. His testimony, his witness, his crew's story, lost for ever. Unless he used the sword in his right hand.

For them, then. For them.

Frank lifted the shield higher and swung at Justin's legs. He hit. Not hard enough. He pulled back, suffered another literal hammer-blow to his upraised arm that almost tore it from its socket, and swung again.

This time he got the right knee. Justin's leg buckled like the ship's landing leg had done. He caught himself before he collapsed, hopped backwards and tested his weight.

Frank pushed himself up, slowly and painfully. There was nothing left to fight over. Yun had gone, M2 was in ruins, and still they were going to duke it out. A proxy war between XO and Frank's crewmates. Nothing at stake but pride.

He couldn't lift his left arm any longer. If he had time, perhaps he could strap it across his chest to protect his suit controls, but he didn't, and he let it hang limp. Instead, he raised his makeshift sword out in front of him, to give him a sense of the space between them.

Justin knocked the end of the sword with a swing of Jim's hammer and Frank made the effort to bring the point back around again. He'd never done this before today, unless kids playing with fallen sticks, pretending to be Jedi knights, counted, which he guessed not. But he could at least turn sideways on, lead with his sword hand, keep his suit and his left arm out of the way of the hammer. Awkward, though: he couldn't see through the side of his helmet, and he returned to a face-on stance when he realized it wasn't going to work.

"We going to do this, then?" he said. "We going to finish this now?"

There was no way Justin could hear him. All the same, the man's eyes seemed to narrow. He knew it was over, too. He knew. He swung the hammer again, connecting with the end of the sword, knocking it aside, and tried to jump forward to hit Frank on the return, but his leg wouldn't take it. He stumbled, and he hastily pushed back, trying to recover his balance.

Frank lunged, the sword point skittering across Justin's carapace just above the controls, heading for his armpit, but he was out of range, and it was Frank's turn to go on the back foot. They were testing each other, seeing what the other could and couldn't bring to the fight.

Clearly, Frank had the reach, and he started to circle, always keeping the sword between him and Justin. Circling meant walking up the slope of the wall, and back down to the midline, and it was obvious from his opponent's painful hopping that Frank had the advantage of maneuverability, too. He could get in and out of range far more easily, just as long as he didn't make a mistake.

Frank could feel the feral part of his brain take over again, sliding between him and conscious decision, turning him into something with just animal instinct; predator and prey.

Was that what he wanted? Was that what he really wanted? Justin's blood on his blade? Revenge, justice, whatever he called it, he was going to kill yet another man, and he didn't have to. No one was forcing him. He could leave it. He could just leave it. Walk away. Let nature take its course.

He was panting with the effort of making a choice. He wasn't at war with Justin. He was at war with himself, and it was time to declare a truce. He wasn't alone any more. He could, conceivably, still go home after this. He'd survived everything, the worst that both Mars and XO could throw at him.

And he could just as easily throw all that away by giving Justin a chance to get inside his guard.

OK. Deep breath. Circle round again. Back to the breach.

He kept his eyes firmly on Justin, parried a couple of abortive attempts to get closer, and finally stood part-way up the wall, one foot on the edge of the curling metal and loose insulation wave that had frozen in place. The buckled fuselage was sharp. He'd need to tread carefully.

But every time Frank tried to back out, he had to straighten up and ward Justin off by brandishing his sword, holding him at arm's length to prevent him from landing a blow. With one damaged arm, it was impossible to escape. But neither did he want to kill again. Justin, however, seemed hellbent on only one of them getting out alive.

Lucy climbed through, and stood next to Frank. It took a little while for him to realize she was there, and a little longer for him to register the gun in her outstretched hand. He looked at her through her faceplate, her thin-lipped expression, her unblinking gaze.

He got the message, even though they couldn't talk. Justin got the message too. He stood, weight on one leg, hammer held low by his side. He stood up as straight as he could. Frank climbed carefully out, teasing his way through the gap in the side of the prone spaceship, and then stood on the sand, waiting for the flash, waiting for the low, distant pop, waiting for Lucy to come out and tell him it was done.

33

[Transcript of Emergency FLIGHT meeting Ares IV Mission Control JPL Pasadena CA 3/10/2049]

GT: I've been up for forty-eight [48] hours straight. Just so you all know. Sound off.

MA: CATO. DSN [Deep Space Network] confirm that signals from the three [3] XO satellites in areostationary orbits are ongoing. ATA confirms this also. No direct communications have been established with MBO.

LS: RIO. It's out of my hands. The U.S. ambassador to Beijing was summoned to explain the situation, and the Secretary of State has been in touch with his Chinese counterpart. The CNSA [China National Space Agency] liaison here has been sequestered in meetings. This is . . . about to explode. Sorry.

WM: ODIN. If they have total computer failure, then they may be too busy to communicate. But given that the uplink is a priority, and that I'm estimating a sol to fix everything, even just to patch it together enough to send a lo-fi message . . . we may be looking at something more serious.

GT: How serious?

WM: Catastrophic hab failure with zero survivability.

PO: ECLSS. I can't see that. The habs are modular, the systems are robust, the personnel trained. And HiRISE2 tell us the infrastructure appears intact.

GT: They're burning more fuel trying to stay overhead than they'd spend in years of station-keeping.

TY: OPSPLAN. I've still got nothing. Though the rovers have moved. They have definitely moved. There are people on the surface.

GT: XO have refused my request to go to Gold Hill in person.

PO: Seriously?

GT: They said the site is "commercially sensitive", but I'm hearing rumors that's not all it is. I have a car out front. Al is meeting me there. Let's see what they say to our faces.

[transcript ends]

He didn't remember much after that.

Fan opening the door to the stand-alone airlock, and Yun taking her first unsteady steps wearing Leland's suit. Her face, livid and puffed, and her eyes... every blood vessel burst.

Frank, arm not just broken, but shattered, and Fan having to heat up a morphine autoinjector in a self-igniting can, to melt the crystals and then inject the contents, almost boiling, into his bloodstream through the already patched arm of his spacesuit.

That had hurt. Hurt a lot: Frank's yell of pain died the other side of his faceplate, and then it faded, leaving him in an almost dreamlike fugue. The pain—well, it might have been there, but he couldn't feel it any more. His mouth had gone dry, and he had a problem with Mars turning when it clearly couldn't do any such thing. He blinked and squinted again. Definitely turning. Slowly, left to right, and then back, in a huge, glacial circle.

He was hauled up onto a buggy, and tied on, much as the M2 prisoners were, except he was on his side, watching the Martian landscape slide by, top to bottom, like he was climbing a cliff that would never end.

It occurred to him that he was actually injured. Properly damaged. Building sites were dangerous places, but he'd always run a tight ship. Everyone knew the score before they started, and workers goofing around with air hoses and heavy machinery got

338

their pink slips. He'd seen some serious shit go down—mangled limbs, staved-in heads, desleeving injuries, crush and puncture wounds—and now it had happened to him. Someone had set about his arm with a hammer. Of course it was broken.

Now everything depended on whether Fan could fix it straight, with what he had. Hell, at least he could trust Fan not to off him. Not like Alice, who'd killed who knew how many with her skewed idea of who should live and who should be helped to die.

That got him remembering them all. Zeus, huge and tattooed and tireless. Marcy, whose enthusiasm eased seamlessly into recklessness. Declan, sarcastic and prissy and smart. Zero, dedicated to his gardening, and still just a kid. Speaking of kids—Dee: he was normal. Out of all of them, he was the one who Frank would have put on a ship back to Earth, had just one space been available. The injustice of it all. Bringing them to Mars, getting them to build the base, then killing them off. Leaving only Brack.

Brack. Did he know what he was getting himself into? Sure he did. He'd signed up for it, all of it, including Phase three. And when he died—when he bled out on the floor of Comms— he'd died with a threat on his lips, "You'll never see your son again", which might yet come true. Frank might not even make it back to Earth.

But look at what he had done. He'd built a place for people to live in. He'd thwarted XO's plans. He'd done his best to help his new crewmates. He'd saved some of them. Not bad for a lifer. Not bad at all.

"Frank?"

He snapped awake without realizing he'd fallen asleep. Fan had his helmet pressed against his. The buggy had stopped moving, and in his eyeline he could see another buggy parked up, and the outpost.

"We need to swap out your life support, and I want to check on your vitals."

Frank took a breath, and another. His head started to clear. "I'm good. Give me a minute."

He'd made it this far. He'd make it the rest of the way.

The inside of the outpost was still a mess. It offended Frank. Jerry and the two so far nameless M2 people were going to do the work putting it right. The missing equipment needed to be reinstalled or mended, and hopefully between them there'd be enough skills to do that. Because it was still a long way from Earth.

According to Fan, Frank wasn't going to die any time soon. That wasn't the end of the doctor's concerns, though, and the only place he wanted to see his patient was in the med bay. That was still a couple of hours away, and while Lucy, Isla, Yun and Fan were able to climb out of their suits and scratch the places that itched, Frank was trapped.

His arm might make it out of his sleeve once, but it sure as hell wasn't going back in again.

But Fan was able to deploy sufficient diagnostic tools through the open back hatch to confirm that Frank's vitals were stable, and administer enough chemicals to keep them that way.

Fan swapped out Frank's life support, and patted him on the back before Frank closed up his suit again. One thumb up was all he could manage. He was still feeling like this wasn't quite his body, and that he was watching everything from one step removed.

Fan boosted him back onto the buggy, checked on the prisoners, and retied Frank onto the roll bars. Then he took the lead down the Santa Clara, with Isla taking over the driving from Lucy. The smoothness of the river bed was a welcome contrast to the rough edges of the volcano. And because there'd been no car chases or derby races, there was enough left in the fuel cell to drive back to MBO, rather than rely on gravity to roll the rest of the way.

One last turn, and they were out of the mouth of the Santa Clara, back onto the Heights, and there was the base, bathed in the pink afternoon sun slanting in from the west. Frank stirred himself from his torpor, and managed a little more upright than the slumped position he found himself in.

Not that it made him any more comfortable. The morphine was wearing off. He could feel his arm again, and not in a good way. It felt sore and hot, like someone was rubbing sandpaper across his skin. The rest of him was just dog tired. This was it. This was the end of it, and the start of something new.

Out of the valley, he could make and receive transmissions again. The clipped chatter between Lucy and Fan. No, wait, that wasn't small talk.

"Fan. Fan, talk to me. Fan!"

The base slewed off to the right. And then out of sight, behind him.

"Frank. Frank, can you hear me? Frank, something's wrong with Fan."

Frank shook himself, and realized that Fan was asleep at the wheel, making the buggy turn in a wide circle. He struggled against the cargo strap that held him down, reached forward and banged Fan's shoulder hard. Fan fell further onto his left side, held in position only by the driver's harness.

His hands fell off the controls. He wasn't asleep. He was unconscious.

Frank gritted his teeth and screwed up his face. OK, think. Think. Then he noticed that the air in his suit wasn't blowing in his face any more. He flipped up the control panel on his chest, one-handed. Nothing. No display. No numbers.

His suit had just turned itself off. If the same thing had happened to Fan's...

Not a coincidence. Surely, not a coincidence.

He had a helmet's worth of air. Less than that. If his scrubbers had stopped working too, then he was going to choke on his CO_2 faster than he'd run out of oxygen. How long did he have? A minute? Seconds?

And Fan was further down that road than he was, because

he'd already passed out, was already suffocating, as soon they both would be, rolling slowly to a stop on the Heights.

OK. Stop breathing. Untie yourself by pulling on the right part of the strap. Climb up and over and restart the buggy. Try and ignore the pounding heartbeat in your ears.

He felt his lungs begin to strain. They urged him to take a breath. Just one more. He loosened the strap enough that he could pull himself up and move around on the lattice frame so that he could reach the controls.

It took him a couple of attempts, and they began to head back the way they'd come. Close enough for the others to run over and help? Frank used his dead hand to hit the harness buckle. Once, twice, and it just wasn't clicking out. He swapped hands, got it first time, but slipped and fell against the chassis, driving what air he had left out of his body.

Fuck.

He had to breathe, and as soon as he did, he needed another. He knew that if he did, he'd not wake up.

He picked Fan up, one-handed, and bundled both of them off the buggy.

They landed together, awkwardly, sprawling in the dust and against the rocks. There wasn't anything else Frank could do. It wasn't pain he could fight against, it wasn't effort that was required: it was the very essence of him craving oxygen and shutting down in its absence. His vision started to gray out. He was mid-faint. He forced himself to his knees, and clawed at Fan's back unit. His fingers caught the recessed latch, and he pulled.

In there was the hard reset button. He'd used it to try and revive Marcy, all the way back on that first trip out. It was all he could remember. Not the order of the buttons, whether it was the left one or the right one he needed to press. The color— one was red, the other green—would have told him, but he was blind and he was sliding down that long, dark tunnel.

Yes, he was panting. Yes, there was air moving in and out. It wasn't doing any good. He slapped his hand down—

He was face-down in the dirt, a bead of sweat hanging from the end of his nose. But he could breathe.

Fresh air blew against his skin, making the sweat-bead tremble. His throat hurt. No, everything hurt. He turned his head slightly and fastened his lips around the water spout. Empty. Goddammit.

"Frank?"

Someone kneeling on the ground next to him, their head lowered to the same level as his, looking sideways into his face.

"Yeah?"

"You OK?"

"Isla?"

"You saved Fan."

His suit had shut down. As they approached the base, his suit, and Fan's suit, had simply turned themselves off.

"That's good."

"The two M2 people…we didn't get to them in time."

Frank got his arm underneath his carapace and heaved. Willing hands pulled at him, and got him as far as sitting, leaning against the wheel of a buggy.

There was Fan, and Lucy, and Yun. And Isla. His eyes were sore, and he blinked rapidly. They were back at the entrance to the Santa Clara.

"What the hell happened?" he asked.

"We don't know. There's a fault with the suits."

"A fault? They turned off. We did nothing, and it was like someone just pulled the plug on us."

Lucy stood with hands on hips, looking behind Frank, across the Heights at the distant base.

"How far from the base were you?"

"Four, five hundred feet."

"Just about the suit's wifi range, right?"

"Mine's less. But yes." Frank remembered being hunted by Brack, out in the cold, dark night, and the only thing keeping him alive was that he was too far from the base for the implant in his chest to connect with the base's automatic systems.

"Fan's suit logged on first. Your suit, a few seconds later. The M2 suits were the same as yours. And the moment they connected with the main computer, they turned themselves off." Lucy reached up and wiped dust from her faceplate. "Sorry, Frank. Looks like you were right."

"Oh, OK. That's nice. I like being right. And Isla has to do my laundry for a month."

"I thought...I don't know what I thought. At least we know what the problem is: XO installed a kill switch, injecting the code through the dish before we cut them off, and left it there to take out anyone returning from M2. There has to be a workaround." She looked at Yun. "Any suggestions?"

Frank took the opportunity to check his suit numbers. Everything seemed OK. Now. OK apart from the dead man and woman they had fastened to the back of the buggy, and the fact that getting within range of the main computer system's wireless transmitter would kill a suit—and the occupant. "Shame we can't call Jerry. Or even if we can, he's tied up."

"What can we try?" Leland's suit seemed crumpled with Yun inside it. She had shorter legs, and shorter arms, and even though the torso was a rigid container, her head seemed lower in the helmet. She looked like shit, and her voice sounded like she'd been gargling with razor blades. But she was still trying. "Use a tablet to access the root?"

Fan handed her his, and she tapped at the screen. It became rapidly apparent, from both her expression and the frequency of her finger movements, that she was having problems. "I'm not locked out. But I've had all my permissions revoked. There's another layer of security immediately behind the initial handshake, and I can't get through it."

She kept on going, while Isla suggested: "We can drive back

344

up to CU1, disable our transmitter chips, drive back down and hope we have enough air to last us that long. Which we might not."

"Just turn off your transmitter," said Frank.

Isla talked over him. "That's the only way we're going to get into the base and reset the system."

"But you can just turn it off from the suit controls," Frank said.

"Because it's automatic. It just logs on to the network. So we need a way of stopping that."

Lucy interrupted Isla. "Say that again, Frank."

"I can turn off my transmitter." He opened up his controls and scrolled through the menu. "See?"

He pressed the button and instantly all communication ceased. He thumbed the button again, and it came back.

"We can't do that," said Lucy.

"Can't you?"

"That command just doesn't exist. Why would we need it?"

"To stop someone fucking your suit over?" Frank dragged himself up and turned himself around so that he could see the base. It was tantalizingly close. "I guess that's never been a thing until now."

"It's sure as hell a thing now. How did XO think they'd get away with this?"

"By making sure you're not alive to tell anyone." He needed a drink. Water would do. Beer would be better. But it was obvious what needed to be done, if how to do it remained opaque. "So which wires do I cut?"

"It's a little more complicated than that, Frank," said Yun.

"You can't go, Frank," said Fan.

"Why the hell not?"

"Because you're high on morphine, you've broken your arm and if something happens to you in there, none of us can come and get you."

"The morphine wore off a while ago."

"Trust me: if it had worn off, you'd be begging me for more. You're hurt, Frank."

"Don't make me regret bringing you back." Frank looked around at the others. "Who else is going to do this? You guys? Or those guys?" He pointed to the back of the buggy.

"We can't, and those guys are dead, Frank."

"Looks like I'm the last one standing who can fix his suit so that it won't kill him." No one else appeared convinced. "Sure, we can all head back to the outpost, pull your comms circuits out by hand in a way you may never be able to repair again, hope our air lasts long enough that we can fix whatever problem there is. Or you can just tell me what to do, I can go and do it, and then you all come over. I know which sounds like the easy way."

Lucy grunted. "Yun. Talk him through it." There were objections, and she shouted them down. "He's an adult. He can make his own poor choices."

"He's not fit for duty," said Fan. "I'm the medical officer."

"Technically, you can't order me around," said Frank. "We don't even work for the same company."

"But you don't work for XO. Not now."

"Let's say I've gone freelance. Just let me do this. I'll be fine."

"Like hell you will." Despite that, Fan shut up and turned away.

Yun stood next to him, the tablet still useless in her hands.

"So what do I do?" he asked.

"There are several ways of doing this. The wireless starts in Comms/Control, and has repeaters in every hab. You could turn them all off manually, but that relies on you finding them all. Did you install them?"

"That was Declan. I think Dee helped."

"If you miss one, the kill signal still gets broadcast. The surest way of disabling it is to turn it off on the main computer."

"But you can't access that."

"I know."

"Can't I just cut the power to the computer?"

"Yes, but it's working on a UPS." When Frank looked blank, she explained. "It's got its own battery. We'd have to wait a day for it to run down."

"Can't I just pull the battery leads out?"

"Again, yes. Do you know where it is?"

"Do you?"

"It's behind a whole lot of panels that aren't meant to be opened. And if you do turn the computer off, there are all the automatic systems that rely on it. We run the risk of everything freezing, the plants dying, and the base atmosphere going wrong, between you turning it off and me turning it back on again safely. So that's Plan B, but there's something else I'd rather try first. It is rather technical."

"If you're asking me to reprogram it, then you've picked the wrong guy. Turning stuff off, I can do that. Silicon Valley shit? Nope."

"Why not give me a chance to explain, and then decide?"

His arm was aching, and it was making him irritable. He took a breath, and then another one. Because he could. "Just keep it simple."

"The new code must have been either installed and activated recently, or installed at a past time and activated only recently. The computer regularly backs itself up. An earlier version of its memory will have the kill switch set to off. All you need to do is load up that version instead of the version that is currently running."

"If you can't get into the computer, what makes you think I'll be able to?"

"Because the keyboard in Comms doesn't go through the wifi system. At that point, you'll have bypassed what's locking me out. Now, you'll need to restart the computer—"

"If I'm doing that anyway—"

"Let me explain, first," she repeated.

"Sorry."

"You interrupt the boot sequence, and you access the system

set-up screen. From there, you can then tell the computer where to look for its operating system. You direct it to a different path, and then let it continue from there. The problem is solved, at least temporarily, with very little interruption of the core life support systems."

"But the kill switch might still be in there."

"Yes, which is why I'll have to find the process afterwards and delete it permanently." Yun tilted her head on one side. "What do you think, Frank? Can you do that?"

"I . . . guess so. You're going to have to go through it, line by line. And what happens if I forget a step? It won't be like I can just ask you to remind me."

"I'll write it all down for you."

"On what?" The tablet was useless. They didn't have paper or pen.

"You, Frank. Hold still."

She turned Frank towards her, and dragged her glove across his partially frosted faceplate, cleaning it as best she could. Then she reached into her—into Leland's—utility belt and held up a stubby pencil. A grease pencil.

And she began to write the instructions Frank would need across the clear plastic, in English, backwards, and right to left.

34

ST: Extraordinary scenes here as hundreds of law officers, acting on a warrant obtained by the Federal Aviation Authority and backed by the FBI, perform an early morning raid on the Denver offices of Xenosystems Operations. XO's chief Paul Leander was taken into custody, and files and computers have been leaving the high-rise Tower of Light ever since.

XO has been under the media spotlight in the last several days due to the failure of its communications links with Mars Base One and the Ares IV mission currently in residence on the red planet, but this raid came right out of the blue. The search warrant cites multiple breaches of the Commercial Space Launch Act, but we don't know exactly what those breaches are, what they mean for XO, or what impact this will have on the astronauts on Mars. This story is developing, and a press conference with FAA officials is scheduled for ten [10] o'clock Mountain Time.

[transcript ends]

Frank was helped up onto the buggy—no point in walking the mile or so to the base—and he settled himself in the seat. The controls relied on squeezing the accelerator paddles, but it'd work just as well with one as with both, and there wasn't anything else he needed to do, even strap himself in. It was straightforward enough, literally as well as figuratively, to drive over to the base, squinting out at the world around the blue pencil-marks across his field of vision.

Whether he'd get there with his suit still working was something else entirely. Yes, he knew he could press buttons on his suit controls that would tell him he'd turned his transmitter off, but whether that was enough, or whether XO had installed some sort of backdoor that allowed them access to his life support without him knowing...

He was about to find out. And there was nothing he could do about that. Either he'd realize in time, and manage to steer the buggy back over to the river, where the others would try and restart his suit again, or he'd black out and just carry on until he hit something. Or fell off the edge of the Heights and into the crater below.

He was back in a world of silence. Whatever he'd done, he'd cut himself off from the voice comms. It was just him and the buggy for now. And he didn't care what Fan said, the morphine was definitely wearing off. He couldn't turn around anyway, to see them all for what might be the last time, but maybe that was for the best, because there were also the two M2 crew lying dead on the ground right next to them. Whatever they were, whatever they'd done, they deserved their names at least. Jerry could supply those.

Frank raised his good hand, then took hold of the controls and eased the buggy away. It rumbled and rocked, carrying him onwards.

The base slowly grew larger, and he caught himself holding his breath. That was stupid. Instead, he took his hand off the wheel, and propped open his suit control pad so that he could see whether it was powered up or blank. Then he carried on, one eye on the diminishing distance, one on the little read-out. If it went dark, he'd know instantly.

It stayed stubbornly on.

Was he close enough? Was he past that point already?

The buggy was slowing to a crawl. That was him. He was easing back on the trigger. He checked his suit again, and it was still fine.

"Fuck it," he said to himself, and purposely closed his fist. The buggy picked up speed and, surely, he was near enough now that if something was going to happen, it would have already happened. There was the base...the base that looked wrong. Deflated. Not all the way, but the outer skin wasn't as taut as it usually was.

XO were trying to kill them slowly, having failed to kill them quickly.

He steered in the direction of the yard and pulled to a halt beside it. Getting down from the buggy was an art he hadn't mastered one-handed. In the end he sat on the edge of the frame and pushed himself off while still holding on. It worked, more or less.

His heels hit the soil, he flexed his knees, he straightened up. He focused on the list in front of his face.

It was only a few skipping strides to the airlock at the end of the crew hab. He hauled himself up the metal steps, and pushed the airlock cycle button.

Nothing happened. He looked at it, and saw the telltale wasn't lit.

Fine. Play hardball then. There was more than one way to open the airlock. Except not this one, because they—no, he— had left the inner door open, precisely so that no one could open the airlock, with or without power.

He needed to stay frosty, when he was feeling anything but.

The cross-hab, then. He climbed down the steps, walked around Comms/Control, and to the cross-hab airlock. The telltale on this airlock was off too, but he should be able to open this one manually. He got his fingers into the recess on the external hatch, gave it a tug, and pulled the lever down to vent any airlock air to Mars.

A whisper of gas crystallized near his feet, turning to ice and falling as glitter onto the top step.

He returned the lever to upright, opened the airlock door, and stepped inside, closing the outer door behind him. There was another lever behind another hatch, next to the inner door. He tugged on it, and the cubicle repressurized with a sudden whoosh. Sound returned, and with it the noise of alarms.

Frank took a moment to check the pressure. It should have been five psi. It was south of four. Breathable, but like being up the top of a mountain. He needed to check on Jerry before he tried anything with the computer.

He entered the cross-hab. The oxygen sensor on the ceiling was chirping away, the bleeping mercifully dulled by his suit's helmet. It was still loud, but just about bearable. He picked up the scuba mask from the top of the life support rack, tucked it under his arm, and hauled the one cylinder of oxygen that remained out of its place on the shelf. Either it had grown heavy, or he'd grown weak.

He let it hit the floor, and he dragged it after him on his way to the med bay.

The door to the examination room was still locked, the bolt on the outside shot home in the hasp on the frame. Frank used the back of his hand to knock it aside and then his shoulder to push through the door.

Jerry was lying on the floor, mostly face-down, his hands still bound behind his back and his feet wound into the blanket he'd been given. He didn't move when Frank barged in, and stayed that way when he was accidentally knelt on.

Frank heaved him over. Jerry's face was flushed red, and reminded him instantly of Dee, and how he'd died, gassed by the CO_2 extinguishers. Could XO have set those off too? Jerry was still breathing: fast, deep, his whole frame swelling and shrinking. He was still alive, but there wasn't much Frank could do but plug in the scuba mask, turn the oxygen on and force

Jerry's face into it. He couldn't work the straps one-handed, and he had to give up on that.

He left him there. He'd done his best—Fan would be able to do so much more if he could just get into the base. Frank's job, his one job, was to do battle with the main computer.

He pulled the door to, just in case that managed to increase the oxygen pressure in the cubicle, and walked quickly through to Comms. He kicked the chair out of the way, then went to the wall where the computer itself was sited. He looked up at his instructions, found the reset button, found that his gauntleted finger was too fat to fit in the depression, and looked around for something small enough to reach.

A coffee spoon handle.

OK, go to the kitchen, open the drawer, rake out a spoon, take it back to the computer, insert it into the hole and press.

The alarms fell silent. Thank God for that.

Next instruction. Get back to the terminal and press down the shift key before the boot sequence is complete.

He was too late. It had been seconds at most to walk around the desk and point his finger. He looked at the distance again, and dragged the console closer, and facing him. He used the spoon again, and watched the monitor go blank for a moment, before it popped up with "no video signal".

He let go of the button, and now he could just lean over and press the shift key.

It worked. He was given a list of options. He selected "advanced options", then the first choice with the recovery mode label. Paranoid about making a mistake, he used the spoon handle on the keyboard, tapping the down arrow key once, and then enter.

The screen flashed and came up with another menu. This time he was going to choose... "root".

This was where shit got real. He had to type in a series of commands exactly as they were presented to him on his faceplate. If he got one of them wrong, he'd have to do it again. If Yun had got one of them wrong, then—what? He'd have to drive back across the Heights and get her to correct her instructions. All the while their base, their food supply, was dying.

He started along the first line, "mount -o remount,rw" and pressed enter. So far, so good. Then into the system files, delete them all—he was sweating, because Yun had told him that he could really screw things up—then copy all the files over from a backup directory. Streams of data washed up the screen, far faster than Frank could read, almost faster than he could see.

The inevitable message, something to tell him he'd failed, never came. Yun's instructions were boilerplated.

He exited the root, then tapped up to "resume". Here went nothing.

It worked. At least, it appeared to work. Scripts ran, the screen went blank, and then icons began to pop up on the screen. The alarms started again, having detected the lack of oxygen in the air, but there were alerts piling up in the action center which, when he opened it, told him that the air plant had just kicked in, that the scrubbers were on max, trying to take out the CO_2, that the airlocks were being set to active. Lights. Music. The works.

Had he managed to remove the suit kill switch, though? The only way he was going to be able to tell was by turning his comms back on. It'd kill him if he hadn't, so he didn't.

He'd done everything he'd come to do. The base should be starting to reinflate around him now, and return to its normal state. He could silence the alarms, but it was a good, audible reminder for everyone not to take their suits off. The noise would stop when the air was safe to breathe again.

All that remained to be done was to check on Jerry, and then head back to the Santa Clara. They'd see soon enough if he'd managed to incant Yun's spell properly.

Jerry wasn't what Frank would have called awake. He was stirring, moaning and coughing, pushing into the mask. He could really do with being untied, and that was something that Frank could manage one-handed.

Back to the kitchen for a knife, and saw slowly through the cable ties, trying not to nick the skin on Jerry's wrists, because he was in enough trouble without getting cut too. The moment the plastic snapped, Jerry coughed and his hands planted on the deck to try and brace himself.

Frank used his good hand to help Jerry find the mask, and hold it to his own face. He wasn't a doctor. He barely knew the basics. It was the best he could do.

He brought his head down and shouted, over the electronic beep of the overhead alarms, over the coughing and panting: "I'm coming back for you, OK? I'm bringing Fan with me. He'll patch you up. Just keep breathing."

Jerry had done bad things, but so had Frank. And if he could work out his salvation, there was hope for everyone. He didn't have to like him. Just to recognize that he'd been there, too, and the way out took both time and effort.

Back to the cross-hab airlock, where the lights on the telltale were back on. Frank should have been able to just open the door and enter, but even in the short time the air plant had been back on, the pressure had increased enough to seal the door shut. He cycled the lock to equalize, and then again to exit into a Martian afternoon, the sun tipping low towards the western wall of Rahe crater.

He had a couple of hours' air left. By the time that was up, the habs should have reinflated. Or at least enough that it wouldn't kill them. He walked back round to the buggy, parked next to the dead transmitter dish, and tried to climb up.

They'd gone through the plan several times. What to do if Frank couldn't access the computer, what to do if Frank couldn't turn off the wifi repeaters, what to do if Jerry had freed himself and holed up inside, everything that might prevent Frank from neutralizing the kill switch threat.

What they hadn't done was plan for his success.

He should, reasonably, be able to climb up one-handed, but goddammit he was tired. And weak. And everything else in between. The top of the chassis was just over head height. In normal circumstances, he could jump that high from a standing start. Right now, if he could make any air at all, he'd consider it a win. The lower part of the frame was four feet up. If he could get his leg onto that, he could probably lever himself the rest of the way. Barring that, it was a long walk back.

He looked up at the buggy again. A ladder. That was all he needed.

OK. He pulled his nut runner from his belt, spent a couple of minutes unbolting the steps leading up to the airlock at the end of the yard, and pulled them, jerking them inch by inch, around and against the side of the buggy.

He could have thought of that a while back, but he was actually pretty pleased to have thought of it at all. He climbed up, stepped carefully across the open tubes and lowered himself into the seat. It took a little careful steering to maneuver the back wheels away from the obstruction, but he still remembered how to do it, and he drove back across the Heights to where the rest of the crew sat waiting for him.

All that knowledge, all that training, and it came down to him. He didn't feel like bragging, though. He was just glad he was in a position, thanks to XO and their prototype suits, to help.

The others were sitting in the sand, or on the buggy, conserving what was in their tanks. But they stood, one by one, as Frank approached, and walked out to meet him.

Lucy climbed up and touched helmets with him.

"Tell me you did it."

"I did it. Worked first time."

"Thank you." She relayed the message, and suddenly everyone looked much happier. Apart from the two dead astronauts lying face-down in the dirt.

"XO had also vented the CO_2 extinguishers, cut the power

to the airlocks, and had started depressurizing the habs. If they could have burned the base down, pretty certain they'd have done that."

"What's the damage?"

"Didn't check the greenhouse, so I don't know about the plants or the fish. Jerry was still alive when I left him, but he was trying to cough up his lungs, so maybe Fan can see to him."

Lucy broke contact. Fan's body language changed—treating a man who'd eaten Jim—and Lucy seemed to spend a while in talking him round. In the end, he flapped his arms in surrender, and went to sit at the controls of the second buggy.

"He'll do it."

"Because you ordered him to, or because he wants to?"

"Does it matter?"

"I guess not. Though our team doctor had a thing about euthanizing her patients, so I'd probably want to get seen by someone who didn't think I was better off dead."

"We've all had a difficult few days, Frank. There's a lot to process, a lot to come to terms with. I'll keep an eye on him, but I don't think Fan's going to deliberately kill someone he's treating, no matter how much he might like to." She straightened up for a moment to look at the base. "You want to try this thing out?"

"You going to be the guinea pig?"

"I can't ask anyone else to do it, can I?"

"Sure you can. But since you're a decent human being, you're stepping up to the plate yourself. Sit where I can see you, and put a hand in the air if your suit craps out. I'll take it slow."

Frank drove forward. He knew he was going to be safe, but having had his suit stop working on him once, he knew what Lucy had to be thinking. Now? If not then, then now? How about now? Surely close enough now.

Then uncertainty. Then hope. Then...Frank had forgotten about it when he had other, more urgent things to worry about. How odd that such imminent danger of death should become normal, but it had. He'd been on Mars, what, nine, nearly ten months? And every day he'd suited up and walked around one of the most hazardous environments known.

Normal. It was normal.

Once upon a time, he'd been concerned that he'd not been able to feel anything. That he was already in the grave. Still. Silent. Here, he was alive, so fully alive.

Perhaps XO had done him a favor after all.

Lucy's hand stayed down. He'd done a good thing. He'd done a bad thing before that, a long time ago. The good didn't cancel out the bad, he knew that, but maybe he'd earned himself some peace.

35

[Transcript of interview with Benjamin Jonathan Cohen, conducted by [redacted—A#1] and [redacted—A#2]. Also present Stephen Buk, Attorney at Law 3/17/2049 Salt Lake City UT]

A#1: Tell me about Luisa.

BJC: Luisa was all of us.

A#2: All of you, or some of you?

BJC: Whoever was on duty. We were working around eighteen [18] hours solid, but we had to get some sleep sometime. And a Mars sol is thirty-seven [37] minutes longer than an Earth day. After twenty [20] days, the day/night cycle completely reverses. No one person could be Luisa.

A#1: So how did you maintain consistency?

BJC: I guess, same way you get a writers' room. People would say "that doesn't sound like Luisa", or "she'd not use that word", and the thing would get written pretty quickly. We knew we had to keep him on board. It was the only way we could get anything done.

A#2: Luisa was the good cop?

BJC: I mean, sure. There's this guy, starved of human contact, starved of female contact. So we kind of did a bit of flirting, make him feel like we were just a bit on his side against the management, that we thought he was getting a bum deal but, you know. Stick with it, champ.

A#2: Champ, or chimp?

SB: You don't have to answer that.

359

A#1: Everyone who was Luisa: they were regular Mission Control people.

BJC: We didn't have a separate Luisa team.

A#1: And you were all in Mission Control for the whole duration.

BJC: [whispered conversation with SB]

SB: My client would like to know what kind of deal might be on offer.

A#1: I'm not certain we need to offer anyone a deal at this stage.

BJC: [whispered conversation with SB]

BJC: Yes.

A#2: The whole duration? From June 2048?

BJC: Yes.

A#1: OK. Let's have some names.

[transcript ends]

It had all come down to knowing where Earth was, and then encoding its movement in a series of equations that the dish motors could follow, to keep the antenna pointed at the correct portion of the sky.

Yun had explained that the problem wasn't trivial. That bypassing the dedicated satellites in orbit and calling home directly on the equipment MBO came with, was complicated precisely because no one had thought the situation would ever arise. That turning an entirely digital system into an analog one, without destroying the ability to switch back, was time-consuming and technically difficult.

She had, of course, managed it within a week. From their initial Mayday, to reaching a lo-fi text-only system, had taken another week. Video was out of the question for the time being, but highly compressed voice messages, sent over the Deep Space Network, was something they could now manage.

Messages from home. Messages from family, from friends, from colleagues. It felt like a huge thing, and it was. And every day, as Mars turned away from the Earth, there was silence for twelve hours.

Frank didn't ignore the event. It just didn't mean as much to him as it did to the rest of the crew. Luisa had gone. XO no longer had any relevance for him. And Lucy was camped out in Control/Comms, trying to relay as much information as possible regarding what had happened.

Sometimes Frank took her food—it was all he was able to do—while she was in the middle of dictating another lengthy transmission. She'd always pause her recording and make some small talk, but it was clear she wanted to continue as soon as she could. He understood there was pressure from NASA, but he wasn't privy to the content, nor the context.

Frank was going to have to wear his inflatable arm cast for four months, and not take it off at all for the first two. Fan didn't have access to an x-ray machine. He didn't have the surgical plates and screws he probably would have used back on Earth, either. It was going to heal crooked, and it was never going to be as good as before, even if everything else went well.

The cast stretched from wrist to past his elbow. He had to wear a sling with it, which meant it was always present in front of him, and he could see, through the transparent covering, his skin turn yellow, then mottled black. It hurt, mainly at night when he didn't have anything else to think about.

He didn't like taking anything for the pain, for…reasons. But sometimes, lying there in the almost-dark, he'd bite his blanket in order to stop himself from crying out. He was pretty certain Fan wouldn't have minded being woken up—Frank had a standing invitation to do so—but so far, he hadn't taken the lifeline offered to him.

In the cold light of day, he wondered why. Yet during the night, he stuck it out. The pins and needles. The random shooting pains. The steady throb. The bone-deep itch. Hurt was now his default. He'd thought it would be better than this. Disappointment added to his discomfort.

The things that Frank couldn't do without two hands—almost everything except greenhouse work and carrying light things—Jerry would do. Frank couldn't go outside. All he'd seen of Mars for the last month was through the little window in the airlock, and yes, it might be an airless red desert where nothing would grow in the toxic, frozen soil, but he missed it. The simple act of suiting up and stepping out, and having a sky over his head rather than a low ceiling, would have been a relief. But there was no way he could do that, and still have the possibility of a working arm at the end of it. Jerry ran his chores, using Leland's suit.

It kept the M2 man busy. It kept him from killing himself, and Frank was no Leland. He could listen, but he wasn't so hot on advice. Jerry'd talk to Frank about who he was and how he'd ended up on Mars. About the people he had waiting for him back on Earth. What he'd wanted to do, and how his idealism about taming a new planet had slowly desiccated in the fine red dust until it was a dried, twisted caricature of what he'd dreamed of before.

There was no emotional attachment. Jerry was a project: they were both survivors of their respective missions. Frank had arrived on Mars already a criminal. Mars had turned Jerry into one. Frank didn't know how he felt about that.

The greenhouse was the only place he didn't feel like a spare part. He could top up the nutrient tanks, take readings, record heights and weights and volumes, and carefully harvest the produce. He could pollinate with a paint brush, move lights higher and lower, plant seeds and, mostly, anything else that needed doing.

It also, incidentally, meant that he spent a lot of time with Isla.

Not that he talked to her much. She had her experiments, which she decided that she had to start again from scratch due

362

to the partial depressurization and atmosphere changes in the hab, and she concentrated on those while Frank carried on the grunt work of growing food.

But she was there, in the background, a presence. A welcome presence. They bumped along together. He knew where stuff was kept and, despite his inertia when it came to learning new things, he'd gotten knowledgeable about the plants he was tending. Mineral deficiencies, mutations, drip rates, germination conditions and harvesting times. She asked his advice. Whether she needed it or not, it made him feel less useless.

Neither of them mentioned that night in the shower.

All the same, it was a memory that Frank treasured. It had made him feel human again.

Yun's days were spent doing what Jim should have been doing. Collecting rocks. Surveying. Digging. Lucy had taken Jim's hammer from Justin. Yun wore it in her utility belt. Frank's utility belt. His suit was a better fit for her than Leland's.

The rule about pairing up had gone out the airlock along with so much else. The worst had already happened. In the spirit of her dead colleagues, she was going to collect as much data as she could, while she could. At some point, someone was going to have to go back up to the outpost, and further still, as far as M2, to retrieve what was left there. Not just the equipment, not just Station seven: the bodies. Whatever remained of Jim. But that was in an undefinable future, not now.

The one time they were all together was at dinner. That wasn't so strange for Frank. His crew had done it. Even Jerry was expected to be there, though he didn't talk much. What does a man say to the friends of someone he's helped eat?

And just when he thought things had settled into a new normal, the greenhouse airlock opened and there was Lucy. She stood there for a while, not catching Frank's eye, nor Isla's, just checking out the health of the hab and its contents. Frank was busy with the nutrients, swapping out nearly empty syringes with full ones. He had to use his teeth to remove the flexible hose, and the C nutrient especially tasted bitter. Isla was taping the seams of a new atmosphere-controlled experiment. Both of them carried on working, expecting to be interrupted at any moment.

It didn't come. Lucy climbed down the ladder to the lower level, and Frank raised an eyebrow at Isla, who shrugged back.

Frank finished the tomatoes, and walked around to where he could see through the grating. Lucy was leaning over one of the tilapia tanks, wafting her hand through the already stirring surface. Her sleeve was dangling, and had wicked up the dark, algae-rich water as far as her elbow.

"You OK?"

She looked up at him, and then shifted her gaze back to the tank. "They want me to call it, Frank."

"Call what?"

"Stay/No Stay."

He was aware of Isla behind him, listening.

"I didn't think the MAV was ready yet."

"Mission Control have calculated that with a reduced crew, the MAV already has enough fuel to make orbit and rendezvous."

A reduced crew, she'd said. That didn't include Jerry. Or Frank. He'd not asked before about that. It looked as if someone somewhere—probably several someones—had made a pronouncement and, well: it wasn't like he was unused to bad news. "Does that mean what I think it means?"

"Things have been happening back on Earth. Serious things. Seriously legal and political things. It's a hell of a mess. There are lawyers and federal agents all over this, and I've tried to insulate everyone here from the shitstorm that's broken out. But they want me to call it, Frank. Today, tomorrow. They've left it up to me." She looked up again. "I don't know what to do."

"I guess you'll do whatever you think best. For your crew."

"We're in uncharted territory, Frank. I'm not going to lie, part of me wants to have nothing more to do with this planet. It's taken two of the best people I know. Then again, I've never run away from anything before."

"No shame in calling it quits," he said.

"You won't be left behind," said Isla, softly enough that only he could hear it. "I won't allow it."

He felt her hand on his shoulder, her fingers digging into the skin and muscle beneath his overalls. A fierce grip. It was almost painful, and that was good. She meant it.

"I need to talk to everyone," said Lucy. "I can't make this decision by myself."

Frank swallowed. "OK. Let me know when you're done."

"You need to be there. Five minutes, kitchen."

She lifted her dripping sleeve and squeezed out the water, then climbed the ladder. She might have given the tableau of Frank and Isla the side-eye before she left, but it was difficult to tell. She seemed to have closed down completely.

Isla squeezed tighter, then let go. He'd be bruised there later, to go with all the other bruises.

"If she tries to make us return without you, there'll be a mutiny."

"Whoa. Just think about what you're saying."

"I know what I'm saying."

"You're on Mars. The MAV is it. If it's leaving, you should be leaving with it. We don't even know, after this, that they'll ever send another."

"All of us, or none of us."

"What if she orders you?"

"Then we disobey her. We have space on the Prairie Rose for you. Even for Jerry. We can wait for another month, two months, and then we can all go."

"Maybe Lucy's just giving you the option. Not because she wants to go herself, but because she thinks you might."

"I'm doing this as much for me as I am for you." She was adamant, and Frank didn't know what that signified. Something for sure.

Brack had once taunted him saying people like him didn't have friends: that he was indelibly marked out—the mark of

Cain—as being different, being other. And yes, while he'd been in prison, that had been true enough. There'd been guards, and there'd been other cons, and why the hell would he want to make friends with anyone in either group?

In his mind, he'd not done anything to earn this generosity. Yet here was someone who was unequivocally on his side. He was conditioned to think, "what does she want?" OK, Frank. Don't overthink it: what if she doesn't want anything?

"I have to stay," said Isla. "To the end of the mission. I'll never get another chance at this. None of us will. I'm so sorry we lost Jim and Leland." He could hear her passion. "But I didn't realize how much this meant to me until I thought it might be taken away."

He tidied away the nutrient solutions, making a note of where he'd got to and pushing in a flag to indicate the last tray he'd topped up: he liked things squared away. That way, if he suddenly died, then the next person along wouldn't curse him for being messy.

She carried on: "The radiation exposure, the reduced gravity, the risks, my age—don't laugh—this is it. I'll never get back to Mars again. People will remember this mission for all the wrong reasons anyway. I understand that. If we turn tail and run now, or in a couple of months' time even, that's all they'll remember. I want them to have something else."

"You don't have to explain it to me."

"I do. Yun feels the same way."

He walked ahead of her, running the fingers of his right hand across the tray of wheat tillers.

"You've talked to her? Of course you have." He suddenly realized what was going on, and turned round. "Wait. You think I've got a vote? I'm pretty certain I don't have a vote."

"You're crew."

"I'm a con, Isla. Guys like me, we don't get a say in stuff like this."

"Most of Yun's equipment is still intact. We can fix what M2 took. She knows this is her only opportunity too. And Fan."

"What did Fan say?"

"'You need a doctor', is what he said."

"That's not great."

"It's enough." Isla looked down at Frank's broken arm. "He's willing to say he can't leave until that's fixed. That's..."

"Four months at least. Maybe six. Does Lucy know you got this all sewn up?"

"No. But if you want to go home, first opportunity you can, then I'll switch. All you have to do is say."

He missed leaning against stuff. Putting both his hands down and just resting his weight against them. "I've no idea what's going to meet me at the other end. You know that, right?"

"I know that," she said.

"Any deal I cut with XO, I blew out when I told you who I really was. They took me out of jail to send me to Mars. There's nothing now to stop me bouncing straight back there. I've another hundred and nine years to serve. I don't think you quite appreciate that that's set in stone."

"We can get you a new lawyer. Another trial."

"The first trial wasn't wrong, Isla. They didn't come to the wrong conclusion. I did what I did, and this base might just be the only place on two planets I get to be free." Then he turned away. "What I'm saying is, don't make any decisions based on what may or may not happen to me. I don't want that."

"We can fix this."

"The only way to do that is to bring back the dead. That's not happening. Not everything is fixable. So just drop it. Please."

She did. She took herself out of the greenhouse, and elsewhere, and left Frank alone. He stood there for a while, then followed.

Jerry was coming in from outside—it was still disconcerting to see Leland's suit without Leland inside it. Maybe they should scrub his name off the carapace. Maybe that would be too much, too soon. Maybe it wouldn't matter if it was just him and Frank in the base.

Jerry opened up the back hatch and eased his head out. "What's going on?"

Frank checked up and down the corridor. "Lucy's got to make the call."

"The call?" Then he got it. "Right."

"It probably won't involve us." He let that sink in. "No reason why it should. Neither of us should be here."

Jerry slithered out backwards, with a dexterity that Frank envied.

"Where does that leave us?"

"On Mars. Where did you think it'd leave us? We look after the base, like we were always supposed to. They go home, like they were always supposed to. Just earlier than they expected."

"Do you think they'll do that?"

"That's what they need to decide. I burned my bridges with anything on Earth a while ago. You? I don't know how space law works, but I'm pretty certain you'll be joining me and the XO board in jail."

Jerry looked away, but Frank could see the muscles on his jawline flex.

"That's not much of an offer," said Jerry.

"Tell me about it. But unless I get anything better, that's the one I'm taking. I've gotten used to pissing with no one watching me."

"Is it that bad?"

"What it is, is gray. Think about that, Jerry. Whatever color is in your life, you'll lose it."

Jerry pulled on his borrowed coverall and racked his kit.

"What am I going to do, Frank?"

"People like us, we get it done to us. Today, we get to sit in and listen to what they have to say. Keep it zipped and take whatever comes. Just like I will. Let's go see how it pans out." Frank used his good hand to drag Jerry along with him to the kitchen. The others were already there, Isla and Fan and Yun sitting on the sides, Lucy standing at the yard-end of the table. Where Frank had sat, all those months ago, facing Declan and Zero and a tableful of shivs.

Frank guided Jerry around to the kitchen end and dropped him in one chair, then took one himself. If he sat just so, he could rest his arm on the tabletop and take the weight off his neck.

Lucy started pacing, first of all without talking, then, eventually, giving them the news.

"The situation is," she pulled a face, "unclear. XO are holed up behind a wall of lawyers. They're not admitting to anything, and are using our old friend, 'commercially sensitive', to cover almost every question they've been asked. They say that M2 acted independently of XO, that they lost contact early in the mission, that they can't be held responsible for the actions of M2 crew. That much is what we know already."

She stopped and stared at Jerry, who looked down at the floor until she resumed.

"Someone will probably manage to pin something on them in a civil suit, negligence or fraud or something like that. That might take years. Key personnel have just disappeared, gone to ground somewhere. Frank: you were reported dead six months ago. That's why you've not been called on to give evidence yet. No one can work out who you really are. Your ashes were disposed of. There's a death certificate for you, for Alice Shepherd, for Marcy Cole and Declan Murray. In the absence of the Phase three files, folk are trying to fill out your crew roster based on what you've told us. Needless to say, there's no one who goes by the name of 'Lance Brack' anywhere near this or any other project. The military are now involved. Sorry, but you cleaned up too well. There's no material evidence here we can point to that corroborates your story. Except for you. If you really are Franklin Kittridge, then someone on Earth will have to vouch for you."

"There's enough of the guys I worked with, in and around San Fran, who can do that. And my ex. And my boy." Frank rubbed the end of his nose. "You want evidence? You've been walking over it for weeks. I did a decent job at getting rid of the blood in the ceiling voids, but sure, there'll be some left. Scrape it out. Bag it. Take it back."

Everyone cast their eyes downwards at the floor, and were silent for a while.

"So that's where we are," said Lucy. "Jim and Leland's families have been informed. We can do precisely nothing about what's going on back on Earth. We might be astronauts, but this is so far above our paygrade…"

She trailed off. She kept pacing, but she said nothing further.

Fan cleared his throat. "So far above our paygrade that what?"

Lucy finally stopped, and rested her knuckles on the table. "That we might as well stay." She waited for a reaction, any reaction. "It has to be unanimous. I'm not going to keep anyone here against their will. We've lost two dearly beloved crew members and friends. We're all still raw about that. I'm worried that none of us are ready to make a decision with such long-term consequences."

"Stay," blurted Isla. She took a deep breath. "I mean, I vote to stay."

"Yun? You've talked to your government. But you still get to choose."

"They have encouraged me to see out the mission, but they are not unsympathetic to the trauma of what has happened to us. I can still perform useful science, even if my original experiments are compromised. I can continue Jim's surveying and sample collection, if you'll permit me. I see this as my one opportunity to live and work on another planet. I wish the circumstances were different, but they are what they are. Stay."

370

Fan shrugged. "Jim and Leland are still here. I'm closer to them if I stay. So, stay."

No one said anything for a long time after that. Then Lucy stirred herself and raised her head.

"Frank? What about you?"

"What about me? It's not up to me. There's not even enough fuel in the MAV for me."

"There will be one day. Don't you want to go home?"

"I've been thinking about that. But I still don't get why you're even asking me. I don't have a say in this. I'm not crew."

"Is it that you're worried about going back to prison? What if I told you that the FBI have intimated that if you turn State's evidence, they could do something. Change the terms of your sentence. Maybe even a pardon."

Yes. That would change things. He'd be tied up with juries and hearings for years, and the Feds would want nothing but his full cooperation. Blowing them out, heading to the east coast? That wouldn't be part of the plan, would it?

And now when it came to it, he didn't know what he wanted to do. He'd endured. He'd survived. He'd changed. And really, what was left for him on Earth? His kid had done without him for a decade, and his ex was a good mother. They didn't need some goddamn hero crashing into their lives after such a long time.

But here? He could do good here.

"You're crew, Frank," said Lucy. "Stay or go. It's your call."

Deep breath. Say it. Say it.

"Stay."

Coda

Dad? Is that really you?

extras

orbit

meet the author

Photo credit: Simon Morden

DR. S. J. MORDEN has won the Philip K. Dick Award and been a judge on the Arthur C. Clarke Award committee. He is a bona fide rocket scientist with degrees in geology and planetary geophysics.

if you enjoyed
NO WAY

look out for

EQUATIONS OF LIFE
Samuil Petrovich: Book One

by

Simon Morden

Samuil Petrovitch is a survivor.

He survived the nuclear fallout in Saint Petersburg and hid in the London Metrozone—the last city in England. He's lived this long because he's a man of rules and logic.

For example, getting involved = a bad idea.

But when he stumbles into a kidnapping in progress, he acts without even thinking. Before he can stop himself, he's saved the daughter of the most dangerous man in London.

And clearly saving the girl = getting involved.

Now the equation of Petrovitch's life is looking increasingly complex.

Russian mobsters + Yakuza + something called the New Machine Jihad = one dead Petrovitch.

But Petrovitch has a plan—he always has a plan—he's just not sure it's a good one.

1

Petrovitch woke up. The room was in the filtered yellow half-light of rain-washed window and thin curtain. He lay perfectly still, listening to the sounds of the city.

For a moment, all he could hear was the all-pervading hum of machines: those that made power, those that used it, pushing, pulling, winding, spinning, sucking, blowing, filtering, pumping, heating and cooling.

In the next moment, he did the city-dweller's trick of blanking that whole frequency out. In the gap it left, he could discern individual sources of noise: traffic on the street fluxing in phase with the cycle of red-amber-green, the rhythmic metallic grinding of a worn windmill bearing on the roof, helicopter blades cutting the gray dawn air. A door slamming, voices rising—a man's low bellow and a woman's shriek, going at it hard. Leaking in through the steel walls, the babel chatter of a hundred different channels all turned up too high.

extras

Another morning in the London Metrozone, and Petrovitch had survived to see it: *God, I love this place.*

Closer, in the same room as him, was another sound, one that carried meaning and promise. He blinked his pale eyes, flicking his unfocused gaze to search his world, searching…

There. His hand snaked out, his fingers closed around thin wire, and he turned his head slightly to allow the approaching glasses to fit over his ears. There was a thumbprint dead center on his right lens. He looked around it as he sat up.

It was two steps from his bed to the chair where he'd thrown his clothes the night before. It was May, and it wasn't cold, so he sat down naked, moving his belt buckle from under one ass cheek. He looked at the screen glued to the wall.

His reflection stared back, high-cheeked, white-skinned, pale-haired. Like an angel, or maybe a ghost: he could count the faint shadows cast by his ribs.

Back on the screen, an icon was flashing. Two telephone numbers had appeared in a self-opening box: one was his, albeit temporarily, to be discarded after a single use. In front of him on the desk were two fine black gloves and a small red switch. He slipped the gloves on, and pressed the switch.

"Yeah?" he said into the air.

A woman's voice, breathless from effort. "I'm looking for Petrovitch."

His index finger was poised to cut the connection. "You are who?"

"Triple A couriers. I've got a package for an S. Petrovitch." She was panting less now, and her cut-glass accent started to reassert itself. "I'm at the drop-off: the café on the corner of South Side and Rookery Road. The proprietor says he doesn't know you."

"Yeah, and Wong's a *pizdobol*," he said. His finger drifted from the cut-off switch and dragged through the air, pulling a

379

window open to display all his current transactions. "Give me the order number."

"Fine," sighed the courier woman. He could hear traffic noise over her headset, and the sound of clattering plates in the background. He would never have described Wong's as a café, and resolved to tell him later. They'd both laugh. She read off a number, and it matched one of his purchases. It was here at last.

"I'll be with you in five," he said, and cut off her protests about another job to go to with a slap of the red switch.

He peeled off the gloves. He pulled on yesterday's clothes and scraped his fingers through his hair, scratching his scalp vigorously. He stepped into his boots and grabbed his own battered courier bag.

Urban camouflage. Just another immigrant, not worth shaking down. He pushed his glasses back up his nose and palmed the door open. When it closed behind him, it locked repeatedly, automatically.

The corridor echoed with noise, with voices, music, footsteps. Above all, the soft moan of poverty. People were everywhere, their shoulders against his, their feet under his, their faces—wet-mouthed, hollow-eyed, filthy skinned—close to his.

The floor, the walls, the ceiling were made from bare sheet metal that boomed. Doors punctured the way to the stairs, which had been dropped into deliberately-left voids and welded into place. There was a lift, which sometimes even worked, but he wasn't stupid. The stairs were safer because he was fitter than the addicts who'd try to roll him.

Fitness was relative, of course, but it was enough.

He clanked his way down to the ground floor, five stories away, ten landings, squeezing past the stair dwellers and avoiding spatters of noxious waste. At no point did he look up in case he caught someone's eye.

It wasn't safe, calling a post-Armageddon container home, but neither was living in a smart, surveillance-rich neighborhood with no visible means of support—something that was going to attract police attention, which wasn't what he wanted at all. As it stood, he was just another immigrant with a clean record renting an identikit two-by-four domik module in the middle of Clapham Common. He'd never given anyone an excuse to notice him, had no intention of ever doing so.

Street level. Cracked pavements dark with drying rain, humidity high, the heat already uncomfortable. An endless stream of traffic that ran like a ribbon throughout the city, always moving with a stop-start, never seeming to arrive. There was elbow-room here, and he could stride out to the pedestrian crossing. The lights changed as he approached, and the cars parted as if for Moses. The crowd of bowed-head, hunch-shouldered people shuffled drably across the tarmac to the other side and, in the middle, a shock of white-blond hair.

Wong's was on the corner. Wong himself was kicking some plastic furniture out onto the pavement to add an air of unwarranted sophistication to his shop. The windows were streaming condensation inside, and stale, steamy air blew out the door.

"Hey, Petrovitch. She your girlfriend? You keep her waiting like that, she leave you."

"She's a courier, you *perdoon stary*. Where is she?"

Wong looked at the opaque glass front, and pointed through it. "There," the shopkeeper said, "right there. Eyes of love never blind."

"I'll have a coffee, thanks." Petrovitch pushed a chair out of his path.

"I should charge you double. You use my shop as office!"

Petrovitch put his hands on Wong's shoulders and leaned down. "If I didn't come here, your life would be less interesting. And you wouldn't want that."

Wong wagged his finger but stood aside, and Petrovitch went in.

The woman was easy to spot. Woman: girl almost, all adolescent gawkiness and nerves, playing with her ponytail, twisting and untwisting it in red spirals around her index finger.

She saw him moving toward her, and stopped fiddling, sat up, tried to look professional. All she managed was younger.

"Petrovitch?"

"Yeah," he said, dropping into the seat opposite her. "Do you have ID?"

"Do you?"

They opened their bags simultaneously. She brought out a thumb scanner, he produced a cash card. They went through the ritual of confirming their identities, checking the price of the item, debiting the money from the card. Then she laid a padded package on the table, and waited for the security tag to unlock.

Somewhere during this, a cup of coffee appeared at Petrovitch's side. He took a sharp, scalding sip.

"So what is it?" the courier asked, nodding at the package.

"It's kind of your job to deliver it, my job to pay for it." He dragged the packet toward him. "I don't have to tell you what's in it."

"You're an arrogant little fuck, aren't you?" Her cheeks flushed.

Petrovitch took another sip of coffee, then centered his cup on his saucer. "It has been mentioned once or twice before." He looked up again, and pushed his glasses up to see her better.

"I have trust issues, so I don't tend to do the people-stuff very well."

"It wouldn't hurt you to try." The security tag popped open, and she pushed her chair back with a scrape.

"Yeah, but it's not like I'm going to ever see you again, is it?" said Petrovitch.

"If you'd played your cards right, you might well have done. Sure, you're good-looking, but right now I wouldn't piss on you if you were on fire." She picked up her courier bag with studied determination and strode to the door.

Petrovitch watched her go: she bent over, lean and lithe in her one-piece skating gear, to extrude the wheels from her shoes. The other people in the shop fell silent as the door slammed shut, just to increase his discomfort.

Wong leaned over the counter. "You bad man, Petrovitch. One day you need friend, and where you be? Up shit creek with no paddle."

"I've always got you, Wong." He put his hand to his face and scrubbed at his chin. He could try and catch up to her, apologize for being... what? Himself? He was half out of his seat, then let himself fall back with a bang. He stopped being the center of attention, and he drank more coffee.

The package in its mesh pocket called to him. He reached over and tore it open. As the disabled security tag clattered to the tabletop, Wong took the courier's place opposite him.

"I don't need relationship advice, yeah?"

Wong rubbed at a sticky patch with a damp cloth. "This not about girl, that girl, any girl. You not like people, fine. But you smart, Petrovitch. You smartest guy I know. Maybe you smart enough to fake liking, yes? Else."

"Else what?" Petrovitch's gaze slipped from Wong to the device in his hand, a slim, brushed steel case, heavy with promise.

"Else one day, pow." Wong mimed a gun against his temple, and his finger jerked with imaginary recoil. "Fortune cookie says you do great things. If you live."

"Yeah, that's me. Destined for greatness." Petrovitch snorted and caressed the surface of the case, leaving misty fingerprints behind. "How long have you lived here, Wong?"

"Metrozone born and bred," said Wong. "I remember when Clapham Common was green, like park."

"Then why the *chyort* can't you speak better English?"

Wong leaned forward over the table, and beckoned Petrovitch to do the same. Their noses were almost touching.

"Because, old chap," whispered Wong faultlessly, "we hide behind our masks, all of us, every day. All the world's a stage, and all the men and women merely players. I play my part of eccentric Chinese shopkeeper; everyone knows what to expect from me, and they don't ask for any more. What about you, Petrovitch? What part are you playing?" He leaned back, and Petrovitch shut his goldfish-gaping mouth.

A man and a woman came in and, on seeing every table full, started to back out again.

Wong sprung to his feet. "Hey, wait. Table here." He kicked Petrovitch's chair-leg hard enough to cause them both to wince. "Coffee? Coffee hot and strong today." He bustled behind the counter, leaving Petrovitch to wearily slide his device back into its delivery pouch and then into his shoulder bag.

His watch told him it was time to go. He stood, finished the last of his drink in three hot gulps, and made for the door.

"Hey," called Wong. "You no pay."

Petrovitch pulled out his cash card and held it up.

"You pay next time, Petrovitch." He shrugged and almost smiled. The lines around his eyes crinkled.

"Yeah, whatever." He put the card back in his bag. It had only a few euros on it now, anyway. "Thanks, Wong."

Back out onto the street and the roar of noise. The leaden sky squeezed out a drizzle and speckled the lenses in Petrovitch's glasses so that he started to see the world like a fly would.

He'd take the tube. It'd be hot, dirty, smelly, crowded: at least it would be dry. He turned his collar up and started down the road toward Clapham South.

The shock of the new had barely reached the Underground. The tiled walls were twentieth-century curdled cream and bottle green, the tunnels they lined unchanged since they'd been hollowed out two centuries earlier, the fans that ineffectually stirred the air on the platforms were ancient with age.

There was the security screen, though: the long arched passage of shiny white plastic, manned by armed paycops and monitored by gray-covered watchers.

Petrovitch's travelcard talked to the turnstile as he waited in line to pass. It flashed a green light, clicked and he pushed through. Then came the screen which saw everything, saw through everything, measured it and resolved it into three dimensions, running the images it gained against a database of offensive weapons and banned technology.

After the enforced single file, it was abruptly back to being shoulder to shoulder. Down the escalator, groaning and creaking, getting hotter and more airless as it descended. Closer to the center of the Earth.

He popped like a cork onto the northbound platform, and glanced up to the display barely visible over the heads of the other passengers. A full quarter of the elements were faulty, making the scrolling writing appear either coded or mystical. But he'd had practice. There was a train in three minutes.

Whether or not there was room for anyone to get on was a different matter, but that possibility was one of the few advantages in living out along the far reaches of the line. He knew of people he worked with who walked away from the center of the city in order to travel back.

It became impossible even to move. He waited more or less patiently, and kept a tight hold of his bag.

To his left, a tall man, air bottle strapped to his Savile Row suit and soft mask misting with each breath. To his right, a Japanese woman, patriotically displaying Hello Kitty and the Rising Sun, hollow-eyed with loss.

The train, rattling and howling, preceded by a blast of foulness almost tangible, hurtled out from the tunnel mouth. If there hadn't been barriers along the edge of the platform, the track would have been choked with mangled corpses. As it was, there was a collective strain, an audible tightening of muscle and sinew.

The carriages squealed to a stop, accompanied by the inevitable multi-language announcements: the train was heading for the central zones and out again to the distant, unassailable riches of High Barnet, and please—mind the gap.

The doors hissed open, and no one got out. Those on the platform eyed the empty seats and the hang-straps greedily. Then the electromagnetic locks on the gates loosened their grip. They banged back under the pressure of so many bodies, and people ran on, claiming their prizes as they could.

And when the carriages were full, the last few squeezed on, pulled aboard by sympathetic arms until they were crammed in like pressed meat.

The chimes sounded, the speakers rustled with static before running through a litany of "doors closing" phrases: English, French, Russian, Urdu, Japanese, Kikuyu, Mandarin, Spanish. The engine spun, the wheels turned, the train jerked and swayed.

Inside, Petrovitch, face pressed uncomfortably against a glass partition, ribs tight against someone's back, took shallow sips of breath and wondered again why he'd chosen the Metrozone above other, less crowded and more distant cities. He wondered why it still had to be like this, seven thirty-five in the morning, two decades after Armageddon.

if you enjoyed
NO WAY
look out for

ROSEWATER
The Wormwood Trilogy: Book One

by

Tade Thompson

Rosewater is a town on the edge. A community formed around the edges of a mysterious alien biodome, its residents comprise the hopeful, the hungry and the helpless—people eager for a glimpse inside the dome or a taste of its rumored healing powers.

Kaaro is a government agent with a criminal past. He has seen inside the biodome and doesn't care to again—but when something begins killing off others like himself, Kaaro must defy his masters to search for an answer, facing his dark history and coming to a realization about a horrifying future.

Chapter One

Rosewater: Opening Day 2066

Now

I'm at the Integrity Bank job for forty minutes before the anxieties kick in. It's how I usually start my day. This time it's because of a wedding and a final exam, though not my wedding and not my exam. In my seat by the window I can see, but not hear, the city. This high above Rosewater everything seems orderly. Blocks, roads, streets, traffic curving sluggishly around the dome. I can even see the cathedral from here. The window is to my left, and I'm at one end of an oval table with four other contractors. We are on the fifteenth floor, the top. A skylight is open above us, three foot square, a security grid being the only thing between us and the morning sky. Blue, with flecks of white cloud. No blazing sun yet, but that will come later. The climate in the room is controlled despite the open skylight, a waste of energy for which Integrity Bank is fined weekly. They are willing to take the expense.

Next to me on the right, Bola yawns. She is pregnant and gets very tired these days. She also eats a lot, but I suppose that's to be expected. I've known her two years and she has been pregnant in each of them. I do not fully understand pregnancy. I am an only child and I never grew up around pets or livestock. My education was peripatetic; biology was never a strong interest, except for microbiology, which I had to master later.

I try to relax and concentrate on the bank customers. The wedding anxiety comes again.

Rising from the centre of the table is a holographic tele-prompter. It consists of random swirls of light right now, but within a few minutes it will come alive with text. There is a room adjacent to ours in which the night shift is winding down.

"I hear they read Dumas last night," says Bola.

She's just making conversation. It is irrelevant what the other shift reads. I smile and say nothing.

The wedding I sense is due in three months. The bride has put on a few pounds and does not know if she should alter the dress or get liposuction. Bola is prettier when she is pregnant.

"Sixty seconds," says a voice on the tannoy.

I take a sip of water from the tumbler on the table. The other contractors are new. They don't dress formally like Bola and me. They wear tank tops and T-shirts and metal in their hair. They have phone implants.

I hate implants of all kinds. I have one. Standard locator with no add-ons. Boring, really, but my employer demands it.

The exam anxiety dies down before I can isolate and explore the source. Fine by me.

The bits of metal these young ones have in their hair come from plane crashes. Lagos, Abuja, Jos, Kano and all points in between, there have been downed aircraft on every domestic route in Nigeria since the early 2000s. They wear bits of fuse-lage as protective charms.

Bola catches me staring at her and winks. Now she opens her snack, a few wraps of cold moin-moin, the orange bean curds nested in leaves, the old style. I look away.

"Go," says the tannoy.

The text of Plato's *Republic* scrolls slowly and steadily in ghostly holographic figures on the cylindrical display. I start to

391

read, as do the others, some silently, others out loud. We enter the xenosphere and set up the bank's firewall. I feel the familiar brief dizziness; the text eddies and becomes transparent.

Every day about five hundred customers carry out financial transactions at these premises, and every night staffers make deals around the world, making this a twenty-four-hour job. Wild sensitives probe and push, criminals trying to pick personal data out of the air. I'm talking about dates-of-birth, PINs, mothers' maiden names, past transactions, all of them lying docile in each customer's forebrain, in the working memory, waiting to be plucked out by the hungry, untrained and freebooting sensitives.

Contractors like myself, Bola Martinez and the metalheads are trained to repel these. And we do. We read classics to flood the xenosphere with irrelevant words and thoughts, a firewall of knowledge that even makes its way to the subconscious of the customer. A professor did a study of it once. He found a correlation between the material used for firewalling and the activities of the customer for the rest of the year. A person who had never read Shakespeare would suddenly find snatches of *King Lear* coming to mind for no apparent reason.

We can trace the intrusions if we want, but Integrity isn't interested. It's difficult and expensive to prosecute crimes perpetuated in the xenosphere. If no life is lost, the courts aren't interested.

The queues for cash machines, so many people, so many cares and wants and passions. I am tired of filtering the lives of others through my mind.

I went down yesterday to the Piraeus with Glaucon the son of Ariston, that I might offer up my prayers to the goddess; and also because I wanted to see in what manner they would celebrate the festival, which was a new thing. I was delighted with the procession of the inhabitants; but that of the Thracians was equally, if not more, beautiful. When we had finished our prayers and viewed the spectacle, we turned in the direction of the city...

On entering the xenosphere, there is a projected self-image. The untrained wild sensitives project their true selves, but professionals like me are trained to create a controlled, chosen self-image. Mine is a gryphon.

My first attack of the day comes from a middle-aged man from a town house in Yola. He looks reedy and very dark-skinned. I warn him and he backs off. A teenager takes his place quickly enough that I think they are in the same physical location as part of a hack farm. Criminal cabals sometimes round up sensitives and yoke them together in a "Mumbai combo"—a call-centre model with serial black hats.

I've seen it all before. There aren't as many such attacks now as there were when I started in this business, and a part of me wonders if they are discouraged by how effective we are. Either way, I am already bored.

During the lunch break, one of the metalheads comes in and sits by me. He starts to talk shop, telling me of a near-miss intrusion. He looks to be in his twenties, still excited about being a sensitive, finding everything new and fresh and interesting, the opposite of cynical, the opposite of me.

He must be in love. His self-image shows propinquity. He is good enough to mask the other person, but not good enough to mask the fact of his closeness. I see the shadow, the ghost beside him. Out of respect I don't mention this.

The metal he carries is twisted into crucifixes and attached to a single braid on otherwise short hair, which leaves his head on the left temple and coils around his neck, disappearing into the collar of his shirt.

"I'm Clement," he says. "I notice you don't use my name."

This is true. I was introduced to him by an executive two weeks back, but I forgot his name instantly and have been using pronouns ever since.

"My name—"

"You're Kaaro. I know. Everybody knows you. Excuse me for this, but I have to ask. Is it true that you've been inside the dome?"

"That's a rumour," I say.

"Yes, but is the rumour true?" asks Clement.

Outside the window, the sun is far too slow in its journey across the sky. Why am I here? What am I doing?

"I'd rather not discuss it."

"Are you going tonight?" he asks.

I know what night it is. I have no interest in going.

"Perhaps," I say. "I might be busy."

"Doing what?"

This boy is rather nosy. I had hoped for a brief, polite exchange, but now I find myself having to concentrate on him, on my answers. He is smiling, being friendly, sociable. I should reciprocate.

"I'm going with my family," says Clement. "Why don't you come with us? I'm sending my number to your phone. All of Rosewater will be there."

That is the part that bothers me, but I say nothing to Clement. I accept his number, and text mine to his phone implant out of politeness, but I do not commit.

Before the end of the working day, I get four other invitations to the Opening. I decline most of them, but Bola is not a person I can refuse.

"My husband has rented a flat for the evening, with a view," she says, handing me a slip of paper with the address. Her look of disdain tells me that if I had the proper implant we would not need to kill trees. "Don't eat. I'll cook."

By eighteen hundred hours the last customer has left and we're all typing at terminals, logging the intrusion attempts, cross-referencing to see if there are any hits, and too tired to joke. We never get feedback on the incident reports. There's no pattern analysis or trend graph. The data is sucked into a bureaucratic black hole. It's just getting dark, and we're all in our own heads now, but passively connected to the xenosphere. There's light background music—"Blue Alien" by Jos. It's not unpleasant, but my tastes run to much older fare. I'm vaguely aware that a chess game is going on, but I don't care between whom. I don't play so I don't understand the progress.

"Hello, Gryphon," someone says.

I focus, but it's gone. She's gone. Definitely female. I get a wispy impression of a flower in bloom, something blue, but that's it. I'm too tired or lazy to follow it up, so I punch in my documentation and fill out the electronic time sheet.

I ride the elevator to street level. I have never seen much of the bank. The contractors have access to the express elevator. It's unmarked and operated by a security guard, who sees us even though we do not see him or his camera. This may as well be magic. The elevator seems like a rather elegant wooden box. There are no buttons and it is unwise to have confidential conversations in there. This time as I leave, the operator says, "Happy Opening." I nod, unsure of which direction to respond in.

The lobby is empty, dark. Columns stand inert like Victorian dead posed for pictures. The place is usually staffed when I go home, but I expect the staff have been allowed to leave early for the Opening.

It's full night now. The blue glow from the dome is omnipresent, though not bright enough to read by. The skyline around me blocks direct view, but the light frames every high-rise to my left like a rising sun, and is reflected off the ones to my right. This is the reason there are no street lights in Rosewater. I make for Alaba Station, the clockwise platform, to travel around the edge of the dome. The streets are empty save the constable who walks past swinging her baton. I am wearing a suit so she does not care to harass me. A mosquito whines past my ear but does not appear to be interested in tasting my blood. By the time I reach the concourse, there is a patch of light sweat in each of my armpits. It's a warm night. I text my flat to reduce internal temperature one degree lower than external.

Alaba Station is crowded with commercial-district workers and the queues snake out to the street, but they are almost all going anticlockwise to Kehinde Station, which is closest to the Opening. I hesitate briefly before I buy my ticket. I plan to go home and change, but I wonder if it will be difficult to meet up with Bola and her husband. I have a brief involuntary connection to the xenosphere and a hot, moist surge of anger from a cuckolded husband lances through me. I disconnect and breathe deeply.

I go home. Even though I have a window seat and the dome is visible, I do not look at it. When I notice the reflected light on the faces of other passengers, I close my eyes, though this does not keep out the savoury smell of akara or the sound of their trivial conversation. There's a saying that everybody in Rosewater dreams of the dome at least once every night, however briefly. I know this is not true because I have never dreamed of the place.

That I have somewhere to sit on this train is evidence of the draw of the Opening. The carriages are usually full to bursting, and hot, not from heaters, but from body heat and exhalations and despair.

I come off at Atewo after a delay of twenty-five minutes due to a power failure from the North Ganglion. I look around for Yaro, but he's nowhere to be found. Yaro's a friendly stray dog who sometimes follows me home and to whom I feed scraps. I walk from the station to my block, which takes ten minutes. When I get signal again, my phone has four messages. Three of them are jobs. The fourth is from my most demanding employer.

Call now. And get a newer phone implant. This is prehistoric.

I do not call her. She can wait.

I live in a two-bed partially automated flat. Working two jobs, I could get a better place with fully humanised AI if I wanted. I have the funds, but not the inclination. I strip, leaving my clothes where they lie, and pick out something casual. I stare at my gun holster, undecided. I do not like guns. I cross the room to the wall safe, which appears in response to signals from my ID implant. I open it and consider taking my gun. There are two magazines of ammo beside it, along with a bronze mask and a clear cylinder. The fluid in the cylinder is at rest. I pick it up and shake it, but the liquid is too viscous and it stays in place. I put it back and decide against a weapon.

I shower briefly and head out to the Opening.

How to talk about the Opening?

It is the formation of a pore in the biodome. Rosewater is a doughnut-shaped city that surrounds the dome. In the early days we actually called it the Doughnut. I was there. I saw it grow from a frontier town of tents and clots of sick people huddling together for warmth into a kind of shanty town of hopefuls and from there into an actual municipality. In its eleven years of existence the dome has not taken in a single outsider. I was the last person to traverse it and there will not be another. Rosewater, on the other hand, is the same age and grows constantly.

Every year, though, the biodome opens for twenty or thirty minutes in the south, in the Kehinde area. Everyone in the vicinity of the opening is cured of all physical and some mental ailments. It is also well known and documented that the outcome is not always good, even if diseases are abolished. There are reconstructions that go wrong, as if the blueprints are warped. Nobody knows why this happens, but there are also people who deliberately injure themselves for the sole purpose of getting "reconstructive surgery."

Trains are out of the question at this time, on this night. I take a taxi, which drives in the opposite direction first, then describes a wide southbound arc, taking a circuitous route through the back roads and against the flow of traffic. This works until it doesn't. Too many cars and motorbikes and bicycles, too many people walking, too many street performers and preachers and out-of-towners. I pay the driver and walk the rest of the way to Bola's temporary address. This is easy as my path is perpendicular to the crush of pilgrims.

Oshodi Street is far enough from the biodome that the crowd is not so dense as to impede my progress. Number 51 is a tall, narrow four-storey building. The first door is propped open with an empty wooden beer crate. I walk into a hallway that leads to two flats and an elevator. On the top floor, I knock, and Bola lets me in.

One thing hits me immediately: the aroma and heat blast of hot food, which triggers immediate salivation and the drums of hunger in my stomach. Bola hands me field glasses and leads me into the living room. There is a similar pair dangling on a strap around her neck. She wears a shirt with the lower buttons open so that her bare gravid belly pokes out. Two children, male and female, about eight or nine, run around, frenetic, giggling, happy.

"Wait," says Bola. She makes me stand in the middle of the room and returns with a paper plate filled with akara, dodo and dundu, the delicious street-food triad of fried beans, fried plantain and fried yam. She leads me by the free hand to the veranda, where there are four deckchairs facing the dome. Her husband, Dele, is in one, the next is empty, the third is occupied by a woman I don't know, and the fourth is for me.

Dele Martinez is rotund, jolly but quiet. I've met him many times before and we get along well. Bola introduces the woman as Aminat, a sister, although the way she emphasises the word, this could mean an old friend who is as close as family rather than a biological sibling. She's pleasant enough, smiles with her eyes, has her hair drawn back into a bun and is casually dressed in jeans. She is perhaps my age or younger. Bola knows I am single and has made it her mission to find me a mate. I don't like this because...well, when people matchmake, they introduce people to you whom they think are sufficiently like you. Each person they offer is a commentary on how they see you. If I've never liked anyone Bola has introduced me to, does that mean she doesn't know me well enough, or that she does know me but I hate myself?

I sit down and avoid talking by eating. I avoid eye contact by using the binoculars.

The crowd is contained in Sanni Square—usually a wide-open space framed by shops that exist only to exploit visitors to the city, cafés that usually cater to tired old men, and travel agents—behind which Oshodi Street lurks. A firework goes off, premature, a mistake. Most leave the celebrations till afterwards. Oshodi Street is a good spot. It's bright from the dome and we are all covered in that creamy blue electric light. The shield is not dazzling, and up close you can see a fluid that ebbs and flows just beneath the surface.

The binoculars are high-end, with infrared sensitivity and a kind of optional implant hack that brings up individual detail about whoever I focus on, tag information travelling by laser dot and information downloading from satellite. It is a bit like being in the xenosphere; I turn it off because it reminds me of work.

Music wafts up, carried in the night but unpleasant and cacophonous because it comes from competing religious factions, bombastic individuals and the dome tourists. It is mostly percussion-accompanied chanting.

There are, by my estimate, thousands of people. They are of all colours and creeds: black Nigerians, Arabs, Japanese, Pakistani, Persians, white Europeans and a mishmash of others. All hope to be healed or changed in some specific way. They sing and pray to facilitate the Opening. The dome is, as always, indifferent to their reverence or sacrilege.

Some hold a rapt, religious awe on their faces and cannot bring themselves to talk, while others shout in a continuous, sustained manner. An imam has suspended himself from a roof in a harness that looks homemade, and is preaching through a bullhorn. His words are lost in the din, which swallows meaning and nuance and shits out a homogenous roar. Fights break out but are quashed in seconds because nobody knows if you have to be "good" to deserve the blessings from the biodome.

A barricade blocks access to the dome and armed constables form up in front of it. The first civilians are one hundred metres away, held back by an invisible stanchion. The officers look like they will shoot to kill. This is something they have done in the past, the latest incident being three years back, when the crowd showed unprecedented rowdiness. Seventeen dead, although the victims rose during that year's Opening. They were . . . destroyed two weeks later as they clearly were not themselves any more. This happens. The alien can restore the body, but not the soul, something Anthony told me back in '55, eleven years ago.

I cough from the peppery heat of the akara. The fit drives my vision briefly to the sky and I see a waning gibbous, battling bravely to be noticed against the light pollution.

I see the press, filming, correspondents talking into microphones. Here and there are lay scientists with big scanners pointed finger-like towards the dome. Sceptics, true believers, in-between, all represented, all busy. Apart from the classified stuff about sensitives and the xenosphere, most information about the dome is in the public domain, but it is amazing that the fringe press and conspiracy theorists have different ideas. A large segment of the news-reading population, for example, believes that the alien is entirely terrestrial, a result of human biological experimentation. There is "proof" of this on Nimbus, of course. There are scientists who don't believe, but they take observations and collate data for ever, refusing to come to conclusions. There are those who believe the dome is a magical phenomenon. I won't get started on the quasi-religious set.

I feel a gentle tap on my left shoulder and emerge from the vision. Aminat is looking at me. Bola and her husband have shifted out of earshot.

"What do you see?" she asks. She smiles as if she is in on some joke but unsure if it's at my expense.

"People desperate for healing," I say. "What do you see?"

"Poverty," says Aminat. "Spiritual poverty."

"What do you mean?"

"Nothing. Maybe humankind was meant to be sick from time to time. Maybe there is something to be learned from illness."

"Are you politically inclined against the alien?"

"No, hardly. I don't have politics. I just like to examine all angles of an issue. Do you care?"

I shake my head. I don't want to be here, and if not for Bola's invitation I would be home contemplating my cholesterol levels. I am intrigued by Aminat, but not enough to want to access her thoughts. She is trying to make conversation, but I don't like talking about the dome. Why then do I live in Rosewater? I should move to Lagos, Abuja, Accra, anywhere but here.

"I don't want to be here either," says Aminat.

I wonder for a moment if she has read my thoughts, if Bola matched us because she is also a sensitive. That would be irritating.

"Let's just go through the motions to keep Bola happy. We can exchange numbers at the end of the evening and never call each other again. I will tell her tomorrow, when she asks, that you were interesting and attentive, but there was no chemistry. And you will say...?"

"That I enjoyed my evening, and I like you, but we didn't quite click."

"You will also say that I had wonderful shoes and magnificent breasts."

"Er...okay."

"Good. We have a deal. Shake on it?"

Except we cannot shake hands because there is oil on mine from the akara, but we touch the backs of our hands together, co-conspirators. I find myself smiling at her.

A horn blows and we see a dim spot on the dome, the first sign. The dark spot grows into a patch. I have not seen this as often as I should. I saw it the first few times but stopped bothering after five years.

The patch is roughly circular, with a diameter of six or seven feet. Black as night, as charcoal, as pitch. It looks like those dark bits on the surface of the sun. This is the boring part. It will take half an hour for the first healing to manifest. Right now, all is invisible. Microbes flying into the air. The scientists are frenzied now. They take samples and will try to grow cultures on blood agar. Futile. The xenoforms do not grow on artificial media.

In the balcony everyone except me takes a deep breath, trying to get as many microbes inside their lungs as possible. Aminat breaks her gaze from the dome, twists in her seat and kisses me on the lips. It lasts seconds and nobody else sees it, intent as they are upon the patch. After a while, I am not sure it happened at all. I don't know what to make of it. I can read minds but I still don't understand women. Or men. Humans. I don't understand humans.

Down below, it begins, the first cries of rapture. It is impossible to confirm or know what ailments are taken care of at first. If there is no obvious deformity or stigmata, like jaundice, pallor or a broken bone, there is no visible change except the emotional state of the healed. Already, down at the front, younger pilgrims are doing cartwheels and crying with gratitude.

A man brought in on a stretcher gets up. He is wobbly at first, but then walks confidently. Even from this distance I can see the wideness and wildness of his eyes and the rapid flapping of his lips. Newcomers experience disbelief.

This continues in spurts and sometimes ripples that flow through the gathered people. The trivial and the titanic are equally healed.

The patch is shrinking now. At first the scientists and I are the only ones to notice. Their activities become more agitated. One of them shouts at the others, though I cannot tell why.

I hear a tinkle of laughter from beside me. Aminat is laughing with delight, her hands held half an inch from her face and both cheeks moist. She is sniffing. That's when it occurs to me that she might be here for healing as well.

At that moment, I get a text. I look at my palm to read the message off the flexible subcutaneous polymer. My boss again.

Call right now, Kaaro. I am not kidding.